A King to Fight

Empire of Israel

Book 2

By Dale Ellis

The *Empire of Israel* series:

A King to Rule

A King to Fight

A King to Die

A King to Unite

Coming in 2020:

A King to Conquer

Table of Contents

Major Characters

The Israelites

Nathan is the Protagonist of the story. At the tender age of twelve, he witnessed Philistine soldiers murder his father. Ten years later, Nathan's quest for vengeance is well underway. His battlefield prowess and closeness to Prince Jonathan quickly earn him a prominent place within Israel's military leadership. However, Nathan soon learns not all battles are fought out in the open and not all allies are to be trusted. Fortunately, God knows how to direct headstrong young men.

Jonathan, Nathan's boyhood friend, is now a prince of Israel, heir to the Throne and a hero to his people. Yet, Jonathan's success has driven a wedge between him and his increasingly paranoid father. Saul both needs and fears his talented son. The two men negotiate an uneasy sharing of power, but the king remains suspicious of anything the prince proposes. This family dysfunction often forces Jonathan to choose between what is best for the king and what is best for the kingdom.

Saul, King of Israel, has painfully discovered how power can warp even an honorable man. As the pressure of ruling Israel mounts, Saul turns away from God and toward ambitious men for guidance. The Philistine seizure of Michmash proved to be the king's breaking point. Saul panicked, ignored instructions from God's prophet Samuel and took matters into his own hands...with disastrous results. Samuel proclaims God's rejection of Saul as king. The Army of Israel begins deserting him. Jonathan takes over from his father and drives off the

Philistines. Yet, these setbacks only increase Saul's determination to hang on to his crown at all costs.

Samuel has been the only man to hold tribal Israel's trinity of high offices: priest, prophet, and judge. After initially resisting, the aged Samuel finally agreed to Israel's request for a king. He anointed Saul, a humble man from Israel's smallest tribe, as God's chosen Ruler. His heart is broken when Saul later rebels against God's instructions. Samuel reluctantly denounces Saul as king and begins seeking another to anoint in his stead.

Beker first rose to prominence as the opportunistic leader of Israel's anti-monarchist faction. Blindsided by Saul's coronation, Beker deftly switched sides and became the indispensable right hand of the new king. Yet Beker continues to play his own game. He sees the growing rift between the king and his son as an opportunity to expand his own power behind the throne.

Abner, the cousin of the king, now commands the Royal Army of Israel. Lacking the charisma necessary to rule, Abner must content himself with helping Saul keep the crown in the family. However, he allows no one else to stand in the way of his personal ambitions. Not Jonathan. Not Nathan. Not Samuel. Even Beker treads lightly around the powerful general.

Jephunneh, war chief of the tribe of Judah, is a staunch ally of Nathan and his future father-in-law.

Laban risked his life twice in the same day for Jonathan. The first time was to help the prince defeat the Philistines at Michmash. The second was to rally the Israelite Army to prevent Saul's execution of his son. This made Laban the perfect man to lead the prince's bodyguards, also known as the ***Renegades***.

However, Laban's job is far from easy as Jonathan makes a habit of going in harm's way.

Ahithophel was a petty bandit chief until drafted as a scout for one of Jonathan and Nathan's secret missions. More kidnapped than recruited, Ahithophel still knows a good thing when he sees it. His promised reward and the insights which he gained into the region's politics will start the enterprising Ahithophel down the road to true power.

Judith is the daughter of Jephunneh, war chief of the tribe of Judah. She has trained almost from birth to be the lady of a great house, in other words, a skilled hands-on manager. Besides reading and writing, Judith learned finance, animal husbandry and agriculture, as well as how to run a large household. She also is well-educated in how to conceive and raise children. Judith is understandably nervous about her betrothal to a man she has never met. But she trusts her father's judgment. Ironically, at age fifteen, she is much better prepared for marriage than her twenty-two-year-old husband, Nathan. Though he may be a great warrior, Nathan still needs someone like Judith at his side.

David, an unknown teenage shepherd, is an unlikely candidate to be thrust into the turmoil of Israel's Royal Court. Only the king's slow descent into madness drives Jonathan to desperately seek a cure for his father through the solace of music. Although David possesses both a melodious voice and skill with the harp, his selection is no accident. Samuel's obedience to God has resulted in this special young man being in the right place at the proper time.

The Philistines

Achish is the Antagonist of the story. He inherited the crown of the Philistine Kingdom of Gath after his father, **Maoch**, was assassinated during the confusion of the Battle of Michmash. Achish quietly pieced together the clues until they implicated Kaftor, King of Gaza, as the murderer. Despite his strong desire for revenge, the young king has his hands full after Michmash. Achish must rebuild his shattered army and fend off the neighboring kings now sniffing around for signs of Gath's weakness. The King of Gath shrewdly develops his *deep strategy*, a long-term plan for vengeance against his enemies and the conquest of their lands.

Abimelek's official title is *Archon,* the chief administrator of Gath. He is also its spymaster, principal diplomat, and unofficial kingmaker. When King Maoch died at Michmash, Abimelek promptly decided that it was in his best interest to place Prince Achish on the Throne. The *Archon* then skillfully eliminated every man, woman and child who might stand in the way of his new protégé. Although Abimelek frequently reminds Achish of the debt he is owed, the *Archon* faithfully serves his monarch. As long as it remains in Abimelek's best interest, of course.

Kaftor is the king of the Philistine city-state of Gaza, the traditional rival of Gath. The unexpected Israelite victory at Michmash proved to be a mixed blessing for the duplicitous monarch. The death of his chief Philistine rival, Maoch, was offset by the loss of Kaftor's entire chariot army to the Hebrews. The King of Gaza still counts several other items to be in his favor. Kaftor currently possesses the largest infantry force in the region. No one suspects his involvement in Maoch's murder.

9

Best of all, Philistia is in chaos. There is always opportunity in chaos, and Kaftor is nothing if not opportunistic.

The good news for **Davon** after the debacle at Michmash was that Achish had promoted him from captain to commander of Gath's Army. The bad news was that Gath no longer had an army, beyond its vaunted chariot corps. However, Davon never backed down from a challenge. By judicious use of his chariots, he would shield Gath from invasion while rebuilding its army from demoralized veterans, soft garrison troops and raw peasant conscripts.

Ashron's success on the battlefield was due as much to his shrewdness as it was to his fighting prowess. Whenever battle lines crashed together, he learned to hang back slightly to study the enemy's tactics. Ashron would wait until he spotted a weakness before plunging ahead to cut down his hapless foe. One day these skills would lead King Achish to decide that Ashron was the perfect teacher for an extremely large student.

The imposing **Goliath** was nine feet of death on two legs. Men had only two choices when Goliath confronted them. They either ran away or died at the giant's feet. Ironically, this burly beast of a man would one day become an intricate part of King Achish's *deep strategy*.

Neighboring Kingdoms

Karaz once was a prominent general in the Hittite Empire. After the Philistines murdered his family, he was forced to flee and become a mercenary. Providence led Karaz to Israel where he helped found an army for the fledgling kingdom and mentored two promising young leaders named Jonathan and Nathan. Unfortunately, Karaz's military successes also created jealous rivals at Saul's Court who conspired to remove him as the Royal Army's commander. Demoted to training Israel's soldiers, Karaz still finds clever ways to subtly support Prince Jonathan and Nathan.

Malia used to command a band of mercenaries from Crete. Kaftor, King of Gaza, hired Malia to assassinate Maoch, the King of Gath. Unfortunately, the Cretan mercenary failed to understand that Kaftor never left any loose ends. Although Malia is dead now, he still has a significant role to play in future events.

Mesha, King of Moab, had many reasons to feel insecure during the first year of his reign. Surrounded by enemies at home and abroad, Mesha was initially grateful when the new King of Israel crushed the Ammonites, a traditional enemy of Moab. However, the Moabites had for several decades occupied valuables lands belonging to the Israelite tribe of Rueben. Mesha knew that a day of reckoning with King Saul was coming.

Hadar was a favorite general of the King of Edom. Great wealth flowed into the Royal Treasury from Hadar's frequent raids on the Israelite tribe of Judah. Even better, Hadar's superior, the commander of the Royal Armies of Edom was nearing retirement. One more victory over the Israelites would ensure Hadar's promotion to that vacancy. It would be his reward for the many years he spent traipsing across the godforsaken desert south of the Dead Sea.

Rehob, King of Zobah, was the leader of the Aramean confederacy which dominated the lands north of Israel. In the years following the decline of the Hittite Empire, Rehob had

11

bullied a dozen of its former vassal states into acknowledging him as their new Overlord. His astute use of threats and taxation had weakened his Aramean allies and made the Army of Zobah the strongest force in the region. As long as Rehob kept his reluctant allies from getting any seditious ideas, his position was secure.

Eliada, a senior general in the army of the Kingdom of Zobah, was known as a cautious man. Fellow officers had mocked his apparent lack of ambition, not recognizing Eliada's carefully cultivated image as a clever ruse. Eliada was just as ambitious as he was competent, but he had recognized King Rehob's paranoia regarding popular generals. Most of his glory-seeking peers were long since disgraced...or dead. Eliada's home city of Damascus was one the Aramean states which chafed under Rehob's rule. Eliada would continue being cautious until the day came when he could make Zobah bow to Damascus.

Rezon, son of Eliada, was a rising star in the Army of Zobah. Barely twenty years old, he already commanded the regiment based in his home city of Damascus. Rezon had learned both caution and patience from Eliada. Father and son would play the long game against King Rehob so that one day the crown of an independent Damascus would be theirs.

Talmai, King of Geshur, ruled a minor state in the Aramean confederacy. He faced an awful dilemma created by the new taxes to be levied on his lands by King Rehob. If Talmai refused to pay, then the Army of Zobah would roll over his small kingdom. If he paid, Talmai would have to drastically reduce the size of his modest army, leaving Geshur even more vulnerable to future depredations. Talmai despaired until a stranger named

Nathan showed up on his doorstep with an intriguing proposition.

Agag, King of Amalek, observed the expansion of the new Kingdom of Israel with growing concern. His ancestors had tried long ago to destroy the Israelites when they were poor refugees in search of a homeland. That costly defeat had made the Amalekites wary of their unwelcome neighbors for centuries. Amalek prospered while the twelve tribes squabbled among themselves and struggled against foreign invaders. Now King Saul had united his nation and seemed to be settling old scores. Agag anxiously wondered if Saul would eventually get around to Amalek.

Prologue

Then panic struck the entire Philistine army at Michmash. It was a panic sent by God. Saul's lookouts saw their army melting away in all directions. Then Saul assembled all his soldiers and went into battle. They found the Philistines in total confusion, attacking each other with swords. The Israelites who had been in the Philistine camp now joined forces with Saul and Jonathan. When the Israelites hiding in the hill country heard the Philistines were running away, they also joined the pursuit. So, the LORD rescued Israel that day.

From the Book of I Samuel, Chapter 14, verses 15, 16, 20, 21, 22 and 23

The otherwise pleasant morning was marred by the screams from hundreds of throats and the smoke from dozens of fires. The mournful sounds and repugnant smells set the youthful Israelite warrior's teeth on edge. Nathan coldly surveyed the debris of the Michmash battlefield in the mid-morning light. The cries of dying Philistine soldiers, many killed by his own hand, had filled the air barely two days ago. The stench of belly wounds remained in his nostrils and his tongue still tasted like blood. Yet somehow today was much worse. Even though these pathetic victims did not speak his language, Nathan understood their message. Agony. Fear. Confusion. Hunger. Thirst. Despair.

These victims were horses. The Israelites were cutting the hamstrings of their rear legs.

The battle winning asset of the Philistine military was their chariot army. They fielded thousands of swift war vehicles while the Israelites possessed none. The saving grace for Israel was that chariots required flat, open spaces to be truly effective. Threatened Israelites could flee to mountain strongholds until the invaders departed with their plunder. The Philistine seizure of the mountain pass at Michmash had eliminated one of Israel's prime defenses. The chariot squadrons which had dominated the Mediterranean coastal plains could now swarm into the lush Jordan River Valley. With this one bold stroke, the Philistines could double the size of their territory while cutting Israel in half.

Fortunately, an aggressive Israelite leader, Nathan's boyhood friend Jonathan, had seized the initiative at Michmash. The prince and Nathan recruited some renegade Israelites to throw the Philistine camp into an uproar. Fearing betrayal, the Philistine kings had turned on each other. The panicked enemy soon flooded the road back to Philistia and became easy prey for the remnants of the Royal Army of Israel supported by their local militia.

Israelite victory had filled the Michmash plateau with hundreds of dead Philistines, thousands of stray horses, and regiments of abandoned chariots. Nathan sensed the clean-up would be just as unpleasant as the battle. The Israelite warriors were not wantonly cruel, but crippling the horses was a military necessity. Israel's rugged terrain was suitable only to small surefooted donkeys. Nathan's people could not afford to feed the horses nor allow them to wander back to Philistia. The chariots were likewise useless to Nathan's people, but invaluable to their enemies. Enemy prisoners were organized to break the chariots into expensive firewood and burn the bodies of the fallen Philistines. The horses were herded back into their thorn bush corrals where men with sharp knives awaited them. The stricken animals would then limp away to eventually expire from thirst. The fate of the Philistine prisoners was less certain, but they too could never return home.

Ironically, Nathan would today play host to men he was recently trying to slay. An unarmed Philistine emissary had approached Michmash at dawn and called out for a truce. It seemed that a Philistine prince wished to beg a favor from King Saul. Nathan understood why an audience was readily granted to the enemy leader. The King of Israel sought to boost his sagging reputation by receiving homage from a defeated foe.

The month had not been kind to Saul. First, his son Jonathan had triggered an all-out war for which Philistia had been far better prepared than Israel. Then came a very public split between the king and his chief patron, the Prophet Samuel. Coupled with the strategically devasting loss of Michmash and followed by mass desertions, Saul's army had virtually collapsed. Prince Jonathan then rallied the Israelites for an incredible victory, while unintentionally undermining his father. Only the intervention of Israel's fighting men had prevented the enraged monarch from executing his own son.

A carefully selected group of dignitaries surrounded King Saul as he awaited the Philistine noble's entourage. Nathan recognized everyone present as either a supporter of the king or someone Saul needed to impress. Abner was Saul's cousin and the commander of his army. Beker was the king's *Yameen*, or right hand, and ran the kingdom's burgeoning government. Abner's appointed officers rounded out the faction staunchly in Saul's camp. The others clustered around the popular, but impulsive, Prince Jonathan. The Hittite mercenary Karaz had founded the Royal Army of Israel, only to be displaced by Abner. The former renegade Laban had led the mutiny which saved Jonathan from Saul's rage and now commanded the prince's bodyguard. As Jonathan's armor bearer and virtual brother, Nathan stood beside his prince. Several local militia leaders also aligned themselves with Jonathan. Of greater significance was the one person conspicuous by his absence. The man who had anointed Saul as king: Samuel the Prophet.

Tension rippled through the Israelite leaders as ten Philistine chariots slowly ascended the pass to the Michmash plateau. Their swords were sheathed, javelins racked, and bows unstrung. A few hundred Israelite spearmen secured both sides of the narrow pass, backed by archers and slingers. The twenty Philistine soldiers would be skewered if they so much as twitched toward their weapons. Even so, an awe of chariots was so deeply ingrained in the Israelite foot soldier as to produce fear out of all proportion to actual numbers.

Nathan stiffened when the first chariot came to a halt. Jonathan's eyes grew wide as Nathan whispered in his ear. The young Philistine leader was Achish, son of Maoch, the King of Gath. Achish's first assignment had been to command the Philistine garrison in the Benjamite town of Gibeon. Jonathan's family was selling donkeys there while simultaneously spying on the Philistines. Providing donkeys to Achish's soldiers had allowed Nathan and Jonathan to track Philistine activities. Nathan was chagrined to remember the man still owed them money.

Achish removed his helmet and dismounted his chariot while his men remained at attention. Beker strode forward to facilitate the necessary introductions and greetings. Achish bowed deeply, while Saul inclined his head slightly. Beker then moved onto business.

"Prince Achish, why have you requested an audience with the king?"

"My father went missing during the recent battle. I beseech the king for permission to search for him. If alive, I will ransom him. If dead, I will take his body home. Either way, I will pay in gold."

Achish noticed the Israelite warriors' excited murmuring at the mention of gold. He smirked in response.

"Of course, I did not bring it with me."

Harsh laughter from Abner interrupted the proceedings.

"Here's our offer, Philistine. Take the body. We'll keep the head."

Nathan suppressed a chuckle as he viewed the various reactions. Achish's face flushed with anger at the insult. Saul glared at his cousin for ruining his regal ceremony with crude behavior. Beker paled as he saw his diplomatic schemes thrown into disarray. Jonathan and Karaz exchanged amused glances. Abner might be a fearsome warrior, but he was no diplomat.

Beker shuffled forward to mollify Achish. The Philistine regained his composure once Beker said the Royal Court needed time to consider his request. Achish returned to his chariot, put his soldiers at ease and shared some wine with them. Once Saul reconvened his advisors out of earshot, Beker immediately put forth his proposal.

"We are in an excellent bargaining position. Besides gold, we should also demand territorial concessions from Gath. Perhaps even negotiate special trade deals. We can expand the kingdom without shedding a drop of blood."

"And expand your power at the same time, eh, Beker?"

"That is mean-spirited, Prince Jonathan. Israel's interests are my interests."

"Anyway, Beker, your supposed *excellent bargaining position* is a delusion. The militia has already gone home. Our soldiers are the remnants of broken units. It would take an entire day just to get them in marching order. If only one of those Philistine kings grows a pair of stones and comes back with a single regiment to call your bluff, we lose."

"The military is not my area of expertise. General Abner, is the situation really as dire as the prince describes?"

Nathan shook his head at how skillfully Beker had slithered out of an awkward position. The man had implied that Jonathan was only guessing and then dumped the entire mess on Abner. The general's lengthy silence served to support Jonathan's analysis. It took Karaz to finally put the point on the end of the spear.

"Well, that's settled. Now what?"

The impromptu conference progressed quickly once Beker's grandiose scheme was discarded. Karaz recommended they convince Achish that Israel's king was now in a position of strength. Saul would prove that by being magnanimous. Since Maoch was undoubtedly dead, Achish would be given his father's body as a gesture of good will. There was some bickering that Saul should receive at least a token payment of gold. Jonathan quashed that argument by asking if the King of Israel should be known as *a seller of corpses*. Saul summoned Achish so that Beker could announce the king's decision. Nathan detected a pained expression on the Philistine's face as he approached. But before the *Yameen* could speak, Achish asked a question.

"Is that really necessary, Beker?"

"Is what necessary, Prince Achish?"

"The horses. You are torturing my horses."

Nathan realized that he and his companions had become hardened to the continuous cries of the crippled Philistine horses. Jonathan stepped forward when Beker turned his head in a plea for assistance.

"Not your horses anymore, Philistine."

"Still, Hebrew, such valuable animals should not be destroyed."

"They're not valuable to us. Can't use them. Can't feed them. We certainly can't let you have them."

"Even if I paid for them?"

"No, but I can sell you all the donkeys you desire."

Achish's head snapped back at Jonathan's last remark. The Israelite prince cocked his head and advanced to within a few paces of his Philistine counterpart. Jonathan's lips spread in a sly grin as recognition slowly dawned on Achish's face.

"You."

"It's nice to be remembered, Achish. And I have such fond memories of our dealings in Gibeon."

"Jonathan. Running the family donkey business for his father Saul. Was he a king then?"

"No. The family's moved up since Gibeon. Still have the donkeys though."

"That is why my tenure there was so frustrating. Donkeys for supplies. Donkeys for patrols. Donkeys for raids. You knew every move I would make."

"Call it good planning. We like to keep our customers satisfied."

"You even have your sour faced friend with you."

"You mean Nathan? Never could hide his feelings about your people. Something to do with his father's murder. He's touchy about that."

"Can we move on? What about my request?"

Nathan knew the plan had been for Beker to defer to Saul on announcing the decision. Unfortunately, Achish had thrown everything off kilter by straying onto the topic of horses. Jonathan, not Beker, was now leading the discussion. Thus, Achish had directed his question to the prince, not the king. The impulsive Jonathan began to answer without a second thought. Saul attempted to interrupt his son but hesitated a heartbeat too long. The result was an embarrassing stammer which the king immediately cut off. This royal gaffe was not lost on the

Philistine prince. Nathan saw Achish's eyes flicker briefly toward Saul as Jonathan continued speaking.

"Here is the king's decree. You will be allowed to search for your father and recover his body. You may keep your gold."

"No ransom?"

"It's your lucky day, Achish. We'll even provide you with an escort."

"Most generous."

"KARAZ!"

"Yes, Prince Jonathan?"

"Karaz, please inform Prince Achish of how the search will be conducted. Then guide him wherever he wishes to go."

"Right. Now listen carefully, Achish, because I'll only say this once. Pick six men. Side arms only. No chariots. No bows. No javelins."

"May I..."

"No."

"You have the manners of a Hittite, Karaz."

"My parents would be pleased to hear that."

"How did you end up among the Hebrews?"

"Some of your Philistines put me out of work. And you *really* don't want me remembering what they did to my family right now."

"Fair enough. Are you our only escort?"

"I'm all you'll need."

Many in the Royal Court seemed shaken by Karaz's rough manners during a supposedly delicate encounter, but Nathan thought the Hittite's performance was flawless. There would be no misunderstandings after Karaz's blunt instructions. Rather than looking offended, Achish had the air of someone who got a much better deal than expected.

Nathan had been standing with his arms crossed up to now. He relaxed and lowered his arms since everything seemed settled. However, Achish's sudden mood change caught Nathan completely off guard. The Philistine's face paled. Achish pointed at Nathan's chest and howled his next words.

"WHERE DID YOU GET THAT?"

A stunned Nathan followed the direction of Achish's finger to the golden medallion and chain around his neck. His battle trophy had been hidden by crossed arms until now. Nathan slowly pulled himself upright and calmly returned Achish's glare.

"I took it from a man I killed in battle."

"*You killed* the man wearing it?"

By this time, Achish's hand was resting on the hilt of his sword. Nathan read the savage look in the Philistine's eyes. He gripped his own sword while carefully considering Achish's question. The wrong answer would most likely result in one of their deaths. Nathan raised his other hand to forestall anyone else's intervention.

"He wasn't wearing it. He dropped it during the fight."

The terse answer drained the fury from Achish's face. Both men relaxed the grip on their respective weapons. Nathan watched the Philistine's countenance shift from anger to curiosity. Achish requested a description of Nathan's opponent and nodded at each detail. However, the last item caused an unexpectedly strong reaction.

"You say there was a *green* streamer on the man's helmet, Nathan?"

"Yes. Do you know him?"

"Not personally. The armor and weapon you describe are common among mercenaries from the island of Crete. However, the green streamer identifies his employer. It is of no consequence to today's business."

"Then why the ruckus, Achish?"

"That medallion symbolizes the power of the Kingdom of Gath. It is only worn by the king."

"So, you thought I killed your father."

"Except, Nathan, the man was carrying it, not wearing it. The Cretan must have taken it from my father's body."

"Which means?"

"As far as I am concerned, it was a prize taken honorably in battle. However, I must have it back. I will pay whatever price you ask."

"No."

"You intend to keep it?"

"No, but I will not sell it."

Nathan lifted the heavy gold chain over his head. He looked longingly at the valuable medallion before tossing it to an astonished Achish.

"Why, Nathan?"

"My father was murdered by Philistine soldiers while I was a boy. I have almost nothing to remember him by. I will not deprive another orphan of a keepsake from his father."

Memories of his father's death nearly produced tears. The touch of a hand on his shoulder brought Nathan out of his reverie. He turned toward the warm smile of Jonathan. Karaz nodded approval from a few feet away. Saul likewise beamed his pleasure, as if remembering simpler days gone by. Abner looked bored. Beker wore his calculating expression. Nathan took the most satisfaction from Achish's incredulous demeanor as he struggled to speak.

"Nathan…are you a prince?"

"No."

"You should be."

Chapter 1 - The Reconciliation

So, Saul asked God, "Shall I pursue the Philistines? Will You give them over to Israel?" But God did not answer Saul that day. Then Saul said, "We will find out what sin has been committed today by casting lots. Even if it was committed by my son, Jonathan, he must die."

The first lot was cast between Saul, Jonathan and the soldiers. That lot fell on Saul and Jonathan, while the soldiers were cleared. Then Saul said, "Cast the lot between me and Jonathan." And the lot fell on Jonathan. Saul said, "May God deal with me severely, Jonathan, if you do not die this day."

But the soldiers said to Saul, "Should Jonathan die after delivering Israel this day? Never! As surely as the LORD lives, you will not harm a hair on his head. He had God's help today." Thus, the soldiers rescued Jonathan from death.

Saul then stopped the pursuit and the Philistines withdrew to their homeland.

From the book of I Samuel, chapter 14, verses 37, 38, 39, 41, 42, 44, 45 and 46

Captured Philistine camp on Michmash Plateau

Nathan crouched before a small fire in front of his tent as he prepared an evening meal of stew. Looking toward the setting sun, Nathan could see the peak where he and Jonathan had overrun the Philistine outpost. He shook his head to think the adventure had occurred barely two days before. It seemed ages ago.

Today's unexpected encounter with Prince Achish had drained him emotionally. Any encounter with a Philistine could bring on nightmares of his father's murder. Yet the spectacle of Achish searching for his own father had produced conflict in Nathan, a confusing mixture of resentment and empathy. The Philistine prince's search for Maoch had been mercifully short and successful. Nathan had refrained from viewing the enemy king's body, but Karaz thought the wounds indicated assassination, not battle. However, that was Achish's mess to clean up, not his. The young man might even be King Achish now, but Nathan had more pressing concerns than Philistine politics.

How had a family quarrel grown into a national crisis which threatened the very existence of the Kingdom of Israel? Many prominent Israelites were dismayed by Saul's recent performance. Their anointed king had begun with a great flourish against the Ammonites, only to flounder against the Philistines. Which action better predicted Saul's ability to rule? The question concerned more than the usual tribal and clan politics; all feared for the future safety of their families. Many whispered that Jonathan had triumphed over the Philistines twice. Why not place the crown on the head of the charismatic young warrior? Yet, others viewed Jonathan's battlefield behavior as recklessness. Had not Jonathan merely saved the nation from a disaster that he had created? A small, but growing, faction favored removing Saul and his entire family from the Throne and starting over.

Fortunately, there was still time to salvage the dynasty. Israelites were by nature argumentative. Any group seeking to depose Saul would struggle to garner sufficient support. A difficult task, but not an impossible one. And, if Samuel chose to intervene, events could move swiftly. It was clear to both Saul and Jonathan that they needed each other if their dynasty was to survive the year. Of course, Nathan was troubled by a more selfish interest. If the royal family fell, so would his dreams of revenge.

"Are you going to eat all of that?"

Nathan spun around to see Jonathan and Karaz approach out of the lengthening shadows. A few hours before, the young prince had decided to confront the king over their recent schism. Jonathan had requested a one-on-one session to hammer out a reconciliation, but Saul wanted his aides to participate. They finally agreed on one advisor each. Jonathan picked Karaz and Saul chose Beker. Although no sentries were posted, the meeting tent was well guarded. Abner, Saul's cousin, lounged beneath a tree with a score of his henchmen. Laban, Jonathan's recently appointed bodyguard, stood watch nearby with an equal number of men loyal to the prince. The glares of these fearsome warriors were enough to keep curious bystanders at a distance. No one outside the royal tent would know the fate of the kingdom...until now.

Nathan dished out two steaming bowls and nodded toward a nearby water skin. Both men drank their fill before enthusiastically digging into the stew. Neither Jonathan or Karaz seemed immediately inclined to share their experiences. Nathan took a few bites of his meal before indulging his curiosity.

"Didn't your father feed you?"

"He was not feeling particularly hospitable when we started. Even less so at the end."

"Still, your negotiations must have been successful."

"Why do you say that, Nathan?"

"No one died. At least, not yet."

Karaz chuckled over Nathan's pithy summary.

"The boy did me proud today, Jonathan did. Best military victory of his young life. Jonathan made concessions on items that Saul would never have given up. In return, he seized valuable ground where the king saw no value. Just like I taught him."

"Yet I suspect, even now, Beker is bragging to Saul about what fools you both were."

"I hope so, Nathan. Saul may have the gold, but Jonathan got the iron."

Both men then explained to Nathan the key points of the agreement with Saul. Everyone agreed the burden of ruling was too great for Saul to bear alone, yet Jonathan could not be allowed to outshine the king. The first issue settled was the prince's position at Court. Jonathan would be confirmed as heir to the throne and second to his father in authority. When Saul was away from Court, the prince would rule in the king's name. In return, Jonathan agreed to always demonstrate his complete support of Saul as king, while restraining his impulsive tendencies.

The next topic was the kingdom's military command structure. Saul would remain as head of the Royal Army, but with Abner as his field general commanding the regular Army regiments. Abner would appoint the regimental commanders, subject to Saul's approval. Jonathan would be Saul's second in command during time of war, but always remain at his father's side. During a national mobilization, Jonathan would lead the semi-independent militia units raised by the Israelite tribes, but only until the crisis had passed. However, Jonathan would be allowed to raise an independent company, with Laban as their captain, to serve as his personal bodyguard. Nathan would be Jonathan's military advisor and have a seat on the King's War Council with the other senior officers. Karaz would both serve as the War Council Chief and train the officers of the Royal Army. However, the Hittite mercenary would never again hold a field command of his own.

Nathan crossed his legs and rested elbows on knees while digesting both his food and this new arrangement. Somehow, he did not feel the same level of enthusiasm as Jonathan and Karaz. Nathan saw no "gold" and very little "iron" for Jonathan. The plain-speaking Karaz instantly sensed Nathan's pessimism.

"Well now, Boy. You look like you just bit into a donkey turd."

"That obvious, huh?"

"As a botched circumcision. Feel free to correct me, Nathan, but we don't intend to depose Saul, do we?"

"Of course not!"

"Of course not. Your God selected Saul. That means we support him. Even though he's mediocre king. Even though he acts rashly. Even though he was publicly embarrassed more

30

than once by *someone here whose name I won't mention, Jonathan.* But mainly because Saul is a good man."

"Is he really, Karaz? He's changed."

"That goes with the crown, Nathan. Being a king is more frightening than it is pleasurable. A commoner can be forgiven for weakness, but not a king. No wonder Saul follows the counsel of visible men rather than trust an invisible God. They whisper what he craves to hear and not what he needs to hear."

"Men like Beker and Abner."

"Jonathan negotiated this arrangement primarily to weaken their grip on Saul. The son wins back the trust of the father. We take some weight off the royal shoulders; we calm his fears. We give good advice; Saul becomes a stronger king."

"Yet, Beker runs the government and Abner commands the army. Where is this "iron" which Jonathan supposedly won?"

"Beker's position is surprisingly weak. His self-appointed title lacks any popular support. His influence is based on bribes, bullying and a shrewd use of the king's name. Beker deludes people into believing they have no choice but to deal with him. Our *Yameen* may be the most hated man in Israel. Most of his allies are only a step away from becoming enemies."

"Sounds like you know the type, Karaz."

"Go to any kingdom, Nathan, and shake a tree. A bushel of Bekers will fall out. His only real power stems from his association with Abner."

"Who has our entire army under his thumb."

"Not entirely. Abner has the field command, but the War Council will choose his battles. And while he appoints the three regimental commanders, I will *train* and *promote* all his junior officers. Thirty captains. Sixty lieutenants. Six hundred sergeants. When I finish, their loyalty will be first to Saul and then to Jonathan. The common soldiers may fear Abner, but few will love him. Besides, Jonathan commands the militias of all twelve tribes. That should keep Beker and Abner from misusing the Army."

"So much for Abner. How does Jonathan put Beker in his place?"

"By using his popularity and infamous charm. As commander of the militias, Jonathan can build strong relationships with the Tribal leaders. As heir to the throne, Jonathan's word carries greater weight than Beker's. The *Yameen* will soon find it difficult to oppose the prince."

Karaz's reassurances helped calm Nathan, but he still had doubts. Politics never seemed to be straightforward. There were always schemes within schemes. If Beker and Abner had overlooked something, Jonathan and Karaz probably had as well. The prince easily recognized Nathan's anxiety and cast a sly smile towards his friend.

"Of course, Karaz has an alternative strategy if everything goes in the dung heap."

"You do?"

"I'm a survivor, Boy. You know I always have a fallback plan. It's both simple and brilliant. We can rid ourselves of this nest of vipers and live a life of luxury."

"And how might we accomplish such a miracle?"

"The three of us go into exile."

The outrageous suggestion immediately distracted Nathan from his dark mood, just as Jonathan intended. Nathan glared at his Hittite mentor in horror.

"That's a terrible idea!"

"Just hear me out, Lad. Saul's not the only one in the market for an instant army. Many kingdoms would be thrilled to hire the men who crushed the Philistines. Why, we could equip and train up our own regiment in less than a year."

"And then what?"

"We depose our employer and place Jonathan on the man's throne."

"How many kings would be that stupid, Karaz?"

"More than you would think. Mercenaries do it all the time."

"And you approve of this insanity, Jonathan?"

"No. But I thought the concept would amuse you."

Nathan's righteous indignation slowly lost ground against Jonathan's beguiling grin. Then he made the mistake of looking at Karaz. The Hittite cocked his head and wiggled his eyebrows twice. It was enough to cause Nathan to release a week of tension in one long laugh. Karaz simply shook his head and sighed.

"Too bad, Boys. I know a couple of small kingdoms to the east that would be *perfect* for us. Remember. You can always change your minds."

Gath's royal palace in Philistia

Though Achish would never admit it, this particular chamber deep within the bowels of the palace still filled him with awe. The dark, undecorated walls were rough-cut stone. A pair of ventilation shafts provided air to the windowless room. A solitary oil lampstand provided the only illumination. The small wooden table and its matching four chairs had been expensively crafted long ago. Now they wobbled and creaked with age. The confined space provided barely enough room to move around. The chamber's most striking feature was its heavily fortified door. The narrow passageway outside rendered battering rams useless; there was not even enough clearance to swing an axe. The room's occupants could be secure in the knowledge they would never be taken alive.

For over twenty years, Achish had lived in this fortress with no idea the dreary room even existed. Not until his father, King Maoch, had summoned him several weeks ago to plot the conquest of Israel. This secluded refuge had been where conspiracies were conceived, assassinations approved, allies betrayed, and armies mobilized. Ironically, this room was the most honest place in Gath. Royal decree forbade any type of lying here. Only truth was to be spoken, no matter how unpleasant, with no penalty to the bearer. Maoch had accomplished more from this worn-out chair at the head of the table than he had from his throne.

Now it was Achish's chair. The thought sent a chill down his spine.

The recently crowned King of Gath waited silently as his two closest allies squeezed into their chairs. Davon, only six years older than Achish, was a battle-hardened soldier. As a young lieutenant, Davon had been assigned to watch over the teenage prince during his first battle. When disaster forced Achish to assume command, Davon served ably as his adjutant. Rapid promotion followed as he helped his prince achieve several notable victories. However, the Philistine debacle at Michmash left King Maoch dead and Gath's infantry regiments shattered. Only Gath's chariot corps remained unscathed. A desperate Achish had made Davon the Commander of the Army of Gath. With this promotion came the dubious honor of building a new army from scratch in only a few months. Their Philistine brethren would not hesitate to invade a militarily weak Gath. It was simply a question of who could finish licking their wounds first.

The older man at the table was a legacy from Maoch. He was Abimelek, the *Archon* of Gath. In years past, *Archon* had been largely an administrative post in the kingdom. Abimelek had used his legendary cunning to expand the position under Maoch. He was respected as Gath's chief diplomat, spymaster, and the king's closest confidant. Abimelek was feared because he performed all the king's dirty jobs. Achish did not trust the *Archon*, but he needed the man's skills. After all, Abimelek had arranged Achish's ascension to the Throne.

35

Achish would never forget that fateful day. He was still wearing his sweat-soaked armor when Abimelek confronted him during the humiliating retreat from Michmash. The *Archon* had arrogantly offered his services as kingmaker, implying that Achish was merely the first on his list of candidates. Abimelek had rushed back to Gath bearing a death list approved by Achish and accompanied by Davon's soldiers to suppress any dissent. Everything was in order when Achish returned to his Capital. All his rivals had been killed. Their surviving supporters were suitably bribed, intimidated, or exiled. Circumstances precluded an extravagant ceremony, so Achish's coronation had been a modest affair.

This clandestine session was Achish's first official function since becoming king. Now that his power was relatively secure, Achish wanted to establish the facts of his father's death. He felt no emotion or grief. This was a cold-blooded affair of state. Whoever had killed Maoch was a threat to the kingdom. His kingdom. Achish had returned to Michmash to retrieve Maoch's body and came away with a mystery as well. He was counting on Abimelek to help solve it.

"I assume you received my inquiry from Michmash, Abimelek. What have you found?"

"We both have separate pieces to the matter of Maoch's death, Achish. I suggest you share yours first. I will then try to fill in the gaps."

Achish hid his irritation at the *Archon's* obstinate refusal to use his proper title in private. Just another way to remind the neophyte king of his vulnerability. Achish described his meeting with the Hebrew royalty, the recovery of his father's medallion and the search for Maoch's body. Achish had also found the body of Uruk, a rugged scout who was the closest person Maoch had to a friend. Neither man had been wounded in battle. The two men were vicious fighters and unlikely to be surprised by an enemy. Conclusion: both had died from treachery, probably together. Achish found the testimony of the Hebrew Nathan to be most significant. Nathan had taken Maoch's royal medallion from a soldier he had killed in battle. The Hebrew's description was of a Cretan mercenary employed by Gaza. None of these disturbing revelations seemed to upset Abimelek. The *Archon* stared briefly at Achish with hooded eyes before replying.

"Now to add my pieces. At your request, I began seeking out the officers from this Cretan regiment. I discovered a curious fact. Fewer than one common soldier in ten of that regiment had been killed. However, all the officers were dead...except one, the second-in-command. The man was badly wounded. Turns out his fellow officers had been assassinated one, by one, after the battle. Only the intervention of the man's bodyguards kept him alive. The assassin was killed in the process."

"Did the man talk?"

"Oh, he became quite chatty after I offered him and his guards protection. The mercenary general had been promised a hefty fee to murder Maoch when a suitable occasion presented itself. The chaos at Michmash provided the perfect opportunity. Your Hebrew friend's victim was undoubtedly one of the four Cretan soldiers entrusted with the deed."

"And their employer?"

"Kaftor."

Achish's fists balled up upon hearing the name of the hated King of Gaza. Kaftor had been Maoch's bitter rival for years. His father had considered the man more dangerous than the other three Philistine kings combined, which was saying a lot. Kaftor was not a warrior but a schemer who struck from the shadows. The method of Maoch's murder was just the scoundrel's style. Achish took notice of the dark look spreading across his general's features. Davon never expressed any love for Maoch, but the man was a soldier. His professional pride undoubtedly took offense at someone killing his king. On the other hand, Abimelek's expression was as tranquil as if discussing the weather. Obviously, the *Archon* had much experience with such intrigue.

"So, where is your Cretan informant now, Abimelek?"

"Alas, Achish, the poor soul died from his wounds."

"And his bodyguards?"

"They also died from his wounds."

Achish snorted in response to his *Archon's* gallows humor. Abimelek knew the power of secrets and how to protect them. With the elimination of these final witnesses, the King of Gaza would think his murderous trail had been swept clean. Assassinating the Cretan regiment's entire roster of officers was excessive, but one of Kaftor's few virtues was thoroughness. When Abimelek next spoke, there was a hint of amusement, as if the man had made a wager with himself.

"So now, *my King*. What do you intend to do?"

This belated use of his royal title gave Achish no satisfaction. He felt Abimelek was toying with him, like a tutor with a dull pupil. Achish pondered the evidence before him. Kaftor had gotten away with murder. Gaza now possessed the largest body of infantry in all Philistia. Gath, on the other hand, was at its nadir. Achish's kingdom was unsettled. Gath's survival depended on fewer than 800 chariots, an untested reserve infantry regiment, some garrison troops, and the hundreds of dispirited survivors of Michmash. Yet Kaftor was not invincible. The man was a cunning strategist, but a second-rate tactician. Losing nearly his entire chariot force at Michmash was a colossal blunder. Kaftor's unsavory reputation would make the other Philistine kings reluctant to ally with him. And Achish possessed a significant advantage over his adversary.

Kaftor had no idea Achish knew the identity of Maoch's murderer.

Meanwhile, Abimelek showed no sign of impatience while awaiting an answer. He seemed content to allow Achish to struggle mentally. Achish suddenly realized the reason behind the older man's composure. If the young king proved unfit, the *Archon* could simply find another patron and place him on the Throne. Achish had no intention of allowing that. There was no doubt in his mind when he finally answered.

"Nothing, Abimelek. I will do nothing."

"Good!"

The older man seemed suddenly energized by Achish's decision. He even smiled for the first time in the secret chamber. Davon had the opposite reaction. The general pounded the ancient table with both fists as he howled.

39

"Good? GOOD? What do you mean good? Our king was murdered. We're practically at war. Our army is a mirage...and don't grin at me like some happy drunk, Abimelek. We must do something!"

"My dear General. There is doing *nothing*. And then there is *doing* nothing. Our wise young ruler has chosen to practice the *deep strategy*. That is what I called *good*."

Achish was pleased to watch as Davon calmed himself and took on a thoughtful countenance. He needed both men to be different, but also to be able to cooperate. After a moment, Davon gestured for Abimelek to continue.

"General, we must look beyond the hill tops and toward the mountain peaks. Our weapons must be patience, watching, listening, posturing and pretense. We will make enemies feel like friends. Our allies must become invisible. Months, perhaps even years, will pass before our efforts bear fruit. Yet this subtle stratagem offers our best hope for complete victory and a delicious revenge. Are we agreed, Achish?"

"Rest assured, Davon, we will be quite busy. It's just that no one outside this room must notice."

"Fine. Both of you have convinced me, but you seem to have overlooked one thing. We must first solve the problems on our *hilltops,* or we will not live long enough to reach the *mountains*."

"Ah, yes. You mean our temporary military weakness. What concerns you most, General?"

"I can handle the recruiting and the training of our new army, Abimelek. But equipment and time are out of my control."

"I have already set some wheels in motion to obtain the necessary equipment."

"Encouraging but understand this. We are doomed if Gaza attacks us before autumn."

"I can assure you, General, you will have at least that long."

"How?"

"I will betray Achish to Kaftor."

This unexpected turn in the discussion caught Achish completely off balance. His mouth opened and closed without uttering a sound. Davon, on the other hand began chuckling. The general's mirth continued as he drew out a wicked-looking dagger and laid it on the table. Pointed straight at Abimelek. For the first time, the *Archon* looked unsure of himself. He seemed more afraid of Davon's eyes than the weapon.

"I deserve that, General. For trying to be glib with you. What I meant to say is that I will approach Kaftor and *offer* to betray Achish."

"How does that buy us time?"

"Kaftor never goes to war if he can achieve his ends by duplicity. The prospect of seizing Gath through my treason will be irresistible to him. Conspiracies by nature require time to mature. There is always haggling about terms, price, and timing.

I can easily lead him along until autumn. He will gladly wait. Remember, he will not suspect we are avenging Maoch."

Davon's only response was to replace his dagger in its sheath. However, Achish was not inclined to let the *Archon* off so easily.

"I have to wonder, Abimelek. What if Kaftor makes *you* an irresistible offer?"

"You have nothing to fear, Achish. I could never come to terms with Kaftor. You see...we are too much alike. Coexistence is impossible. Ultimately, Kaftor would have to kill me before I killed him."

"This is comforting to know."

"No, my King. If I betray you, it will have to be with someone totally different."

Chapter 2 - The War Council

After Saul began to rule over Israel, he fought enemies on every side: the Moabites, the Ammonites, the Edomites, the Arameans and the Philistines.

From the book of I Samuel, chapter 14, verse 47

Captured Philistine Camp on Michmash Plateau

King Saul and Prince Jonathan had quickly agreed on the gravest threat to their dynasty. Despite the recent victory over the Philistines, the Nation's confidence in their king's military leadership had been severely damaged. A swift victory was required to restore the people's trust. Mounting a campaign to provide that victory would be the War Council's next task.

Two days after the alleged royal reconciliation, Saul's War Council convened inside a former Philistine noble's tent in the abandoned enemy camp at Michmash. Royal attendants had looted rich wine, plush chairs and exquisite tables from nearby Philistine tents for the comfort of those participating in today's session. Since the Council was intended to bring together all the leaders of a campaign, its membership was fluid. Permanent members were Saul as king, Jonathan as his second-in-command, Karaz as his War Chief, Abner as his Field General, Nathan as the prince's advisor, and the regimental commanders, currently three. Any tribes providing militia for an engagement would also have a representative on the Council, but they would be brought later as needed.

Samuel would also have been a permanent member, but the current rift between the prophet and the king precluded his attendance.

Saul wished to convene the War Council sooner, but Karaz had begged extra time to prepare. The Hittite viewed the War Council as just another battlefield. Karaz was wary of Abner and his appointed commanders since they constituted half of the Council. Although Nathan had been added to provide more balance, Abner still possessed great leverage. However, Karaz knew astute planning could offset an opponent's numerical advantage. So, the War Chief had privately met with Jonathan and Nathan to hone their strategy.

As War Chief, Karaz presented the session's agenda to Saul. In accordance with the king's mandate for an immediate military campaign, three simple questions would be discussed. First: Who would be attacked? Second: What would be the scope of the attack? Third: How soon could the attack be mounted?

Nathan was already privy to Karaz's approach and appreciated it both for its simplicity and its effectiveness. The choice of foe would dictate the type of campaign. The selection of the foe and the campaign type would determine the time needed to prepare. If the required preparation time was longer than the king desired, the Council could then modify the type of campaign or even select a different foe until all three elements satisfied Saul.

Abner wasted no time in laying out his vision for Israel's next war. The Philistine military had been crippled at Michmash. It was time to permanently eliminate the Philistine threat before they recovered. While the Royal Army under Abner cleared the Philistine garrisons out of the passes and roads leading to Philistia, Israel's national militia would be mobilized. The path would lay open for Saul to lead over one hundred thousand warriors into battle. The speed of this unexpected invasion would prevent the decimated Philistine armies from uniting for a common defense. The Israelites would strip the enemy's land bare of food during their advance. One Philistine city after another would fall before them. Israel would hail Saul and the neighboring kingdoms would fear him. Saul would finally bask in the glory he was due. Abner wanted to move before the end of the month.

By the time Abner finished, Saul was nodding his agreement. As expected, each of the three regimental commanders heartily endorsed Abner's strategy. Even Nathan would be shouting his agreement if Karaz had not previously explained why vengeance on the Philistines must be deferred for now.

Nathan reflected on how Abner's presentation matched the man's true nature: shock the enemy by hitting hard and fast. Just as predictably, Abner also sought to curry favor with the king. The general chose the Philistines as adversaries knowing it would appeal to Saul. It was also exactly the plan Karaz had anticipated the man would espouse. Now, Abner would see what happened when a well-prepared opponent refused to be shocked and provided some surprises of his own.

Abner's first surprise came when Karaz remained silent and Jonathan began speaking. After spending much of his speech eying Karaz, the general seemed taken aback when the young prince challenged him instead. Nathan knew this too was part of Karaz's strategy to boost Jonathan's prestige.

45

"Tell me Abner. Are you proposing to fight both Philistia and Egypt?"

"Egypt? What does Egypt have to do with anything?"

"Your one hundred thousand men will need to move along the road through the Beth-Horan pass in order to strike quickly into Philistia. The exit from the pass is controlled by the fortified city of Gezer. For generations, it has been garrisoned by Egyptian soldiers...a great many Egyptian soldiers."

"Jonathan, I... we are not going into Philistia to fight Egyptians. Our men will simply bypass Gezer."

"What if the Egyptians will not let you pass?"

"Of course, they allow us to pass! They would be fools to take on our army!"

"They would be fighting our militia, Abner, not our army. My last question still requires an answer. What if the Egyptians decide not to allow us to invade one of their loyal vassals? What if they move into the Beth-Horan pass, or any easily fortified strong point, before our militia arrives? Could our militia fight their way past hundreds of veteran Egyptian soldiers?"

"Forget the militia! I would use our three Army regiments to force a passage anywhere that it might be necessary."

"Three weak regiments?"

"They will be strong enough for the job! Satisfied?"

"Yes, Abner, I am. Now back to my first question. Are you prepared to war on both Philistia and Egypt? For I seriously doubt Pharaoh will allow our Army to slaughter one of his garrisons."

For an instant, Nathan feared Abner would strike Jonathan. The general had obviously never even considered the possibility of Egypt's involvement. Naturally, no one could predict if the Egyptian garrison would fight, but such a glaring oversight was embarrassing to Abner. And it allowed Jonathan to neatly steal the initiative. The prince then pressed his advantage before Abner could think a way out of his predicament.

"Abner, we can discuss the Egyptian issue later, but I have more questions. I agree with you that we have a decided numerical superiority over the Philistine infantry. Yet, the Philistines still possess a formidable chariot force, and the ground favors them on the coastal plains."

"We can keep our men in a formation that Philistine chariots will find difficult to assault without support from their infantry. We will give battle only when conditions favor us."

"True, such tactics could protect our men. However, the mobility of chariots would allow the Philistines to cut off our lines of supply and communication."

"I have already said that our men can live off the land. We could go weeks without any supplies from home."

"Abner, when is the next harvest in Philistia? My understanding is their crops were planted recently, and it would be several months before they could feed our hungry soldiers. Do you propose delaying our attack until then?"

Nathan could see the general's mounting frustration in the face of Jonathan's pointed questions. But never one to admit failure, Abner pressed on.

"No, I will not delay. Even if you are correct, the Philistines will have last season's grain in their warehouses and livestock in their fields. We will simply adjust our objectives based on the available food. If the situation becomes critical, our men can withdraw to positions where we can feed them."

"I see. Well, Abner, I have just one final question. Why should our Army fight to capture passes and roads which lead to places we may not be able to hold?"

Abner leaned back in his chair in bitter silence. Words were not necessary as the general's eyes effectively conveyed his anger. When Abner turned his hostile stare on the silent Karaz, Nathan assumed he blamed the Hittite as well. The general was only partially right because both Jonathan and Nathan had contributed their own ideas to Karaz's. However, Nathan observed Saul growing increasingly annoyed by Jonathan's apparent defeatism. The king came to the aid of his embattled general.

"Jonathan, do you have a better alternative?"

"I do, Father. I propose that we attack three other kingdoms instead."

"Son, your jest is in poor taste."

"I am quite serious, Father. We can achieve the victories you seek by attacking the Moabites, the Edomites and the Arameans. Not together, but one after another in rapid succession."

Jonathan's words seemed to energize Abner. Nathan assumed that the general saw a chance to redeem himself in Saul's eyes.

"This is your proposal? Instead of attacking one weak enemy, you propose to attack three strong neighbors? Jonathan, how can you...."

Saul interrupted Abner's tirade by raising his hand for silence while studying his son's face. Jonathan refused to flinch under the king's stern gaze. Saul's expression slowly changed from annoyance to thoughtful consideration.

"Explain why three wars would be better than one war."

"They give us the greatest possible gains for the least amount of effort."

"A noble goal, Jonathan, yet how could your plan surpass Abner's?"

"What troubles the twelve tribes most, Father? That substantial lands allotted to them by Joshua are occupied by enemies along our northern, eastern and southern borders. Our people there are continually threatened by raids or demands for tribute. By expelling the Moabites, the Edomites and the Arameans from even small areas, we not only enlarge our borders, but also increase the security of our interior."

"That is also true of our western border with Philistia. Most would prefer that we expel the Philistines first."

"Except that dealing with Philistia would require an enormous effort for rather modest gains. Put Abner at the head of one hundred thousand men next month, and he will drive back the Philistines. But will he wipe out the Philistine armies in a single blow? Even Abner doesn't promise that. Our militia must return home for the harvest, followed by next year's planting. The Royal Army alone cannot hold the flat plains of Philistia against chariots. They would be forced to withdraw to defensible mountain passes when the militia left. The Philistines would spend the next year recovering their strength and re-taking everything Abner gained."

Nathan studied the impact of Jonathan's words on both Saul and Abner. The general's disagreement was obvious, but evidently he could not refute the prince's logic. The king's response was altogether different. Saul looked like a man desperately seeking a solution. All listened as Jonathan pressed his advantage.

"And there is the question of provoking Egypt, Father. Pharaoh would not grieve if every single Philistine were killed, so long as Egypt's coastal trade routes remained secure. But...Egypt might feel threatened enough to attack us if those trade routes came under our control. However, the Moabites, the Edomites and the Arameans are not Egyptian vassals."

"You have not mentioned the Ammonites. They are also on our eastern border, between the Arameans and the Moabites."

"Father, when you crushed their army at Jabesh-Gilead, it initiated an Ammonite civil war. It will be years before they want anything to do with Israel."

"Who do you recommend we attack first?"

"The Moabites. They are between the Edomites to the south and the Arameans to the north. We would be in a position to prevent the other two kingdoms from coming to Moab's aid and uniting against us. Once Moab is subdued, Edom would be isolated in the south and ripe for the next attack. This would leave the Arameans alone to face us in the north. In each battle, we will enjoy the advantage in numbers by fighting them one at a time."

"I see. Abner, how soon could your three regiments move against Moab? To summon all the tribal militia will require..."

"Father, only one Army regiment will be needed against Moab if it is backed by the normal militia levy from the tribe of Rueben."

"That's barely ten thousand men! "

"That size force should be sufficient for all three campaigns. Our second regiment, supported by the militia levy from Judah, will be used against Edom. Our third regiment, with militia from Manasseh, will fight the Arameans."

"But Jonathan, why not use all our forces at the same time?

"There are several reasons, Father. Speed and surprise are essential. They are more easily achieved with ten thousand men than with one hundred thousand. Don't forget that the Royal Army regiments are in disarray; we need time to rebuild them. Karaz can reorganize the First Royal Regiment for Moab in a month. He would then prepare the Second Royal Regiment during the Moab campaign and the Third Royal Regiment during the Edom campaign."

"True, but what can they accomplish against the armies which our enemies can field?"

"Each force can win, if given achievable objectives. We are not conquering an entire kingdom or retaking all the disputed lands. But...there are significant areas which we can pry away from our neighbors now and hold. Seizing these territories will restore the confidence of our tribal elders in the Crown."

"And where are these valuable lands that can be recaptured so easily?"

"I don't know yet."

Nathan groaned at Jonathan's blunt answer to Saul's question. Abner roared like some wounded beast. Even Karaz winced. Yet Jonathan appeared pleased with himself. Saul was so shocked that he spoke barely above a whisper.

"You don't know?"

"I intend to spy out the land before each campaign. The local population knows where the enemy is strong and where he is weak. They see how complacent their foes have become after years of easy occupation. That is why the border clan elders have been begging for help. Anyway, Karaz will use this time to reorganize the First Royal Regiment for Moab. Father, I promise you. There will be no attack without your approval."

After the War Council adjourned, Saul hosted its members to a lavish evening meal featuring sumptuous Philistine delicacies which had not yet spoiled. Afterwards, Nathan and Karaz went to Jonathan's tent to review the Council's decision. Upon entering the oil lamp lit enclosure, Nathan saw the young prince seated at the head of the table with golden goblets and a wine skin. As Jonathan began serving his guests, Nathan gave voice to his suspicions.

"Jonathan, winning over your father was not surprising, but the last thing I expected was for Abner to end up endorsing our plan. This sudden change of heart was truly amazing to behold, unbelievable, in fact. What think you, Karaz? Is Abner plotting something?"

"Of course, Lad! He is still Abner, after all. It just took the dullard awhile to realize that he can't lose."

Nathan considered Karaz's words as he drank from goblet. Jonathan noted his friend's puzzlement and responded.

"Abner knows either we will fail, or we will succeed. If our plans come to naught, the three of us are finished as leaders. Abner will be more powerful than ever. Unfortunately, many good men could be dead, including us."

"But if we succeed, then Abner is finished."

"No, Nathan. Abner still profits from our success, just to a lesser degree. As Commander of the Armies of Israel, he can take credit for all battlefield victories. That is why Abner started playing our tune."

Karaz quietly nodded, obviously pleased with his former pupil. Nathan was still concerned but tried to see light along the dark path before them. He finally took a deep breath and swallowed his fears.

"Then let's get busy. These wars aren't going to start themselves."

Chapter 3 - The Bandit

A bandit is a villainous scoundrel who spreads lies. He winks at you while signaling an ambush with his hands and feet. He plots evil deceit and stirs up dissension.

From the book of Proverbs, chapter 6, verses 11 to 14

The main Plateau of the Reubenites

Nathan believed at that moment he was enjoying the most spectacular view on God's earth.

The journey across the rugged plateau of the tribe of Reuben had been arduous, but worth the effort. Before him to the west, the sun was setting behind the Judean mountains and highlighting the waters of the Dead Sea nearly two thousand feet below the ledge where Nathan was perched. Turning to his left, Nathan gazed down on the Arnon River flowing into the Dead Sea through the deepest gorge he had ever seen. Two miles away, on the south side of the Arnon, he beheld another equally high plateau that was home to the people Nathan had come to fight – the Moabites.

"Almost makes you forget your blisters, doesn't it?"

Jonathan's words brought a smile to Nathan's face as his friend came alongside. Both men had gone without sandals the past few days rather than risk a fatal fall on the steep, treacherous paths, but such risks were necessary for spies traversing this terrain.

Nathan had departed with Jonathan from Michmash the previous week accompanied by Laban and seventy-eight men of the prince's newly formed bodyguard. Their destination was the border between the tribe of Reuben and the Kingdom of Moab, roughly fifty miles away. The need for secrecy was so great that the Elders of Reuben had not been notified of their coming. Nathan was pleased with the number of men Jonathan had selected for their mission. Their party was large enough to impress the local clans, but small enough to avoid the Moabites. They crossed the Jordan River just north of the Dead Sea where the lands of Benjamin and Rueben shared a narrow border. Avoiding the rivers and valleys that crisscrossed the Reubenite heartland, the small band continued west to the main trade route known as the King's Highway. They then turned south skirting the eastern edge of Reuben toward Moab until reaching Dibon, the southernmost town still under Reubenite control.

Nathan had the men set up camp just beyond the town walls while Jonathan entered Dibon to greet the local magistrate. The town would not only be a resource for food and water, but also for contacting tribesmen with knowledge of Moab. Dibon offered another advantage: remoteness. Jonathan would not have to deal with the Reubenite leaders until he was ready.

Now as he and Jonathan took in the grand vista before them, Nathan asked the question weighing most heavily on his mind.

"Jonathan, do you think we really can take back any of this land?"

"I'm sure of it. Look at the river."

Nathan spent several thoughtful minutes studying the area indicated by Jonathan. He compared the high plateaus occupied by Reuben and Moab to two great fortresses separated by a plain. He and Jonathan stood near the narrowest portion of the plain where the Arnon emptied into the Dead Sea. The plain quickly widened from two miles to over ten miles as it stretched toward the eastern desert. The land was fertile. That was evident from the numerous villages on both sides of the river. Little wonder the Moabites had gradually encroached on it over the years. Suddenly, Nathan became aware of the most significant feature within his view.

"The river flows much closer to Moab, practically at the base of their plateau. That's it, isn't it?"

"Yes. The Reubenites should be able to extend their border to the river. What's preventing them? Moab must hold some advantage over Reuben."

"And how do we find this advantage?"

"Simple. We spy. We pray. We spy some more."

Two days later, Jonathan and Nathan were back at their main camp and hard at work. Nathan organized Laban's men into scouting parties while Jonathan charmed the locals. The prince met with the elders of Dibon, old warriors, traveling merchants, shepherds, and outlying villagers. Each evening, Nathan and Jonathan shared their discoveries. As the days passed, Nathan could see the pieces of a plan coming together.

The Kingdom of Moab was similar in many ways to the tribe of Reuben. The territory of each was roughly forty miles long and thirty miles wide, although where their eastern borders ended, and the desert began, was extremely vague. Their populations were nearly equal in number. Water was in short supply, but the fertile land and the winter rains produced one good crop a year for both peoples, as well as abundant grazing for animals. Both lands were protected against invasion by the Dead Sea to the west and rugged mountains to the north and south. Although there were no mountains to the east, an extensive desert discouraged any major incursions into either country.

The terrain left only one place for both Moab and Rueben to expand...the Arnon River Valley. But as Nathan had observed days before from the high Reubenite plateau, nearly all of this land was on Rueben's side of the river. Nathan also learned from his scouts that the river was a magnificent defensive barrier. The Arnon flowed through steep gorges which would be almost impossible for an army to cross. Yet despite their decided advantage, the Reubenites had allowed the Moabites to gain the upper hand here. Why?

The answer was the city of Aroer.

Aroer sat at a strategic location along the King's Highway, the great inland trade route between Mesopotamia and the Red Sea. More importantly, it was north of where the great road crossed the Arnon River. The city was the Moabite advantage for which Nathan had been diligently searching. Whoever held Aroer decided who would be allowed to cross the river, thereby controlling the Arnon River Valley. Somehow, an earlier generation of Reubenites had allowed Aroer to slip into the hands of the Moabites.

Nathan could imagine all too easily how this had occurred. Although similar in strength to the tribe of Reuben,

Moab benefited from a strong king and a standing army. The leadership of Reuben, on the other hand, lacked unity and would muster their tribal militia only when necessary. Unfortunately, as Nathan well knew, by the time the militia could assemble, it was often too late. The Moabites had apparently found an opportune moment to seize control of Aroer before the Reubenites could mount an effective challenge. Having obtained a solid foothold north of the river, the Moabites began expanding into the valley. Sometimes the Moabites confiscated land for their own use; other times the Moabites were content to exact tribute from the now isolated Reubenite families. Attempts by the Reubenite militia to expel the first Moabites from the valley had been crushed by veteran Moabite soldiers based in Aroer.

Nathan knew that the disunity of Reuben was merely a reflection of the Nation's overall history of dysfunction. Lacking a centralized government, the other Israelite tribes had been free to ignore Reuben's calls for assistance. Even worse, the southern border clans who had lost land to Moab received only lukewarm support from their fellow Reubenites. The better-organized Moabites continued their expansion into the valley as resistance lessened and then ceased altogether. No one could tell Nathan how many soldiers Moab originally used in its conquest, but it appeared that the King of Moab was now holding the disputed territory with a surprisingly small number of soldiers.

After ten days of reconnaissance, the last of Laban's scouts returned to Dibon. Nathan summarized their information for Jonathan over a campfire that evening. Jonathan leaned back against a large rock and closed his eyes as Nathan finished.

"So, Nathan, Aroer is the key to everything. If a Reubenite village resists, soldiers from Aroer come out to punish them. If Reuben sends in their militia, the Moabite Army invades the valley through Aroer. It's worked so well that Reuben doesn't even try anymore."

"I agree. What do we do?"

"Capture Aroer."

"With eighty men? Not bloody likely, Jonathan. Even if Karaz sends us a regiment, I give us only one chance in three."

"We could also call up the Reubenite militia."

"One chance in four then."

Jonathan laughed, then grew serious.

"We're taking that city, Nathan. The problem is we don't know enough about it. We just need to get some good men inside."

Nathan leaned forward with his elbows on his knees and gazed deeply into the flames. His mind searched intently for a way to get the elusive information. His solution was so unorthodox that Nathan clapped his hands with excitement.

"Not *good* men, Jonathan. We need some *bad* men."

The wilderness near the city of Aroer

Ahithophel sat bolt upright in his dark tent and tried to discern what had disturbed his sleep. The six Israelite families

60

he led had managed to survive among the Moabites largely because of his survival instincts. His small band had become skilled in the arts of camouflaged campsites, invisible fires and trails without footprints. Their lives would be simpler if they did not dwell so near the city of Aroer and the King's Highway, but Ahithophel wanted to be near where they worked.

Ahithophel and his people were bandits.

Everything appeared normal at first to Ahithophel. His wife was still asleep in their bedding, as were Ahithophel's young son and infant daughter. His ears finally told him what was amiss: the sound of a large crackling fire just outside the tent. Ahithophel crawled noiselessly away from his bed until he could slowly pull back the lower edge of the tent flap. Someone had indeed added fuel to his family's fire pit and turned its smoldering embers into blazing flames. After Ahithophel's eyes had adjusted to the bright light, he could make out two seated figures facing his tent on the opposite side of the fire. The stranger on the left was cooking a small piece of meat on the end of a long stick. The other sat motionless as if waiting for someone to greet him. Ahithophel was certain both were men, but not his men.

The fools on watch would suffer for their incompetence, but Ahithophel knew that must wait. The bandit chief hurriedly pulled a cloak over his bare shoulders and drew his sword before walking out into the firelight. The two men looked up at Ahithophel but seemed undisturbed by his drawn blade. They were unmistakably warriors. Ahithophel could see both carried swords but kept them in their sheaths. He edged closer to the fire until he could see the men clearly.

The stranger on the right possessed a young face but had the eyes of a much older man. His skin and clothes bespoke a rugged life in the outdoors, as did his rough hands and muscular limbs. Yet he wore a striking gold chain around his neck and a magnificent ring on his left hand. Obviously more than a common soldier, perhaps he was a mercenary officer.

The young man on the left was no less impressive physically but lacked any signs of wealth. He took his eyes off Ahithophel only to check the progress of his cooking. Evidently satisfied, the man pulled out a wicked looking dagger and sliced a small portion of the meat. After tasting it, the man cut a larger piece of meat and extended the slice on his dagger for his companion to eat. It was clear to Ahithophel that the man on the right was the leader. However, this cook was no slave as the manners of the two men bespoke equality.

All these insights still failed to answer Ahithophel's most urgent question: *what to do next?* He doubted that he could defeat both men in combat, perhaps not even one of them. Ahithophel also knew he would already be dead if they so desired. Since his mysterious visitors obviously wanted something, hospitality seemed the most prudent course of action. Ahithophel shrugged his shoulders and sat down cross-legged by the fire with his sword across his lap. He would find a way, somehow, to gain the upper hand. Knowing his fellow bandits were nearby gave Ahithophel a measure of confidence.

"I rarely get to entertain guests."

The Leader snickered before responding.

"Your home is hard to find."

The Cook swallowed his last bite and joined in.

"Took us almost an hour."

"Yet few would dare risk their lives by coming to my camp uninvited, especially if there were only two of them."

The Leader's eyes glowed amusement in the firelight as he responded.

"Small minds are too easily impressed by large numbers. God can use two men to put an entire army to flight. Three hundred men once..."

The Cook rolled his eyes.

"Gideon again?"

The Leader glared at the Cook but did not continue. The meaning of this exchange was lost on Ahithophel, but he always took advantage of disunity whenever he could.

"So then, are you two counted among the great warriors of legend?"

Surprisingly, the Cook provided the response. Between bites, he nodded toward his Leader.

"He is. I just clean the blood off his sword."

Ahithophel smiled. It appeared he might be dealing with a pair of boastful fools after all. Now was the time to get serious.

"Then demonstrate your prowess for me. I can call a score of my armed men..."

"You have eleven men."

The accuracy of the Leader's words caused Ahithophel to blink in surprise. He felt as if he had been stabbed and began to sweat as the Cook joined in to twist the imaginary dagger.

"Unless you count the five boys not yet ready to bear arms."

Ahithophel's eyes darted between the two strangers who appeared both calm and menacing. Ahithophel's fist tightened on his sword as fear gripped his heart. He failed to keep the desperation out of his next words.

"I have but to shout and my men will be upon you!"

When this threat failed to elicit a reaction, Ahithophel hesitated in confusion. As the silence dragged on, the Leader spread his hands apart while raising his eyebrows. This gesture clearly meant he was waiting for Ahithophel to shout for help. Getting no response from the bandit chief, the Leader put his fingers in his mouth and gave a shrill whistle.

Armed men immediately poured forth from the bandit tents and encircled the group sitting at the fire. Ahithophel's brief sense of relief evaporated as he realized the men were not his. The tallest man in the group came to a halt one pace behind and to the side of where the Leader sat. He leveled his javelin directly at Ahithophel. Resigned to his fate, the bandit chief tossed aside his sword.

"My men...dead?"

The Leader spoke over his shoulder to the tall man.

"Well, Laban, are they?"

"No, my Prince, they are merely restrained. Just as you ordered."

This hint at the Leader's identity nearly overwhelmed Ahithophel. Even along this remote frontier, word had spread of a mighty prince of Israel. The Leader's age was right, his appearance matched the stories, and only one thing seemed out of place to Ahithophel.

Why would a prince be screwing around in this godforsaken wasteland?

Ahithophel could not think of any reason that would favor his gang of bandits. Their best hope was that this was a chance encounter. Ahithophel took a deep breath to calm himself and decided to find out if his worse fears had come to pass.

"Are you Jonathan, the son of King Saul?"

The cook chuckled at Ahithophel's obvious discomfort.

"He's a well-informed thief, Jonathan. Those are the best kind."

"Manners, Nathan, we must be polite to our host, even if he is a bandit."

Ahithophel's mind was racing as things began falling into place. The stories said Prince Jonathan had selected a boyhood friend to be his strong right arm, undoubtedly Nathan the Cook. Ahithophel had originally discounted as wild tales the rumors of a Philistine army at Michmash having been broken by only two men. But after meeting Jonathan and Nathan in the flesh, that account suddenly seemed more believable.

What truly frightened Ahithophel was the skill of Jonathan's men. His own followers had eluded the Moabite patrols for years. Yet these outsiders had found Ahithophel's most secure camp and soundlessly subdued his men. While most men were drawn to banditry by desperation rather than skill, the profession tended to quickly kill off the foolish and the weak. A group of highly trained trackers such as Jonathan's men would only be used against a foe considered to be extremely dangerous. Ahithophel felt he needed to quickly address this issue if he were to survive.

"My Lord, my Prince Jonathan, I..."

"What is your name?"

"My Prince, it is Ahithophel, my Lord..."

"Ahithophel, I'm in a hurry. For simplicity's sake, call me Jonathan. Call him Nathan. Call him Laban."

"Of course...Jonathan. You call me bandit and thief, but the Moabites have driven my people from our homes and killed our loved ones. To avenge ourselves, we have taken up arms against them. To survive, we raid their caravans and villages. We have never shed a drop of Hebrew blood or taken a morsel of food from our brethren. If you come to destroy us as bandits, you are misinformed."

Even though the sun would not rise for hours, perspiration rolled down Ahithophel's face as he tried to read the expressions of Jonathan, Nathan, and Laban. The bandit chief knew that he had overstated his case, especially the part about not harming any other Hebrew. Ahithophel and his men never asked the nationality of their victims. Still, what he said was mostly true, the important part of it anyway.

"Ahithophel, I have not been misinformed. I know what you are. That is exactly why we are having this discussion...and why you are still alive."

A wave of relief washed over Ahithophel, only to be replaced by confusion.

"My...uh...Jonathan, what exactly are we discussing?"

"I need someone to guide four men, including Nathan and me, on a reconnaissance of Aroer. A man experienced at slipping past the Moabite patrols, day or night. He must know every road, path, goat trail, ravine, and gully around Aroer. He must be able to lead us secretly in darkness to the very gates of the city. That man, Ahithophel, is you."

"Jonathan, your request does me great honor, but..."

"Did that sound like a request?"

Despite the fire before him, Ahithophel felt a sudden chill as he considered the implications of Jonathan's words. This was not a request to decline, but an order to be obeyed. No one would question the prince's legal right to execute bandits for any reason, even if they masqueraded as patriots. Ahithophel doubted Jonathan would execute the women and children, but disobedience would certainly doom him and his men. On the other hand, there had to be benefits to a successful mission. A rich city like Aroer provided wonderful opportunities for plunder. The bandit chief resolved to make the best of the situation.

"I understand."

"We leave as soon as you are dressed. My men already have supplies. I want to be in a good position to observe the garrison at Aroer before dawn."

"For how long?"

"Three days and nights should suffice. Oh, there is one other thing."

"Yes?"

"Your people will remain here, under Laban's protection, for as long as I deem necessary. They will be safe and comfortable. Laban will even untie your men twice a day, so they can relieve themselves."

"You fear betrayal, and for good reason. Moabite gold would be very tempting."

"Ahithophel, serve me well, and I promise your people enough gold to start a new life. One without banditry."

Outside the Moabite controlled city of Aroer

Three days later, Nathan peered over the edge of the low ridge and repeated his study of Aroer for the one hundredth time. He did not expect to find anything new, but every detail had to be fixed firmly in his mind. Jonathan deemed it too risky to make records. The discovery of maps or other incriminating writings by the Moabites would doom their mission. The information collected so far had been both useful and surprising.

68

The first surprise occurred when Ahithophel told them of a fortified enemy camp containing over two hundred soldiers on Moab's side of the Arnon River. At this spot, the riverbanks were less steep and the river shallow enough to create the ford used by caravans following the King's Highway. Men and animals could easily wade across, but not heavily armed soldiers. Any force seeking to invade Moab here would be decimated by archers on the south bank. Of greater concern to Nathan was the possibility of these Moabite soldiers ambushing the Israelites attempting to recapture Aroer.

The second surprise was that the garrison of Aroer was quartered outside the city walls. Most likely, the original defenders of Aroer lived at home and did not require a barracks. The first Moabite overlord probably thought it too costly to build housing for his soldiers within a crowded city. Years of quiet had given the Moabites no cause to change this decision. Some three hundred Moabite soldiers occupied earthen brick barracks built along the wall's southern face near the main city gate. The garrison had been reduced over the years, since the barracks could easily house twice the current population. Nathan rarely spotted Moabite officers within the barracks area. The officers apparently enjoyed more luxurious accommodations inside the city walls.

Nathan carefully noted the routines of the garrison over the past few days. Every four hours, squads of sentries relieved their comrades at the city gates and atop its walls. Fewer than fifty soldiers stood watch within the city during the day and no more than thirty at night. The four sentries at each of the two outposts along the main road were relieved on the same four-hour schedule. The Moabites also sent frequent patrols into the western river valley. Ahithophel told him each patrol of twenty men lasted between seven and ten days, depending on their destination. The ox-drawn wagons went out with food for the Moabite soldiers and came back with plunder from the Reubenites.

A thorough reconnaissance of Aroer included the terrain outside the city. Jonathan and Nathan had spent their second day spying out the best approach to Aroer. They soon agreed a large Israelite force required the well-traveled road running between Dibon and Aroer. Any other route would take too much time and sacrifice the vital element of surprise. Fortunately, a secluded area existed two miles from Aroer where the Israelites could secretly assemble for their final push toward the city. Walking further down the road, Nathan and Jonathan came across their first obstacle – the small Moabite outpost on a ridge one mile from Aroer. Four sentries carrying trumpets were stationed in a rough circle of boulders slightly above the road. Nathan could see why the Moabites had selected this location. Besides having a clear field of view, the outpost was visible from both the walls of Aroer and the next road obstacle – a similar outpost only half a mile from Aroer.

Passing the second outpost a short while later, Nathan noted that it too was on a ridge, above the road and manned by four sentries. He and Jonathan continued along the road as it ascended to Aroer. Like most cities, Aroer was located on the highest point in the barren landscape. Attacking soldiers would have no cover as they ran the final half mile uphill to the main city gate. More unpleasant observations were made as they neared the city.

Nathan and Jonathan halted before Aroer's main gate and looked left toward the garrison compound located outside

70

the city walls. The Moabite barracks were not as exposed as they first appeared. Nathan could now see a deep ravine which provided as much protection to the barracks area as any wall. The ravine limited the approach to the garrison compound to a narrow neck of land near the main city gate. Ten paces left from the city gate, a man-high stone fence running the one-hundred-foot distance from the ravine edge to the city wall blocked the entrance to the garrison compound. A fifteen-foot-high watch tower overlooked the wooden gate which provided the only access through the stone fence. Nathan could now understand why the Moabites were content with this arrangement. With only a few minutes warning, the garrison could easily cross the short distance from their compound and enter Aroer before an enemy assault force arrived.

Nathan slid down from his perch on the ridge overlooking Aroer to a shady spot where he tried to envision how the city might be taken. Certain facts were obvious. A warning from either outpost on the road to Aroer would doom the assault to failure. The Israelites must rush half a mile up over open ground to reach the city. Upon arriving at Aroer's main gate, the attackers would turn left, breach the garrison compound's wooden gate and catch the Moabites still in their barracks. The Israelites must do all this before an alarm was raised. Nathan sighed as he remembered Karaz's saying that a plan which had no room for mistakes also had no room for success. He did not even want to consider how to get into the city itself or what to do about the Moabite force south of the river.

The coming night marked the end of their planned reconnaissance of Aroer. Once the sun set, Nathan would slither back to the remote cave Ahithophel had recommended for their camp. Ahithophel proved invaluable, but the bandit chief had also been under constant watch. The more he was around this thief, the better Nathan came to understand him. A cautious man could work with Ahithophel on the basis of mutual benefit, but only a fool would trust him. Nathan never forgot that Ahithophel's loyalty lasted only until the bandit could cut a better deal.

The evening meal in the shadowy cave was simple fare as usual, but it was warm and there was enough to fill Nathan's stomach. Ahithophel wanted to slip into Aroer and supplement their diet with some stolen Moabite delicacies, but Jonathan was firm in his refusal. After the bandit was safely tucked away in the cave with the two bodyguards, Jonathan invited Nathan out under the stars to discuss strategy. While the night was beautiful, Nathan knew the real reason was that Ahithophel could not be trusted with their plans. Once both men had settled down on a ridge overlooking Aroer, they shared the day's discoveries. Satisfied there was nothing more to glean from further reconnaissance, Jonathan began discussing their options.

"So, Nathan, what's in our favor?"

"First, the Moabites are cheap. They cut corners on both Aroer's defenses and its defenders. Second, their garrison is bored and lazy."

"Think our men are better than theirs?"

"I do, Jonathan. Karaz is readying the First Royal Regiment for battle. We know the terrain better. Our men excel at night movements."

"What if your cheap, lazy Moabites simply withdraw behind their walls and wait us out? We don't have the supplies or equipment for a siege."

"Then we can't let that happen, can we?"

"So, what do we need, Nathan? Leave out the Reubenite militia for now, and just count on a single Royal Army regiment. Also assume we need to prevent the Moabites at the river ford from coming to Aroer's assistance."

"A siege is out of the question. We must take the city in a single assault. That means by surprise, which means after dark. A night attack would catch the garrison sleeping outside the city walls, without their officers. We kill the garrison in their compound, and no one is left to defend Aroer's walls."

"The trick, Nathan, is to get our men close enough without being detected. We must slip by two road outposts, an impassable ravine, and a stone fence to even get at the garrison. Can we avoid using that road?"

"Only if you attack with mountain goats."

Nathan and Jonathan spent the rest of the night debating specific tactics. By the time the sun rose, they did not have a plan so much as a series of choices that must be made on the spot, based on how the Moabites reacted. After directing Nathan to get a few hours rest, Jonathan announced his next move.

"Today, you and I depart for Gilgal to meet with the War Council. We'll take half my body guard and Ahithophel. Laban will stay behind with the rest of our men to shepherd our little flock of bandits."

"Aren't you rushing things, Jonathan? I fear the Council will reject us."

"The War Council will approve our plan because one powerful person will support it, no matter what it is."

"Who? The king? Karaz?"

"Ah, Nathan. So wise in the ways of war, yet so innocent in politics. I am counting on Abner, of course. He will convince the War Council for us. Victory increases his power as General of the Royal Army. Defeat removes us as rivals."

"But do we have even a plan to propose?"

"Nathan, it is a long walk to Gilgal. That will give us something to pass the time."

The Royal Army of Israel's Camp at Gilgal

A week later, Ahithophel was extremely impressed by his initial view of the royal military camp at Gilgal. It was not just the spectacle of a thousand soldiers in training, but the presence of an even greater number of civilian workers. Everyone scurried about like ants streaming forth from their hill. A small army of stone masons, carpenters and common laborers busily constructed living quarters for people and warehouses for the supplies pouring in daily from an endless stream of ox-carts. Others were installing cisterns to capture the land's irregular rainfall before it was lost. A sizable bazaar had sprung up where all manner of human needs could be supplied and satisfied.

Gilgal's new manufacturing center especially caught Ahithophel's eye. The bandit chief had never seen so many skilled tradesmen in one place. Most activity centered on the recently built metal forges in the heart of the camp. For now, the forges produced only the Royal Army's most urgently needed items: iron swords and bronze spear points. The inquisitive Ahithophel soon learned the operation was run by Kenite iron workers "liberated" from the Philistines by Jonathan. These craftsmen were supported by a horde of laborers since each master blacksmith required at least ten other skilled workers. Once the forges began producing armor, helmets and shields, the number of workers would be doubled and then redoubled.

As a bandit leader, Ahithophel appreciated the importance of having a secure base of operations. Guarded by mountain ranges and vast deserts, the plains around Gilgal had been the traditional marshaling area for the warriors of Israel. Now King Saul was establishing a permanent armory and supply base from which his armies could go forth to smite Israel's enemies.

Ahithophel was not offended by his exclusion from the discussions Jonathan and Nathan were having with the other military leaders. Instead, Ahithophel searched for profitable uses for his time. Although two of Jonathan's bodyguards were always in his shadow, Ahithophel found that he was allowed free run of the camp. He stumbled across his first enrichment opportunity quite by chance.

It was a training session led by a tough-looking veteran named Karaz. As Ahithophel listened from a distance, he learned the group of men gathered in a semicircle before Karaz were all officers or sergeants from the same company. No one paid him any notice, so Ahithophel quietly slipped into the rear rank of observers. Even his two watchdogs seemed eager to attend Karaz's lecture.

The morning's topic was how to maneuver infantry to take a fortified position. Starting with only the bare area of sand before him, Karaz used a long stick to outline locations and features as he explained their significance. He then added two different colors of rock to represent the attackers and the defenders. The growing enthusiasm in Karaz's voice was evident as he moved his attacking rocks into position for the climatic charge, even sounding the actual signals on a *shofar* made from an oversized ram's horn. Karaz's embellishments were greatly appreciated by his audience, including Ahithophel. Once the defending rocks had surrendered, Karaz patiently fielded questions from the company leaders. Having satisfied the curiosity of his listeners, Karaz directed them to return to their company, repeat the exercise for their men and carry out the same maneuvers during the afternoon training period. As the departing soldiers thanked him, Karaz gathered up his rocks, smoothed out the sand and prepared for his next batch of students.

Ahithophel, and his two escorts, followed the other men from the class area to the large open field used for training. He had not asked Karaz any questions, for none were necessary. Although never trained as a soldier, Ahithophel still recognized what Karaz had depicted in his sand drawings – the city of Aroer. Ahithophel was now privy to what only a handful of people in all Israel knew. The city of Aroer was to be attacked by the Royal Army and its garrison put to the sword. The Moabites would be expelled from the Arnon River Valley and the land restored to the tribe of Reuben. The only question in Ahithophel's mind could not be asked of anyone in this camp.

Should he slip away and betray this plan to the Moabites, or keep silent and profit from an Israelite victory?

Ahithophel mulled over his options as he watched three companies of the Royal Army march out to separate locations on the Plains of Gilgal. Each company separated into two platoons with one being the attacker and the other acting as defender. The opposing platoons engaged in mock combat with spears and wooden shields. Ahithophel soon recognized that each platoon was acting as one of the rocks in Karaz's lecture. Ahithophel watched the three companies repeat this exercise over and over. By the end of the training period, the soldiers were quite proficient. Ahithophel surmised the attack against Moab could occur very, very soon.

For the midday meal, Ahithophel invited himself to the Royal Army's officers' mess, reasoning that they ate better than the common soldiers. It was here that he fortuitously discovered an excellent way to gather information. Misunderstanding the role of his two watchdogs, the other soldiers assumed Ahithophel must be quite important to merit a constant bodyguard. Ahithophel never corrected this false impression and eagerly gleaned all the available army gossip. He then spent the afternoon confidently swaggering around the camp, with his escort in tow, while questioning a diverse group of people, ranging from common laborers to tribal elders.

The day provided Ahithophel with significant insights to both the Royal Army and the politics of the new kingdom. He readily identified several different factions vying for power behind the throne. Ahithophel was shocked to realize how insecure Saul's dynasty really was, for many he met would not weep if the crown passed to a different tribe. Ironically, these experiences made Ahithophel decide not to become a Moabite traitor. Ahithophel did not know how to benefit from his new knowledge yet, but there was much profit to be made in Israel for someone as skilled in intrigue as he.

The Commanders' Pavilion at Gilgal

Nathan once again marveled at Jonathan's political savvy as he witnessed the daylong proceedings of the War Council at Gilgal. Word of Jonathan's return from Moab had reached the king at his capital in Gibeah the previous day. Saul, Abner, and the commanders of the other regiments arrived in the training camp by mid-morning. No Tribal Elders had been invited for reasons of secrecy. Even the *Yameen*, Beker, was absent. These leaders might take offense at their exclusion, but a victory would salve any injured feelings.

The session began with the reconnaissance of the Moabites. Nathan was asked to provide specific details about Moabite military strength and the city of Aroer. Jonathan then presented his plan to overcome the Moabites at Aroer with a nighttime assault by the First Royal Regiment. Once Aroer fell, the Reubenite militia would clear out any remaining pockets of opposition in the Arnon River Valley. Nathan sensed the other council members, except for Karaz, were pessimistic about their chances of overcoming Aroer's garrison.

Nathan and Jonathan knew their tactics here were incredibly risky but presented their proposal with outward confidence. Laban's stealthy scouts would move ahead of

Abner's regiment and silently capture the two outposts on the main road to Aroer. While Abner covered the last half mile to Aroer in darkness, a dozen of Laban's best men would cross the deep ravine bordering the city and infiltrate the garrison compound. They would quietly eliminate the Moabite sentries and open the gate for Abner's men. Even so, Nathan's stomach churned as he considered how delicate the timing was. If Abner were late, the Israelites holding the garrison gate would be overcome. If Abner were early, the alarm would be raised. Then the garrison would kill the Israelite infiltrators and block Abner's attack.

Ultimately, Jonathan's strategy was based on a crucial assumption: that Aroer would immediately surrender once its garrison was slaughtered. The lightly equipped Israelite regiment would lack the necessary siege equipment to force the main gates to the city. Assuming all the other possibilities for failure had been overcome, Nathan would gladly confront this final challenge.

Despite his misgivings, Nathan watched as the deliberations play out just as Jonathan had predicted. Abner, of course, asked very hard questions. Jonathan provided reasonable answers. Nathan could see the general positioning himself to be blameless in the event of a disaster. Jonathan soothed Saul's fears by pointing out all the opportunities the Israelites would have to safely withdraw with little or no loss. Nathan suspected Saul thought even a safe retreat to be humiliating, but that the shame would fall on Jonathan. As Jonathan predicted, Abner's resistance gradually decreased, and the regimental commanders followed their general's lead. All rehearsed very nicely. With a nod to Karaz, Abner finally endorsed the proposed attack on Aroer.

Indeed, Karaz had performed a near miracle with his rapid rebuilding of the Royal Army after so many had deserted prior to the battle at Michmash. Karaz chose to abandon the old regimental organization and start from scratch. Karaz first identified the most capable officers and warriors in the army. He then divided these skilled veterans into three groups. Each group would serve as the cadre for a new regiment. The remaining soldiers were assigned at random to one of the three reorganized regiments to evenly distribute the remaining talent. Two understrength regiments were left under Abner's command to hold the vital pass at Michmash while Karaz took the eight hundred men of the First Regiment east to Gilgal for training. New recruits would bring the regiment up to full strength. This regiment also included the first company to have completed the training in swordsmanship, which Karaz intended the entire army to receive.

Saul polled his War Council one final time for their opinions and found it to be unanimous in its support for attacking Aroer. The king then questioned Karaz and Abner about the necessary logistics and timing. Both men agreed that the First Royal Regiment could be ready to depart Gilgal in three days and be in position to take Aroer ten days after that. Jonathan was proposing that he leave immediately for the border when Saul interrupted him.

"No, Jonathan, you will not be returning to Moab."

Silence descended heavily within the tent. Nathan leaned back to see how the other council members responded to this unexpected turn of events. Only Abner seemed unsurprised by Saul's words. After a moment, Jonathan recovered enough from his shock to speak.

"Father, does this mean you are cancelling the campaign?"

"Not at all, Son. However, Moab is but a single step in our overall strategy. Jonathan, you did a masterful job in laying the foundation of our coming victory. I need you to do the same for Edom, our next foe. While Karaz prepares the Second Royal Regiment, you will be spying out the Edomite weaknesses."

"Who will lead our men?"

"Abner. He is quite capable of following your plans."

"But he has never seen the terrain."

"Nathan seems well acquainted with Aroer. He will serve as Abner's advisor."

"Father, the Reubenite Elders have not been told of our intentions. They will need time to raise their militia."

"I will accompany the Army as it moves through Rueben. We will raise the militia along the way."

"We agreed that commanding the militia is my responsibility."

"Nonetheless, Jonathan, this is the price of my approval."

Nathan followed Jonathan out of the cool night air into the latter's darkened tent. He sat down on a stool as his friend lit a pair of oil lamps. Jonathan then slumped into a chair without a word, staring vacantly at the table before him. The young prince had barely uttered a word during the evening meal with the other members of the War Council. Only

Jonathan's eyes moved when his tent flap was pulled back and Karaz strode in. The older man pulled another stool up to the table and studied his companions for a moment.

"Such moping! I'd hate to see how you two Boys handled a real setback."

"You know I should lead this campaign, Karaz. This is almost more than I can bear."

"I missed when your mission changed from helping your father to overthrowing him."

"That's not what I meant!"

"Oh, so you thought that Saul had stopped fearing your success? That Abner was no longer ambitious? Have you forgotten the previous War Council? We made them both back down from fighting the Philistines. In return, they keep the three of us separated and in the background. Lad, what did you expect them to do?"

Burning anger still filled Jonathan's eyes. Nathan's mood matched his friend. Karaz let them both stew awhile before attempting to soothe his former pupils.

"Moab is merely the first destination on a very long road. Be patient! You can't win every war in the first battle. Take what you can, when you can."

"Karaz, Jonathan's power is based on his battlefield success. What if Abner appears to deliver the victories instead of Jonathan?"

"For the first time, your squabbling tribes have united behind a king. The kingdom needs Saul. Saul depends on Abner. We need them. They need us. One day, Jonathan will be ready to wear the crown, but not now."

"But Abner may be more trouble than he is worth."

"Nathan, reliable men with talent are rare. Few men in Israel are better than Abner, and most are far worse. True, his ambition still exceeds his skill, but Abner can succeed if a strong hand holds him in check."

"Saul has grown more arrogant, insecure, and petty since Abner came along."

"A king has few friends. Flatterers seek to deceive him. Jealous rivals wait for him to stumble. Plotters try to undermine him. The weight of a crown has broken many a man. If we try to remove Abner, Saul may crumble. I think we can tolerate an Abner or two."

Nathan exchanged glances with Jonathan. They both knew Karaz was at his most unbearable when he was right. Their reluctant nods pleased Karaz.

"Good. Now, do you Lads have any anything else I can help you with?"

"Well, I was not going to mention it, but there is a small problem with my bodyguards."

"Oh?"

"Yes. They do not want to be called *bodyguards*. Seems that is what louts who protect brothels are called in the

Canaanite language. The other soldiers taunt them unmercifully."

"And just what do those *renegades* expect to be called?"

Both Nathan's and Jonathan's heads popped up at the same time. Each grinned at the other and nodded in agreement. Once again, the hoary Karaz had come through for them.

The next morning, Jonathan departed Gilgal for the border of Edom with forty of his newly christened *Renegades*. The unique unit name had been enthusiastically embraced by all concerned. Nathan and Ahithophel remained behind to guide Abner and the First Royal Regiment to the Reubenite town of Dibon. Before the final thrust to Aroer, they would pick up Laban and the rest of *Renegades* from the bandit camp. Confident that Ahithophel had no chance to escape, Nathan finally shared his plans with the bandit chief. Ahithophel not only showed no surprise at the news, but also had some valuable suggestions. Nathan especially liked Ahithophel's idea to eliminate the Moabite sentries at the one mile and half mile outposts simultaneously, instead of one after the other. Still, Nathan harbored no illusions about the man. There might be mutual benefit in their collaboration, but no trust...not by either of them.

Chapter 4 - The Moab Campaign

Moses and the Israelites camped in the desert that faces Moab toward the sunrise. They set out from there and camped along the Arnon River, which is in the desert and flows into the Amorite lands. The Arnon River is the boundary between Moab and the Amorites.

From the book of Numbers, chapter 21, verses 11 and 13

Moses gave to the tribe of Rueben and the tribe of Gad all the territory north of the city of Aroer which is near the Arnon River Gorge, including half the hill country of Gilead and all its towns.

From the book of Deuteronomy, chapter 3, verse 12

Outside the Moabite-occupied city of Aroer

Ten days after leaving Gilgal, an anxious Nathan peered through the darkness behind an outcropping of rocks on the ridge south of Aroer. He studied the makeshift outpost which the Moabites maintained along the road roughly one-half mile from the city. The faint starlight revealed a circle of small boulders rolled together to provide a bit of shelter from the wind for the Moabite sentries. No fire was visible, but that was to be expected. Flames would have ruined a lookout's night vision. Unfortunately, there was no sign of the four Moabite soldiers normally on duty. An experienced scout like Nathan should have spotted them by now. Either the men's field craft was exceptional, or something had gone very wrong this night.

Sucking in a deep breath, Nathan closed his eyes and willed himself not to panic. The entire campaign would succeed or fail because of his choices during the coming minutes. Had the Israelite soldiers been detected? Were those sentries already rousing the garrison at Aroer? Nathan instantly rejected these unhelpful thoughts, knowing they would only paralyze his thinking. His mind instead locked onto the cold, hard facts. It was too late to withdraw. The entire Israelite force was already committed. Following the plan offered the only way to victory. Nathan opened his eyes. He knew what had to be done.

Twelve of the elite *Renegades* sprawled in the dirt behind Nathan, waiting to overcome the sentries. If all went well, Nathan would light a small torch where it could not be seen from Aroer. That would signal Laban and his *Renegades* to assault the other Moabite outpost sitting one mile from Aroer. Once those sentries were eliminated, Laban would light his own torch. Abner's regiment then would arise from its hiding place and guided by Ahithophel, proceed down the unguarded road toward Aroer. At the same time, a runner would race to Dibon to summon King Saul and ten thousand Reubenite militia.

The most complicated phase would begin after Abner's arrival at the half-mile outpost. Nathan would combine Laban's *Renegades* with his own and lead them in near darkness toward the Moabite garrison outside the walls of Aroer. They would slither across the deep ravine protecting the garrison compound as silently as snakes. It was imperative that Nathan's infiltrators swiftly overcome all the Moabite guards before an alarm was raised. Meanwhile, Abner's soldiers would advance like ghosts up the road to Aroer. If God were merciful, Nathan's men would open the compound gate just as Abner arrived. What happened after that was anyone's guess.

But first Nathan had to find those four whore-begotten Moabites who were supposed to be on duty.

Nathan crawled alone toward the circle of boulders with his head down, relying only on his ears. With only three feet remaining to the nearest boulder, he heard a cough. Nathan instantly froze in place and listened even more intently. The next sound was totally unexpected: snoring. Nathan rose to a crouch and peered over the rock with one eye. Seeing nothing at first, Nathan rose slowly to his full height. Amazingly, all four Moabite soldiers were stretched out inside their outpost, sound asleep.

Nathan never even heard his own men approach; the curious *Renegades* simply materialized at their leader's side. They looked like a pack of happy wolves once Nathan set them loose. The four Moabites throats were slit before Nathan could take a second breath. He was soon waving a newly lit torch toward where he hoped Laban waited.

After extinguishing the flame, Nathan reclined against a boulder both to restore his night vision and release some pent-up tension. The night's work was far from over, but he had accomplished an essential task. Nathan was anticipating the arrival of Laban's crew when his name was urgently whispered from above. Looking up, he saw a sight that chilled the marrow of his bones.

A line of four torches was slowly winding its way down the road from Aroer.

Nathan was dumbfounded. The Moabites had always changed the lookouts every four hours, and the current watch was only half over. He feared Moabites on the city walls had somehow spotted his men. Yet, no warning trumpets had sounded, and the approaching party seemed to be a small one. Nathan turned toward the four Moabite sentries now in a state of a permanent sleep. Perhaps this change in routine was merely intended to keep lax soldiers alert. Sending the next watch earlier than expected would discourage soldiers from sleeping on duty.

The cause was unimportant. Nathan had mere minutes to devise a plan of action. His first ideas were all bad ones. Ambushing the Moabites would awaken the garrison. The discovery of an abandoned outpost would still raise an alarm. Nathan even considered trying to talk his way out of trouble in the darkness, except a password would probably be required. However, that stray thought led Nathan to a possible solution. He gathered his men for a desperate gamble.

On the Road from Aroer to Outpost 1

The young Moabite lieutenant had first heard the disturbing rumor that morning from a soldier facing discipline for theft. To avoid his well-deserved public whipping, the man offered up a closely held secret. The sentries at Outpost 2 always covered for the men at Outpost 1 so they could sleep through the watch. Since the entire garrison rotated through both outposts, each man was guaranteed being able to sleep half the time he was assigned this boring, isolated duty. Of course, the fools thought they could get away with it forever. While he had no sympathy for these malingerers, the lieutenant knew their dereliction of duty would bring down their officers as well if the commander learned of it.

The informant gratefully accepted double watches for a month in place of the whipping. The lieutenant kept this new intelligence to himself until tonight when he was the duty officer. Midway through the second watch, he commandeered eight of the garrison compound sentries to replace the outlying soldiers. By unexpectedly changing the watch early, he would catch the culprits in the act. Their punishment would straighten out the rest of the garrison. He might even get transferred back to Moab as a reward for his diligence.

The decision to carry torches was a calculated risk. The lieutenant wanted to cover the half mile to the first outpost as quickly as possible, even though his party might be spotted. Of course, if all four sentries were asleep, the extra light would not matter. He soon could make out the dark circle of boulders coming up on his right side, positioned about ten feet higher than the road itself. There was no sign of activity. The lieutenant then spied something which confirmed all his suspicions.

The light from the flickering torches reflected off the helmet and armor of a Moabite soldier curled up between two boulders. The soldiers behind the officer either snickered or groaned at the sight. Leaving his men in the road, the lieutenant climbed up toward the prostrate man. Three other armored figures stood up from the rocks, apparently awakened by his approach. Silently, they slid down to the road below to join the other soldiers. The lieutenant would deal with those three shortly, but first, there was the man lying at his feet. The officer drew back his foot to deliver a swift kick to the sleeping man's ribs.

The Moabite lieutenant was caught totally unaware by the swift movement of the prone figure. This seemingly helpless man not only dodged his kick but also grabbed his leg as it swung past and flipped him to the ground. Lying on his back, the stunned lieutenant tried to call for help, but found the air forced from his lungs by a knee on his chest. A dagger thrust to the throat permanently silenced the hapless officer.

Nathan pushed the Moabite helmet back from his head and looked into the dying eyes of the foe beneath him. He rose quickly to aid his companions, but found the other *Renegades* had the situation well in hand. As Nathan expected, the other Moabite soldiers had been paralyzed at the sight of a supposed comrade murdering an officer. Wearing the armor of the sentries they had originally killed, three of Nathan's men slipped up and slit three more Moabite throats. Nathan's other men rose from their concealment and made quick work of the five remaining Moabites.

The Israelites anxiously stared at the city of Aroer for several tense moments. They gradually relaxed as it appeared their actions had gone undetected. Nathan ordered the four torches gathered up and carried out of sight. Anyone watching from Aroer's walls would assume the Moabite patrol had paused briefly at this outpost before proceeding along the road. Nathan's attention was soon drawn in the opposite direction by the distant sound of footsteps in the cool night air. Nathan hoped the noise signaled the arrival of Abner's force, but he took no chances. Nathan placed the torches, so they illuminated the road and melted into the darkness with his men. Figures soon appeared and paused at the edge of the light. Nathan breathed a sigh of relief when he was able to make out Laban's face in the gloom. He sheathed his weapon and walked into the light to greet the *Renegade* commander. That was when Laban unexpectedly lunged forward with his javelin. Nathan was so shocked by this unprovoked attack that he barely dodged in time. It came to Nathan in a flash: he was still wearing the Moabite armor! He quickly shed the helmet and used it to parry Laban's next thrust.

"Laban! It's me!"

Laban stepped back, keeping his weapon at the ready. After a few seconds, he rested the butt end of his javelin on the ground and growled at Nathan.

"Jonathan would never forgive me for skewering you, Nathan. Even though you deserved it."

"Apologies, Laban, but I had a good reason."

"Just warn me if you decide to join the Moabite army again."

Both men laughed to relieve the tension of this near fatal mishap. Suddenly, Nathan grew quiet while he stared long and hard at the Moabite helmet in his hands.

Garrison Compound outside the walls of Aroer

The Moabite sergeant in charge of the garrison sentries had many reasons to feel uneasy this night. First, the eager young duty officer had decided to change the watch schedule for the two outposts. The sergeant would not have minded, except the lieutenant had taken eight of his sentries instead of rousing the men on the next relief watch from their sleep. After the duty officer departed, the sergeant sent one of his few remaining sentries to the barracks to find replacements. He knew this would take time. Soldiers were naturally reluctant to leave their warm beds, especially to cover someone else's watch. The sergeant was manning the garrison tower all by himself when he spotted torches coming up the road to Aroer. He knew this could not be good news. The lieutenant had not had time to travel to both outposts and back. The mysterious group made the sergeant's stomach churn, for he had only three men to defend the compound gate.

The sergeant felt relief when he could finally make out men in Moabite armor led by an officer. He was about to give the night's password and countersign challenge when he noticed something odd. Whenever the outpost watches were changed, eight soldiers would leave and eight would return. The sergeant now counted the officer leading sixteen men toward the garrison gate. This meant that both outposts were unmanned! Something was definitely amiss, but why did it have to happen on his watch? When the soldiers halted before the gate, the worried sergeant forgot all protocol and simply asked the question foremost on his mind.

"Sir, is there anything wrong?"

An extended silence followed. Sweat collected inside the sergeant's armor at this lack of response. Finally, the officer roared like an angry beast.

"OPEN THE DAMN GATE!"

The sergeant nearly fell off the tower. Obviously, the young officer was furious about the lack of a password challenge and rightly so. The sergeant called his three men over to unbar the garrison gate while he scrambled down from the tower. He thought nothing could be worse than being on the bad side of a pissed-off lieutenant. The sergeant quickly found out how wrong he was.

Moments later, Nathan pulled off his Moabite helmet as he walked back through the gate while his men disposed of the four dead Moabite soldiers. He wanted nothing to interfere with either his vision or hearing. The garrison compound was so quiet that Nathan feared someone might actually hear his rapidly beating heart. So far, his impromptu change in tactics seemed to be working better than he dared hope. Instead of sneaking blindly through the ravine, Nathan had boldly marched his infiltrators up to the garrison gate dressed in Moabite armor. The simple question from the guard tower had briefly stymied Nathan, as he knew an extended conversation could prove fatal to him and his men. In the end, Nathan had shouted out exactly what was on his mind at the time. When the gate opened, Nathan's men praised him as a genius. Only he knew it was an act of desperation, not inspiration.

Abner's first company arrived a few moments later. Following Nathan's instructions, they advanced the final one hundred yards in single file, out of sight of the main city gate. These were the First Royal Regiment's best assault troops – men who had completed Karaz's elite sword training. Nathan met briefly with their captain to give final instructions. One third of the company would be kept in reserve to block the gate. The rest of the swordsmen would delay their attack on the garrison until either Nathan signaled or the Moabites raised an alarm. The element of surprise was crucial for the Israelite swordsmen would be outnumbered two to one by the garrison troops. Nathan had considered using more companies, but he feared they would only get in each other's way in the darkness. When the next Israelite company sent word they were in position,

Nathan knew it was time for the final phase to begin. In a few minutes, the battle would pass completely out of his control.

Nathan slipped his pilfered helmet over his head. He had one final task to perform as a Moabite soldier.

Main Gate to the City of Aroer

The Moabite captain responsible for Aroer's city walls had dispassionately observed the comings and goings from the garrison compound. He was curious, but not overly concerned, about the early change of the outpost sentries. The duty officer would undoubtedly justify his actions in the morning. The apparent abandonment of both road outposts was most irregular, but no alarm had been raised. Resisting the urge to leave his own post, the captain nervously paced back and forth above the city gate. His patience was soon rewarded when a lieutenant trotted over from the garrison compound with a squad of Moabite soldiers. The captain assumed the officer's unfamiliar voice meant he was one of the recent replacements.

"An Israelite army is approaching the city. Open the gates so the garrison can enter."

Now everything made sense to the captain. If an enemy were spotted, the outpost sentries would naturally fall back from their outposts to Aroer itself. Meanwhile, the garrison must enter the city and prepare for a siege. The captain wanted to ask how long before the Israelites arrived when he noticed the lieutenant had left. The torches on the wall revealed a score of Moabite soldiers now waiting to be admitted to the city, with more men behind them in the darkness. The captain promptly ordered the city gate to be opened.

The Moabite captain had second thoughts moments later when a shrill trumpet call erupted from the garrison compound. Trumpets were used to turn out the garrison, but this call was wrong. Instead of the expected signal to assemble with weapons, the trumpeter had ordered an immediate attack. The captain moved from the torches illuminating the gate to see better in the surrounding darkness. As his eyes adjusted to the gloom, he realized a large body of men was moving into the garrison compound, not out of it. The captain shouted for the gate to be closed as he rushed down the nearest ladder. He was horrified by the scene awaiting him on the ground.

Eight Moabite soldiers struggled under the weight of the heavy beam used to bar the doors of the city's main gate. Before the men could drop the beam back into place, they were swept aside by a torrent of Israelites pushing open the massive doors. Recognizing that the gate was lost, the captain despaired of summoning help. The score of sentries manning the city walls were the only other soldiers in Aroer, besides the handful of Moabite officers scattered throughout the city. Hesitation proved fatal to the captain as he was swept away by the flood of invaders.

Garrison Compound outside the walls of Aroer

Nathan stood holding a torch just outside the city, watching for Abner's arrival. He had already shed his Moabite helmet and armor to avoid any fatal misidentification. The sounds of battle now echoed from the garrison compound to his right and the city gate to his rear. Nathan resisted joining either fight for now, only because he and Abner needed to determine how best to use the bulk of their forces. Nathan had already committed the first three Royal Army companies: one company to the garrison compound and two more into the city. But the outcome was in doubt, and Abner still controlled the remaining seven companies. Nathan was relieved to see Abner approach with his personal bodyguard and the First Royal Regiment's commander, Bicri. He quickly briefed the general and his subordinate.

"Excellent, Nathan, the battle goes well for us. Should I send in another company against the garrison?"

"I want to go in there and judge for myself, Abner. Leave a company in reserve here. I'll use it if needed."

"Very well, you shall have it. Bicri, you will take three companies to block the Arnon River crossing. Prevent any Moabites from crossing the river in either direction. I will take the other three companies into the city."

"Yes, General! But what if I find the Moabites still sleeping on the other side of the river?"

Abner's only answer to Bicri's question was a predatory grin. Bicri's expression matched his general's as he departed into the darkness. Abner then faced Nathan as if daring him to comment. It was obvious to him what both the general and Bicri had in mind. Jonathan's plan prohibited sending any Israelite soldiers across the Arnon River. However, Bicri had not asked permission to cross the river. Likewise, Abner had not given any permission. There was nothing for Nathan to protest, yet he knew that Bicri intended to capture the enemy outpost on the

96

other side of the Arnon. Of course, Bicri was a fool to expect Abner's full support based solely on a grin. If the risky assault succeeded, Abner would claim all the credit, making Jonathan appear timid in the process. If Bicri failed, the regimental commander, alone, would face possible execution for disobeying orders.

Nathan had no intention of giving Abner any satisfaction in this matter. He abruptly handed his torch to Abner. This action caught the general off guard, and he accepted the torch like a common servant. Nathan gave Abner a grin and then trotted off toward the fighting in the garrison compound. It suddenly struck Nathan that he had no idea where Ahithophel was, but he let the thought pass. The bandit posed no threat of betrayal because his golden reward was yet to be paid. Nathan could rely on the security of mutual benefit. He briefly reflected that dealing with Abner was much like dealing with Ahithophel, except that the bandit chief was far more consistent.

Laban was waiting with his thirty-eight men just outside the entrance to the garrison compound. Nathan led them through the gate and tried to make sense of the battle within. The scene was partially illuminated by some ox carts and other wooden structures that had been set ablaze. Thirty paces from the gate, Nathan found the remnants of a battle line where the garrison had first offered resistance. The bodies on the ground indicated that the Israelites had broken through a thin crust of Moabite soldiers before assaulting the barracks. Judging from the badges of rank on the dead, the garrison had already lost what little leadership had been present.

A short distance ahead, Nathan came across thirty Israelites of the company's reserve assigned to prevent a breakout by the garrison. He identified himself to a young lieutenant and a grizzled sergeant before turning his attention to the main action before them. Many bodies, mostly Moabite, littered the open area, increasing in number closer to the actual fighting. Nathan deduced that the other Israelite swordsmen had moved swiftly through the Moabites at first, but then their progress slowed as more of the garrison left the barracks. The combatants were now concentrated at the narrowest point in the compound between the steep ravine and the city wall. The battle had temporarily stalled here with the Israelites unable to punch through their foe's greater mass, and the Moabites failing to bring their full might to bear in such tight quarters. Although initially relieved, Nathan knew time would favor the more numerous Moabites unless the Israelite swordsmen were reinforced. It was then he realized the additional company promised by Abner's was nowhere to be seen. Nathan moved closer, searching for a way to break this deadlock in the Israelites' favor.

Nathan saw Karaz's training and discipline being used to good effect by the Israelite warriors. Fighting in teams, Israelite shields skillfully blocked opponents' blows and created opportunities for deadly counterattacks with their swords. By contrast, the Moabites in the front line seemed poorly prepared. Most of their men were armed with only a sword or a spear while the rest were using a variety of improvised weapons, such as stools, buckets and pieces of wood. One large man was even swinging a heavy chain over his head with some success. Nathan reasoned those Moabites taking the time to put on full armor arrived on the scene much later than those who had responded immediately, armed with whatever was at hand. However, the crowding and confusion now kept these armored soldiers near the rear and out of the fight. Nathan knew at any moment the poorly armed Moabites could simply fall back behind their better equipped comrades. They could then retrieve their own armor and make a real fight of it, with the Moabite heavy infantry slowly chewing up Israelites. The Moabites seemed to have no leader to sort out their chaos, but that could quickly change. Feeding the available Israelite reserves into the battle line would merely prolong the current situation, which was unacceptable to Nathan. The Israelites needed a quick victory, not a stand-off.

Nathan saw only one possible way to break the stalemate. A hard-hitting group of soldiers might force enough of a gap at the end of the Moabites' left flank for some Israelites to slip along the city wall and attack the enemy's rear. Nathan thought to use the *Renegades* for this task until he noticed the lines of strain on Laban's face. These men had already spent hours crawling through rough terrain in the darkness, laying ambushes, and guiding their fellow soldiers for long distances. They were exhausted and could not carry the weight of this mission alone. Nathan then looked to the company reserve behind him: fresh men, eager for battle. He wanted to use both them and Laban's men, but someone needed to block the compound's gate. A resolute Nathan began issuing orders.

First, Nathan told Laban that his men were now the reserve. Laban was to use his own judgment regarding how to commit his men to the fight. Nathan then grabbed the young officer by the tunic and pointed where his thirty soldiers were to go. He ordered the veteran sergeant to the rear to encourage the other men forward. Nathan then drew his sword and led his small band into combat.

A handful of soldiers at the end of the Moabite line tried to stop Nathan's advance, but they rapidly fell under the swords of his companions. After squeezing by along the city wall, Nathan suddenly found himself on open ground about ten paces behind the oblivious Moabites. He spread his thirty men out as much as he dared before launching them at the center of the garrison's battle line. The surprise was complete as the Israelites slammed into the backs of the unwitting Moabites. Nathan knew he was taking a great risk, for these were the most heavily armed enemy troops. But few things frighten a soldier as much as the realization that he is surrounded. Instead of turning on Nathan's small force, the panicked Moabites began shoving forward to escape the new threat. This action in turn bunched the other garrison troops so tightly that most of them were unable to move, much less fight.

Nathan stepped back from the fighting to ascertain how the overall battle was going for the Israelites. Looking beyond the mass of Moabites, he saw a wide gap unexpectedly appear in the Israelite battle line on the other side, revealing the open compound gate beyond. Nathan grinned wolfishly as he recognized that the captain of the Israelite swordsmen was employing one of Karaz's favored tactics. The Moabites also saw the gap and surged towards it like water through a burst dam. Desperate soldiers in the rear began slaying their fellow Moabites to improve their chances for escape. Once past the thin line of Israelite swordsmen, many fugitives tossed their weapons aside and ran toward the promise of survival offered by the open gate.

Only to run straight into Laban's *Renegades*.

Laban had positioned his men closer to the ravine in anticipation of a Moabite breakout. The thirty-nine Israelites hit the flank of the fleeing mob, pinning them against the walls of Aroer. The Moabites still had a three to one advantage, so Laban's men eschewed prolonged, individual combat. Instead, they inflicted a single wound on a Moabite before engaging their next foe. Chopping a leg muscle ensured the victim would not travel far. A deep cut to an arm allowed the man to flee, only to collapse later from blood loss. Nathan doubted more than handful escaped into the night unscathed.

The fighting slowly petered out until the only men standing in the compound were Israelites. Nathan recalled his exhausted soldiers and organized small groups to search the barracks for food and water. He was anxious to learn how Abner and Bicri had fared, but Nathan needed to tend to his immediate command first. Roughly one hundred and thirty Israelites had walked through the garrison gate that night. The captain reported twenty-seven men of his company failed to answer when called, while Laban could not account for nine of his. Nathan hoped the daylight would reveal some of these to be wounded, but too weak to respond. Several dozen more men were thought to be wounded, but the darkness made this difficult to ascertain.

The morning light exposed the full extent of the slaughter, leaving Nathan numb. One hundred and eighty-six Moabites lay within the confines of the garrison. Those not yet dead when counted were swiftly dispatched by the Israelites. Nathan could see more bodies on the road leading to the Arnon River. The captain and his uninjured men began following blood trails in search of any garrison survivors. Laban's men were left behind in the compound to sleep and care for the Israelite wounded.

Inside Israelite-occupied Aroer

Nathan was extremely concerned about the lack of news from Abner. The general should have at least attempted to confirm that the Moabite garrison no longer posed a threat. So, the next morning, he entered Aroer in search of the elusive general. Nathan found the city itself to be deathly quiet at first. A dozen dead Moabite soldiers just inside the main city gate had been the only evidence of a battle. The lack of Israelites guarding the entrance to the city was most disturbing. As he walked through the streets of Aroer, Nathan was struck by the total absence of its residents. The first sign of life was a group of Israelite soldiers looting a private house. They seemed unconcerned by Nathan's appearance and readily directed him toward Abner's new headquarters in the former governor's palace, before returning to their plunder. He passed many other soldiers engaged in similar activities before he reached a palatial building facing the city's main square.

The two guards standing watch at the ornate entrance were the only signs of military discipline to be seen. Nathan was so tired at this point that he was not even annoyed about waiting until Abner gave permission for him to be admitted. As he was escorted to the general's quarters, Nathan noticed the numerous expensive baubles left in place, at least for the time being. He found Abner wearing a purple robe and reclining on a luxurious couch while enjoying a sumptuous breakfast. He seemed amused by Nathan's appearance.

"Well, well, Nathan... I've seen better looking beggars."

"The Moabites look worse. Wiped out their entire garrison. Half my men were casualties, and half of those are dead."

"Very sad, Nathan, but really a small price to pay for an entire city."

"How much of a price did your men pay, Abner?"

"Only two killed, praise be to God! Jonathan's intelligence was extremely accurate. Only a handful of soldiers defended the city. The Moabite officers immediately went into hiding once they knew all was lost. The local populace is being quite helpful in tracking them down. They will make good hostages to ransom."

"I hope six companies were enough for you to capture an undefended city, Abner. Yes, I noticed you pulled the one company you promised. I guess you needed more men to loot adequately."

"Nathan, be reasonable. I have thousands of inhabitants to subdue. A show of force is necessary."

"I doubt those inhabitants have as many weapons as the garrison I fought, with only *one sixth* as many soldiers as you kept for yourself. Abner, you didn't even care enough to find out how my men were doing!"

"Because of the great confidence I have in you! But you are correct, it was a grave oversight. Really, Nathan, I have no desire to offend. Look, you have fought hard and need a well-deserved rest. Allow me to put you up in one of the royal apartments here, with some delicious food and great wine. And help yourself to any valuables you desire."

For the first time, Nathan really noticed the grime and dried blood which encrusted his body. His skin itched, his stomach ached with hunger and his muscles burned with fatigue. He spent a moment taking in the sight of Abner basking in comfort and luxury. Nathan finally turned without a word and walked silently from the palace.

At that moment, he wanted nothing more than to be with Laban's men and share their squalor.

Two days later, Nathan prepared to depart Aroer and rejoin Jonathan. Saul was due to make a triumphant entry at midday and then to formally turn the captured city over to the Elders of Reuben. The Reubenite militia had already begun to sweep the remaining Moabites from the Arnon River Valley. Nathan heard that Saul planned to post two companies of the Royal Army at Aroer to bolster the Reubenite militia. The local populace was already hard at work converting buildings confiscated from their Moabite owners into garrison barracks within the city walls. Nathan wondered how long it would take the Israelite defenders to become as lax as the Moabites had been.

The festive atmosphere was somewhat muted by the heavy Israelite losses suffered at the Arnon River. As Nathan had foreseen, Bicri crossed the Arnon under cover of darkness with his three companies hoping to surprise the Moabite stronghold defending the ford. The ambitious regimental commander had marched directly into a trap, losing the equivalent of an entire company, as well as his own life. It gave Nathan a good reason to leave before Saul arrived. He did not want to be present when Abner excused himself to the king from any blame. True, Bicri had exceeded Abner's *verbal* orders, but not the general's *implied* orders. Since a confrontation over this issue would accomplish nothing, Nathan preferred to be absent.

Nathan had just completed his final obligation in Aroer...paying off Ahithophel. Nathan was still baffled as to how the bandit chief managed to convince Abner's officers that he was a person of great importance. He found Ahithophel ensconced in an opulent suite in the governor's palace, just down the hall from Abner's quarters. No words were exchanged between them. Nathan simply made eye contact from the doorway, tossed the small purse of gold on the floor and then left. Nathan was certain of only one thing regarding the transaction – none of that gold would ever be used for honest purposes. But such matters were the concern of princes, not armor bearers.

Main Gate to the City of Aroer

As he exited the city, Nathan spied the small caravan formed by his traveling companions waiting by the side of the road. Twenty-six of Laban's men were fit to travel and rejoin Jonathan's body guard. Nathan planned to request from Karaz a dozen of his best trainees to bring Jonathan's escort up to full strength. It saddened him a little to realize replacing good men would become a regular occurrence.

The survivors from the First Royal Regiment were seated on either side of the road, where the ground gently sloped upward to Aroer. Nathan paused at the top of the slope to examine a low platform built from the wooden doors of the old garrison gate. He was told that Abner planned to address his victorious soldiers from it. Words of glorious praise would flow from the platform down to deserving men below, although Nathan suspected that most of the praise would remain at the top with Abner. He was about to join Laban when a deliciously insane idea occurred to him. Immediately ten reasons to do it flashed across his mind, followed by ten reasons not to. One last thought convinced him to act.

Karaz always said, "Never pass up a good opportunity."

Abner could leave his headquarters in the city at any moment, so there was little time for Nathan's subterfuge. Putting on his sternest expression, he strode toward the four soldiers positioned around the platform to keep away the curious. He pretended not to notice the guards as they nervously observed his approach. Nathan's precise relationship with the Royal Army was rather vague, yet it was common knowledge that he frequently gave instructions to their general. Like most soldiers, the four men knew better than to get on the wrong side of high-ranking officers. They made no move to obstruct Nathan. Within seconds, he was standing on the platform, facing hundreds of men.

Once in place, Nathan was at loss how to proceed. Most of the soldiers lounging on the hillside were unaware of his presence, as there had been no fanfare to announce him. However, he was soon delivered from his predicament. The group closest to the platform happened to be the company of swordsmen Nathan had led in the garrison fighting. He was recognized by the young lieutenant whose men had attacked the Moabite rear. The officer stood to his feet, drew his sword and shouted.

"NATHAN! NATHAN!"

More than fifty other survivors from the company joined their lieutenant's cheer.

"NATHAN!"

All eyes turned toward the platform as Nathan's name spread through the assembly like a grass fire. Nathan seized the moment and held up his arms for silence.

"Soldiers of the Royal Army of Israel! It has been my privilege to fight beside you in this glorious victory. Today, I must leave you to join Prince Jonathan on another important mission for the king. He will be pleased to hear his strategy was successful, and I will tell him of your bravery. He will then sing your praises to his father the king!"

Spontaneous cheers rose from over eight hundred throats. Abner would soon stand in this very spot and claim the victory as his, but Nathan was satisfied that now credit would also go to Jonathan. However, he had only seconds to finish and flee.

"Hail, King Saul! Hail, Prince Jonathan!"

While the soldiers echoed this cheer, Nathan trotted toward his caravan. Laban waited for him with a look of deadly seriousness.

"Fine words, Nathan. The soldiers loved them. Are we in danger?"

"Not if we leave immediately."

Laban needed no more encouragement to get his men and the pack animals moving towards the King's Highway. Their destination was Judah where they would find Jonathan somewhere along the border with Edom. Before Aroer was out of sight, Nathan witnessed Abner berating the hapless guards in charge of the platform. He was not worried about the consequences of stealing Abner's thunder. By taking the initiative and speaking the truth, Nathan had put the general on the defensive. If Abner wished to diminish the joy of his soldiers and to create a dispute with the popular heir to the throne, that was his choice.

Inside Israelite-occupied Aroer

Even before receiving his wages from Nathan, Ahithophel had decided no one else would ever learn of his windfall. Ahithophel reclined on the couch in his apartment and weighed the gold nuggets for the fourth time. The amount was always the same, but handling this newfound wealth was intoxicating. Ahithophel planned to exchange one of the smaller gold pieces for enough copper to send his fellow thieves into absolute ecstasy. While Prince Jonathan may have expected his little band of thieves to purchase farmland, Ahithophel had no intention of spending the rest of his life looking at the rear ends of goats. He had better things for his people to do.

Ahithophel was not actually sure what they would do next, but the gold could only help. He looked again at the best accommodations he had ever enjoyed and sighed reluctantly. One thing was certain – he must leave Aroer before Saul arrived. It would not do to have the king or one of his attendants point at Ahithophel and ask, *"Who is that stranger?"* The Army officers who had treated him so richly would not appreciate learning they had been duped by a pauper. Besides, the renewed Israelite military presence here would make banditry less profitable. Ahithophel knew he would have a suitable destination in mind by the time he collected his followers and their families.

The arrival of Prince Jonathan at his campfire had opened a new world to Ahithophel – politics. He was not interested in titles or offices, but the power behind it all fascinated Ahithophel. In the past few weeks, he had come to understand how readily available power was in Israel to a clever man, unburdened by a conscience. Ahithophel had observed powerful politicians firsthand and recognized their skills as being very similar to those of a thief. In this case, those skills had less to do with dishonesty, and more to do with ruthlessness and cunning, traits Ahithophel had in abundance. Those men of power merely benefited from opportunities previously denied to Ahithophel. Perhaps this gold would provide him with similar access.

The royal palace of the Kingdom of Moab

Mesha, King of Moab, walked the walls of his fortress city of Kir as he pondered the disastrous news from Aroer. He always felt secure in his impregnable capital high in the mountains of central Moab, although there had already been much to make Mesha insecure during his brief reign. Thirty-year-old Mesha had ascended to Moab's throne the previous year when his uncle died without a male heir. The dead king's two daughters had been bypassed and the crown had gone to Mesha as the eldest nephew. The other cousins who had sworn their allegiance to Mesha at his coronation in the morning were plotting his overthrow before sunset. The truth was that Moabite law may have put Mesha on the throne, but only the support of the Army's senior commanders kept him on it. With threats from Israel and Ammon to the north, desert raiders to the east and Edom to the south, Moab's generals would support the strongest military leader.

And now Aroer was lost. What would his generals make of it?

Mesha simply lacked the resources to remedy all of Moab's weaknesses. His royal predecessors had allowed Aroer's defenses to languish for the same reason. Moab had an effective, but small standing army. With mountain ranges protecting her northern and southern borders, and the Dead Sea forming a barrier to the west, most of Moab's soldiers guarded the vulnerable eastern slopes. Mesha dared not call out Moab's militia yet, for fear that many of their leaders would prove more loyal to his cousins than to him. He felt compelled to place his few Army reserves where they would discourage any uprisings. Mesha needed time to consolidate his own position first. There had been virtually nothing left to reinforce Aroer.

Mesha shook his head in frustration. Ignoring Israel as a potential threat had been a safe choice once. Moab never provoked its Reubenite neighbors much. True, his people had occupied some land in the Arnon River Valley and, yes, the Army collected tribute from the Israelites living there. But Moab did not want Rueben destroyed any more than a man would butcher the cow giving him her milk. The land of Rueben formed a nice buffer against both Ammon and the other Israelite tribes. Mesha had even been grateful when the new king of Israel defeated Nahash before the Ammonite king could turn his eyes toward Moab. While the Israelite victory over the Philistines at Michmash had been a masterstroke, Mesha assumed Saul would still have his hands full with them. In retrospect, Mesha saw he had made a grievous error by underestimating Saul. The Israelite king somehow sensed where Moab was most vulnerable and pounced. This Saul was proving to be a brilliant strategist, but Moab's recent military setback was not without benefit.

Mesha's chief rival for the throne, an incompetent cousin, was captured by the Israelites at Aroer.

The man was next in the line of succession after Mesha. He had more vanity than talent, but that trait made him the perfect "cat's paw" for others with little royal blood, but much ambition. The cousin had been made the governor of Aroer as a political sop to Mesha's jealous rivals. It was a comfortable assignment, in a quiet area with experienced subordinates to keep the man out of trouble while he lived in wanton luxury. Despite all these safeguards, the fool had still managed to make a gift of his domain to the Israelites. His cousin proved to be both a curse and a blessing to Mesha. The Arnon River Valley was a costly property to lose, but his rivals could hardly use it as an excuse to remove Mesha from the throne. Not when their preferred replacement had lost it and gotten himself captured in the bargain.

That still left Mesha with few options to rectify the situation. The Reubenites could easily hold the land north of the

Arnon River now that they possessed Aroer. Any Moabite army would face the unenviable task of forcing a river crossing against stiff Israelite resistance. Even if successful, his army would then have to fight with their backs to the river. The facts were plain: Mesha could not risk his remaining military strength to retake Moab's lost stronghold. Besides the conspirators at court, Mesha's other chief concern was that the desert jackals to the east would smell blood and encroach on Moab's borders. They were not especially strong as individual tribes, but the eastern portion of Moab was highly vulnerable to invasion. Mesha needed to consider the economic factors as well. Saul could punish Moab by blocking its access to the trade goods traveling down the King's Highway. Both the rich and the poor in Moab might demand Mesha's head over that.

The safety of his cousin as a hostage was yet another reason not to provoke Saul with military action. Secretly, Mesha wanted to offer Saul a bag of gold for returning his cousin alive to Moab and two bags for returning him dead. But the political reality would not countenance such an act, delightful as it was for Mesha to contemplate. He must arrange for the safe return of his cousin, but not too soon. The Hebrews could be blamed for delaying negotiations. Let the fool languish in chains for a few months, as his support at Court slowly withered like leaves in the hot desert sun. His cousin would return home in shame, broken, finding his influence irreparably damaged.

Mesha then tried to look at the current situation from Saul's viewpoint. The Israelites most likely had resources for only one campaign at a time. Which of their neighbors would be viewed as offering the best balance between vulnerability and reward? Moab could easily hold off Israel at the Arnon River. The Ammonites were currently in the midst of a civil war but might rapidly unite if invaded. The Philistines had crawled back home to lick their wounds, although they still possessed formidable forces. That left the Arameans to the north, and both the Edomites and Amalekites to the south. Mesha's intuition selected Edom as Saul's next target.

This realization offered Mesha a quick way to strike back at Saul. After returning to his chambers, Mesha called for a scribe to send a warning letter to Edom. While he waited, Mesha realized he could survive one major setback, such as Aroer, but not two. His desire for revenge against Israel was great, but he had to be cautious and focus on an aggressive defense for the near future. He then compared Israel to Moab. Their kingdom was still a new institution in Israel. In time, it would be stricken with internal divisions. Rivals for the crown would inevitably arise just as they did in every other mature kingdom. Somewhere in Israel, lived a man whom Moab could one day support to overthrow Saul. Mesha merely had to be patient until that man revealed himself.

When the chamberlain announced the scribe had arrived, Mesha hesitated. Edom and Moab were traditional rivals. Was Israel actually more of a danger now than the smaller, but prosperous Edom? Perhaps a weakened Edom would be less likely to nibble away at Moab's boundaries. Mesha sent the scribe away and instead asked his chamberlain to bring food and wine. For now, there was nothing he could do against Israel. No, Mesha would wait until he found the proper ally before confronting Saul.

Chapter 5 - The *Arabah*

So, Joshua conquered the entire land: the hill country, the Negev, Goshen, the western foothills, the Arabah, and the mountains of Israel.

From the book of Joshua, chapter 11, verse 16

Along the border between the land of Judah and the Kingdom of Edom

It took Nathan and his small caravan nearly a week to catch up with Jonathan south of the Dead Sea in Judah. The prince had been operating out of Tamar, a small town marking the effective limit of Judean control along the border with Edom. While Laban and his men settled into the nearby camp with the rest of Jonathan's bodyguard, Nathan met with his friend. He was eager to learn of the Edomites, but Jonathan insisted on hearing about the Moabite campaign first.

"Tell me all about the capture of Aroer, especially what Abner doesn't want me to know."

"You already heard we took it?"

"I knew two days ago."

"Did somebody swim the Dead Sea?"

"A few of my Reubenite spies slipped through Moab and across Edom with the news."

"The fools are lucky to be alive."

"Don't tell them that, Nathan. I need to send them back the same way."

Nathan then went on to describe in detail how the Israelites overcame Aroer's sentry outposts, its garrison, and the city walls. The part where Nathan dressed as a Moabite soldier especially amused Jonathan. The prince was most distressed by the losses to his bodyguard, the *Renegades*. Jonathan knew each dead man by name.

Jonathan's mood darkened upon learning that most of the Israelite losses occurred because of Commander Bicri's foolhardy crossing of the Arnon River. The man's job had been to block Moabite reinforcements from reaching Aroer; invading Moab itself had been strictly forbidden. The Moabites allowed all three Israelite companies to cross the Arnon unmolested. At daybreak, Bicri's men were ambushed by the Moabite garrison. Discipline simply evaporated. The Moabite infantry pursued their hapless foes into the river where they became easy targets for the archers. Over one hundred Israelite bodies lined the river banks. Jonathans eyes flamed as Nathan finished.

"So, you're telling me that Abner gave no actual order. Even has you as his witness. That crafty bastard subtly goaded Bicri into assaulting a Moabite stronghold. He knows it. We know it. But the one man who could have accused our feckless general is conveniently dead. I almost admire Abner's perfidy."

"Sorry, Jonathan, I couldn't think of a way to stop him."

"Not your fault. Not your job. You had your hands full, Nathan. Nothing stops Abner. Frankly, you're lucky he let you live."

115

"But I'm worried about the next campaign. Abner will be even bolder and more arrogant now."

"Yet, despite this appalling incident, all we can do is tighten Abner's reins during the Edom campaign."

"So, what have you discovered for us in Edom, Jonathan?"

"Nothing that will do us any good."

Jonathan drew a rough map in the sand to illustrate what his reconnaissance had disclosed. The disputed territory was called the *Arabah*, an arid depression bordered on the west by the Judean mountains and on the east by the highlands of Edom. Its northern edge began at the Dead Sea and extended over one hundred miles south to the Red Sea. The *Arabah's* flat plain was thirteen miles wide for most of its length but narrowed to six miles near both its northern and southern ends. Seizing the *Arabah* posed only one problem, but it was a big one.

With only a few notable exceptions, the *Arabah* was completely worthless.

The first exception was the *Arabah's* value as a defensive barrier. It received less than an inch of rainfall in a *wet* year, and the barren desert was always unbearably hot. Even if an invader managed to survive this inhospitable wasteland, he would have to fight his way through the surrounding mountains. Several dry riverbeds provided passage through the mountains, but these were easily defended. An army would likely perish from thirst before it fought its way out of the *Arabah*.

116

The second item of value in the *Arabah* was an oasis within sight of Mount Hor, about thirty-five miles south of the Dead Sea. It was the only haven for hardy travelers braving the harsh climate of the central *Arabah*. Edomite control of this strategic oasis allowed it to serve as a base for raids into southern Judah.

Lastly, there was the crown jewel of the *Arabah* – the *Ghor*. This natural wonder ran twelve miles south from the Dead Sea and was six miles across at its widest. The northern half of the *Ghor* nearest the Dead Sea consisted of impassable mud flats and stinking salt marshes. But the remainder of the *Ghor* resembled the Garden of Eden. These thirty-six square miles formed a basin where the runoff from hundreds of square miles of arid land congregated before flowing into the stagnation of the Dead Sea. The countryside was covered by masses of tangled vegetation fed by streams flowing in all directions. Generations before, the Edomites had conquered the city of Zoar, allowing them to rule this paradise.

The cause of Jonathan's frustration was apparent to Nathan. There were only two objectives worth acquiring: the Mount Hor oasis in the middle of the *Arabah* and the lush *Ghor* farther north by the Dead Sea. But only the *Ghor* could possibly justify a costly military operation. However, taking the *Ghor* necessitated capturing its fortress of Zoar first... and Edom was much closer to the city than Israel. Anything the Israelites seized in the *Arabah* could be retaken by the Edomites with only half the effort. As their discussion went around and round, Nathan felt like a fox chasing his own tail.

Whatever was worth taking in the *Arabah*, Israel could not hold. Whatever Israel could hold in the *Arabah* was not worth taking.

Nathan and Jonathan finally left their tent to share the evening meal with their men. Nathan inhaled the cool, crisp desert air and studied the stars. Identifying the constellations always helped clear his mind. It struck Nathan that this endeavor against Edom was the reverse of the Moab campaign where the geography had favored the Israelites.

Nathan suddenly halted in his tracks. A stratagem Karaz often used when studying a map now came to mind. *Go to the other side of the table and see things from your opponent's point of view.*

"Jonathan, we have been going about this all wrong."

"In what way?"

"We need to stop thinking like Israelites and begin thinking like Edomites."

This deceptively simple statement released the creative tides within both men. Ideas came rapidly over their first bites of food. The half-eaten meals were soon forgotten as Jonathan began pitching various plans to his friend. Nathan would search diligently for the flaws and propose alternate tactics. Slowly, a viable plan began to take shape. Hours later, Nathan moved closer to the campfire's warmth while Jonathan outlined his final strategy. He could only shake his head in wonder after his friend finished.

"It's a typical *Jonathan plan*. Bold. Risky. Full of holes. Good luck convincing Karaz."

"He's your problem, Nathan. I need to rally Judah's militia, so I can't go to Gilgal now. Karaz won't trust anyone else, but you."

"Assume I convince Karaz. What if he can't support us in time?"

"Karaz is the least of my concerns. That man always finds a way."

"Don't forget, Jonathan, everything depends on the Edomites. What if they decide not to cooperate?"

"We get our men to safety. Then face the consequences."

"Speaking of consequences, Jonathan, here's a big one. You agreed not to provoke a war without Saul's consent."

"Quite right Nathan. I promised my father. So, *I* can't be the one to provoke the Edomites, *now can I?*"

Nathan leaned forward and stared intently through the flames at Jonathan. After all these years together, words were often not necessary. He gleaned everything he needed to know from the face of his friend. Nathan finally nodded, satisfied he understood what Jonathan expected of him. He called out into the darkness.

"Laban!"

"Yes, Nathan?"

"Laban, the prince has dismissed you and the *Renegades* from his service."

Nathan was amused to see one of the most fearsome men in all Israel look like a lost child.

"He has?"

"Yes. You're working for me now."

Royal Army of Israel base at Gilgal in the Jordan River Valley

Three days later, Nathan's weary feet rested in Karaz's tent at Gilgal. After covering fifty miles of rough terrain, he greatly appreciated the cushion, food and drink provided by his host. Nathan soon launched into his presentation while Karaz absorbed every detail without comment. At the end, Karaz leaned back and shook his shaggy head before speaking.

"One thing about our Jonathan – he never makes small mistakes. How did you Boys ever come up with such an outlandish idea?"

"Jonathan remembered how you recaptured the city of Qadesh from the Philistines."

"Qadesh! Why would he ever think...look, tactically, Qadesh was totally different from..."

Karaz lapsed into silence and stared off into the distance. Nathan recognized that his mentor was comparing the past and the present situations in all respects. When Karaz's eyes finally came back into focus, he grunted his understanding, if not yet his acceptance.

"So, Jonathan thinks that this affair with the Edomites might play out the same way. He could be right, but what about his father? Saul may decline to make the necessary long-term commitment."

"Once we win the prize, Jonathan doubts his father will simply give it back to the Edomites. Or disappoint a tribe as important as Judah."

"I agree with him, providing we succeed. Then there will be forgiveness all around. Very well, Nathan, what does Jonathan require of me?"

"Move the Second Royal Regiment undetected through Judah to the southernmost end of the Dead Sea. Then wait for instructions from Jonathan."

"When will your provocation occur?"

"One week from today, Karaz."

"Allowing time for the Edomites to respond, I'll have at least two weeks. Should be enough time to get the Second Royal Regiment in position. In fact, I guarantee it. How certain is Jonathan that the Edomites will move against Kadesh-Barnea in Judah?"

"That area will appear to be the source of the Edomites' irritation."

"If they go somewhere else, we're in some pretty deep dung. But that's Jonathan's worry."

"Expect any trouble with the Second Royal Regiment's commander? He's Abner's man, after all."

"Nathan, the man's rarely even here. Usually off visiting his concubines. Doesn't want to be bothered until his regiment is ready."

"Sounds like Bicri's twin."

"Apparently, their clan has too much inbreeding. This so-called commander will be no problem. As far as he's concerned, I'm taking the regiment on a training exercise."

"What if he goes running to Abner after you leave?"

"To tell Abner what? That he misplaced his regiment and doesn't know where to find it?"

One mile from the Mount Hor oasis

Nathan instigated the war with Edom one week later, just as promised.

He had met up with Laban's *Renegades* at a secluded site on the Judean side of Mount Hor. Including the replacements Nathan recruited from Gilgal, there were eighty-nine Israelites in the camp. Laban had been reconnoitering the oasis for several days. Thirty to forty Edomite soldiers occupied the crude clay brick barracks near the tranquil waters which nourished dozens of palm trees. Several small caravans pitching tents for the night added perhaps another hundred temporary residents. At moonrise, Nathan led his eager warriors from Mount Hor toward the peaceful oasis.

The assault plan was simplicity itself. A few stealthy *Renegades* eliminated the six sentries while the remaining

Israelites surrounded the sleeping garrison. The bleary-eyed Edomites were overwhelmed before most could grab a weapon. Seven of them were slain, but Nathan was pleased that all four officers were captured alive, as he ordered. Twenty-two dispirited enemy survivors were herded into an open area and forced face down on the sand. Laban took a few men to evict the other oasis residents. These hastily fled on their camels into the dark desert night, leaving substantial merchandise behind. Though none of the frightened people realized it, the Israelites were being merciful.

For the real performance was about to begin.

Nathan announced to the captive soldiers that he was Simon from Kadesh-Barnea and claimed the oasis in the name of the tribe of Judah. The prone Edomite prisoners were positioned so they could see little but hear everything. Ten men were assigned to guard the prisoners while the remaining Israelites were divided into four groups. Nathan then started these groups marching in a large circle while talking loudly among themselves every time they drew near to the prisoners. The men guarding the prostrate Edomites would then greet each passing body of men as if for the first time. The parade lasted almost an hour, simulating the arrival of hundreds of Israelites at the oasis.

Nathan finally called a halt to the marching and signaled Laban to begin the finale. The ten Israelite warriors guarding the captives already knew their roles. Laban then pretended to be the newly arrived Israelite commander with Nathan as one of his officers.

"Captain, who are these dirt eating pigs?"

"The Edomite garrison, Sir."

"Why are they still breathing? Execute them at once!"

The Israelites then used their spears to jab some of the Edomites lying helplessly on the ground. Their screams of pain caused every prisoner to bolt out of the circle. Laban and a few other Israelites pursued them into the darkness. Nathan strolled over to a newly built campfire to wait until the shouting stopped. He looked up when Laban returned a short time later.

"So far, so good, Nathan. I made sure all four officers escaped, just like you wanted. We killed most of the common soldiers to make it look good, but a few still got away. Want us to hunt them down? Good practice for the new men."

"No. It'd look suspicious if the only survivors were officers. Think they can find their way toward Edom in the dark?"

"We chased them in the right direction."

"On foot, they should reach their nearest outpost by tomorrow night. That gives us two days before the first Edomite scouts get here. Feed the men and let them sleep till noon. Then set up our pickets. They must keep the Edomites from learning how few we really are."

"Pretty nice place here, Nathan. Plenty of water and shade. Those merchants left behind some expensive food and wine. This should be some cushy duty for the next week...at least until the Edomite army shows up."

The royal palace in the Philistine Kingdom of Gath

Achish, King of Gath, followed one of Abimelek's servants into the *Archon's* chambers. Davon, his military commander, and Abimelek were already inside the antechamber, reclining on plush couches. Although the general immediately stood and bowed to his sovereign, Abimelek merely nodded to acknowledge Achish's arrival. The young king chose to overlook this minor display of arrogance by his minister. He saw no benefit in giving the older man the satisfaction of provoking the royal temper today. Besides, the three most powerful men in Gath were gathered to hear some vital news. After Achish was comfortably seated with refreshments, he brusquely motioned for Abimelek to get on with it.

"To begin, my Friends, I am pleased to confirm that our intelligence about the Hebrews proved accurate. They did indeed move against Moab rather than Philistia. Kicked the little bastards south of the Arnon River in a single night."

"Their army is that good?"

"To be honest, General, their victory was not as impressive as one might think. The Moabite garrison there had grown soft and sloppy over the years. Also, night maneuvers are one thing at which the Hebrews have always been very, *very* good. By the way, Achish, your idea to track their army's purchase of donkeys was an inspired suggestion. Might I ask what made you think of it?"

"No, Abimelek. You may not ask."

Now it was Achish's turn to enjoy the irritation etched on the *Archon's* face. He had learned a hard lesson about secrets and donkeys from the Hebrews. As a young officer, Achish was gulled by their spies into revealing his plans through the rental of their animals. Wherever his Philistine soldiers went, the Hebrew donkeys went as well. Achish had no intention of sharing that embarrassing bit of information with his frequently annoying subordinate. He shrewdly changed the subject to keep the *Archon* off balance.

"So, Abimelek, where and when do you expect the Hebrews to go next?"

"My people are still sifting through the rumors and gossip, Achish. Where? Definitely not Philistia, at least not in the short term. Edom seems most likely, although the Amalekites and the Arameans are also in the mix. When? That is more difficult. Even their Army commanders seem confused."

"And what does that suggest?"

"That the Hebrew leadership is divided. Indeed, their Moab success may have been mostly a stroke of luck."

"Then we can put the Hebrews aside until you learn something useful, Abimelek. Now your invitation implied you had news about weapons to re-equip our Army. That is what I really came for."

Abimelek snapped his fingers in response. Two husky servants shuffled into the chamber bearing a heavy table covered by a thick blue cloth. They maneuvered their burden between the three couches before silently departing. Achish raised a questioning eyebrow toward the *Archon* but received only a smirk for an answer. Now the young king really was in danger of losing his temper. Gath's infantry had been nearly exterminated at Michmash and their equipment lost to the Hebrews. Davon had been hurriedly rebuilding the shattered regiments, but desperately needed weapons and armor for his raw recruits. This was no time for Abimelek to suddenly be coy. Achish tightened his jaws and spoke.

"Well, *Archon*, where are my weapons?"

"Right in front of you."

"Do not toy with me, Abimelek."

"Achish…. just look under the cloth."

Red-faced, Achish lifted the nearest corner of the cloth and peeked underneath. He immediately dropped it as if a coiled viper lay there. The shocked king then seized the covering with both hands and flung it into a corner. Davon silently rose and stared at the table slack jawed. Abimelek chuckled quietly.

Ingots of gold. Bars of silver. Glittering jewels. More than enough to fill a chest measuring a foot on all sides.

"I apologize, Gentlemen, if I misled you. No, the actual weapons were not on this table. However, the wealth you see should be enough to equip five regiments with armor, helmets, swords, spears, shields and all the other sundry essentials of war."

"How on earth did you obtain all this, Abimelek?"

"I cannot tell you."

"I insist."

"NO, Achish. It's for the safety of us all. If there is even a hint that Gath was behind the theft, *we die*."

"The people you robbed are that powerful?"

"And they have long memories. Everyday this treasure remains in our possession is one too many. If Davon will give me a list of his needs, I will make the necessary arrangements."

"Give *you* my list? Don't you trust me, Abimelek?"

"For the record, Davon, I trust no one. However, it would give the game away if the Commander of Gath's Army were suddenly flush with wealth."

"But not the *Archon* of Gath?"

"Not at all. For I will transform all these precious baubles into more common stuff. Wheat. Olive oil. Iron. Wine. Merchandise that will move invisibly through various merchant warehouses to reemerge as your tools of war."

"So, Abimelek, only you will ever know the entire story."

"It is one of the few joys of my profession."

The royal palace in the Philistine Kingdom of Gaza

Kaftor's mood was so foul that he barely tasted the expensive wine he was sipping and spilling down his robes. One of his favorite days of the year had become an utter disaster. Several years before, the King of Gaza had made a secret covenant with the Pharaoh of Egypt. Kaftor would protect

Egypt's interests in Canaan, especially from the ambitious Maoch of Gath. In return, Pharaoh would send a generous chest of treasure once a year to Gaza. This well-guarded caravan from Egypt had arrived today to deliver the fourth such chest.

To preserve the secrecy of the agreement, only Kaftor and the Egyptian ambassador had been present in Gaza's treasury with the sealed strongbox. First, the King of Gaza measured its dimensions to be sure he was not being shorted. Next, he checked the integrity of the metal seal bearing the Pharaoh's *cartouche*. Satisfied, Kaftor broke the seal, inserted his key in the lock, opened the lid and beheld the contents in speechless horror.

Rocks and scrap metal. Enough to simulate the weight and sounds of more valuable materials while in transit.

The Egyptian ambassador had pissed himself on the spot. The man pleaded his innocence and readily agreed to allow his guards to be interrogated by Kaftor's experts. The king waited for the results but sulked as he realized any answer would be meaningless. The Pharaoh's seal had arrived unbroken. Any theft or subterfuge had occurred in Egypt. Kaftor looked up when his chamberlain entered the room.

"Well?"

"My King, the interrogators separated the Egyptians and questioned each one under duress. Their stories were all consistent. They know nothing of the theft."

"Not surprising. They would not dared have come here if they did."

"What are your wishes, my King?"

Kaftor stared for a moment at the worthless chest. He mulled over various possibilities but thought the simplest one was the most likely. Pharaoh had undoubtedly decided to break their agreement. The box of rocks was intended to humble the King of Gath and serve as a reminder of who was the lord and who was the vassal. Well, Kaftor knew exactly how to respond to such an insult.

"Release the Egyptians. Have them return the chest to Pharaoh...with the ambassador's head in it."

The royal palace in the Philistine Kingdom of Gath

Abimelek's pleasant mood greatly enhanced the flavor of the delicate wine he was savoring. Today's meeting with King Achish and General Davon had gone extremely well. The Hebrews were leaving Gath alone for the time being. Once Davon had rebuilt the kingdom's army, Abimelek could end the phony conspiracy he initiated to woo Kaftor of Gaza. The charade had succeeded in every possible way. Seduced by the possibility of an effortless takeover of Gath, Kaftor had neglected his own army. Abimelek even managed to unearth the itinerary of the caravan bringing Egypt's annual bribe to Gaza. Deprived of Pharaoh's treasure, Kaftor would struggle for many months, perhaps even years, to bring his army back to full strength. A priceless bonus would be the wedge driven between Egypt and Gaza.

The *Archon* wished he could have witnessed Kaftor's reaction upon opening the chest of trash. The man must be going mad trying to solve the robbery. That was the thing about strong boxes. Everyone focused on their sturdiness, their locks and the seals.

But no one ever paid any attention to *the hinges*.

Chapter 6 - The Edom Campaign

Esau (also called Edom) gathered his wives, sons, daughters, and every member of his household, as well as his herds and all the goods he had acquired in Canaan. He moved far away from his brother Jacob, because the land where they lived could not support both their herds. So, Esau, the father of the Edomites, settled in the hill country of Seir.

From the book of Genesis, chapter 36, verses 6 to 8

The Mount Hor oasis in the Arabah desert west of Edom

Hadar hated riding camels.

Chariots were impractical in the unmercifully hot *Arabah*. Their horses required too much water. Donkeys were the same and even slower. That left camels. Spitting, biting, stinking camels. And Hadar always grew sores on his butt from rocking to and fro like a drunken sailor in a storm.

Still, the Edomite general admitted that camels offered one enjoyable benefit. Their height gave Hadar a wonderful view of the mighty Edomite host under his command. The King of Edom was greatly alarmed that the Israelites had grown so bold as to seize his valuable oasis. He entrusted Hadar with over half of Edom's standing army to not only reclaim the lost possession, but to also inflict a frightful vengeance on the thieves. Admittedly, the general had selfish motives in accepting his king's commission. The present commander of the Royal Armies of Edom was growing elderly and senile. His forced retirement loomed. Soon there would be a power struggle between Hadar and two other senior Edomite generals. A quick victory over the Israelites would ensure Hadar's promotion to the vacancy.

Hadar viewed with pride his mile-long column as it departed the recently recaptured Mount Hoar oasis, bound for Kadesh-Barnea in Judah. Over two thousand heavy infantrymen marched in their companies across the arid plain of the *Arabah*. With few exceptions, everyone else in Hadar's command walked, including the food. Hundreds of sheep followed behind the soldiers as meals on the hoof. The animals had been allowed to drink their fill at the oasis, for most would receive no more water during the campaign. The number of sheep taken was sufficient to feed Hadar's soldiers for three days. After that, the Edomite army would live off what they scavenged from the Israelites. Behind the sheep, came an ox train hauling five thousand skins of water. This water, combined with what the soldiers themselves carried, would supply the column until it reached Judah.

The rearguard of the Edomite army contained the most miserable men under Hadar's command. Both his regimental commanders used this assignment as a punishment detail for those officers and men who had fallen out of favor. These troops ate the dust of the entire column, but that was merely the start of their miseries. Edomite soldiers were trained to march and fight without sandals, since unshod feet usually provided a man with better traction. Every man soon built up sufficient calluses to provide protection from almost anything they walked on. However, calluses could not shield against what a soldier might step in. The men of the rearguard traveled an endless road coated with dung and urine deposited by the thousands of men and animals ahead of them. Soldiers new to the detail would attempt to step around the worst piles and puddles. After a while, they simply gave up and accepted their lot in life.

Accompanying the men on foot were forty riders on camels. A dozen of these were Hadar's aides, men who could rapidly distribute the general's orders to any part of his army. The rest were scouts, mostly Midianite raiders, hired for their familiarity with the desert. Besides guiding the Edomites across the *Arabah* to Kadesh-Barnea, they screened Hadar's expedition from unpleasant surprises. The Midianites also knew the location of wells in the Judean desert. This knowledge made the Midianites extremely valuable. Less than an inch of rain fell on the *Arabah* in an entire year, and the baking sun could sweat water from a man almost as fast as he could drink it.

Water was vital to Hadar's success.

Naturally, the general had built his entire schedule around water. That was why Hadar had moved so quickly to recapture the lush Mount Hor oasis from the Israelite occupiers. Fortunately, the Israelites were so intimidated by the Edomite army that they had fled without a fight. Hadar had spent an entire day at the oasis to refresh his men and animals while every water skin was filled to bursting. The Edomites required water for three days until they reached the wells beyond the Judean mountains bordering the western edge of the *Arabah*.

Hadar left two companies to hold the oasis in the unlikely event that he needed to fall back on it. The Edomite column then departed the oasis just before dark, planning to march during the night to reduce the amount of water consumed by the men. His soldiers would sleep tomorrow during the hottest part of the day for the same reason. When they awoke at sunset to begin the second day's march, the

Edomites would refill their personal water skins from those carried by the ox train. The empty ox carts would be escorted back to the oasis, so their water skins would be refilled as insurance against future need. Hadar's men planned to reach a mountain pass before sunrise the following day. The Edomites would then sleep a few hours, traverse the pass, and make a forced march to reach the first Judean well by midday. Hadar would take a couple of days to rest his soldiers and secure their base. Then the Edomites would unleash their vengeance across southern Judah.

During this first night, the Edomite column tracked the Israelites fleeing westward from the oasis. Hadar was mildly annoyed at having so little information about his opponents. The escaped garrison officers reported an attack on the oasis by hundreds of Israelites, but close questioning revealed the men had actually seen very little. The Midianite scouts were little better, saying the Edomites were either following a large body of men trying to conceal their tracks or a small number who were extremely careless.

Hadar understood why the oasis had been an attractive target for the Israelites. It had long served as a convenient base from which Edom launched raids into the more lightly defended portions of Judah. The practice had evolved over the years as the kings of Edom delegated raiding to private enterprises. The typical raiding party was composed of an assortment of desert scum and mercenaries led by former army officers. Camels were the preferred mode of transport for these small bands which needed to strike quickly and flee even more swiftly. Wealthy Edomite nobles funded the raids in return for a share of the profits. Officially, the Crown was paid one-fifth of the loot, but probably received much less. However, the raiders dared not be too greedy or else they would be denied the use of the oasis upon their return.

A troubling thought came to the general's mind the next afternoon while his soldiers refilled their water skins from the ox train in preparation for the night's march. What if the Israelites planned to raid the fertile valleys of Edom? These were lightly guarded now and easily accessible from the *Arabah*. The primary reason for holding the Mount Hor oasis and the *Ghor* in the first place was to shield these valuable Edomite lands. Such a change in Hebrew strategy could be troublesome. Would the Israelites now begin using camels for military purposes as well? Hadar immediately rejected such ideas. Obviously, the Israelites had expected only a modest Edomite effort to retake the oasis, not an entire army coming to lay waste to Kadesh-Barnea. Whatever the Israelite ambitions had been, Hadar would put an end to them.

The Judean mountains west of Mount Hor oasis

Carrying every last drop of available water, the Edomite column had continued their westward trek while the empty ox train returned to the oasis. An hour before dawn, the Midianite scouts reported sighting the mountain pass through which the Israelites had fled into Judah. The timing pleased Hadar greatly. His entire force should be able to negotiate the pass after a brief rest and then march five more miles over the desert plain to camp at the first Judean well. The general had no inkling that his meticulous schedule would fall apart within the hour.

Hadar's miseries began shortly thereafter when word came of a large body of men approaching from the Judean plain. His Midianite scouts estimated it would reach the narrowest part of the pass well before the Edomites. The general had his soldiers fall out while he evaluated the situation. The last thing Hadar wanted was to fight a prolonged battle on unfamiliar ground with tired, thirsty troops. In addition, the constricted terrain would greatly aid the Hebrew defenders. The Edomite heavy infantry would undoubtedly grind down the Israelite militia, but it might take more time than Hadar could afford. Yet, delaying his advance introduced additional complications. The Hebrews *might* receive more reinforcements, and his men would *definitely* have less water.

Hadar finally decided to gamble on a lightning effort to clear the pass before the Hebrews could fortify their position. Hadar sent forward three companies, one after another, to batter through the enemy militia. When the first company was exhausted, it would immediately withdraw to be replaced by the second, which would later give way for the third. Hadar hoped in this way to slaughter enough of the Hebrew militia to panic the survivors into retreating. The general watched as his three most experienced captains and their men marched off into the pass. The sun was just starting to creep over the eastern horizon when the first sounds of battle reached the anxious Edomite horde.

It was late morning when remnants of the three Edomite companies staggered back from the pass. The senior captain reported his men initially made good progress, killing at least three Hebrews for each Edomite lost. There were simply too many of the militia. Instead of running, the Hebrew militia had retreated up the pass to throw rocks and roll small boulders down on the fatigued Edomites. The noise of combat echoed off the rocky cliffs and hampered the Edomite officers' efforts to direct their men. Once the Edomite ranks cracked, mobs of Hebrews overwhelmed individual soldiers. A withdrawal was finally ordered.

At midday, Hadar resumed his assault on the pass, but with even less success. The number of Hebrew defenders had grown from hundreds to thousands. Blood flowed down the stony path to the place where the general stood. His experienced eye saw an inevitable Edomite victory, but it would come at too high a cost in both men and water. Even if Hadar took the pass, the Hebrews might still prevent the Edomites from reaching a well before dehydration incapacitated his men. The general briefly consider a tactical withdrawal to the oasis, but quickly dismissed the idea as defeatist. His king had entrusted Hadar with Edom's best soldiers. His promising career would end in shame if Hadar were driven off by some Judean rabble armed with rocks. Hadar needed to find an alternative...and soon.

Midianite scouts were hastily dispatched north and south to search for an unguarded passage. Their camels provided Hadar with a significant advantage since his enemies seemed to be moving on foot. The scout leader returned three hours later to report that a suitable pass had been found four miles to the south. No enemy forces were in sight, and several scouts had been left behind to watch both sides of the pass. If any Israelites appeared, the scouts would signal with a smoky fire. Hadar hurriedly issued his orders. He would remain with his first regiment and continue contesting this pass to pin the Hebrews in place. The Midianites would guide Hadar's second regiment through the southern pass and maneuver behind the enemy. Within a few hours, the Israelites would either retreat or be crushed between both Edomite regiments.

Four miles south of the Edomite Army

Nathan crawled on his belly over the sharp rocks to join Jonathan in staring down on the four Midianite scouts in the empty pass below. The camels knelt on the ground allowing the riders to rest in their shade. One pair of scouts was positioned at the bottom of the pass and the other pair was at the top, where they could observe any movement from the Judean plain. After a few minutes, both men slithered back to a ravine where a score of other Israelites waited. Eight were *Renegades* who arrived with Nathan only minutes before. The rest were from Jonathan's Judean militia. Jonathan stopped far enough away from the group to take Nathan's report in private.

Jonathan learned that Nathan and the *Renegades* had left the comforts of the oasis a day before the Edomite vanguard arrived. Leaving a trail which a blind donkey could follow, the Renegades hurried to the first pass which the Judean militia would defend. The next day, Nathan's men were careful to leave no signs as they circled back to the oasis to begin their surveillance of the Edomite army. Waiting until the main Edomite column was out of sight, the *Renegades* massacred their water caravan returning to the oasis. Most of these Edomites were not soldiers so the fighting was short and brutal. Even the oxen were killed, lest they wander back to the oasis and alert the Edomites there. While Nathan took a small escort to find Jonathan, Laban led the rest of their band north to take up their next positions.

"Good job with the ox train, Nathan. Now our Edomite friends will think we really have them surrounded. How soon will the *Renegades* be ready?"

139

"Laban's men should be in place by tomorrow morning."

"Excellent. He must keep the Edomites blind to anything east of their army. The *Renegades* must ensure their scouts never return."

"These are Laban's hunting grounds. A rabbit won't get through."

"One last request, Nathan, and then off you go. Would you mind eliminating those Midianite scouts down there for me?"

"My boys will enjoy the challenge. However, I'm curious. The Edomite army should be here shortly. Your dozen companions back there look pretty fierce, but are they enough?"

"Two thousand Judean militia are assembling a mile west of here. *They'll* be enough."

Edomite camp east of the Judean mountains

For Hadar, it had been a day of good news, bad news and worse news. The good news came when his first regiment finally forced their way through the original pass shortly before sunset. The fanatical Hebrews were evicted only after much loss of life on both sides. Standing at the top of the pass, Hadar was now frustrated by what he observed. His enemy was withdrawing in good order across the dusty plain to a nearby ridge, an excellent position from which to harass the Edomite column as it moved toward the nearest well. His own thirsty

140

soldiers were exhausted from the uphill fight. Hadar had no choice but to wait for assistance from his other regiment.

An hour later came the bad news that an even larger Israelite force was blocking the second Edomite regiment to the south. The entire situation was turned on its head. Hadar's rescue force was itself in need of rescue. It had been folly to divide his army without knowing exactly where his enemy was. The general closed his eyes and took a deep breath to calm his rapidly beating heart. The day could still be salvaged, provided their water held out. Fortunately, Hadar had the foresight the previous day to send one of his aides by camel to the oasis to bring back the ox train loaded with water. Traveling all night, it would arrive by tomorrow morning. Unfortunately, the Edomites would be able not spare any water for the thirsty oxen. Hadar would have to slaughter them to feed his men and save the sheep for later.

The worst news of the day arrived several hours before dawn and effectively ended the Edomite invasion of Judah. Hadar's aide returned to report coming across the remains of the ambushed ox train. Falling back on the oasis was no longer an option for the Edomites, not with an enemy force of unknown size to the east. The general realized he had led his army into a cunning Hebrew trap. The question was how to escape it. Should he head northeast, bypass the oasis, and head directly toward the safety of Edom? The risk was that the enemy force to the east might move north to cut him off, leaving his army trapped between them and a pursuing horde of Israelite militia. Moving directly north seemed more inviting. There appeared to be no opposition between him and the city of Zoar in the well-watered land of the *Ghor*. This route was longer to water but, with his troops refreshed, the general would feel secure enough to turn and face anything the Hebrews sent against him.

Hadar desperately needed more information before gambling on a direction for his army. He dispatched five of his Midianite scouts to the east in search of the enemy. Meanwhile, his troops would head directly north, away from the Israelite militia and toward the fortress of Zoar in the lush *Ghor* region. If his scouts found nothing, he would turn his army northeast to take the shorter route home.

After recovering his other regiment from the southern pass, Hadar set his entire army in motion. Hundreds of Israelite militia followed the Edomite column at a safe distance. Hadar's heavy infantry could easily scatter the poorly armed Israelites, except it would be a waste of both time and water. The enemy militia would undoubtedly melt away into the nearby foothills, only to reassemble when the Edomites resumed their marching formation. Hadar intended to keep his men moving through the night, but his second regiment had spent the entire day marching or fighting. Its men began collapsing from fatigue a few hours after sunset. Without fuel for fires, Hadar made a cold camp and posted triple the customary number of sentries. This did not deter the Israelites from making a series of probing attacks that denied rest to the Edomites.

When none of his Midianite scouts returned from the east, Hadar planned to send more out the next day. However, the rising sun revealed the remaining Midianites and their camels had abandoned the Edomites to their fate. Now tactically blind, Hadar had no choice but to continue north toward Zoar. Discipline was already becoming a problem as an increasing number of fights broke out over the dwindling water supply. One man was beheaded for trying to steal the water and another for hoarding it. Hadar knew such extreme measures had only a limited effect. Unless they reached water before sunset, his army would disintegrate during the coming night.

The scorching march to Zoar was surprisingly uneventful for most of the day, but Hadar's anxiety only increased. The pesky band of Israelites to his rear was increased by a steady stream of reinforcements descending from the Judean passes. He realized by midmorning that the Israelites were not pursuing him to Zoar. They were driving him. Hadar did not want to consider that his enemy might know more about what lay ahead than he did.

The oppressive heat relentlessly drained the strength out of the thirsty Edomites and with it, their courage. From atop his camel, Hadar could see his soldiers were leaving a trail of discarded equipment. The leggings and forearm protectors were the first to go, followed by an increasing number of helmets and mail armor. Since this was a flogging offense, Hadar was disturbed to see so many men flouting the regulation. Yet, fatigue turned the strongest men into cowards. Hadar could feel the growing dread among his troops as their future grew ever more uncertain.

The unmistakable scent of water in the late afternoon told Hadar his army was approaching the final descent toward the *Ghor*. He knew, of course, water itself had no odor. People actually smelled things around the water such as rotting plants, dung left by thirsty animals or dead fish decaying in the mud. The sagging spirits of the exhausted Edomites lifted as word spread through the ranks. Then Hadar looked up to see one of his aides galloping towards the head of the column. He had sent men forward on the few remaining camels to serve as a protective screen. As the aide drew near, he shouted that the enemy had been sighted ahead.

Hadar lurched back and forth in the saddle as his own camel raced forward, finally stopping at the beginning of the steep descent into the *Ghor*. Despite the sudden danger, he was distracted by the dramatic change in the terrain before him. The desert sand continued downward for a few hundred feet until it encountered unbelievably lush vegetation. His attention quickly shifted to where his aide now pointed out a large body of Israelites arrayed in a battle line a short distance ahead. He estimated at least one thousand men blocked the most direct route to the city of Zoar. Although only light infantry, the Israelites were well equipped with shields and spears. The discipline apparent in their well-ordered ranks indicated these were not ordinary Hebrew conscripts. Even with the Edomites' significant numerical advantage, Hadar seriously doubted his weary foot soldiers could force a passage through such men. Yet, the Edomites could ill afford to be caught between them and the pursuing militia.

Then Hadar looked to his left and spotted his army's salvation. Not half a mile distant, flowed the first of many small streams which emptied from the Judean mountains to water the *Ghor*. Once there, his men could establish a strong defensive position. Each company would need only minutes at the stream to drink and fill their water skins. Within an hour, the scales of war would shift back in favor of the Edomite army. Hadar would bypass the Israelite regiment before him. His refreshed men could march north along the edge of the *Ghor*, before turning east to pass between the *Ghor's* verdant expanse and the mud plain covering the final six miles to the Dead Sea.

Water would no longer be an issue as they crossed stream after stream. The Edomites would leave their Israelite pursuers behind and reach the safety of Zoar before dark.

The general and his escort hurried their camels toward the approaching Edomite column and turned it toward the narrow stream. Looking down from his saddle, Hadar gave instructions to the commander of his lead regiment. The first four companies were to set up protective skirmish lines on both sides of the water. The rest of the regiment would refill the water skins, one company at a time, in order to remain combat ready. Each company in the skirmish lines would be relieved for their turn at the stream by a company with water. The commander acknowledged his orders and jogged away to catch up with his lead companies.

Hadar then rode to the rear of the column to find the commander of his other regiment. He already had chosen the spot where a few hundred men could be positioned to block the approach of either Israelite force. Hadar was in the midst of giving orders when he heard the shouting of men and the clamor of fighting from the direction of the stream. He swiftly turned his camel round and rode toward the uproar. There Hadar found his worst nightmare being acted out in the harsh light of day.

No Israelites were present, only Edomites. Instead of skirmish lines and ordered companies, he saw hundreds of men crawling over each other to reach a small stream less than four feet wide and no more than a foot deep. Men lying down to lap the precious water were stepped on by men leaping into the stream itself to get a drink. The soldiers were soon packed together so tightly that it was nearly impossible for a man to bring a handful of water up to his mouth. Hadar closed his eyes in despair as he realized how naive his plan had been. Driven mad by thirst, men in the lead companies must have broken ranks as soon as they saw water. Once the stampede began, their officers would have been unable to make themselves heard over the tumult, assuming they did not join in themselves. The horror was made complete when the men furthest from the stream began using their swords to hack their way through the crazed Edomite throng.

Hadar instantly recognized that the first regiment could not save itself from destruction. Its men knew only one thing...life-saving water was just ahead of them. Lacking the general's vantage point from atop a camel, they could not see the near impossibility of reaching the stream. The regiment would continue to tear itself apart until most of its members were dead. Only then would the survivors be able to pull away the bodies and enjoy a cool drink. The only solution was to bring in officers and troops from the other regiment to restore order.

Leaving his aides to do what they could at the stream, Hadar rode back to collect his other regiment. He was horrified to see that the Israelite militia had closed to within a hundred yards of the rear of the Edomite column. A single Hebrew shofar blared forth a signal which was picked up by dozens of others. Thousands of Israelites shouted and charged the Edomites. The general watched helplessly as confusion consumed his last functional regiment. The rearmost Edomite companies stood fast, the companies at the front ran to join the first regiment at the stream, while the rest remained paralyzed with indecision. The dehydrated rear guard held out for a few minutes before being overrun by the screaming Hebrew horde. The remaining companies then took flight as well. The general whacked his camel with his whip and joined them.

The Edomites fleeing the Israelite militia bypassed the mob at the stream and kept running. The sight of comrades running for their lives woke many from their murderous frenzy. Most began fleeing immediately, but some hesitated too long and were run down by the Hebrews. Other Edomites were so pitifully thirsty that they continued to drink even as they were being stabbed by their foes.

Hadar used the speed of his camel to get in front of the Edomite survivors. He directed them north to the beginning of the mud plains and then eastward to Zoar. The dispirited soldiers were willing to follow anyone offering escape from certain death. It helped that they passed more sources of water. The Edomites were so spread out now that the fatal crowding at the first stream was not repeated. They also enjoyed a respite from their pursuers while they drank. Like most part-time soldiers, the Israelite militia lacked the discipline to refrain from looting the dead, slaughtering the wounded, and running down stragglers. The general viewed the remnants of his army with dismay. Hadar estimated less than half his original two thousand men had made it this far. Even worse, Hadar failed to find a single intact company. His command was reduced to hundreds of individual stragglers with dubious value as soldiers.

The general was hopeful of reaching Zoar without further incident when hundreds of Hebrews stepped out from one of the *Ghor's* great palm tree groves and approached the Edomite column's right flank. It was the same regiment of professionals the Edomites had faced earlier. The Hebrew leader had chosen his battleground well. The Hebrews stood on firm dry ground while the Edomites maneuvered in a kind of miry clay. Hadar saw retreat was impossible. The mud behind the Edomites grew thinner as it neared the Dead Sea and, even a few hundred feet away, it might not be able to support a man's weight. The Edomites had no choice – they must stand where they were and fight.

Hadar and his camel-mounted aides doggedly attempted to form their bedraggled refugees into a battle line. Surprisingly, the Israelites did not charge, but advanced at a rather leisurely pace. The reason for the delay soon dawned on Hadar. The opposing commander was giving the Edomites time to become afraid. His own anxiety level grew with each step the Israelites took forward. Fearful Edomite soldiers began drifting away from the battle line and farther out onto the mud flats. Soon most of his force was struggling north towards the Dead Sea through calf-deep mud. Hadar watched in horror as some men blundered into deep, mud covered pits. Those pathetic wretches fought vainly against the sucking muck pulling them down until their throats filled with mud that muffled their screams. The discipline of the Edomite battle line crumbled at first contact with the Hebrew regiment. As the last of their officers died, the survivors also fled into the deadly mud. The general and his aides retreated on the camels to a safe distance and watched the dreadful finale.

The Hebrew commander finished the battle with great economy of effort. He divided his men into groups of three and spread them out along the edge of the mud plain to wait out the Edomites. At first, the muddy fugitives painfully tramped east toward Zoar; however, the Israelites benefited from better footing and easily matched the progress of their prey.

Whenever an Edomite collapsed in exhaustion, three Israelites would wade out into the mud to finish him off. If there were other helpless victims nearby, the Israelites would wait patiently for the best time to strike. Realizing they could never make Zoar this way, groups of fatigued Edomites formed up to come back out of the mud and challenge the patiently waiting Hebrews. These unfortunates never had a chance as the Hebrews always gathered more than enough men to overwhelm each slogging band of Edomites.

Consigning his remaining men to their fate, Hadar turned his back on them and rode to meet his own in Edom.

The Governor's palace in Israelite occupied Zoar

Nathan contemplated how few armor bearers ever faced the kind of day that he would today.

A week had passed since the outnumbered defenders of Zoar meekly submitted to the Israelite army. Along with the Second Royal Regiment's officers, Nathan waited in the former governor's palace for the arrival of King Saul and General Abner. The reunion would not to be a pleasant one. Undoubtedly, the king would demand to know why a major battle had been fought without his knowledge, much less his permission. It threatened to bring back memories of Jonathan's unauthorized attack on Geba and rip open barely healed wounds in the royal family. Nathan's job was further complicated by the fact that he had to face Saul and Abner alone.

The king had shown a tendency of late to make rash decisions when angered. He might cancel the upcoming campaign against the Arameans as a demonstration of royal authority. However, the king could not interfere with the plans of Jonathan and Karaz if both men were absent. Already, Karaz was back in Gilgal rebuilding the Third Royal Regiment while Jonathan travelled to northern Manasseh to scout the Arameans. Therefore, it became Nathan's lot to remain behind to soothe Saul's injured pride and help the king to see recent events in the proper light. At least that was the hope.

Abner presented a different type of challenge. The general would feel threatened that his soldiers had performed well under someone else's command. Several hundred men of the Judean militia died defending the passes leading to their homeland, but the Royal Army suffered only a handful of casualties. Not even the battle-hardened Karaz had expected the thirsty Edomite army to totally disintegrate at the first stream they reached in the *Ghor*. Still, the Israelite soldiers believed the resulting slaughter was due to Karaz's brilliance. Abner had always been jealous of Karaz. No doubt the general would try to take out his frustration on Nathan.

Fortunately, Nathan knew a few tricks.

First, Nathan had made arrangements to put Saul in the best possible mood before their meeting. Laban would meet the royal entourage outside the *Ghor* and guide them by the longest possible route, giving Saul and Abner an extended tour of the most desirable portions of the king's newest acquisition. As Saul approached the palace, he would be cheered by thousands of soldiers and militia. The presence of the victorious officers with

Nathan should also induce Saul and Abner to behave in a professional manner.

The sound of shofars preceded the honor guard escorting the king and his attendants into the grand hall where Nathan stood at attention with the other soldiers. Saul stepped forward to be greeted by Nathan, closely followed by Abner and another man. Nathan assumed the third man was Zerah, the missing commander of the Second Royal Regiment. Nobody seemed to be sure of what to do next, as the Royal Court was still developing its protocols. Nathan took the initiative by bowing to Saul, an action immediately copied by the officers behind him.

"Greetings, my King. Greetings, General. "

Nathan paused slightly while considering how to address Zerah. He decided on a frontal assault.

"You must be Zerah. Your soldiers look forward to finally meeting you."

One of the officers behind Nathan stifled a laugh. Zerah turned a deep shade of crimson at the seemingly innocent innuendo. Nathan saw he had correctly judged that the man lacked the wit to recover his dignity. Zerah had been smoothly neutralized.

One down, two to go.

Abner then turned to Saul and received a slight nod from his royal cousin. Apparently, Abner wanted to launch the first volley at Nathan. The general could not even wait for a private venue. That suited Nathan. He preferred witnesses to be present.

"I do not see Jonathan or Karaz present. I assume they fled and left you alone to face judgment for their actions."

"Not at all, Abner. Jonathan and Karaz are away carrying out the War Council commands. I was given the honor of explaining how the king's soldiers...your soldiers ...won a great victory for Israel."

Abner flushed at Nathan's display of quiet confidence. Jonathan and Karaz had always been the vocal ones in council meetings. The general never dealt with Nathan as an equal before and obviously had expected to roll right over the younger man.

"Those are not the actions I meant, Nathan. Only the king may decide when to go to war. Only I may lead the Army into battle. At the very least, Jonathan has usurped his father's authority, and Karaz has challenged mine."

"I wasn't aware that Jonathan had declared war on anyone. This war was declared by the King of Edom when the Edomites invaded Judah."

"You twist my words. Jonathan attacked the Edomites without his father's permission."

"Only after the Edomites entered Israelite territory and the Elders of Judah requested his assistance. The prince is the commander of Israelite's militia, including Judah's. Therefore, Jonathan usurped no one's authority."

Nathan watched calmly as Abner clenched his jaw in frustration. Reluctantly accepting that he had been outmaneuvered on the war issue, the general chose to attack on a different front.

"Jonathan conspired to have Karaz seize control of a Royal Army regiment and send it against the Edomites without my permission. This cannot be denied!"

"Karaz didn't *seize* control of anything, Abner. The Second Royal Regiment was already under his command at Gilgal. After its training was completed, the War Council expected Karaz to deliver the regiment to Judah anyway. Karaz did not inform you of his exact schedule because it was not his responsibility. That was Zerah's job. After all, you appointed him as your regimental commander.

"Don't quibble over words, Nathan. The regiment was not to fight until Saul and I were there to take command. Jonathan agreed to this during the last War Council."

"Now who's quibbling, Abner? None of us knew the Edomites would invade Judah. The tribe was fighting for its survival. Their Elders begged Jonathan for assistance. The only help available was the Second Royal Regiment. Jonathan had no choice but to send for the regiment, and Karaz had no choice but to bring it. Be honest. Would you have denied the Judeans' plea?"

"All right...I would have ordered the regiment to move to Judah. But that changes nothing. The offense consisted of Karaz sneaking the regiment away from Gilgal without its commander, Zerah. That Hittite stole a command that he was not entitled to!"

"If Karaz meant to steal the regiment, why did he first send a runner to Zerah's home? Karaz did not leave until his man returned without Zerah. Incidentally, where were you, Zerah? Your wife thought you were at Gilgal with your men."

When Zerah wilted under Abner's glare, Nathan knew the rumors about the man's philandering were true. He decided to press his advantage with Abner.

"Tell me, Abner, what should Karaz have done instead? Allow the Judeans to suffer and die until Zerah *girded up his loins* for battle?"

Nathan's double meaning caught the fancy of all present. In fact, the regimental officers were grinning openly at the predicament of their erstwhile commander. Abner had been humiliated by Zerah. But the general never gave up in battle, even when it appeared to be lost. Abner intended to loose his last remaining arrow at Nathan.

"You are a clever boy, Nathan. Perhaps you can answer a question that has bothered both the king and me. The Edomites have not shown this much aggression for many years. Why did they choose to launch this invasion now?"

Finally, the general was close to hitting his target, the one weakness in Jonathan's grand strategy. Nathan, not Jonathan, had been the one who usurped the king's authority to start a war, albeit for the best of reasons. Jonathan had distanced himself from the attack on the Edomite oasis garrison and Nathan's men covered their tracks well. Still, both Saul and Abner suspected Jonathan of provoking the Edomites. Nathan had performed well thus far today, but if he faltered now, his friend was doomed.

"Abner, you will have to ask the Edomite commander that question. He never took me into his confidence."

Nathan could feel Abner's eyes as they searched his face for clues. The general had been stymied by Nathan's answer, but apparently sensed a weakness somewhere. Abner continued to probe.

"Then, Nathan, it truly is a shame the Edomite commander is not here, isn't it?"

Abner's words triggered a sudden flash of inspiration in Nathan. The idea seemed insane, but the general may have inadvertently provided him with a way of escape. Nathan was sure of only one thing...he had nothing to gain by being timid.

"Actually, Abner, he is here. Would you like to meet him?"

Abner blinked twice in his confusion. The general had not expected his question to be taken literally. Realizing the entire room was staring at him, Abner numbly nodded his head in assent. Nathan whispered instructions to two guards. The men left the room and returned moments later with a small table and a large clay pot. One guard placed the table directly in front of Abner and the other put the pot on it before returning to their posts. Everyone watched in fascination as Nathan rolled up his right sleeve and removed the clay lid. He reached into the pot and pulled out a dripping object that had been soaking in wine. Abner gasped in astonishment when he finally recognized what Nathan was holding...a human head.

"Abner, his name is, or rather was, Hadar. The King of Edom sent the head of his defeated general to Saul as a trophy."

Nathan continued to hold Hadar's head before Abner as if inviting him to question the dead man. The shocked silence in

155

the chamber was broken as a few soldiers began laughing. Soon the entire assembly was roaring their approval of Nathan's jest. Abner bowed his head slightly toward Nathan, an acknowledgement that the younger man had stolen the moment. Nathan replaced the head in the jar when the general silently turned to take his place behind Saul.

Two down, one to go.

Saul took a moment to regain his composure after unexpectedly meeting poor Hadar. Nathan could still see a keen mind at work behind the king's eyes. Abner was an imposing man, but deep thinking was not his strength. Nathan knew the day's greatest challenge was yet to come.

"Nathan, I now recognize the necessity of fighting Edom when we did and as we did. That still leaves many problems for me to solve. Israel is not prepared to fight an extended war with Edom. I believe we could ultimately conquer them, but at a cost that would leave us easy prey for the Philistines and our other neighbors. Fighting to keep the lands we have just captured from the Edomites might have the same effect. Yet, if we simply withdraw, we invite their vengeance."

"Sire, perhaps I can ease some of your worries. An ambassador from Edom is waiting in the next room to make a peace treaty with you. The King of Edom will agree to halt all raids into Judah and cede to Israel all land, towns and cities of the Ghor, as well as the Mount Hor oasis. In return, all he asks is that Israel not retaliate against Edom."

"Very generous of them. Why would they agree to such terms?"

"Sire, the Edomites acknowledge that Israel has stolen their strategy. Imagine that the entire Arabah rests on a giant table. By taking the Ghor and the oasis at Mount Hor, we have turned the table around on the Edomites. Not only is Judah now beyond their reach, but our forces can invade Edom's valleys where their most fertile lands are located. Israel can now act against Edom, as Edom has acted against us these many years."

"I'll assume for the moment what you say is true, Nathan. What keeps the King of Edom from changing his mind next year?"

"A few days ago, two of the four regiments in Edom's field army were slaughtered. The King of Edom will be hard pressed to fend off the Moabites and the Amalekites for the next few years. He has no choice except to agree to Israel's terms if Edom is to survive. In truth, the only way for you to hold the Ghor permanently is if the cost for Edom to take it back is too great. Judah cannot do this alone. At a minimum, Sire, you must fortify Zoar and garrison it with your soldiers."

"What if I choose not to make such a commitment?"

"Saul, the Elders from Judah are waiting outside. You can tell them yourself that you are giving everything back to the Edomites. Just imagine how the families of their dead will receive that news from their king."

Nathan saw the anger in the king's eyes at such blunt words. It was also the first time Nathan had publicly called him Saul since being crowned king. Nathan had chosen this moment to force an important decision on his sovereign. Saul could either rebuke Nathan as an impertinent youth or accept him as a valued counselor. Whichever action Saul chose, he could never go back to the other. The silence hung thickly in the hall for many heartbeats.

"We can't very well do that, can we Nathan? Given two years, I think we can make Zoar well-nigh impregnable."

Nathan merely bowed to Saul, but inwardly he felt a great relief at the king's smile. Nathan had not only stood up to his sovereign, but also addressed the man as an equal, and gotten away with both acts. In effect, Saul had given Nathan a promotion that put him on equal footing with Abner in the eyes of the Army and the Royal Court.

The assembly soon broke up as Saul personally thanked every officer in the Second Royal Regiment. Nathan's final function in Zoar was to host a sumptuous banquet that evening in honor of the king. The following morning, Nathan would take his leave of Saul to join Jonathan in northern Manasseh. Saul would enjoy having another king pay him homage through the treaty negotiations. Abner would stand at the head of his soldiers and receive the gratitude of the entire tribe of Judah. Despite their new-found camaraderie, Nathan knew both Saul and Abner would be pleased over not sharing the glory with Jonathan, Karaz, and especially him. Nathan planned to sleep that night with no regrets.

All in all, it was not a bad day's work for an armor bearer.

Chapter 7 - The Diplomatic Spy

The Israelites did not drive out the people of Geshur and the people of Maacah. They live among the Israelites even to this day.

From the book of Joshua, chapter 13, verse 13

Western Shore of the Sea of Galilee

Jonathan had chosen a secluded, but pleasant, site for his first meeting with Nathan since the Edomite campaign. The two men ate their midday meal on a gently sloping hillside, relishing a magnificent view of the Sea of Galilee's western shore. Water was a precious commodity. The thirst-quenching bounty of this deep blue, fifteen-mile-long lake always awed Nathan. Growing up in more arid lands, Galilee seemed like Paradise. Instead of seeking shade from some dusty boulder, Nathan and Jonathan reclined on soft, green grass beneath a leafy tree and relished a cool breeze off the placid waters. Thriving vineyards and orchards dotted the verdant landscape up and down the shoreline. The eastern shore only a few miles away, exhibited similar signs of prosperity. It was a shame that beautiful land was currently under Aramean control.

After the food and drink were consumed, Jonathan asked about Edom. The location for their lunch had been selected not just for the lovely scenery but to also avoid the prying ears of others. The prince allowed Nathan to share his adventures without interruption. Nathan could see his friend was pleased by most answers, and downright amused by others.

"Nathan, confronting Abner with the head of an Edomite general was brilliant. And hilarious."

"Didn't feel hilarious at the time. I was all out of tricks, Jonathan. If Abner had kept probing, we could all have been charged with treason. You. Me. Karaz."

"Fortunately, you took advantage of our good general's weak point. The man cannot stand being laughed at. The king is my real concern. Does my father suspect we goaded the Edomites into this war?"

"Not sure. He seems to have chosen to focus on the outcome rather than the cause."

"We can live with that...literally. Nathan, you're showing a flair for politics. Maybe I should delegate more of this to you."

"So, my reward for performing an unpleasant task is... that I get to do it more often?"

"Consider it the price of leadership. Ready for our next exercise in treason?"

"Absolutely. You've had the *Renegades* lurking around the Arameans for weeks. Found anything?"

"Maybe, but I want to hear your ideas first, Nathan. How would you deal with the Arameans?"

"I'd eliminate their greatest threat to us."

"Which would be?"

"Our territory east of the Jordan River. They've been forcing our people back across the river for years. Now is the time for Saul to push back."

"How far would you push?"

"All the way to Mount Hermon, Jonathan."

"Over fifty miles? Both ambitious and risky, Nathan."

"You've been a bad influence on me."

"So, you're going after the *Bashan*, a large, fertile plain. Excellent chariot terrain, of which the Arameans have several thousand. Our militia would run at the sight of them. The Royal Army would stand and be slaughtered. Try again, my Friend."

"How about simple and safe, then? We seize one of their small valleys on Naphtali's northern border. No room for chariots there."

"The Arameans wouldn't need chariots. They could wait in their mountain passes and then cut our men to pieces."

"You're teasing me, Jonathan. You've already decided. What is it?"

"You're looking at it."

Nathan spent several fruitless minutes searching around the Sea of Galilee for Jonathan's objective. He grew annoyed at the sly smile on his friend's face. Finally, Nathan lifted his eyes toward the distant horizon, and all became clear. His jaw dropped in disbelief when Jonathan grinned.

"You can't mean...that!"

"But I do."

Jonathan nodded toward the thousand-foot-high plateau several miles beyond the eastern shore of the Sea of Galilee.

"It has to be here, Nathan. The Golan Heights. Nothing else the Arameans hold is worth the effort."

The remainder of their afternoon was consumed by a lively debate. Both did agree on one issue. Whoever possessed the Golan Plateau controlled the rich lands east and south of the Sea of Galilee. That "whoever" was currently the Kingdom of the Arameans. The pass leading down from the Golan city of Aphek allowed their chariots to roam where they pleased. All the Israelites needed was a foothold in the Golan Heights to block that access. Nathan immediately saw two problems with Jonathan's brainchild.

The first was the need to capture an easily defended mountain pass from the Arameans. Nathan doubted Israel's Royal Army could force a passage by direct assault. Jonathan countered by suggesting the numerous river gorges and ravines might allow the Israelites to bypass any prepared defenses. Nathan had no doubt the *Renegades* could get through, but a whole regiment was another matter entirely. However, this issue was moot unless a solution was found for Nathan's second problem.

Nathan argued that even if the Royal Army established a foothold, they were doomed. That vast plain, the *Bashan*, lay eastward from the Golan Heights. Enemy regiments could easily stream across it from the various Aramean vassal kingdoms. Israelite maneuvering would be restricted to a single, winding mountain road. Even gravity would favor the Arameans. If the Israelites were pushed off the Golan Plateau back into the pass, they would be defending uphill while the Arameans attacked downhill. However, Jonathan presented Nathan with an intriguing idea.

"Nathan, remember Karaz's lesson about *My Neighbor's Neighbor*?"

"That neighbors are often rivals? I sure do. You think his little proverb applies here?"

"That's what I want you to find out."

"I'll need something to bargain with."

"I think I can arrange that."

City of Aphek in the Aramean Golan Heights

A fortnight later, Nathan had transformed into a prosperous wine merchant leading a small caravan up the Golan pass toward the Aramean-held city of Aphek. The twelve men tending his three ox-carts and their jars of wine were some of the thirty *Renegades* supporting Nathan's mission. The rest mingled unnoticed in the multitude of travelers with business in Aramean territory. Laban was about an hour ahead on the road, looking for the unexpected. Nathan knew the expected dangers were deadly enough.

Nathan's caravan soon came to the narrowest point of the pass, about a mile west of Aphek. Here, for the next quarter mile, the pass was barely fifty yards wide. Nathan estimated a full company of Aramean soldiers was camped nearby. A squad currently manned the small guard post used to collect tolls. Nathan's generous gift of wine distracted the thirsty sentries from finding the weapons hidden in his wagons. He diverted his caravan into Aphek a short while later. Under the cover of watering his oxen and selling wine, Nathan dispatched his *Renegades* spies into the city.

The first thing Nathan noticed about Aphek was its lack of walls. Apparently, the Arameans felt the surrounding cliffs and the restricted approach were sufficient defense. He found it difficult to disagree. Nathan passed the garrison area on his way to the marketplace. He noted earthen-brick barracks capable of housing several hundred soldiers. He soon found a suitable space to set out his wine jars and began looking for customers. Now that his band was in Aramean territory, Nathan needed to be rid of the encumbering ox carts. Nathan intentionally allowed himself to be bargained down to acceptable, but exceptionally low, prices. Sales proved to be brisk and his inventory was gone before sundown. He even struck a deal to sell the oxen and their carts the next day. Nathan decided to frequent the taverns in search of news while his small caravan made camp. Its location outside the town allowed Laban and a few of the Renegades to scout the surrounding gorges and ravines for alternative routes around Aphek.

Silver and free drinks made the locals eager to answer Nathan's seemingly harmless inquiries. Surprisingly, the local gossip revealed that the Aramean troops holding Aphek were from the Kingdom of Zobah far to the north, instead the nearby Kingdom of Geshur. Nathan knew that the Arameans were really a loose federation of tribes known as *Aram-Zobah*. The Arameans were nominal vassals of the Hittites, much as the

164

Philistines supposedly served Egypt. As Hittite influence declined, the various Aramean cities declared themselves to be kingdoms, albeit rather small ones. The Kingdom of Zobah had emerged as the dominant power and was currently bullying the smaller kingdoms into submission. The King of Zobah had claimed half of the fertile plains of the *Bashan* and key cities such as Aphek for himself. Nathan doubted this expansion pleased Zobah's neighbors. As a bonus, he learned of a location that would be perfect as a base for his operations. When Nathan arrived at his camp after midnight, Laban was waiting for him by an inviting fire.

"Decided to spend the night with us peasants, my Lord? I doubt we have any suitable accommodations."

"Next time, Laban, you can play the rich man. So, what did you *peasants* find out today?"

"The pass near Aphek is paralleled by two river gorges. One runs to the north of the city and the other runs to the south. There are several ravines lining the gorges where a man can move up and into the pass behind Aphek."

"You said *a man*. What about a regiment?"

"Maybe. If they traveled undetected during the night. If they used both gorges. Half the men come through the north gorge and the other half through the south one."

"You're suggesting two separate attacks, through mountains, in the dark. It could be a disaster, Laban."

"That's why I'm just a peasant and you are the *Aluf*."

"Well, we just need to keep looking. Find a good hideout for us yet?"

"One day from here in Geshur's territory. It's a desolate place where nothing grows. Nearly twenty miles of rocky ridges, huge boulders and deep caves. An army couldn't find us. It's called the *Lejah*."

"Doesn't that name mean *refuge*?"

"Yes, Nathan, but only for evil or truly desperate men. The *Lejah* is full of fugitives, murderers and thieves."

"Then our boys should feel right at home."

Aramean Wastelands of the Lejah

The *Lejah* proved to be everything Laban had promised...and less. The *Renegades* were accustomed to harsh conditions, but the near total absence of life was unnerving. Nathan wondered if Hell was like this for the unrighteous. He mentioned this thought to Laban as they searched for a camp site. The *Renegade* leader chuckled before replying.

"If I owned both Hell and the *Lejah*, I would sell the *Lejah* and live in Hell."

The next morning Nathan sat down to breakfast with Laban and six other *Renegades*. He awaited the return of a dozen men who had been sent to scout the nearby Kingdom of Geshur. The remaining Israelites watched over the camp from places of concealment. The *Renegades* had no intention of learning the hard way how the *Lejah* had earned its sinister reputation. Nathan avoided looking at their foreboding surroundings while he spoke with Laban.

"What have you learned about our neighbors?"

"Over fifty men live within a mile of our camp. At least a dozen of them are watching us right now."

"Should we be worried?"

"Probably not. No sign of any organization. Many of them are alone, and the rest belong to small groups, most likely for self-defense. Still, I don't advise strolling around by yourself."

"I wonder why a bandit chief like Ahithophel hasn't moved in and taken over."

"Because, Nathan, there's nothing worth stealing here. Men come to the *Lejah* to hide, not become wealthy."

"Still, that many men must know a few things we would find useful."

"They seem rather shy."

"Let's invite them to breakfast."

The three ragged men had been watching the newcomers from behind a high ridge since sunrise. Inhabitants of the *Lejah* quickly learned the value of stealth or they died. Naturally, the three were shocked when a brawny man unexpectedly arose from the rocks behind them. The stranger asked them if they were hungry. When they numbly nodded their heads, he waved them towards the newcomers' camp and walked away as silently as he had come.

The nine residents of the *Lejah* responding to Nathan's invitation proved to be an odd mixture. There were several men Nathan could not help but pity, while he wouldn't turn his back on others. He and Laban manage to get the strangers to talk about themselves between bites of food. Nathan noticed several of their guests furtively glancing around, obviously coveting the Israelites' food and possessions. However, they appeared intimidated by the rugged *Renegades* silently standing watch. After listening for an hour, Nathan came to an astounding conclusion. Not a single man in the *Lejah* had ever committed a crime. Whether accused of theft or murder, each fugitive could cite a prior injustice to justify his actions. Of course, the well-used weapons they carried seemed to argue against their innocence. Nathan hid his skepticism and listened sympathetically but kept probing with discreet questions. After hearing a cattle thief's tale of woe, Nathan caught Laban's subtle signal and walked over.

"Nathan, have you talked to that man, the one whose fine clothes have seen better days?"

"No. Who is he?"

"Until a month ago, he was an officer in the palace guard at Zobah."

"Indeed...what brings him here?"

"He made a powerful enemy...something about a pregnant girl, an angry father and castration."

"Laban, a man hears many things in a palace."

"Just what I was thinking."

Smiling, Nathan picked up a wine skin and walked over to his new-found friend.

The royal palace in the Aramean Kingdom of Geshur

Talmai, King of Geshur, inhaled the cool morning air as he walked out on his broad balcony into the sunlight. He tried to shake the fuzziness from his head after yet another sleepless night. There had been many such nights since the proclamation arrived from Zobah about the new taxes being levied on Geshur. All the *Aram-Zobah* kings supposedly paid taxes for the benefit of their entire Federation. In reality, the King of Zobah benefited more than all the other members combined. Talmai had watched in frustration as the entire *Aram-Zobah* was being gradually absorbed into the Kingdom of Zobah.

Geshur had not always been dominated by Zobah, located some fifty miles to the north. Talmai's father had been the first of the Aramean nobles to break away from the Hittite Empire. This bold action had exposed Hittite impotence in the region, and additional Aramean kingdoms soon sprang into existence. Disease took his father's life only two years later, but the man had laid a solid foundation for his son. Talmai was now thirty-three years old, with a decade of experience on the throne. It was infuriating for him to watch his father's legacy slip away.

Rehob, King of Zobah, had been the last Aramean vassal to rebel against the Hittites, but proved to be the most cunning. Over the preceding years, he had used bribery and assassination to obtain the loyalty of the Aramean army commanders serving under the Hittites. When Rehob declared his independence, the new Kingdom of Zobah possessed the single largest military force in the region. He moved swiftly to annex nearby Damascus and, with it, control of the lucrative trade of the King's Highway. Using this additional wealth, Rehob bullied the smaller Aramean states into accepting Zobah's control over the fertile plains of the *Bashan*, the strategic Golan Heights and the prosperous lands around the Sea of Galilee. When Rehob formed the *Aram-Zobah*, none of the other Aramean kingdoms dared not to join it.

Now taxation would be Zobah's newest weapon, making it nearly impossible for the smaller Aramean kingdoms to maintain standing armies. The Kingdom of Geshur had survived this long only because of its two thousand infantry and two hundred chariots. Talmai could pay that many soldiers only through great sacrifices in other areas, but even those would no longer be enough. The proposed taxes would require Talmai to release nearly half Geshur's army. No doubt Rehob would use Geshur's own tax money to add those unemployed Geshurite soldiers to Zobah's army. Of course, Talmai could always go to war over the taxes, but his chances for success seemed remote. Even his attempts at diplomacy had borne little fruit. Three years ago, Talmai had married a daughter of the King of Maacah, seeking an alliance with Geshur's immediate neighbor to the north. The love match was of little help. Maacah's army was only half the size of Geshur's and facing the same tax burden. Rehob's scheme to strengthen himself while weakening his opponents seemed unstoppable.

Unless stronger allies could be found, Talmai would have no choice but to submit.

Talmai's gloomy thoughts were interrupted by distant shouting in the vicinity of the city gates. From the second story balcony, Talmai could see people gathering in the streets, but not the cause of the disturbance. He was on the verge of asking his chamberlain to investigate, when dozens of people began rushing into the palace square, obviously fleeing from something. Yet, the growing crowd, while agitated, was not panicked. The source of the disruption soon came into Talmai's view.

A block of men, five abreast and six ranks deep, silently advanced through the square toward Talmai's palace. Their clothes were common, but no one would mistake them for peasants. Their professional demeanor and confident air, as well as the sword each wore, clearly marked them as soldiers. Very good ones to Talmai's experienced eye. They were preceded by a tall, well-dressed man, most likely their captain. Talmai could hear excited sounds from his palace guard echoing through the halls as they hurried to the main entrance below the balcony. The lead stranger stopped before the palace steps, and his men halted five paces behind him. Talmai assumed a commanding pose as he called down to the bold intruder.

"You there! Who allowed you to enter Geshur under arms?"

The tall leader looked up at the sound of Talmai's voice. The king was surprised to discern a youthful face behind the man's beard. Instead of immediately answering Talmai's challenge, the man gestured to his followers. Their ranks parted, and four soldiers stepped out from the center. They carried forward another man, bound and gagged. They casually tossed their pathetic burden to the ground before closing ranks.

Talmai recognized the man sprawled on the dusty pavement as a Captain of the Guard. The leader then pointed down at the struggling Geshurite officer.

"He did."

"You're an arrogant bastard."

"I hear that a lot."

Talmai could not help laughing at such bold impudence. In only a few minutes, this stranger had cleverly managed to both gain the king's attention and demonstrate that he was someone to be reckoned with. Talmai instantly recognized the quality of the young man and hoped he had a good reason for today's transgressions. Talmai thought it would be a shame to have him executed.

"Why have you come?"

"I have business to discuss with the King of Geshur."

"What kind of business?"

"Private business."

Talmai silently searched for clues to the enigma now before him. Soldiers implied an army. The young man was clearly an emissary for someone important, but for whom? This stranger evidently believed his private business so vital to Geshur that he could risk offending its king. Business so secret that it was for the king's ears only. Talmai's pulse quickened as he grasped an additional fact.

"You're a Hebrew?"

"Since birth."

It was difficult for Talmai to maintain his composure as exciting possibilities flooded his thoughts. This Hebrew's business might benefit Geshur. First, he must find out what was being offered, and at what price. Talmai called for his chamberlain.

"Hamar! Prepare the best food and wine for the men of...of...What is your name, anyway?"

"Nathan."

"For the men of Nathan. See to their comfort while I discuss business with my new friend. Oh, Nathan, if you wouldn't mind untying my officer, he can escort you to my chambers."

Chapter 8 – The Battle Before the War

Hear, O Israel! Today you go into battle against your enemies. Do not be fainthearted or afraid. Do not be terrified. Do not panic before the enemy. The LORD your God goes with you to fight your enemies and give you victory.

From the book of Deuteronomy, chapter 20, verses 3 and 4

Town of Hammath on the Western Shore of the Sea of Galilee

A fortnight passed before Nathan rejoined Jonathan in Hammath, a town renowned for its healing hot springs. Nathan felt his three days of negotiations with the King of Geshur were more stressful than a year of surviving in the wastelands of the *Lejah* would have been. Their final agreements were actually quite simple. Both Israel and Geshur would end up doing things they each really wanted to. The catch was that each kingdom had to patiently wait for the proper time to act. Dealing with Ahithophel, Abner, Beker and other rascals had prepared Nathan well for his new role as a diplomat. No trust between Israel and Geshur had been required in the agreements; mutual benefit would drive both nations' actions. Nathan found the similarity between politics and banditry to be unsettling.

Upon their safe return, Jonathan had released the *Renegades* from duty for ten days, with a shekel's weight of silver in each man's purse, as a reward. Jonathan had even granted Nathan a good night's sleep before starting a grueling planning session. Nathan was confident he had executed the *Neighbor of my Neighbor* strategy just as Jonathan hoped. The question was whether the Israelites could now do anything with it.

The next morning, Nathan began describing the pass to Aphek, the Aramean defenses in the Golan, and his observations about both the land of Geshur and its king. The prince's neutral expression seemed to indicate *so far, so good*. Taking a calming breath, Nathan then broached his unauthorized treaty with Talmai, the King of Geshur. Jonathan was not angry, but not overjoyed either.

"And I thought that I had a reputation for exceeding my instructions. Nathan, when I advised you to work on your diplomatic skills, this was not what I had in mind."

"But you are not repudiating my treaty, are you?"

"At the risk of insulting a potentially useful neighbor? No, but I am not your worry. A treaty with a king can only be made by another king. Until my father approves it, your treaty is worthless. He would reject it out of hand if I told him now."

"So...we just get him to approve it later, Jonathan. After we win. Just like with the Edomites."

"Nathan...Nathan. Are all my sneaky habits rubbing off on you?"

"I strive to learn from the best."

"Since you leave me no choice, how do we make your treaty work for us? Israel must act first against the King of Zobah while Geshur observes from a safe distance. This King Talmai only supports us if we succeed. If he chooses to do nothing, we are lost. He could even sell us out to Zobah. You have brought me a lot of risk, Nathan."

"I couldn't very well expect Talmai to stick his neck out just for my promises. Israel must initiate this war. If we fail, we are on our own...but how isn't that how it always is? Look, Jonathan, the King of Geshur is no fool. He knows Zobah is going to swallow him whole. We are his last hope."

"What does Talmai know of our plans?"

"That Israel wants the Golan Heights, but not how you plan to take it. I couldn't tell him, because even I don't know what goes on in that royal head of yours."

With a sly grin, Jonathan outlined his vision for the coming campaign. Nathan was impressed by its audacity... and its hazards. Yet his diplomatic efforts in Geshur just might be the final piece required for Jonathan's grand strategy. Nathan's analysis of his friend's scheme was both brief and blunt.

"Your father will be anxious. Abner will be furious. Karaz may whip us. I can't wait to tell them."

"Good. Let's call out the militia."

The Plains of Galilee west of the Golan Heights

The time Jonathan had spent cultivating the Elders of the northern tribes paid off handsomely. Naphtali, Gad, Issachar, and Manasseh answered the prince's call to arms with nearly twenty thousand militia. More than half came from Manasseh, which was not surprising. It was the largest tribe of the group and stood to gain the most from the coming campaign. Within a few days, Manasseh's volunteers had begun flooding into Jonathan's encampment east of the Sea of Galilee. The men from the three more distant tribes required a full week of travel. Most of the militia were on hand when Saul, Abner and Karaz arrived with the Third Royal Regiment. The three men had no inkling the militia would already be present. Nathan had anticipated the negative reactions of Saul and Abner, but even Karaz seemed displeased. After congregating inside Jonathan's tent, the king wasted no time in calling his son to account.

"Have you learned nothing? Are your promises worthless? I can't allow you to start wars behind my back!"

"What war is that, Father? The one which your War Council has already declared against the Arameans? I have started nothing. No blood has been shed, no border has been crossed."

"No, but you assembled your own army without my consent."

"The use of militia was always part of this plan and *you* made me their commander. Unless you *specifically* instruct otherwise, I decide when and where to muster them. They now await *your* orders."

Jonathan's bold defense reduced the fretful king to sullen silence. Seeing his cousin's hesitation, Abner leaped into the fray.

"Stupidity, Boy, is never..."

"I AM YOUR PRINCE! You may disagree with me, General, but *always* with respect!"

Even Nathan was taken aback as an outraged Jonathan gripped his sword, ready to unsheathe it in an instant. Abner actually took a step backwards in reaction to this unexpected challenge. The general looked to Saul to rebuke his son, but that hope was in vain. Abner's disrespect to the royal heir was too much for the king to excuse. After an awkward silence, Abner sidestepped the issue.

"What I mean... your camp is easily watched from the Golan Heights. The enemy knows your strength and your every move. You have cost all of us the element of surprise."

"I know."

"Even now, the Arameans may be moving their army down the pass from Aphek to attack us."

"Good."

"There's nothing good about it! Once their chariots get down on the plains, they will..."

Abner was interrupted by a firm, restraining hand on his shoulder. He turned to see Karaz glaring directly into his eyes.

"If you don't mind, Abner, I would like to hear what Jonathan has to say first. Then we can decide what to do about him."

Chapter 9 - The Aramean Campaign

So, the Aramean ministers advised their king, "The Hebrew God is a god of the hills. That is why they were too strong for us. But if we fight them on the plains, we will be stronger than them."

From the book of I Kings, chapter 20, verse 23

Outside the City of Aphek in the Aramean Golan Heights

Eliada had earned his reputation as a cautious general; first, leading Aramean levies in the Hittite Empire's wars against Egypt, and now, in the service of the Kingdom of Zobah. Fellow commanders had mocked his steadiness in combat as unimpressive, even fainthearted. Yet, Eliada always looked beyond the battlefield. Early on, he had recognized King Rehob's paranoia regarding popular and ambitious generals leading his armies. So here he was now, the king's senior general, while most of his glory-seeking peers were disgraced...or dead.

Standing just west of Aphek, Eliada beheld thousands of his soldiers marching down the pass towards Galilee. Eight days ago, word had reached the palace in Zobah of a horde of Israelite militia massing along their common border. King Rehob had charged Eliada with striking the first blow. His orders were simple: scatter the Israelite rabble and ravage Galilee. Rehob then assigned Eliada five of Zobah's eight infantry regiments, but only one of its five chariot corps. The suspicious King of Zobah trusted even a loyal general only so far. Keeping four chariot corps in reserve was Rehob's insurance in the event a victorious Eliada became tempted by treasonous ideas. The king had undoubtedly planted assassin-spies within Eliada's own bodyguard, but the general would eventually sniff them out. Such men always tried too hard to appear loyal. Truth be told, Eliada was secretly more ambitious than anyone else in the fragile Aramean Federation. At the right time, he would make his move, just as he always did. Until then, Eliada just needed to be successful... and cautious.

The rearguard of Eliada's infantry was on track to reach the Galilean plain well before sunset. His chariots would remain up on the Golan plain, east of Aphek, until the Aramean camp had been secured at the foot of the pass. The four companies of the Aphek garrison would hold the pass open in the unlikely event of an Aramean retreat. Even so, Eliada left nothing to chance. His engineers were currently supervising the garrison in digging additional field fortifications in the narrowest portion of the pass.

Eliada walked with his aides to a ridge with a sweeping view of the Galilean plain far below. Directly ahead some ten miles distant, the Sea of Galilee dominated the western landscape. Eliada looked to his left and spied several large Israelite encampments on the far side of the Jordan River, just south of the huge lake. Looking right, he witnessed his lead companies exiting the bottom of the pass. Eliada meticulously pointed out to his officers where and how they would engage the Hebrews. He visualized the undisciplined Hebrews militia pinned in place by his heavy infantry, while five hundred Aramean chariots swung around to attack their rear. The fighting would be over in a matter of minutes, to be followed by a bloody pursuit of the demoralized enemy. Yet another cautious triumph to be added to Eliada's legend.

Satisfied nothing had been overlooked, Eliada departed Aphek with his escort and began the downward trek.

A Ridge south of the City of Aphek

Nathan peered from his hidden perch overlooking Aphek as the last Aramean regiment disappeared down the rocky trail towards Galilee. Nathan recognized his continued observation of the city was essentially futile. The Israelites were already committed to capturing Aphek tonight. Even if ten thousand enemy soldiers appeared in the next hour, Nathan could do nothing to prevent the coming assault. Discovering that the fearsome Aramean chariot squadrons remained behind on the Golan Plain was an unexpected bonus. God willing, those chariots would never join up with their infantry. Nathan still fretted. A single Israelite mistake could still doom the entire operation.

Remembering yesterday's War Council session did cause Nathan to grin. Saul and Abner were both appalled to learn of Jonathan's intention to lure an Aramean army down onto the Galilean plains. The prince believed that their large body of militia, on terrain favorable to chariots, would prove irresistible to the Arameans. Karaz, the wily mercenary veteran, had observed that so much bait required a very large trap. Jonathan had confidently assured one and all that such a trap would be sprung at Aphek.

At the end of the War Council, Nathan finally disclosed the terms of his secret treaty with the Kingdom of Geshur. Saul had blanched upon hearing the agreements made in his name with King Talmai. Nathan had asked if he should return to

Geshur and retract them. After a long period of contemplation, during which even Abner was not allowed to speak, the king answered with a firm *NO*. Nathan then looked Saul directly in the eye. He assured the king that he would not regret this decision.

Looking down on slumbering Aphek, Nathan wished he felt the same bravado right now.

Nathan prayed that the *Renegades* were even now guiding Abner and the Third Royal Regiment through trackless ravines and gorges toward Aphek. The general needed to make his final approach to the city after dark and ambush its garrison. With the Israelites blocking the narrow pass below Aphek, the Aramean army in Galilee would find itself surrounded, outnumbered, and cut off from their chariots. No matter which way the invaders moved, an Israelite force stood poised to attack their rear. Although pleased at having a major role in the coming battle, Abner still pointed out the obvious weakness in Jonathan's tactics: the Arameans had other soldiers. If a single enemy regiment approached from the Golan Plain, the soldiers of the Third Royal Regiment would be the ones snared in a trap.

Abner needed to slip nearly one thousand soldiers into Aphek with both speed and stealth. The *Renegades* had discovered two rugged river gorges which paralleled the Aphek pass, one to the north and the other to the south. Several small footpaths climbed up and over the steep walls of the gorges and into the pass behind the city. However, it seemed unrealistic to expect an entire regiment to traverse either in a single night.

For that reason, Abner had split his regiment in half. Guided by Laban and twenty *Renegades*, the regimental commander and five companies were assigned the northern gorge. Twenty more *Renegades* were leading Abner and his other five companies through the southern gorge. The other forty-two *Renegades* waited with Nathan to prevent some sentry or passerby from stumbling into the Israelite columns. Every Israelite was to be in position for the assault three hours after sundown. Meanwhile, Saul, Jonathan, and Karaz were noisily advancing with nearly twenty thousand militia into positions near the enemy encampment. With luck, the commotion would draw the Arameans' attention away from Aphek. However, experience had taught Nathan to expect half their people to be behind schedule and the other half to be in the wrong place. He did see a bright side: it should confuse the hell out of the Arameans.

A restless Nathan could not help making one final reconnaissance of the enemy positions. Half a mile west on his left, sat the camp of the Aramean company guarding the narrowest portion of the pass. In the gloom, Nathan could barely make out the hastily dug fortifications, some sort of earthen wall. Aphek lay directly ahead to the north, with the garrison's barracks visible on the western outskirts of the city. At least three Aramean companies were in residence. Nathan viewed with special interest a two-story building located about fifty yards to the right of the barracks area. This served as the quarters of the garrison's officers. Those Arameans were the target of his band of *Renegades*. Completing his survey, Nathan looked right to see where the pass widened before it joined the broad Golan plain. Although not visible, hundreds of Aramean chariots bivouacked just a few miles distant.

Three taps on Nathan's right shoulder from a *Renegade* lookout signaled the arrival of Abner's vanguard. He discerned at least a full company already waiting below in the darkness, with more men strung out in the gorge behind them. Abner was the first to scale the rocky slope. After a quick update from Nathan, the general began sending his soldiers the final few hundred feet up the treacherous footpaths from the river gorge. Several *Renegades* directed the weary Israelites to a secluded ravine to rest until the actual attack. Abner did not even grace Nathan with a smile before joining his men. Nathan watched with mixed feelings as the sturdy general disappeared into the shadows. The man lacked manners, but Abner was still Israel's most formidable warrior.

Nathan then set several of the *Renegades* to constructing a three-sided fire pit, with the open side facing into the pass. The stone walls would block the view of Aphek's sentries. Laban would build a corresponding structure on the opposite side. Lighting a small fire would signal that all the soldiers on that side of the pass were in place. Once the second fire appeared, the Israelites would move against their assigned objectives. Nathan shivered slightly in the cool night air as the most difficult phase was about to begin.

Twenty *Renegades* and two companies of the northern unit would attack the Aramean company camped in the pass and seize the new fortifications. The remaining northern three companies would dig in east of Aphek to deny the Aramean chariots entry to the city. The heaviest fighting was to be handled by Abner's southern unit. The general would attack the enemy barracks with his five companies. Given the element of surprise, Abner's men intended to slaughter the three hundred Aramean soldiers before they could be organized.

Nathan and his *Renegades* intended to give them that opportunity.

184

As each dark hour passed, Nathan felt he aged another year. The soldiers' movement out of the southern gorge were progressing much too slowly. He feared the northern unit was experiencing similar delays. The noise of sliding rocks and several sickening thuds indicated yet another Israelite had lost his footing and fallen back down the slope. All motion around Nathan ceased, for fear that the disturbance had alerted the Aramean sentries. After long minutes had passed with no sign of activity in Aphek, Nathan signaled the men to keep moving. At least a dozen men had already been lost during this final climb, but their injuries, or deaths, had gone unnoticed by the enemy. Nathan seethed with frustration. Their chosen approach was challenging enough in daylight and the men simply could not be rushed in the dark.

As the time for the assault came and went, men were still negotiating the narrow river gorge. Nathan impatiently sought out the *Renegade* counting the soldiers as they passed over the ridge. The man's report was alarming.

Only one hundred ninety-seven men.

Nathan closed his eyes in pain. It was barely two companies. The coming sunrise would find Israelites still in the southern gorge. He assumed the northern unit was just as bad off. Nathan visualized the inevitable outcome. The Aramean sentries would sound the alarm while Abner's men floundered. The garrison's heavy infantry would don their armor, form ranks and drive out the disorganized Israelites. Abner's hungry and thirsty survivors would wander the Golan Plain until the Aramean chariots ran them down. Conflicting thoughts crowded Nathan's mind, but one fact was unmistakably clear.

Decisive action was needed now, or the Third Royal Regiment was doomed.

Forcing calmness which he did not feel, Nathan summoned three *Renegades* and went in search of Abner. Nathan found the man in a heated discussion with his officers. The general's fierce expression indicated that Abner had reached the same disturbing conclusions. Catching sight of Nathan, Abner directed his rage toward the younger man.

"Your prince really knows how to prepare a trap. Unfortunately, he sprung it on my soldiers! I see no way out of this abomination!"

"Then be silent, Abner. I will tell you what to do."

Eventually there would be a reckoning with Abner over Nathan's hastily chosen words. However, he had no regrets; the general was on the verge of hysteria. True, word of Abner's humiliation would spread like a grass fire among the common soldiers. Yet, there was simply no time for Abner's petulance. Nathan's one advantage was that his aggressive response caught the general off guard. Abner glowered for a moment before responding.

"What do you propose...*armor bearer*?"

Ignoring Abner's taunt, Nathan addressed the three *Renegades* at his side.

"Cross over to the far side of the pass. Seek out Laban. Take different routes. Tell him to watch for my signal fire, then attack the Aramean company camped in the pass with however many soldiers he has. Whatever happens, those Arameans must be kept separated from the garrison. They can even be allowed to flee down the pass. Laban can forget about their chariots; we'll deal with them later. Understood? Then go!"

Each man vanished into the night. Uncharacteristically, Abner had not disputed Nathan's abrupt assumption of command, or even questioned Laban taking over the northern unit. Nathan wasn't quite sure what to make of the general's sudden acquiescence. The man either agreed with Nathan's orders, or he believed Nathan would be held responsible for their failure. Perhaps both statements were true regarding the wily general. Deciding the future would have to take care of itself, Nathan faced Abner.

"I'll give Laban twenty minutes, then light the signal. Prepare your men to attack the barracks, General."

Abner locked eyes with Nathan before silently stalking away. Nathan released a deeply held breath. Cold sweat ran down his armpits. The entire campaign faced disaster if the mercurial Abner went his own way. Of course, the campaign might already be doomed no matter what Nathan did. He was on the verge of tears, when one of Karaz's Hittite proverbs came to mind. The pithy saying did nothing to improve the situation, but it did make Nathan laugh.

The gods of battle enjoy pissing on your plans.

Nathan gave Laban as much time as he dared. In a few hours, Israel's chances of victory would fade with the rising sun. Two hundred and twenty-four soldiers were now available for Abner's assault on the barracks. The only hope for the out-numbered Israelites' lay in absolute surprise. Nathan briefly considered adding his forty *Renegades* to Abner's force, but quickly rejected the idea. Their original mission was even more vital now. If Nathan and his little band were successful, the enemy would be decapitated.

Ten pairs of *Renegades* were now poised along the edge of the ravine nearest Aphek. A second group of forty rested a short distance behind them. The sound of crunching sand and gravel farther back in the ravine meant that Abner's men were moving into position. Nathan doubted that the temperamental general would consider abandoning the plan, but a great sense of relief still washed over him. When the time came to advance, Nathan lit the small signal fire.

The twenty *Renegades* sprinted toward Aphek. Their task was to eliminate the Aramean sentries. He and Abner merely looked at each other, nodded and trotted off in different directions. Nathan hurried to the end of the ravine to join his forty men. Hopefully, Laban was in motion as well.

Nathan rushed his band of *Renegades* toward the Aramean officers' quarters. If these men were captured or killed, the soldiers Abner faced would be leaderless. Nathan hoped to keep the senior officers alive. Their knowledge of the Aramean strategy might prove invaluable. The *Renegades* slowed as they entered the shadowy streets of Aphek. Nathan noticed the bodies of several Aramean sentries sprawled in the alleys. Nathan halted his men behind the building nearest to their objective and cautiously peaked around its corner. The two-story building had a single entrance which faced to Nathan's left. Four sentries were stationed near the door, although three appeared to be sleeping. Nathan grinned wickedly. This lack of discipline indicated all the officers were safely asleep. He assumed the front door was barred, but that was of no concern. The Israelites were really interested in the four first-story windows on the side directly across from Nathan.

At Nathan's direction, the *Renegades* quickly divided into five groups. One group would silence the four sentries while the other groups each went through a different window. Nathan's squad had three extra men for a special task. While the other *Renegades* subdued the first floor, the men with Nathan would rush to the second floor where the more valuable prisoners probably resided. Nathan and the first three men up the stairs carried swords to deal with any armed resistance. The rest of his companions bore wooden clubs to take the remaining Arameans alive.

Just as the *Renegades* moved into the open, excited shouting came from the direction of the garrison area. Nathan resisted the urge to check on the Israelite assault against the barracks. That was Abner's problem now. His job was to get his men inside the adjacent building before their prey was aroused. The architect's desire to provide adequate light and ventilation greatly benefited the raiders. Nathan led his eleven men through the leftmost window. He jumped up and landed one knee on the windowsill while gripping its sides with both hands. Nathan then pulled his other leg over the sill and hopped down into the dark room.

Moving out of the way of the next man, Nathan drew his sword and gave his eyes a few seconds to adjust to the dimness of the building's interior. His ears confirmed *Renegades* were scrambling through the other windows. The area around Nathan appeared to be a kitchen. A faint glow from last night's cook fire provided enough illumination to reveal that the first floor was one large room. There were several large wooden pillars supporting the ceiling and numerous occupied beds scattered about. The stairs were located along the far wall. Nathan and his group began threading their way through the various obstacles. The sounds of life and death struggles began as he rushed up the steps. The *Renegades* repeatedly yelled the Aramean phrase they had practiced all day.

"Lie down and live!"

This command had two intended benefits. First, it encouraged the Aramean officers to surrender. Second, it helped the Israelites identify their comrades in the dark. Unfortunately, the cry also woke up the Arameans on the second floor. A small oil lamp dimly lit the room where Nathan found himself confronted by two naked Arameans holding swords. However, neither one moved against Nathan. When the first man questioned him in Aramean, Nathan realized he had been mistaken for a member of the garrison. Nathan quickly thought of a clever way to answer the confused man's query.

Nathan silently pointed toward a window.

When both men turned to look outside, Nathan struck. He slashed down on the nearest man's sword arm and lunged inside the reach of the other. Nathan wrestled the second man to the floor before smashing the hilt of his sword into his opponent's face. Their shrill screams alerted the other Arameans to the identity of the Israelites bounding up the stairs. Nathan heard yelling and the thud of clubs against flesh for a moment. Then, there were only the sounds of painful moaning and heavy breathing. The victorious *Renegades* unwound the ropes wrapped around their waists and swiftly bound their new prisoners.

The first floor was also secured by the time Nathan descended the stairs. Thirty-two Aramean officers had been sleeping in the building. There were eighteen bruised and bloody survivors, although four were not expected to see the next sunset. The junior officers on the first floor had put up the hardest fight and suffered the most casualties. Most importantly, the garrison commander and his two of aides living upstairs were taken alive. The *Renegades* had suffered two killed and six wounded.

The bound Arameans were piled into a corner of the first floor. As Nathan waited, he noticed an iron poker used to stir the cook fire. In a moment of inspiration, Nathan used the poker to stir the dormant flames to life before jabbing its tip into the hot embers. He became aware again of the sounds of battle drifting over from the garrison area. The *Renegades* assigned to kill the sentries soon rejoined Nathan. He now counted forty-seven men fit for battle. After assigning four men to guard the prisoners and care for his wounded, Nathan led the rest toward the fighting.

Nathan halted his men when the garrison area came into view. It appeared Abner had at least partially succeeded at surprising the more numerous Arameans. Yet, his instincts told him the outcome was still in doubt. Nathan estimated barely an hour remained before sunrise. The enemy chariots might decide to pay a visit then. Nathan decided to throw his remaining *Renegades* into the fray. He pointed his sword toward the battle and issued a challenge.

"Let's show Abner's men how to take a city!"

The *Renegades* roared their approval, drew their weapons and sprinted away. But before Nathan could take a

191

step, strong hands grabbed his shoulders and threw him on his back. Furious, he looked up to see a burly *Renegade* sergeant towering over him. The man thrust a beefy finger in Nathan's face.

"Laban thought you might try something stupid. He said to tell you this. *'Nathan, don't you think we can handle this? An Aluf has better things to do.'*...Well, do you?"

Nathan laughed despite his annoyance. Sheepishly, he nodded and extended his hand. The gruff sergeant grabbed Nathan's arm, pulled him to his feet and clapped him on the shoulder. As the big *Renegade* trotted off to fight, Nathan saw the wisdom in the man's words. Then he remembered the enemy officers waiting to be interrogated. He smiled.

That iron poker should be red-hot by now.

Several hours later, Nathan walked out of the former officers' quarters into the bright morning sun. He was fatigued, but well pleased with the information gleaned from the Arameans. The senior prisoners confirmed all the Aramean infantry were exactly where Jonathan had hoped and that they lacked any chariot support. Even better, the nearest Aramean reinforcements were over four days of hard marching away. As Nathan expected, he did not have to burn anyone with that hot poker. Merely holding its steaming tip near a man's eyes or genitals did wonders to loosen his tongue.

Encouraging reports from the various Israelite units around Aphek had also made their way to Nathan throughout the morning.

The northern Israelite unit had experienced even worse delays than Abner's men. The frustrated regimental commander was happy to allow Laban to sort out the mess. Barely one hundred soldiers had been available to Laban when Nathan ordered him to attack on the pass. The additional twenty *Renegades* turned out to be a godsend. As the Israelites advanced silently toward the Aramean fortifications, Laban knew his prospects were grim. Not only were the Arameans nearly equal in number to his force, but the enemy had been roused by the noisy fighting in Aphek. Laban was down to his final trick: aggressiveness. With a score of howling *Renegades* in the forefront, the Israelites charged out of the darkness and into the enemy camp. Their battle cries echoed around the pass and confused the Arameans as to the true number of their attackers. Finding their fortifications offered no protection to an attack from the rear, the defenders soon broke and fled down the pass toward Galilee. Although his men now begged to join their comrades fighting in Aphek, Laban had refused. The newly won position must be held at all costs against an Aramean counterattack. Laban chafed at this military necessity, not knowing his action had already laid the foundation for an Israelite victory.

Meanwhile, Abner's attack on the garrison had indeed caught the Arameans in their beds, but the enemy hastily rallied. Many enemy soldiers died defending the barrack entrances, so comrades could don their armor. Soon the battle began to swing against the Israelites. The Aramean heavy infantry gradually pushed Abner's more lightly armed men back. If the Aramean company routed by Laban had been present, the Israelites would have surely been overwhelmed. Instead, the timely arrival of Nathan's forty-three *Renegades* tipped the scales in Abner's favor. These agile Israelite warriors swarmed the Arameans' infantry in the open ground before they could assume a proper fighting formation. Time and again, several *Renegades* would isolate an armored enemy and then cut him down from behind. After half the garrison had been slain, the surviving Arameans barricaded themselves in the compound's largest building. A bloody stalemate appeared likely until one of the *Renegades* suggested searching a nearby barn. A short time later, laughing Israelites clambered onto the roofs of the holdouts' barracks with torches and lamp oil. The soldiers poked holes in the mud brick ceilings through which oil and fire were dropped down. The flames and smoke promptly drove the luckless Arameans into the waiting arms of their executioners.

Fortunately, Abner recognized it was not time to celebrate. The general learned two more Israelite companies had climbed out of the gorge. Abner quickly marched these soldiers to the east side of Aphek to block chariots from the Golan Plain. The general's instincts proved to be on the mark.

An hour after sunrise, five Aramean chariot squadrons attempted to retake the Aphek. A mile from the city, they found nearly three hundred fresh Israelite troops waiting to greet them. In the narrow confines of the pass, the outcome of any battle was obvious. The Aramean chariots would first be slowed, then swarmed by Abner's foot soldiers. The enemy horsemen withdrew without a fight. Nathan guessed the chariot commander would never sacrifice his valuable resource needlessly.

The crucial stronghold at Aphek was now theirs. But for how long?

The Israelite margin of victory had been by less than a knife's edge. Nathan believed the besieged enemy garrison would have attempted a breakout if they had known how few healthy Israelites opposed them at the end. The piecemeal arrival of the Third Royal Regiment had resulted in horrendous casualties. Abner would be fortunate to muster more than six hundred fit soldiers this day.

The *Renegades* had also paid a heavy price. More than eighty of these fearsome warriors had charged into the pass last night. Only fifty-one Renegades rallied to Nathan's trumpet call that morning. Surprisingly, the sight of Laban limping badly affected Nathan more than the other deaths. A great deal of shouting was required before Laban agreed to lie down until his bleeding stopped. The incident served to reinforce how much Nathan depended on his stalwart subordinate... and the unique skills of his company. There were only eight other healthy *Renegades*, currently serving with Jonathan as bodyguards down in Galilee. Karaz had assured the prince that finding replacements for the *Renegades* would never be a problem. There was no shortage of army volunteers for this elite band. Nathan's concern was that hard-earned experience was being lost faster than it could be cultivated in the new recruits. He resolved to use these special troops more carefully in the future.

The streets of Aphek were silent as Nathan strolled west in search of Abner. Most of the residents remained in their homes, although a few had fled into the surrounding hills. The Israelites were instructed to leave anyone alone who behaved peaceably. As he passed the barracks area, Nathan smelled cooking and observed the victors moving into their dead foes' quarters. Naturally, the *Renegades* had already claimed the Aramean Officers' building with its comfortable beds and even better food. A sentry advised Nathan to seek Abner at the fortifications in the pass.

His initial view of the Arameans' defenses left Nathan unimpressed. The enemy had simply placed a packed dirt wall, about four feet high, in the narrowest point of the pass. He headed towards a tall figure coated in mud and blood looking over this crude barrier toward Galilee. Only his height and shield identified the man as Abner, but no amount of grime could disguise he was a true man of war. Nathan wondered if his own filth made him look as impressive. Abner stooped slightly from fatigue, but he still managed to tweak Nathan.

"Oh...there you are. Manage to get a nap in?"

Nathan's rude gesture made the older man chuckle. When Abner declined further comment, Nathan turned his blood-shot eyes toward the enemy breastworks. Both men studied the terrain in silence, attempting to anticipate coming events. Nathan's opinion of the fortifications improved as he identified several unexpected features. The Arameans had dug a ditch four feet deep and six feet wide across most of the pass. The earthen wall before him had been created by heaping all the dirt on Aphek's side of the ditch. Nathan was impressed. The results were both simple and effective. Because of the depth of the ditch, an attacker coming up the pass toward Aphek from Galilee would face a barrier nearly eight feet high. Anyone trying to scale the wall would only claw away a few handfuls of dirt before falling back into the ditch. Meanwhile, the defenders could easily lean over the wall to stab their assailants, while risking minimal exposure. The pass was barely one hundred yards wide here. One hundred soldiers could hold off an army indefinitely from behind this well-sited entrenchment.

Surprisingly, the Arameans had not extended the ditch for the entire width of the pass. They had begun their digging at the rocky slope on Nathan's right, or the north side of the pass, but stopped some ten yards short of its southern boundary. Here, both the ditch and wall took a sharp left turn and continued on for another twenty yards in parallel to the pass's southern rocky face. Obviously, the open gap on the left allowed the movement of troops and supplies, but Nathan saw no reason to angle the ditch and wall combination. Why not add a gate instead? He set that puzzle aside only to notice another one.

The Arameans had randomly dug a score of broad, shallow pits in front of the ditch. The nearest pits came within five yards of the ditch, and the furthest ones were no more than twenty yards away. Nathan wondered if these excavations were unfinished, for the pits themselves were rather pathetic obstacles. A man could easily step in and out of any of the pits, if not simply walk around the few blocking his way. Karaz always cautioned against assuming your foe was stupid. So, Nathan used his training to visualize how a battle might take place here.

In his mind, Nathan imagined the Aramean regiments advancing one behind the other up the pass from Galilee. The rocky slopes here would force the enemy to attack on a narrow front. The commander would send forward his first regiment, arrayed one hundred men wide and ten ranks deep, against the earthen wall. Somewhere between one hundred yards and fifty yards out, the regiment would begin its charge.

Before coming to an abrupt stop.

The purpose of the pits now became clear to Nathan. They were meant to break the momentum of a charge. The first rank of soldiers would spot these shallow obstacles, but not the men following. The second and third ranks would be tripped up by depressions less than a foot deep and then be crushed by the stampeding rear ranks. The bulk of the regiment would be halted by the piles of bodies blocking their advance. At the best, the attacking waves would slow to a walk and attempt to pick their way through. Karaz always sang the praises of even rudimentary fieldworks. Nathan now saw the proof.

Nathan had to assume his enemy would eventually reach the ditch. Now the earthen wall would provide an effective dam against the attacking tide... except in one place. Nathan's eyes were drawn left, to the large defensive gap along the southern rock face of the pass. The Aramean attack must flow in that direction, irresistibly drawn, like a river, to the only possible place where it could surge again. Nathan now grasped the reason for angling back the ditch and wall along the gap. Like the neck of a wine jar, the open left flank would funnel the attackers into a deadly killing ground. An Israelite shield wall would be waiting here, plugging a space where no more than ten of the enemy could confront them at a time. Meanwhile, the Arameans would face a deadly gauntlet as they crowded into the gap. Scores of Israelites, protected by that angled twenty yards of ditch and wall, would rain down arrows, javelins and stones on their exposed flank.

Only one thing disappointed Nathan: the Arameans already knew every detail of the Aphek defenses. Unexpectedly, this realization sent a thrill of excitement through his tired body. Of course, the Arameans knew, they built the thing! But the fortifications had been constructed for their use...not Israel's.

That very knowledge would discourage the Arameans from ever attacking Aphek from Galilee. The potential slaughter would force the Arameans to go somewhere else, perhaps even into Jonathan's trap! Nathan now fully grasped the meaning of another of Karaz's lessons.

Fortifications could win battles merely by existing.

Nathan was unaware that he was laughing aloud until he noticed Abner's confused look. The general listened intently to Nathan's excited explanation. Within minutes, the pass was echoing with the laughter of two exhausted men.

Galilean Plains west of the Golan Heights

Eliada strode into the oversized tent where his senior officers now stood to attention. He had been awake for hours, ever since the first garrison survivors began streaming into the Aramean base camp from Aphek. The Aramean general had immediately dispatched scouts into the pass, and their report had just arrived. Aphek had fallen. There was no sign of the Aramean chariot corps. Hundreds of Israelites were now manning the pass's defenses. Eliada's subordinates listened in grim silence as he dispensed the shocking news. Eliada was more disturbed by his officers' pessimistic mood than the loss of the city. Such setbacks usually provided excellent opportunities for the experienced tactician. Despite a few impressive achievements, this Hebrew king was still a battlefield novice. Eliada would patiently wait for his opponent's inevitable missteps and salvage the situation. This mishap was merely the first roll of the dice in a complex game.

Therefore, Eliada's main concerns were gossip and rumors. Being cut off from one's homeland was a serious matter, but not necessarily fatal. However, a general loss of confidence within the Aramean army now could be. The nervousness of a captain invariably begat cowardice in his soldiers. Eliada resolved to prevent that crisis by stiffening the quaking knees of his officers. He began by giving quiet, confident orders to his steadiest regiment commander.

"Jaulan, have your men ready to march within the hour. Leave everything behind except weapons and three days of food."

"Consider it done, Sir! We'll retake Aphek by supper."

"You're not going to Aphek. I want your regiment to move east through the Yarmuk River Valley as rapidly as possible."

"How far?"

"Until you reach the plains on our side of the mountains. Meanwhile, the other four regiments will break camp. Derah, your men will carry the equipment left behind by Jaulan. In three hours, the rest of the army will follow him up the Yarmuk River."

Eliada waited patiently in the awkward silence that filled the command tent. The Aramean officers cast furtive glances to each other. Jaulan finally broached the question Eliada knew was in all their minds.

"Sir, then how will we get back Aphek?"

"We won't. Not now, anyway."

Protocol was abandoned and replaced by surprised gasps and frantic whispers. Eliada could sense his officer's moods wavering between confusion and anger. Eliada was not surprised when Derah challenged him. The man had powerful patrons but was the least intelligent of all the Aramean regimental commanders.

"So, you make us slink back to Zobah in shame? This is what happens when our king selects a commander with caution instead of courage!"

Eliada strolled over to stand a few inches from Derah. He was accustomed to criticism of his cautious nature, but by his peers or superiors, not by subordinates. It was time to put this ass back in his pen. Eliada hovered silently, like a hawk, until the first beads of sweat dripped down Derah's face. His opening words were all the more chilling for their softness.

"Derah, do you know how many Israelites are at Aphek?"

"No...Sir."

"Interesting. Apparently, your courage does not care about numbers."

Eliada now turned his back on Derah and began eyeing his other subordinates. His voice gradually increased in volume and intensity with each sentence.

"Derah would have us attack our own defenses before Aphek. We would wreck at least two regiments in the process, but we would most definitely get through. Only to go nowhere! Why? Because thousands of Israelite militia would be hounding us all the way up the pass! And unless the Israelite commander in Aphek is stupid enough to disband *his* army, *our* army would be trapped. Is this what your courage looks like, Derah?"

"Sir, I meant...uh..."

"Naturally, Derah, a courageous leader like you sees yet another alternative to retreating. You would lead our five thousand infantrymen out onto the open plains of Galilee against four times as many Israelites. Now a cautious commander would wait for chariot support, but apparently your courage has no need for chariots...or food for that matter. Because the Israelites at Aphek would storm down the pass, destroy our camp and take our army from behind. Your courage, Derah, would have no one slinking back to Zobah. Because we would all be dead."

"Look, Eliada, you have..."

"Tell me, Derah, does your courage always look like *disaster*!"

Eliada had strode full circle to resume his place in front of Derah. His final sentence ended in a shout which rattled loose objects. To Eliada's astonishment, Derah could not keep his tongue still. An affliction common among men whose stones were larger than their brains.

"But, Sir, won't the enemy militia simply follow us into the river valley?"

"Most likely. And that, Derah, will be your problem. Your courageous regiment will serve as the rearguard...as well as carrying the equipment of Jaulan's men."

Eliada searched the faces of his other subordinates. All stood rigidly at attention after the brutal humiliation of their fellow officer. Derah had voiced all their fears and looked ridiculous for having them. Then Derah's soldiers would guess their miserable assignment at the rear was due to their commander's big mouth. Eliada knew the lower ranks always found a way to repay such abuse. However, the important thing to Eliada was that his officers had forgotten to be afraid. Now to give them hope.

"Anyway, who said we were going back to Zobah? I never did. Because we are not. We are merely leaving this death trap to seek a proper battlefield. This war is just beginning! You have your orders."

Eliada's performance had its desired effect. His officers departed the tent in good spirits, except for Derah, confident their general had the situation well in hand. Eliada sat down and drank deeply from a wineskin when he was finally alone. There was no reason to mention the damaging countermove he feared the Hebrew commander would make. Whether or not his opponent was that clever, Eliada had no choice but to send his army up the Yarmuk River.

Chapter 10 - The Betrayal

I called to my allies, but they betrayed me.

From the book of Lamentations, chapter 1, verse 19

Golan Heights Pass west of Aphek

Nathan scrambled up a rocky promontory slightly more than a mile down the pass from Aphek. He currently enjoyed an unobstructed view of the vast Israelite militia encampment on the Galilean Plain far below. Ignoring the burning in his muscles, Nathan hastened his ascent. Barely six hours had passed since Aphek had been seized from the Arameans by the Third Royal Regiment. However, the previous night's vicious fighting was only the opening move in a rapidly expanding conflict. This nondescript chunk of stone over which Nathan now crawled was the most significant piece on the Golan Heights right now. It was here Nathan would learn whether the Israelite cause was still viable or hopelessly doomed.

A stiff breeze shifted direction across the rock face and blew a whiff of cooking smoke toward Nathan. He assumed it came from the *Renegade* lookouts. A moment later, Nathan stood upon a small mesa roughly twenty yards across. Abner and Laban were perched near the cliff's edge, staring intently toward Galilee. Nathan was impressed the wounded *Renegade* leader had managed the steep climb on a bad leg. Apparently, he would have to tie Laban up to keep the man from bleeding to death. A few yards away, three other *Renegades* shared a meal around the small fire which had earlier caught Nathan's attention. The west wind was even stronger at the top and covered the sound of Nathan's sandals crunching on the gravel until he was almost on top of the other five men. Abner walked back to the fire when he became aware of Nathan's approach. The general scooped some steaming stew into a wooden bowl and handed it to Nathan before resuming his watch. Coming from the gruff soldier, Nathan thought this simple act to be high courtesy indeed. His stomach found the warm gruel unexpectedly satisfying as he gulped it down. Hunger satisfied for the moment, he joined Abner and Laban in their vigil.

Although much activity was visible within the Aramean camp, its purpose was still unclear. Jonathan and the militia in Galilee were closer and would discern the enemy's intent first. The challenge was how to communicate between the Plains and the Heights so that the Israelite militia and the Third Royal Regiment could coordinate their actions. So, Jonathan and Nathan had settled on the idea of signal fires. Once the Aramean Army was committed to an action, Jonathan would light one, two or three fires from his encampment. Nathan would interpret their meaning before committing Abner and his soldiers to action.

A single fire meant the Arameans were advancing up the pass toward Aphek. Abner's regiment would then man Aphek's fortifications and prepare for a bloody fight. Meanwhile, Jonathan would assault the enemy camp with the Israelite militia. The theory was that the Arameans could not advance and fight a rearguard action simultaneously. Hopefully, the enemy army would be trapped in the barren pass and forced to surrender once their water and food ran out. The worst possible outcome for Israel would be for the Third Royal Regiment to be destroyed at Aphek. The Arameans could then escape, obtain reinforcements, and return to Galilee with a vengeance.

Two fires would be lit if the Arameans chose to fight the Israelites on the Galilean Plains. Nathan knew this was the outcome which Jonathan feared most. The Israelite militia would be launched in a massive charge to surround and overwhelm their enemy while Abner's regiment descended to attack the Aramean rear. However, the Aramean soldiers' training and discipline gave their smaller force many advantages over even a huge formation of militia. If the Third Royal Regiment could be tied down at the bottom of the pass, the remaining Aramean regiments might sidestep the militia's onslaught and outflank it. The Israelite militia units would be destroyed one by one until the survivors finally surrendered.

The most desirable outcome, at least to Jonathan's way of thinking, would be indicated by three fires. The Yarmuk River Valley ran eastward from Galilee to Aramean territory and was easily accessible from the enemy encampment. A prudent commander might choose to escape from the trap, instead of fighting his way out. The enemy general could preserve his army by retreating east along the river, reach safety within a few days and return to Galilee under more favorable circumstances.

Unless Nathan's various schemes began to bear fruit.

The *Renegades* had already located an easily defended chokepoint in the valley where a few hundred men could block an entire army. The path there was more readily traversed than the treacherous route to Aphek had been. Abner's men should be in position long before the first Aramean scouts arrived. With Jonathan leading the Israelite militia in pursuit, the Arameans would discover both ends of the valley to be firmly sealed. Yet, an Israelite victory here was by no means assured. Even if all went according to plan, Nathan would still be required to pull off one final miracle.

A shout from Laban pulled Nathan's attention back to the present situation. A column of smoke was starting to curl skyward from the designated spot near Jonathan's camp. Nathan's stomach began to churn. Despite all the disadvantages they faced, the Arameans might still decide to slug it out with the Israelite Army at Aphek. Nathan was considering his own chances of surviving that bloody fight when a second fire began to burn. He involuntary released a sigh of relief, but now felt Abner's growing tension. The general was anxious to know if he had to start his men down the pass to rescue the militia. Blindly attacking an enemy's camp posed many hazards.

Then, a third wisp of smoke began to rise. The Arameans were retreating up the Yarmuk River Valley! Nathan could already make out some militia units advancing on the Aramean camp. The three leaders exchanged smiles and clasped arms before departing on their various errands. Nathan would rush most of the *Renegades* into the valley to ambush the Arameans' advance guard and delay their column. A few *Renegades* would guide Abner and seven of his understrength companies down to the chokepoint in the Yarmuk Valley. However, there was always the chance of an Aramean ruse. For now, Laban would remain in Aphek with the three companies which suffered the most casualties. God willing, the first of several thousand Israelite militia would reach Aphek by midafternoon. They would assume the defense of Aphek, allowing the three Army companies to rejoin Abner. Laban had grudgingly agreed to remain in Aphek until his leg healed. Of course, Laban would be the one who decided what *healed* meant. Nathan reflected on the vagaries of war as he skidded down the slope. Out of all the various options, the enemy commander had chosen the most conservative one.

Once again, another of Karaz's lessons had proved to be true. Most men *became* generals by being audacious, but they *stayed* generals by being cautious.

The Yarmuk River Valley east of Galilee

Eliada's next meeting with his commanders took place along the northern slope of the Yarmuk Valley in a secluded nook providing a modicum of privacy. The session began with Jaulan's report to Eliada, although it was already common knowledge in the Aramean Army. The Israelites had ambushed Jaulan's lead elements four hours after his regiment entered the valley. The Arameans stubbornly pushed on, suffering dozens of casualties during the afternoon from concealed archers and slingers. Just before sunset, Jaulan found the Israelites waiting in force where the Yarmuk River took a sharp bend in a confined portion of the valley. The site was well suited for defense. The Arameans were obliged to wade twenty yards across a swift, knee-deep river and ascend a steep bank before engaging their foe. Dozens fell to enemy arrows and javelins in the cold water. The Israelites had little trouble dispatching those fatigued Aramean survivors who emerged from the river. Attempts to outflank the enemy position by way of the valley slopes likewise failed, for the Israelites had already secured the high ground. Jaulan allowed three of his companies to be badly mauled before admitting the futility of these efforts. He then ordered his battered regiment to withdraw and await the arrival of their general.

In contrast, the remainder of the Eliada's army had completed the journey unmolested. Thousands of Israelite militia had been content to shadow the Aramean column as it snaked along the Yarmuk River. Their pursuit ended at a particularly tight passage nearly a mile behind the Aramean rearguard. The Israelites were at this very moment busily blockading the narrow ravine there with boulders, logs and dirt. The Aramean tactical situation was apparent to the rawest recruit.

Eliada's five infantry regiments were now under siege.

The general noted various levels of anxiety in all the men in attendance, with one exception: Derah. The outspoken regimental commander not only radiated renewed confidence but seemed to have won back the support of a few other officers. Eliada almost laughed at the irony of Derah benefitting from the enemy's successes. Well, if the current situation was a surprise to Derah, it was not to Eliada. The Israelite commander had made an obvious countermove to the Arameans' retreat into the Yarmuk Valley. No oracle was needed to divine this basic maneuver. Any army that could ascend the treacherous mountains to Aphek would find it even easier to descend them. Eliada had entered this potential trap with eyes wide open. While being the best of several undesirable options, it still temporarily passed the advantage to the Israelite dogs. If he was to recover the initiative, Eliada must first reestablish dominance over his own pack of curs, especially Derah. Fortunately for Eliada, Derah's own mouth continued to betray him. The man's opening comment could not have been more fortuitous if Eliada had dictated the words to him.

"I must apologize, Eliada, for my previous criticism of your caution. Great courage is required to fight a battle on two fronts. Otherwise, why lead us into a trap?"

"Your apology is appreciated, Derah. However, I have no intention of fighting here."

The confused look on Derah's face almost made up for the peril Eliada now faced.

"What? Don't you...it seems I must be blunt with you, Sir. Your strategy has doomed our men! If we do not fight, there can be no escape!"

"Derah, if we do fight now, there will be no escape."

"Do you propose we all just fall on our swords?"

In contrast to Derah's near hysteria, Eliada's voice remained calm, almost relaxed. He broke eye contact with his troublesome subordinate and turned to address the group.

"Can someone please explain why it is better to be trapped here than trapped before Aphek?"

"I see two reasons, Sir. First, we can defend ourselves more easily. Second, there is an abundant supply of water."

Derah whirled around to identify Eliada's supporter. His eyes blazed when he realized the words came from a senior captain named Burak, Derah's own second-in-command. Burak ignored his immediate superior's angry glare and continued to face his general. Eliada recognized the younger officer had decided to risk his career by throwing in his lot with him against

210

Derah. This Burak was apparently both ambitious and intelligent. Eliada made a mental note of the man's qualities.

"Well said, Burak. This is a much better place to wait out the enemy."

This brief exchange between Eliada and Burak further infuriated Derah.

"So, what if the Israelites can't reach us here? The men will soon grow hungry. But wait... there is a river at hand. Do you plan to go fishing, Eliada?"

"An excellent suggestion, Derah. Fishing might extend our supplies for a day or two."

"Don't mock me, Eliada. We face disaster here!"

Eliada slowly walked back to lean into the face of his accuser. He shook his head as if he were lecturing a slow-witted child.

"Then, Derah, I suppose it is a very good thing that assistance will soon be here. I sent ten messengers to Zobah by different routes *before* we broke camp yesterday. Within a week, ten days at the most, King Rehob will be moving westward through the Yarmuk River with a relief force. Between us, we will squeeze the Israelites out of the valley like virgin oil from new olives."

Eliada stepped back to see signs of courage returning to his other officers. He swiftly gave his orders for the day.

"Meanwhile, have your men rest, care for their weapons...and fish."

While the morale of his departing officers could have been better, Eliada felt it sufficed for now. Derah would find little support if he harbored any thoughts of mutiny. Eliada was more disappointed that only Burak grasped the Aramean situation was not as dire as it first appeared. The general found a solitary ledge among the rocks where he could peacefully observe the Yarmuk's flow and consider his next moves.

Eliada recognized the Hebrew king, or one of his generals, was indeed a gifted amateur, but an amateur, nonetheless. Like most novice commanders, an initial battlefield success had encouraged the man to overreach. The stunning capture of Aphek was an example of brilliant tactics, but poor strategy. The Hebrews were now just as trapped in the Yarmuk Valley as the Arameans were. The difference was that King Rehob's reinforcements would soon break the deadlock in Eliada's favor. The enemy soldiers who now blocked Eliada's eastward retreat would be forced to stand and die in a vain attempt to prevent Eliada and Rehob from joining forces. Eliada could then leave a strong Aramean rearguard to keep the remaining Israelite militia occupied. Meanwhile, the bulk of the Aramean host would exit the eastern end of the valley and swing north to unite with the chariot corps camped on the Golan Plain. This combined force would swiftly retake Aphek, clear out the pass, sweep down the Galilean Plain and block the western end of the Yarmuk Valley. The besieging Israelites would then find the gaming table had been turned around. Any of their militia escaping slaughter in the valley would be run down on the plains by the Aramean chariots.

Eliada returned to his tent shortly before dark, satisfied with his vision of the future. The temporary seizure of Aphek would cost the Hebrew leader his best military formation, the lives of thousands of his militia and the entire region of Galilee. After such losses, at least a generation would pass before any Hebrew could even consider challenging the Aramean Federation.

Sitting in his tent six days later, Eliada conceded that the Yarmuk River had done little to relieve the hunger pangs of his army. Fishing was not a bad idea; it simply was an inadequate one. Fish turned out to be scarce in the mountain streams that time of year. At least attempting to fish gave his idle soldiers something to do besides think of their stomachs. The Arameans had consumed their last regular meal during the third day in the valley. There had been almost no time to accumulate food stocks in Eliada's base camp before the Aramean supply line was cut at Aphek. Small game and edible vegetation rapidly disappeared on both sides of the river in the vicinity of the hungry camp. Efforts to gather food from farms in the countryside proved futile. Even large Aramean foraging parties were attacked soon after they ventured beyond the picket lines.

The Arameans could not even enjoy the Yarmuk's cool, clear waters. Hundreds of Israelite soldier made a daily show of urinating upstream from where the Arameans drew their water supplies. This disgusting habit, though annoying, had so far made no discernible difference in the water's taste. Still, Eliada felt queasy every time he drank from the river.

Apart from harassing the Aramean foragers, the Israelites showed little aggressiveness. Eliada's scouts estimated Jaulan had encountered at least one regiment of Israel's regular army on the first day of the attempted retreat. These Israelite soldiers had since been augmented by hundreds of additional militia. Eliada was particularly surprised the enemy had not yet requested his surrender. It seemed as if the Israelites were also waiting for something to happen. Eliada judged the spirits of his soldiers to be good, considering the circumstances. That could rapidly change if their relief did not arrive in a few days, as their general had so confidently guaranteed.

Frantic shouting abruptly interrupted Eliada's thoughts. He pulled back the tent flap to see men pointing toward the eastern end of the valley. Using his hands to shield his eyes from the morning sun, Eliada made out three shadowy figures walking out from the Israelite defenses. He was astonished to identify the trio as two Israelites casually escorting an Aramean soldier. The presence of a distinctive pouch around the Aramean's neck caused Eliada to correct himself a few moments later. The man was not a mere soldier; he was a courier from the Royal Court in Zobah. This fact deeply concerned Eliada, for he could think of no good reason for Israelites to help deliver his king's mail. Halfway between the two armies, the Israelites turned back and allowed the courier to proceed alone. Eliada rushed back to his personal tent to prepare. He charged a squad of his bodyguards with bringing the courier directly to him, and no one else. His officers were ordered to await the news from Zobah in the command tent. The last thing Eliada desired at this moment was to deal with Derah's distractions.

A few minutes later the courier was ushered inside the general's tent. Eliada instructed his bodyguards that no one was to disturb this meeting on pain of death. The courier politely, but firmly, asked to see Eliada's signet ring. Satisfied with the general's identity, the courier bowed and handed over a leather pouch emblazoned with Zobah's royal crest. King Rehob had dispatched this courier and two others on the same day that Eliada's plea for reinforcements arrived in Zobah. The Israelites had intercepted the man the night before. Upon seeing the courier's pouch, the Israelites had taken him straight to the Aramean camp.

Eliada found the behavior of his enemies to be puzzling indeed. There had been no attempt to interrogate the courier. Of course, this would have done the Israelites no good since only illiterate men were selected to carry the King's messages. But Eliada wondered why the Israelites had not even tried. He opened the pouch and removed a small scroll still bearing the unbroken seal of King Rehob. This too was most curious because Eliada always read any captured enemy documents. After dismissing the courier, he cracked the seal and unrolled the scroll to reveal a lengthy Aramean poem. After studying some seemingly random symbols in the margins, Eliada began extracting the real message from his king. He painstakingly scratched out each word with a stylus on a soft clay tablet. Eliada rechecked the bewildering message three times, but it always came out the same. He was so dumbfounded that he consumed an entire wineskin before confronting his officers.

A hush fell over the assembled Aramean officers later when Eliada entered the command tent. The only sounds were the crackling of leather and the clink of armor scales as the men rose to their feet. Their commander's expression indicated that the news from Zobah was not good. Eliada could think of no better way to proceed than to read the transcribed text directly from his clay tablet.

REINFORCEMENT IMPOSSIBLE

MAKE BEST POSSIBLE TERMS

RETURN WITH YOUR ARMY INTACT

The message was so startling that even Derah was speechless for a moment. Eliada used the stunned silence to take control during its discussion.

"Our first task is to open negotiations with the Israelites. Their initial terms will dictate our next actions."

Eliada was disturbed to see nearly half the heads of his audience turn towards Derah. The man needed no additional encouragement to challenge his general.

"Hunger steals more of our strength each day, Eliada. The Israelites have grown complacent. A bold strike to the west now can break their militia."

"The king has commanded us to parlay, Derah."

"And if they refuse? Time favors our enemy. I doubt the Israelites will be in a hurry to talk."

A calm voice unexpectedly interrupted the nascent power struggle.

"The Hebrews might be ready sooner than you think, Derah."

All eyes turned toward Derah's second-in-command, Burak. The young captain was peering through the open tent flap toward the eastern Israelite defenses. Eliada led the rush outside for a better view of the company of Israelites now marching their way. Trumpets throughout the Aramean camp spread the alarm. Most of the enemy soldiers halted some two hundred yards away and sat down on the ground. Ten Israelites advanced for another fifty yards to a shady spot beneath a rocky outcropping where they began preparing a meal. Their intent was clear. They were daring the Arameans to come out and talk.

Eliada knew this convenient invitation indicated the Israelites had somehow anticipated Rehob's instructions long before they arrived. There could be only one answer: treason. Aramean treason. Eliada seethed inwardly at the arrogance and cunning of the Israelites. They had made use of traitors to maneuver his army into an impossible situation. Now the gloating Israelites were waiting for Eliada to come crawling. He selected nine bodyguards as an escort while angrily rejecting the demands of his officers to accompany him. Eliada could not afford to argue with his subordinates during any negotiations. He must focus all his attention on the Israelites.

The ten Israelite emissaries leisurely ate their food while observing Eliada's approach. He grudgingly admired how his foes subtly demonstrated that they now held the upper hand. Eliada reassured himself during the brief walk by listing the advantages he could summon during the coming negotiations. He doubted the Israelites could keep their militia forces intact for much longer. His army was still quite formidable. Most commanders would be reluctant to pay the price in blood required to wipe out five Aramean regiments. The Israelite toll would be even higher if they left the Arameans no alternative but death. By the time he came face to face with his opponents, Eliada was convinced an honorable resolution was just a matter of agreeing on the right price.

Now that he could see the Israelites up close, Eliada was glad he brought sturdy bodyguards instead of his older officers.

Eight of the most intimidating men he had ever seen stood up as the Arameans drew near. The way their lips curled into grins after studying his bodyguards was especially disquieting. Two men wearing well-worn armor, but no helmets, remain seated in front of the other Israelites. Eliada judged one man to be in his forties but thought the other might be only twenty years of age. He assumed the Israelite delegation consisted of the commander, one aide and eight guards. Eliada signaled his own men to halt ten paces before the Israelites. He walked slowly forward until he stood a few feet away from the seated men. A lengthy silence ensued, during which Eliada focused on the older man. Eliada was slightly taken aback when it was the younger who requested his identity.

"I am Eliada of Damascus, General to King Rehob, and Commander of the Army of Zobah."

"The top man, are you? Good. Saves a lot of time. I am Prince Jonathan, son of Saul, King of Israel. This is Abner, General of the Army of Israel."

Eliada's mind reeled briefly as he realized how badly he had misjudged the situation. He tried to recover by hurriedly studying the face of this youthful prince. Eliada cursed himself for missing obvious clues to the true nature of the young man seated before him. The piercing eyes, confident manner, commanding voice, combined with Abner's deference, all pointed to Jonathan as the powerbroker. This young man might even be the architect of the calamity now facing the Arameans. Eliada tried to start over with Jonathan by making a simple request.

"May I please be seated, my Lord?"

218

"You won't be here that long."

"Negotiations of this type can be quite lengthy."

"You're not here to negotiate, Aramean. You're here to receive my orders."

Jonathan's brusque manner convinced Eliada to respond in kind. He could not allow himself to be treated as a supplicant.

"And why should I take orders from a boy?"

"You already know why."

"Let's set that issue aside for now. Exactly what do you think you can make me do, Hebrew?"

Jonathan's response was both brief and blunt. Eliada experienced an unfamiliar combination of anger...and fear.

"You can't possibly expect my men to submit to that! There must be room for us to negotiate!"

"I do. And there isn't."

"We would rather fight to the death!"

"You might, Eliada. Few of your soldiers will."

Jonathan and Abner both rose to their feet while Eliada sputtered in a wordless rage. As the Israelite guards fell in behind them, Jonathan offered one final observation before turning to leave.

"You Arameans have a truly remarkable army. Apparently, your soldiers grow stronger the longer they starve."

A harsh dryness suddenly filled Eliada's throat. After a few seconds, he finally croaked out a single word.

"Wait."

It was nearly an hour before Eliada reconvened his interrupted officers' meeting. Finalizing the surrender arrangements required only minutes. Eliada had mostly listened while the Hebrew prince dictated the time, location and procedures. He took some consolation in being able to obtain one concession from Jonathan. Yet even that small victory was troubling. Eliada thought he detected a mischievous look in the prince's eyes as he agreed. The reason for delaying the start of his meeting was simple. Eliada needed time to regain his composure before explaining the unpleasant details to his staff.

As soon as he closed the tent flap, Eliada perceived the first sign of trouble. Upon his entry, all his subordinates remained seated and continued their conversations. The second was the interruption of his opening remarks.

"Here are the surrender terms as presented by the Hebrew Prince Jonathan. First..."

"Sir, we already know them. That's what we have been discussing."

Eliada looked at the speaker, Jaulan, in bewilderment. Seeing disbelief on his general's face, Jaulan proceeded to accurately list every detail of the proposed surrender.

"Who told you this, Jaulan?"

"While you were away, the Israelites released a score of our soldiers captured at Aphek. These men were given the terms of surrender and told that our survival depended on honoring them."

"How many of our soldiers know of this?"

"It's spreading through the camp like a grassfire."

Eliada reluctantly acknowledged the shrewdness of this Prince Jonathan. The young man had skillfully driven a wedge between the Aramean leaders and their men. Eliada knew even the most distasteful surrender terms could be accepted by a common soldier, if his survival were guaranteed. Eliada's worst fears were promptly confirmed by Burak.

"Sir, I spoke with the senior sergeant in my regiment. He fears the men might follow us into battle but surrender as soon as the fight turned against them."

Burak's comment unleashed an immediate firestorm of disagreement. Nervous officers began firing off accusations, first at Burak and then each other. The meeting descended into chaos.

"You cowardly fools! What if the Israelites betray us? We would be helpless! Have your soldiers thought of that?"

"The Israelites gain what they want more easily by keeping their word, than by breaking it. That's the beauty of their proposal."

"Burak speaks unpleasantly, but he speaks truly."

"You both make me sick! If your men lack discipline, be men and deal with them! My regiment would never submit like sheep!"

"Wonderful. You can lead the attack."

"Have you lost both your stones *and* your brains? Just lop off the necessary number of heads!"

"Mass executions? Ohhh, that should amuse the Hebrews."

"ENOUGH!!!"

Eliada rarely raised his voice during a conference, so his unexpected shout hushed the assembly. If Eliada could not bring his demoralized commanders to heel, a formal surrender would be superfluous. The Israelites could simply sit back and watch as the Arameans disintegrated.

"King Rehob ordered me to seek terms that will preserve our army. I have done so. Regarding the Hebrew terms, I have already agreed to them. There is nothing more to discuss. Prepare your men to move out one hour after sunrise tomorrow."

A sullen silence greeted Eliada's dismal proclamation. The general used the interlude to survey his audience. Even Eliada's most reliable subordinates were struggling to accept the inevitable. The less loyal men were undoubtedly considering how best to lay this disaster at Eliada's feet and walk away blameless. But if his commanders somehow held their regiments together now, Eliada could deal with their recriminations later. It was then that he noticed Derah. Uncharacteristically, the opinionated regimental commander had not uttered a word since Eliada's return. He paused before Derah and made eye contact.

"So quiet, Derah?"

Eliada could now sense a barely controlled rage building within Derah. The officer abruptly rose and leaned into the face of his general. Derah's voice was low, but full of menace.

"I save my words until we reach Zobah. There, everyone will give an account to the king...*Everyone!*"

"Then choose those words carefully, Derah. They may be the death of you."

The thinly veiled threats created an immediate stir among the other Arameans who feared the two men would come to blows. When neither backed away, several officers moved to intervene. Burak whispered something into Derah's ear but was roughly shoved aside by his superior. Jaulan placed a restraining hand on his fellow commander's arm, which Derah shook off before stalking out of the tent. After the raucous exit, every eye turned to a flushed Eliada.

"You have your orders. Dismissed."

One by one, the officers took leave of their general and departed. Eliada was not surprised to see Burak lingering until the very end. He and the young officer exchanged a long, meaningful look. Burak then bowed deeply before slipping out of the tent. Eliada experienced an odd sense of relief now that he was alone. The oppressive pressure of command had magically evaporated. There were no battles to plan, no decisions to make and no arguments to win. Still, Eliada was not one to waste time. He decided to take refuge in some cool wine and a warm bed before tomorrow's unpleasantness.

After a refreshing night's sleep, Eliada reached the designated Yarmuk River crossing at the appointed hour after sunrise. His army stretched out over a mile behind him in the valley, with Jaulan's regiment in the lead. Eliada wanted his best formation at the front if the enemy attempted any treachery. He could see a group of Israelites some twenty yards away on the opposite side of the Yarmuk. At the sound of an Israelite *shofar*, Eliada crossed the cold knee-deep river with Jaulan's first company. This simple procedure would be repeated over and over throughout the day. One *shofar* blast... one Aramean company crossing the river. The Israelites had cleverly chosen the tight river bend to discourage the surrendering Arameans from changing their minds and attempting a mass charge. Once across the river, numbers favored the Israelites.

Prince Jonathan and General Abner were nowhere to be seen among the waiting Israelites. Instead, a young man named Nathan was in charge. Eliada quickly discerned Nathan possessed traits similar to Jonathan. Such a person was always to be respected, despite his youth. Eliada also recognized Jonathan's and Abner's rough looking guards standing behind Nathan. They were in the company of fifty or sixty other Hebrews who appeared just as menacing. He was bemused to hear Nathan calling them *"renegades"*, but the men treated this insult like a title of honor. Upon hearing distressed voices, Eliada turned and winced as the first humiliation of his soldiers began.

The surrendering Arameans were made to pass single file between two lines of these rugged Hebrews, so they could be disarmed. First, their spears were collected and stacked in piles on the left. Any Aramean who hesitated felt a sword tip in the back from a Hebrew on the right. A few paces later, swords were confiscated, followed by shields, helmets, and finally, body armor. When one man undressed too slowly, three Israelites knocked him down and peeled off his scale armor as if they were skinning a rabbit. Although there were nearly two Aramean soldiers for each Israelite, no one made a move against any of these fierce looking "renegades". Eliada followed his dispirited troops as they gathered up their remaining possessions and moved on to the next humiliation.

Eliada came upon an enemy regiment drawn up in companies a short distance away. One company was busily engaged in robbing the disarmed Arameans while their comrades looked on in amusement. Every sack, pouch, bedroll, and suspicious clothing bulge was carefully inspected. The purloined gold, silver and jewels were placed in a common pile on a blanket, most likely to be split up later. However, individual Hebrews kept other items that caught their fancy, such as clothing, sandals, cookware or tools. Any Aramean making a fuss soon found himself stripped naked and sent on his way. Once Jaulan's first company had been thoroughly pillaged, the Israelites gathered up their booty and left. Another Israelite company took their place and went to work on the second Aramean company to come through. Eliada was impressed by such well-organized thievery. By rotating their troops in this manner, each Israelite soldier should be able to loot at least five Arameans.

Eliada's single concession from Jonathan was visible several hundred yards beyond the Israelite encampment. There Eliada could make out well-armed Aramean soldiers: two companies of infantry and a squadron of chariots, wearing either the colors of the Kingdom of Geshur or the Kingdom of Maacah. When Eliada expressed concerns for the safety of his unarmed soldiers the previous day, Jonathan had permitted him to request protection from nearby Aramean allies. This modest force from Geshur and Maacah would escort Eliada's army all the way back to Zobah.

Eliada was startled to notice Nathan standing at his side, watching as the Arameans were stripped of their valuables. Although the Israelite's stealth was impressive, Eliada's pride would not allow him to admit being surprised. He chose to mask his discomfort with small talk.

"So, Nathan...Why aren't your *renegades* sharing in this plunder?"

"They requested the job of disarming your soldiers. They get to have their pick of your best weapons that way."

"Men who prefer a fine blade over shiny baubles, are they? Well, my officers and I appreciate being able to keep our personal weapons."

"You're going to need them, General."

When Nathan noted the sudden look of alarm in Eliada's eyes, he chuckled.

"Not because of us, Aramean. Jonathan thought you needed protection from your own men. They might decide to avenge themselves on the officers responsible for their predicament."

Eliada's blood chilled as he considered the implications of Nathan's casual observation. The general determined to have his bodyguards arm themselves with some stout cudgels... right after he promised them a bonus for his safe arrival in Zobah. He would advise his officers to take similar preventive measures, all except Derah, of course. Eliada already had someone watching over the insubordinate officer.

Nathan watched as the Aramean general wandered off toward the waiting escorts from Geshur and Maacah. The impish rascal in him longed to see Eliada's reaction when he learned everything his erstwhile allies had in mind. Nathan ignored the urge, knowing his presence would betray Israel's hand in the matter. He would have to let his imagination suffice. As for Eliada...

The enemy general would undoubtedly find the hot, dusty journey home to be more pleasant than his arrival.

Chapter 11 - The Fruit of Betrayal

God raised up Rezon, son of Eliada, against Solomon. Rezon had fled from his master the King of Zobah. He then became leader of a band of rebels when David destroyed the armies of Zobah. Rezon's men captured Damascus and settled there. So Rezon ruled the Arameans and fought against Israel.

From the book of I Kings, chapter 11, verses 23 to 25

The royal palace of Zobah, Aramean Federation Capital

"You surrendered *all* your weapons and armor?"

Eliada had expected the first words out of King Rehob's mouth to be something similar. One part of his mind registered that Rehob's embedded spies had already made their reports. Another part determined to find out who they were, but that minor matter must wait, perhaps forever.

Eliada was presently on trial for his life.

Rehob had wasted no time having Eliada disarmed and escorted under guard to an inner chamber of the royal palace in Zobah. The general was not even permitted to wash away the eight days of road grime. Eliada had spent his journey rehearsing this very meeting over and over in his thoughts. Survival depended on his ability to anticipate the king's accusations and to provide a few surprises of his own. Caution would not benefit Eliada this day. However, he was aggressive when the occasion called for it. Today was definitely one of those.

"Sire, your message ordered me to bring back your army. It said nothing about their arms. You ordered me to make the best terms possible. I made the only terms possible."

Rehob's clenched jaw told Eliada that he had successfully parried the king's opening thrust. But his sovereign's angry countenance indicated Eliada's life still hung in the balance. Even if Eliada won every argument, the king could still have him executed. The embattled general faced a true dilemma. Somehow, Eliada must defend himself without overly antagonizing Rehob.

"You were sent to capture Galilee, Eliada, not get trapped in a valley! You were incompetent!"

"If you really believed that, Sire, I would already be dead."

"None of this would have happened if you had held Aphek!"

"As you just stated, Sire, Galilee was my goal. Holding Aphek was never my responsibility."

"Don't quibble, Eliada. You knew Aphek's importance."

"Sire, I built field fortifications in front of Aphek and left a corps of chariots behind it."

"Apparently, General, that was not enough defense."

"Is *that* what Aphek's governor told you yesterday? Strange, but *the Hebrews* appear to have no problems defending his former capital."

Rehob appeared shaken by Eliada's knowledge of the former governor's whereabouts. *Too bad*, mused Eliada, *but Rehob is not the only one to employ spies*. The man had been secretly ransomed back from the Hebrews and quickly sequestered in a remote outpost. Normally, an embarrassing royal appointee would be killed quietly, but Eliada knew that convenient option was not open to the king. The hapless Governor of Aphek was, after all, a relative of the Queen. Yet, it seemed extreme to abandon an entire army just to save face for a family member. Obviously, Rehob was concealing something bigger. Something Eliada might turn to his advantage.

"There is no reason to discuss the governor, Eliada. That subject is closed."

"Very well, Sire, then let us discuss what is really important. You need me. I need answers."

"You forget yourself, General. You are not here to question me."

"Sire, I can't help you if I am kept ignorant of essential details."

"What details?"

"You had the opportunity to relieve my army and crush the Hebrews. Instead, you abandoned us. That means you faced some greater threat. I may be able to overcome that threat, but only if I know what it is."

Rehob furrowed his brow while considering Eliada's request. Apparently reaching a decision, the king poured two cups of wine and handed one to his general. Not exactly a reprieve, but still a good sign. Eliada could not let down his guard yet, but Rehob's sudden hospitality hinted the general had found some leverage.

"The same day your request for help arrived, Eliada, I learned Geshur and Maacah were moving their armies into my territory in the southern Bashan."

"The *same* day, Sire? A curious coincidence. What was their reason?"

"With your force cut off, both kings claimed the entire Bashan was open to a Hebrew invasion. Their troops would keep the land in Aramean hands."

"Sound reasoning, Sire. We must keep the Hebrews out of the Bashan. However, the timing is most suspicious. It implies advance knowledge of the Hebrew plans for Aphek."

"My thoughts exactly."

"Assume our allies conspired with the Hebrews, Sire. You still could have sent me reinforcements."

"Combined, Geshur and Maacah can field over three thousand soldiers. Eliada, they could have easily ambushed your relief column from the Bashan. Zobah would lay naked to attack, a risk I could not take. Your army became expendable. Most reluctantly, of course."

As Eliada sipped his wine, the missing pieces fell into place. Rehob had annexed a large portion of the fertile Bashan for Zobah by bullying the minor Aramean rulers with his larger army. The King of Geshur and his father-in-law, the King of Maacah, were obviously in league with the Hebrews. The benefits of this collaboration were clear. The two smaller

Aramean kingdoms could expand while Zobah was weakened. In return, the Hebrews would gain a foothold on the Golan Heights, allowing them to control all Galilee. A brilliant strategic move for their foes, yet only the beginning of troubles for King Rehob.

Eliada now understood Rehob's initial reluctance to confide in him. The mere existence of this conspiracy posed a significant threat to Rehob's power. If the other Aramean kings learned of it, they would be tempted to join in and effectively end Zobah's hegemony. Instantly, Eliada perceived an additional reason for the humiliation of his army, one which Rehob still concealed. Admitting knowledge of it could cost Eliada his life. For his own safety, Eliada realized he must appear to accept his king's half-truths...at least for now.

"At least, Sire, our weapons were expendable. It is easier to forge swords than to replace veteran soldiers."

"Fortunately, my chariots were untouched, and I have three fully armed regiments in reserve. We can hold out until you rearm your five thousand men, Eliada."

"Only three thousand returned to Zobah with me."

"Your losses were that great?"

"I lost only a few hundred to the Israelites. The rest were taken by the Geshurites and the Maacahites."

This unexpected news rattled Rehob so much that he spilled wine down the front of his expensive robes. He collapsed onto a nearby stool and turned a pallid face toward his general. Eliada could barely hear his king's next question.

"Two thousand killed?"

"No, Sire, hired."

"Hired?"

"After being released by the Hebrews, my troops came under the protection of our supposed allies. However, the Kings of Geshur and Maacah also greeted my men with cartloads of silver. Ten shekels-weight of silver, plus a hefty pay increase, were offered on the spot to any soldier of Zobah who entered their service. Over eight hundred of our men swore allegiance to Maacah, over a thousand to Geshur."

"Traitorous dogs!"

"The men felt betrayed and abandoned, Sire. And with good reason."

"They should have trusted their king's judgment!"

"Most did, but your average soldier has a very simple view of the world, Sire. Besides, our neighboring kings are the real culprits. Their scheme was a marvel of simplicity and efficiency. Each new hire made them one soldier stronger while making you one man weaker."

"You admire them!"

"No, Sire, but I always respect my enemy. I just don't understand the source of their sudden wealth."

"That should be obvious to such a gifted mind as yours, General."

Eliada ignored Rehob's sarcasm and visualized the current locations of the various military units. The answer came to him in an instant. Eliada could barely avoid chuckling as he responded to his petulant king.

"Of course! Their recent acquisitions in the Bashan! Revenue from the wheat alone will finance their new regiments. Once again, more for them and less for you."

"I dread to ask, Eliada, but do you have any more insights to share?"

An idea immediately popped into Eliada's head. A way to snare two birds with the same net.

"Sire, I regret to report that one of my regimental commanders has gone missing. A man named Derah."

"His family is quite influential. What do you mean by *gone missing?*"

"He disappeared while passing through territory now occupied by Geshur. His senior captain brought the regiment back to Zobah. It does make me wonder."

"Wonder what?"

"Well, Derah was a hindrance throughout the entire campaign. I cannot help wondering if he was in league with the Geshurites. He conveniently disappeared in their territory."

"Hmmm... so the traitor sought refuge with his new friends. It would explain much. Who took over Derah's regiment?"

"His name is Burak, Sire."

"Can he be trusted?"

"Absolutely, Sire."

"Very well, Make his promotion permanent."

"A wise decision."

"Eliada, take one of my private chambers here in the palace. Ask for anything you want: food, drink, women, anything. Tomorrow, you will begin rebuilding my army."

"You are most generous, Sire."

"You'll earn it. We should regain our strength in a year."

"Longer."

"Why longer?"

"I wouldn't count on your collecting that proposed tax increase of yours, Sire. From anyone."

Eliada decided to postpone sampling the palace pleasures offered by King Rehob. He needed to discuss these recent revelations with someone trustworthy, but not here. The palace had too many ears and an abundance of spy holes. So Eliada was pleased to find his eldest son, Rezon, pacing in the foyer.

A look of profound relief came across Rezon's face when he spotted his father. Eliada had many reasons to be proud of this strapping young man. Only in his mid-twenties, Rezon had already risen to the rank of captain in the Damascus Regiment. His son's career needed no assistance from Eliada. Rezon's success was due entirely to his own strength, cunning, and intelligence. Eliada abruptly hushed his son's attempted greeting and pointed to the nearest exit. Rezon nodded and fell in step with his father.

Upon emerging from the palace onto the public square, Eliada noticed a platoon of soldiers lurking in an alley. He recognized them as tough veterans from Rezon's own company. At a signal from Rezon, the soldiers silently dispersed into the crowd. Eliada's raised eyebrow elicited a sheepish shrug from his son just as they plunged down a busy side street. After many twists and turns, both men slipped into a familiar ramshackle inn.

Rezon followed his father across the crowded, noisy main room. The tiny gold piece which Eliada flipped to the proprietor seemed to vanish in midair. Both men were ushered upstairs to a quiet back room. A serving girl laid out food and drink before rushing out as swiftly as she had rushed in. Eliada latched the door before speaking.

"So, my Boy, you were prepared to storm the palace and rescue your poor father. With what...almost *thirty* men? I don't know whether to be impressed or appalled."

"I won't even bother next time if all you're going to do is mock me, Father. Besides, I had a very good plan."

"The trouble is that once you start a rebellion, Rezon, you must be prepared to finish it. Kings tend to be very sensitive about that sort of thing. You might even have won today, but what about tomorrow?"

"Well, actually, Father, I was counting on you to take over from there."

Both men stared seriously at each other for a moment before bursting into laughter. Tears were running down Eliada's face when they finally began to eat.

"Seriously, Father. What happened in Galilee?"

"What have you heard?"

"That you blundered into a Hebrew trap."

"Anyone believe it?"

"Not after you left the palace with your head on your shoulders, they won't."

Between bites, Eliada shared with his son details of the failed campaign and Rehob's excuse for his devastating failure to act. He was pleased to see how readily Rezon grasped all the implications. The young man was also sharp enough to catch the inadequacy of the king's explanation of his inaction.

"Rehob couldn't really believe Geshur and Maacah would attack other Arameans. The rest of the Federation would unite against them. Those two kings would lose everything."

"Son, Rehob was not afraid of Geshur. Not Maacah. Not even Israel."

"Then what was he afraid of?"

"Me."

"You?"

"Rehob feared I would take his reinforcements, crush the Hebrews and then march on Zobah. The soldiers of Geshur and Maacah might even have joined me."

"The muddy waters begin to clear, Father. To Rehob's thinking, sacrificing your army was the only way to ensure he remained in control."

"Ironically, Rehob has doomed his dynasty."

"Because Rehob was wrong about you?"

"No, because he was right. Given those reinforcements, I *would* have deposed Rehob."

"Rebellion does not suit your cautious nature."

"Sometimes it is the most cautious path to take. Imagine, Rezon, my leading thousands of soldiers to Zobah in triumph. Would Rehob have given me a chance to prove my loyalty? No. *I* would be dead by nightfall, and *you* would join me before sunrise. Either we go or Rehob goes."

"What do you have in mind?"

"A Kingdom of Damascus...our kingdom. It will be a long road. Most likely, I will lay the groundwork, and you will wear the crown. You are well on your way to commanding your Damascus Regiment. I have secured the loyalty of another regimental commander, a man named Burak. Get to know him."

"I just had a disturbing thought, Father. What if this conspiracy did not originate in either Geshur or Maacah?"

"Then, Son, someone in Israel is more dangerous to us than Rehob."

Chapter 12 – The Love of Politics

After the Judge Jephthah of Gilead died, Ibzan of Bethlehem replaced him as the Judge of Israel. He had thirty sons and thirty daughters. Ibzan married off his daughters to men outside his clan. He also brought in young girls from outside his clan to be wives for his sons. Ibzan judged Israel for seven years.

From the book of Judges, chapter 12, verses 7 to 9

King Saul's House in Gibeah

Nathan heard raucous laughter behind him while departing the king's private chamber. Karaz was undoubtedly telling yet another ribald Hittite tale. It reminded him of the old days: Saul, Jonathan, Karaz and himself happily eating, drinking, planning, and joking. Nathan hoped it meant the wounds were healing that the king and the prince had inflicted on each other. Victory had a way of turning rivals into boon companions, if only until the next conflict. He hoped the reconciliation of Saul and Jonathan would be more enduring. Nathan knew there would always be more disagreements, defeats and enemies.

But for the time being, Nathan was contented.

Guest Quarters on King Saul's Estate in Gibeah

Beker, *the right hand* of the King of Israel, was discontented.

Certainly, the *Yameen* was not dissatisfied. Nor was he displeased. Both those emotions would have implied some failure on Beker's part. In fact, his success over the past few years had been breathtaking. Beker had originally been the leader of a powerful anti-monarchy faction known as the *Highlanders*, so named because most resided in the more secure mountain regions of Israel. Then came the fateful day when the Prophet Samuel overturned the entire political structure of the twelve tribes.

Saul, an unknown farmer, from a minor family, in the smallest tribe, had been anointed king. Both the timing of the proclamation and the selection of the individual had been political master strokes by Samuel. Israel was being pressed on all sides by encroaching neighbors. By selecting a tall, handsome leader with a nonexistent powerbase as Israel's king, the wily prophet held the Nation in the palm of his hand. Beker had been caught off guard as much as anyone in the twelve tribes. Yet while he might be outmaneuvered, Beker was rarely defeated. He had swiftly denounced his former allies and offered his services to the fledgling king. Saul had no army, no wealth, no government...truly a king without a crown. Finding his new sovereign surrounded by chaos and confusion, Beker had created his own position of *Yameen* out of thin air. He then swiftly set about constructing the sinews of a kingdom using outrageous promises, skillful lies, subtle threats, and the occasional assassination.

Beker's bureaucracy grew by fits and starts in parallel with those of the new monarchy. National apathy had nearly ended Saul's rule before it took root. It required a glorious victory over the Ammonite invaders to win for Saul the hearts of his people. However, that success also drew the unwanted attention of the expansionist Philistines. Even though Israel won the resulting war by a whisker, the dynasty itself faced collapse.

After a serious falling out, Saul was publicly denounced by his chief patron, Samuel. The impetuous Prince Jonathan had been nearly executed by his increasingly paranoid father. Mass desertions had shattered the Royal Army of Israel.

Ultimately, the king and his heir had negotiated a tenuous sharing of power. This instability within the royal family unintentionally played to Beker's strengths. The *Yameen* was a master at pitting his competitors against each other. Not being a warrior, Beker stayed clear of the military arena. The *Yameen's* most warlike act had been to undermine the Hittite mercenary, Karaz, and replace him with Saul's cousin, Abner, as General of the Royal Army. His relationship with Abner was typical of Beker's style: allowing his allies to have the glory in public as he amassed power in secret. Meanwhile, Beker's agenda flourished. His administration reaped wealth for the Crown while increasing the number of influential appointees beholden to the *Yameen*.

Ironically, Israel's recent battlefield victories caused Beker's grip on power to slip. Supported by the cunning mercenary Karaz and the precocious Nathan, Prince Jonathan had proposed an aggressive series of campaigns against the Moabite, Edomite, and Aramean kingdoms. The rise of Jonathan's cadre was a direct threat to the *Yameen's* influence. Yet, Beker had supported these military adventures, but with an ulterior motive. Winning three wars with Israel's small and rebuilding army seemed unlikely in the extreme. A single military disaster would discredit the prince and restore Beker's desired balance of power. He even persuaded Abner to acquiesce to his young rival's plans. The general was Beker's insurance against the unforeseen. Even if all Jonathan's campaigns succeeded, Abner would take the credit.

Alas, it was the unforeseen elements which now made Beker discontented.

The self-absorbed Abner had allowed the prince's protégé, Nathan, to emerge as the hero in the victory over the Moabites. Karaz managed to bamboozle Abner's indifferent subordinate commanders and commandeer their regiments without the general's knowledge. Jonathan had somehow provoked the Edomite army into walking into his trap before Abner could arrive on the battlefield. Most surprisingly, the resourceful Nathan had achieved a diplomatic coup leading to the surrender of an entire Aramean army. Jonathan's gambles paid off beyond everyone's dreams. Valuable territory was reclaimed. New revenues flowed to the Crown. Useful alliances were sealed. The kingdoms of Canaan trembled at Israel's might.

The *Yameen's* mistakes were all too apparent in hindsight. Beker had greatly erred by distancing himself from Jonathan's risky ventures. Abner, Beker's supposed minion, seemed content to share the glory with his prince. As a result, Saul was again seeking advice from the gifted Jonathan, the heathen Karaz and even the beguiling Nathan. True, the situation was not a total loss for Beker. New lands brought new opportunities for him. There were political appointments to sell, additional resources to control and a larger bureaucracy to govern. Yet Beker feared being reduced to *just* an administrator. His informants had already heard whispers referring to him as the *royal errand boy*. His office of *Yameen* was a self-appointed one after all. He possessed only the power others were willing to ascribe to him. Beker knew all too well that one day he might hear these dreaded words.

Thank you for your service, Beker. We will take things from here.

Fortunately, the government functioned smoothly, and everyone was happy for the time being. Beker determined not to waste this precious breathing space and began formulating a plan. The king must be made more dependent on his *Yameen*. The prince must be subtly distanced from his father. Perhaps *distracted from his father* was a better strategy. Abner must tighten his grip on the army. Beker doubted he could turn Karaz, and killing the Hittite would be too problematic. Besides, Karaz's only influence was through Jonathan. Limit the master and limit the servant. Nathan was a mystery. The man was completely loyal to his friend Jonathan but had always been cordial to Beker. Could he put Nathan to use one day?

Beker poured himself some wine before reclining on a plush couch. Perhaps he was looking at his problems the wrong way. Other kings had to deal with young, talented sons. What did they do? They educated them. They gave them military commands. They made them governors. They...

Beker jerked up so quickly the wine stained his expensive clothing. His thoughts raced. *Yes, Jonathan! But what about Nathan? Why not him too? Yes, both of them at the same time!* Beker looked at the empty goblet in his hand, hurled it against the wall and howled in triumph.

He might have been outmaneuvered, but Beker was far from defeated.

Nathan's home on King Saul's Estate in Gibeah

The early morning summons from Jonathan had roused Nathan from a sound sleep, and an even better dream. The scanty message said only to come to his friend's home immediately. Nathan's last three months since the successful Aramean campaign had been spent in the Kingdom of Geshur, nurturing the new alliance with Israel. Jonathan had given him a warm welcome on his return to Gibeah and promised Nathan at least a week without any official duties. He grumbled to himself during the short walk from his family's quarters to Saul's residence. The promised holiday from *official* duties had been filled with *unofficial* ones. Nathan had barely been allowed a day to catch up with his mother and sister. Nathan surmised that someone felt an urgent need to hear about his activities in Geshur. His news could easily wait a few hours, or a few days for that matter. Undoubtedly, one of the Royal Court denizens wanted a private briefing so he could impress others with his knowledge of confidential affairs.

Nathan soothed himself by recalling the success of his mission to Geshur. The secret alliance he had originally brokered between Israel and King Talmai was only the beginning. Now that their common adversary, the Kingdom of Zobah, had been neutered, disagreements arose between the victorious allies. Talmai sought to limit both the number of Israelite soldiers garrisoned at Aphek and where they could venture out onto the Golan Plains. The Israelite tribes demanded that Talmai honor their claims to the disputed lands south of Geshur's new holdings in the Bashan. In particular, King Saul wanted Talmai's guarantee that other Aramean kings would not be allowed to cross Geshur on their way to invade Israel. Serious negotiating was still required to harvest the fruits of victory.

Enter Nathan.

Jonathan had approached him one day with a beguiling smile, honeyed words and a host of compelling arguments. Nathan was the only Israelite the Geshurites would trust. Only Nathan truly understood King Talmai. None of Saul's other advisors had shown as much aptitude for diplomacy. Nathan felt his resistance gradually worn down until escape was hopeless. He made one final protest as Jonathan closed the trap.

"Nathan, there is simply no one else like you."

"Jonathan, I know what you really mean. *Nathan is smart enough to do the job...and dumb enough to take it.*"

"That sounds like a YES to me!"

How he hated politics! True, Jonathan was giving him yet another chance to shine at Court. However, any success in Geshur would only encourage the prince to burden him with even more odious missions in the future. Eventually, Nathan's innate sense of responsibility took over and he pursued the new assignment with his customary vigor.

Truth be told, there was much to like about his mission. Nathan found King Talmai to be a pretty decent fellow once you got him away from the negotiating table. Most of Nathan's stay was spent touring the Golan Heights and the farmlands of the Bashan with Talmai. Disagreements were shortened when both parties viewed the actual terrain as each presented his arguments. Scribes and mapmakers were present to capture every detail in their discussions. Nathan finally journeyed home with an agreement that should receive Saul's blessing. As its closing statement optimistically described, *this accommodation between our two peoples will endure forever and ever.*

The last phrase was pure dog vomit.

Nathan knew it and so did Talmai, but both kingdoms desperately required stability along their common frontier. Eventually, one kingdom would overshadow the other. *Forever and ever* would then come to an end. The stronger would impose a new arrangement on the weaker. Hopefully, this would take place in a peaceful manner where both parties benefited. Of course, the one on top would benefit more, but that was the way of the world. May the best king win.

Although the morning sun was barely visible over the horizon, Nathan saw that Saul's home was already buzzing with activity. An elaborate celebration scheduled for midday would commemorate the recent victories over the Moabites, Edomites and Arameans. Levites and priests scurried about setting up altars and preparing the appropriate sacrifices. A host of stewards were preparing refreshments for the large crowd of dignitaries expected to attend. The fledgling monarchy was indeed riding high after its nadir following the fighting at Michmash.

Everywhere Nathan looked, there was evidence that Jonathan's strategy of swift, limited conquests had paid off handsomely. Influential leaders from all parts of Israel jostled with each other in their efforts to obtain the king's favor. An endless flood of wealth poured into Gibeah, accompanied by generous donations to the Crown of land, herds, and flocks. A newly constructed palace was rising on a hilltop above Saul's residence. Housing for the growing bureaucracy was springing up in Gibeah. Soldiers guarding the premises were arrayed in new iron scale armor and bronze helmets. The appearance of improved swords, javelins and shields all indicated that the expanded armory in Gilgal was engaged in full production. Nathan shook his head as he compared this newfound affluence to Saul's original ragtag Court.

The sentry posted at Saul's front door irritated Nathan by brusquely demanding that he state his business. Nathan muttered *I live here* and pushed his way past the dismayed guardian. Fortunately, Jonathan appeared and greeted him by name. Nathan winked impishly at the chagrined soldier before following the prince to the dining area. They joined Karaz at a table overflowing with breakfast delicacies. Nathan helped himself to some bread, cheese and fish before indulging his curiosity.

"So, what's worth interrupting the best dream I've had in months?"

"We're going to pick out our wives today, Nathan."

"OUR WHAT?"

"Wives."

"Close your mouth when you're eating, Boy. You heard correctly. The king commands you and Jonathan to marry."

"I have no idea where to find a wife, Karaz, even if I wanted one."

"Relax, Nathan, it's all been arranged."

"Somehow, that only makes things sound worse. Why is Saul doing this to me?"

"*For* you, Lad. He's doing it for you."

"Fine. Why is he doing it for me?"

"Don't sulk. Our King is riding high now. However, people's memories are fickle. Saul needs to secure long-term benefits from his current popularity. A time-honored way is through political marriages. Two marriages, twice the benefits."

"But Jonathan is a prince. I'm not. So why me?"

"Jonathan's brothers and sisters are either not old enough or unsuitable for a political marriage. There are some alliances Saul must make *now*. Besides, Nathan, you're just as good as Jonathan for the king's purposes. You're practically part of Saul's family, just not a legal member of it."

"Like a bastard son, you mean."

"Think of it as an adoption."

"I'm not ready for marriage."

"Who is? Look at it this way, Nathan. You're a prominent member of the king's household. Many wealthy and influential clans will gladly give a daughter for such a link to the royal family. In return, Saul gains many favors, as well as their loyalty."

"How long have you known of this scheme, Jonathan?"

"My father told me last night. It was not a pleasant conversation."

"And what made Saul decide to include me?"

"When I said, *If I have to marry, so does Nathan!*"

"Always got my best interests at heart, don't you?"

"Think nothing of it."

"I won't."

"Excuse me? Do you boys need to whine some more? Or can we please get down to business?"

"Karaz, I can't afford a wife."

"Normally, you acquire one first. Then pay for her the rest of your life. Except in your case, you need not worry about that."

"Lucky me."

"Behave yourself, Nathan, or you'll get the ugliest one."

"Not if Jonathan get first choice."

"Actually Lads, you both should have very good pickings. Members of the Court have spent weeks scouring the nobility of Israel for suitable brides. The final list has been culled to thirty-four prospects. The odds greatly favor at least two of them not being cows."

"Thirty-four! I couldn't even talk to thirty-four women in one day."

"As I said before, it has all been arranged. The young ladies are invited to an informal banquet after today's assembly. You and Jonathan will be seated where you can see and hear them, but not be seen yourselves. People will be available to answer any questions either of you may have. Then after the banquet, choose one."

"Karaz, I'm with Nathan on this. That's not enough time."

"The alternative is for the king to choose for you. Some very complex negotiations depend on your betrothals being announced two days hence. Typically, political marriages are sealed before the groom ever sees the bride. So, you two are quite fortunate. Rarely does a young noble have any voice in the matter."

"So, suddenly I'm a noble now?"

"Yes, Nathan. Better get used to it."

Nathan expected his friend to laugh at Karaz's last statement, but Jonathan's expression remained deadly serious. Nathan felt a heavy burden descend on his soul. He barely felt adequate to look after his mother and young sister. Now a wife was to be added to the mix. Yet it was not so much the marriage, but the status of nobility that was most troubling. Nathan had originally aligned himself with Jonathan's family to avenge his father's death at the hand of the Philistines. Nathan always assumed that partnership could be ended anytime he wished. Now, he faced becoming permanently ensnared in Saul's dealings. As one of the king's nobles, Nathan would relinquish what little control remained in his life. This proposed marriage represented a turning point. Noble or commoner? No matter which Nathan chose, he could never go back. He took a deep breath and voiced his surrender.

"If something is inevitable, make the best of it."

"Nice to see you still remember at least one of my lessons."

"Well, Jonathan, are you in or out?"

"I'm a prince. Apparently, I was always in."

"One thing more, Boys. I sense other reasons Saul wants you both married."

"Wonderful. There's more."

"He seeks to limit your meddling in royal affairs."

"How so?"

"Apparently, you Hebrews have a custom that a man can't go to war during his first year of marriage. He is to stay home and *cheer up* his wife. I think that means get her pregnant."

"And keep us out of Abner's hair. Anything else?"

"Saul probably hopes you two will enjoy *cheering up* those nubile young wives so much that you'll lose interest in politics."

"Well, Nathan, sounds like a challenge to me. Can we be both great leaders *and* great lovers?"

"I intend to give it a *very* good try."

The Grounds of King Saul's Estate in Gibeah

The afternoon banquet for prospective princesses was indeed well arranged, just as Karaz had promised. The Hittite mercenary guided Nathan and Jonathan to a room with a window overlooking the festivities. The food had been cleverly placed so the young ladies were obliged to pass within a few feet of where the young men lurked. Although the sun hid the room's interior in deep shadows, Nathan and Jonathan could clearly see everyone and hear everything outside. Five members of the Royal Court were already present in the room. Karaz introduced them as the committee responsible for selecting the women in attendance. Nathan could not help comparing the event to a livestock auction where the animals were paraded around before the bidding commenced. He was pleased to see most of the young women were truly attractive, and a few could even be described as strikingly beautiful.

As for the rest, Nathan concluded their families must be *extremely* wealthy.

While Jonathan began asking questions almost immediately, Nathan spent the first half hour just surveying the field. Whenever a girl caught their eye, a committee member would step forward to provide her name along with pertinent information on her father, family, and personal talents. At one point, Jonathan asked Karaz if his own sisters would go through a similar process when they came of age.

"Oh no, Jonathan, a king's daughters are much too important to be married off in such a fashion. Most likely, your sisters will be reserved for a husband with great military strength."

"Is that customary?"

"To quote a venerable proverb: *To a king, a beautiful daughter is worth more than ten thousand soldiers. Even an ugly one is worth five thousand.*"

"I think half of your so-called proverbs are really Hittite jokes."

"It makes little difference. Hittite humor is superior to most nations' wisdom."

"What about my sister, Karaz? Will she get the princess treatment?"

"That depends on you, Nathan. You are the head of her household, not Saul. Your sister's marriage prospects will be linked to your personal success."

Nathan was scowling over this additional responsibility when a lilting voice captured his attention. He found himself staring into deep, dark eyes accompanied by fine facial features, flawless skin, and rich brown hair. Nathan realized how intense his reaction was when a committee member appeared at his elbow without being summoned. The girl's name was Deborah, sixteen years old from the tribe of Benjamin, but all the other details escaped Nathan's memory. He was entranced by beauty which drove away all his reservations about marriage. Nathan continued to study the other women, but Deborah had already become his standard for comparison.

Nathan's home on King Saul's Estate in Gibeah

As soon as the betrothal banquet came to an end, Nathan hurried away in search of his mother. He found her in their rooms preparing the evening meal. Excited words tumbled from Nathan's mouth.

"Mother! I have found a wife!"

"Oh?"

"Yes, Saul arranged for me to see some of the finest girls of the best families in all Israel. He said I could marry whichever one I wanted!"

"Did he now?"

"He certainly did! I picked a lovely girl from Benjamin. Her name is Deborah."

"Did you now?"

"I'm going to marry her!"

"Is that right? Tell me all about her while we eat."

Nathan described Deborah in glowing terms as he wolfed down his food. In his excitement, he paid little attention to his mother's reactions. It only occurred to him later that Miriam had displayed surprisingly little curiosity over her future daughter-in-law.

The long night passed with no dreams and little sleep for the impatient Nathan. Karaz had warned that their weddings might not occur for many months after the betrothals. Nathan was taken aback to learn that the extended time was not for the nuptials, but to give the guests time to prepare their wedding gifts. Even more surprising, neither Nathan nor his bride would ever see the most significant gifts. In a *political* marriage, the truly important details were never disclosed. Ambitious men with something to barter for royal influence would be drawn to his wedding like ants to honey. Hidden behind the facade of Nathan's wedding would be a complex exchange of pledges and promises between the various parties. As king, Saul could broker a multitude of deals where gold, titles, land and power changed hands. Saul expected to profit much while spending little. It would all depend on how well the king could leverage the initial relationship with his new in-laws. The value of these transactions would escalate as related agreements were made and passed from a family to its clan, from a clan to its tribe and finally from that tribe to other tribes.

One thing Nathan need not be patient for was his betrothal. At the end of the day, Saul was to preside over a great feast to honor the Tribal Elders who had attended the victory celebration. Saul would announce Jonathan's betrothal, and then Nathan's, before adjourning the assembly. Nathan was disappointed to learn that all the bridal candidates, including his Deborah, had already departed Gibeah. A combination of customs, superstitions and negotiations would keep the bride and groom apart until the actual ceremony. At least having their union officially sanctioned would provide Nathan with some closure.

The banquet was held that evening in the great hall of the partially completed palace. Nathan felt ill at ease in the crowded room for reasons unrelated to his impending marriage. First, he was wearing the finest set of clothes he had ever possessed. One of Saul's stewards had delivered them that afternoon without explanation. Nathan assumed it was an early wedding gift and was intrigued by how an anonymous tailor knew his exact dimensions. Second, Nathan found himself unexpectedly cast as a celebrity. Strangers kept popping out of the noisy throng to greet him and sing his praises. Such were the benefits to being Saul's almost-as-good-as-a-son.

Nathan was unable to talk with Jonathan before everyone sat down to eat. They had exchanged smiles across the hall, but Nathan thought his friend seemed tense. Both were seated at the king's table, but not close enough for a private conversation. Nathan settled into his food and, as others continued to vie for his attention, he soon forgot about the prince. Good food, drink and conversation combined to relax Nathan. As the meal drew to a close, Saul stood to address the attendees. After some perfunctory remarks, the king finally came to the part of the evening which most concerned Nathan. Saul beckoned Jonathan and another man to come stand at his side. Nathan supposed the stranger must be his friend's future father-in-law. He thought Jonathan looked a little pale, despite his broad smile.

A sudden realization turned Nathan's veins to ice. He had no idea whom his friend had selected. What if Jonathan had also chosen Deborah? As a prince, his selection would supersede anyone else's. Nathan felt his lips tremble as he considered this possibility. It would explain why his friend seemed standoffish that evening. As beautiful as Deborah was, even Jonathan would feel guilty about robbing his best friend. Nathan forced his hands to relax when he felt his fingernails digging into the wooden table. He sat helplessly as he listened to Saul's introductions and feared the worst.

Moments later, Jonathan was formally betrothed to Naomi, from the tribe of Ephraim. A woman Nathan had never heard of.

The crowd stood to its feet and roared approval as Jonathan and his new father-in-law hugged each other. Nathan began to laugh hysterically before congratulating the prince. The raucous celebration slowly subsided as Saul gestured for Nathan to come forward. He was joined by a distinguished looking gentleman about fifty years of age who had obviously been quite handsome and strong as a youth. Nathan barely heard Saul introducing them both to the assembly. He had no need to listen. Nathan immediately recognized Jephunneh, leader of Judah's militia.

Jephunneh had been at Nathan's side during the great victory over the Ammonites. Icy fear swept over Nathan again. He could find no trace of Deborah in Jephunneh's features. And Deborah was from Benjamin, not Judah. He tried to reassure himself that Jephunneh must be a relative standing in for Deborah's father. However, the next words dashed Nathan's false hopes.

"Nathan Ben-Jotham, I heartily accept your proposal of marriage to my daughter *Judith*."

Jephunneh may have said a few more congratulatory words, but Nathan never heard them. He was struggling to stay on his feet. Nathan became dimly aware of distant cheering and Jephunneh hugging him. He responded numbly to the warm embrace. Jephunneh's voice was full of concern as he whispered in Nathan's ear.

"Are you ill, my Son?"

"No, I'm...I'm just overwhelmed."

"I understand. It was the same for me."

258

Somehow, Nathan avoided blurting out *I bet it wasn't.* Instead he meekly waved to the adoring crowd. Nathan caught the prince's eye but failed to see any surprise. As soon as the great hall began to empty, Nathan seized Jonathan's elbow in an iron grip and propelled his friend into an empty chamber.

"You knew."

"I know many things."

"About my Deborah."

"Ah, yes, your Deborah. I did know about that."

"When?"

"The same time I found out about my Jael."

"You mean Naomi."

"No, I mean Jael. I am going to marry Naomi, but the woman I selected was Jael."

"Then why did...but how could..."

"Nathan, it's painfully simple. Our mothers picked out our wives for us."

"Our mothers...you're taking this surprisingly well."

"I didn't this afternoon."

"Then why was that cattle show staged for us yesterday?"

"Politics. Every tribe needed to believe one of their daughters could become a future queen. In reality, only the

259

tribes of Judah, Ephraim and Manasseh were ever in the running. Once that was settled, our mothers went into action."

"Jonathan, I nearly wet myself when I heard the name Judith. You should have warned me!"

"Why? So, you could brood like some miserable sod awaiting execution? I did you a favor, my Friend."

"Don't expect gratitude."

"Complain to your mother, not me. She thought your precious Deborah was an overindulged child incapable of handling adult responsibilities."

"That's pretty harsh."

"It was high praise compared to what my mother said about Jael."

"Saul promised us our choice. A king keeps his promises!"

"Nathan, have you forgotten how determined our mothers can be?"

Nathan exhaled in frustration and leaned back against the nearest wall. The wisdom of Saul's strategy was undeniable. The marriages would bind a large southern tribe, Judah, and a wealthy northern tribe, Ephraim, to the monarchy. Then two loving mothers went to work screening the eligible candidates for their sons. The whole process vexed Nathan, but could he really have done any better? He recognized a similar pain in his friend's eyes. Nathan reproached himself for being so selfish.

Jonathan grieved his own loss. He looked into Jonathan's eyes and managed a weak grin.

"Saul never stood a chance, did he?"

"My father is only a king outside our home."

"Think there's any wine left?"

Chapter 13 - The Wedding

So, Rebekah and her maid servants mounted camels and left her home to return with Abraham's chief steward.

Isaac had just returned home from the Negev. He was going out into the field that evening to pray when he saw camels approaching. Then Rebekah saw Isaac for the first time. She dismounted her camel and asked Abraham's chief steward the name of the man coming to greet them. When the chief steward said it was his master, Rebekah covered herself with a veil.

The chief steward then told Isaac how he had found Rebekah. Isaac brought her into the tent of his mother Sarah where he married Rebekah. She became his wife and he loved her.

From the book of Genesis, chapter 24, verses 61 to 66

The City of Hebron in the Tribal Lands of Judah

Two months later, Nathan and his conflicted emotions were resigned to marry a total stranger. A royal entourage accompanied him, his mother, and his sister on the two-day journey from Gibeah to Judah. Although the king was standing in for Nathan's deceased father, Saul would use the ceremony to strengthen the bond between his dynasty and what was arguably Israel's strongest tribe. Nathan spent most of the trip commiserating with Jonathan. His repeated requests to meet Judith before the wedding had all been politely, but firmly declined. Hearing that Jonathan experienced similar frustrations regarding his Naomi provided little consolation. His friend's wedding was still another six weeks in the future. Apparently, hashing out the details for a prince's nuptials took longer than it did for a mere noble. Both young men equated marriage with an inevitable execution. It was best to just get the whole thing over with.

His future in-laws owned an impressive estate near the prominent Judean city of Hebron. The location itself was eloquent testimony to Jephunneh's prominence within his tribe. The wedding guests arrived before sunset when Jephunneh's magnificent residence seemed to glow from countless lamps and torches. Nathan was amused to find his body reacting as it would before any battle. The closer to contact with the enemy, the more at ease he felt. At least he had nothing to complain about. Judith's family had spoiled him horribly during the day. Yet another anonymous benefactor had provided the fine wedding garments which Nathan now wore. Should he express his thanks before he and Judith were consummated...or afterward? It was just one of many questions now crowding his mind.

This night would be the first time Nathan had ever been alone with a woman not of his own blood. Of course, he understood sex. It was impossible not to while growing up around sheep, cattle, and donkeys. And there was no lack of stories to acquaint teenage boys with the human aspects. During these impressionable years, Nathan had been strongly encouraged to maintain his celibacy by both family and community. It also helped that most Hebrew fathers *aggressively* protected their daughters' purity. His military service allowed Nathan more independence, but the idea of sharing prostitutes with other soldiers always repulsed him. To his mind, sex and love must be as different as military tactics were from military strategy. Nathan finally determined to approach his wedding night as he had his first battle: by following his instincts.

Murmuring guests already filled the great hall when Nathan and Saul assumed their assigned positions. Everyone stood and crowded in as closely as possible, leaving only a narrow lane open to the main entrance. Seating was unnecessary since the actual ceremony would be quite brief. A week of festivities would begin outside as soon as the newlyweds departed the room. While friends and relatives feasted, Nathan's marriage and countless political deals would all be consummated.

Nathan was caught off guard when a sudden hush spread throughout the room. Jephunneh and a small, veiled figure had entered the hall. Nathan gathered as many details as possible while the pair slowly drew near. His bride was clothed from head to toe in gaily colored robes. He could tell little about her physically except that she was some six inches shorter than himself, moved gracefully, and did not appear to be overweight. When Jephunneh and his daughter halted two paces away, Nathan noticed a striking feature just above the veil.

Judith had bright sea-green eyes.

While Jephunneh and Saul recited the customary pledges made between the heads of two families, Nathan focused on the young girl standing before him. Her eyes showed no fear; in fact, they seemed to be studying Nathan as intently as he was her. He made out fine, delicate features beneath the veil. When their eyes locked, Nathan felt that an intelligent mind was probing his. Judith met the grin spreading across Nathan's face by shyly lowering her gaze.

That was when Saul nudged him.

Nathan blinked and turned toward the king. When Saul silently nodded forward, Nathan realized Jephunneh had already extended Judith's arm toward him. As polite giggling swept through the audience, Nathan belatedly moved to take his wife's hand. Judith entwined her arm with Nathan's and took her place beside him. They stepped together to a small table containing a single loaf of bread and a solitary cup of wine. Nathan broke off a small piece of the loaf and handed it to his wife to eat. Judith consumed her bread before breaking off a piece for her husband. After both bride and groom drank deeply from the cup of wine, the simple ceremony was complete. Arm in arm, the couple walked toward the exit accompanied by shouts of congratulations and blessings.

Nathan was now a married man.

While the celebrations began in earnest, Nathan and Judith were conducted from the brightly lit building to their bridal chamber. They would observe a tradition which harkened back to the nomadic roots of the Patriarchs. As Isaac had taken Rebekah to his mother's tent, the two newlyweds would spend their wedding night in a nearby tent prepared by the groom's mother. It was distant enough for privacy, but close enough for observation. Nathan wondered if that last detail was to prevent panicked husbands from attempting an escape in the darkness. He put away such cynical thoughts as they neared the open tent flap. A single hanging oil lamp warmly illuminated the simple interior to reveal a comfortable bed laid out on the ground, several cushions, a small table with food and some chests for clothing. Nathan led the way inside and Judith closed the tent flap behind them. Nathan then pretended to examine each and every item in the tent while he waited for his instincts to give him at least a hint of what to do next. He prayed it would not be a long wait.

Nathan's stalling tactics were interrupted when the lamp was unexpectedly extinguished, plunging the tent into inky blackness. He instinctively moved to re-open the tent flap and obtain at least some light from the night sky. Instead of finding the coarse fabric, his hands settled on warm flesh. Most of Nathan's body stiffened in confusion, but his fingers continued to explore their new discovery. He felt a passionate breath caress his throat as soft hair brushed against his right cheek. Nathan felt his clothing being loosened and pulled away, one layer at a time. When his disrobing was complete, Judith gently kissed her husband on the lips and pulled him down toward their bed.

His young bride's enthusiasm initially caused Nathan to wonder if this was not her first experience. However, a painful gasp immediately convinced him of her virginity. Nathan found a slower pace to be more satisfactory for them both. A short time later the two young lovers were rewarded with climactic satisfaction. He was amazed at how exhausted the brief experience left him. He rolled onto his back and felt Judith slide alongside as she contentedly nuzzled his neck. Nathan's eyes grew heavy, as he was lulled by Judith breathing in harmony with him.

Nathan was almost sound asleep when Judith came after him a second time.

A cool breeze across his bare back awoke Nathan from his pleasant slumber the following morning. His foggy mind registered that the front and rear tent flaps had been partially opened to provide both ventilation and light. Hearing his name called softly, Nathan turned over and gazed up into the smiling face of...HIS MOTHER!

Totally disoriented, Nathan abruptly sat up and anxiously surveyed the tent's interior. A young girl of fifteen or sixteen years of age waited with a robe in her arms a few feet behind his mother. The lovely stranger wore a matching ankle length woolen robe and an enigmatic smile. Nathan slipped into the garment which the girl draped over him as he felt the bedclothes being pulled out from under him. He watched in confusion as his mother wadded up the sheets. Miriam gave the young couple an approving glance before exiting the tent with her burden.

The girl crossed her arms and cocked head to one side as she unabashedly examined Nathan in the morning light. He was immediately impressed by this display of confidence and boldness from one so young. Nathan drank in all the features of her beauty. Lustrous brown hair that reached her waist. Small, but strong looking hands. A well-proportioned body. A smoothly sculpted face completed by a delicate nose and full lips. And eyes as green as the Mediterranean. Nathan finally broke the awkward silence with the first words to come to his mind.

"If you are not Judith, I will be greatly confused...and disappointed."

Nathan was rewarded with melodious laughter.

"Ah yes. My veil gave me an advantage over you last night, Nathan. How ironic. We managed to become *very* well-acquainted without ever being properly introduced. Fear not, I am Judith. Your wife."

Judith gestured to the low table where a simple meal had been laid out. Nathan discovered he was famished after the previous evening's exertions. He pulled out a pair of cushions and sat down with his wife. Nathan helped himself to some bread while watching Judith peel fruit and slice cheese for their first breakfast together. She extended Nathan a plate and he wasted no time consuming the plain, but satisfying, fare. Judith was quite hungry as well, but she dined in a more genteel manner than her husband. Waiting until his bride was finished, Nathan began to indulge his curiosity.

"I am surprised that you did not speak to me last night."

"Why, Nathan? You were doing everything right."

Nathan's embarrassed blushing was met by the same delightful smile he first noticed at their wedding, but now without any trace of shyness. He found the tone of Judith's voice to be just as pleasing as the rest of her. Nathan was surprised by how much he enjoyed her saying his name aloud. He decided to switch topics.

"Judith, what happened to our bedding?"

"It is customary to present them to the heads of both families immediately after sunrise. They are the proof of my virginity."

"Of course. The traces of your blood."

"Those spots mean that you are the true father of any children I will bear."

"Still, I was not expecting *my* mother to collect them *when* she did. It was embarrassing."

268

"It could have been much worse, Nathan."

"How?"

"It could have been *my* mother."

"Both beautiful and witty. Why did I not notice you among the other prospective brides?"

"That absurd display at the king's home? My mother told me how the wives were really to be selected. I saw no reason to parade around like a lamb up for auction."

"So, what *did* you do?"

"I found a shady spot in the garden where I could rate my competitors."

"Yet, you managed to impress my mother."

"The first time I spoke with Miriam was last night."

"Now I'm confused. Again."

"It's simple, really. Why waste time talking to me? Miriam went straight to *my mother*!"

"Amazing. The people planning our future bypassed both of us. I guess we were lucky they invited us to our own wedding."

"It's an old story. Age and experience versus youth and enthusiasm."

"One thing concerns me though, Judith. Between Jonathan and me, would I have been *your* first choice?"

"Does it matter?"

"I guess not, but it brings up another question. I'm at least seven years your elder; yet you seem better prepared for marriage."

"I come from one of the most prominent families in Judah. Therefore, I have spent my entire life training to be the lady of a great house."

"Including your skills in love?"

"Naturally. Our first child will be the true bond between our families, as well as the basis for any political alliances. Skilled lovemaking ensures children, and last night was only the beginning."

"So, the only reason for our marriage is to produce offspring?"

"Didn't I show you any other reasons last night?"

"Several, actually."

"Anything else, Husband?"

"I am ashamed to admit this, but I have no idea what happens next."

"Don't worry. I memorized the entire week's events. Oh, it will be great fun!"

"I've already had great fun."

"Do you want to hear about them or not? We have the entire morning to ourselves. Actually...it's meant to allow our guests time to recover if they celebrated too excessively. Then, we have our midday meal with everyone in the main house. After that, we receive the first of our wedding gifts. Tonight, there will be a great feast with music and entertainment. This routine will be repeated every day, for seven days. Except on the Sabbath, of course."

"Are we really getting that many gifts?"

"Yes and no. An entire week is for the benefit of the gift-givers. They will each make a great show of presenting their gift, followed by everyone praising and admiring it."

"Do we need to prepare anything?"

"No, Nathan, we just show up and look happy."

"How soon until the first event?"

Judith appeared lost in thought for a moment. Then she stared intently at Nathan. Without breaking eye contact, Judith slowly rose and loosened the belt holding her robe in place. She shrugged her shoulders, allowing the garment to slide off and fall around her ankles.

"Not for a while."

Nathan enjoyed his wife twice more that morning. The noon meal was well-timed, as the vigorous activity left both ravenous. The problem of what to wear was easily solved. Nathan and Judith eagerly explored the two chests of clothes conveniently placed in the tent. He selected a fine hand-woven tunic and a luxurious white robe edged with the purple trim normally reserved for royalty. Judith chose flowing, colorful garments and gold jewelry that enhanced her natural beauty.

Nathan was pleased she no longer wore a veil, as he greatly enjoyed gazing on her smiling face. Arm in arm, the exuberant couple traversed the short distance to the main residence.

The midday meal had been laid out in the same hall where they had wed the night before. It would also serve as the site for the presentation of the wedding gifts later. A steward showed Nathan and Judith to the position of honor at the main table, positioned on a small platform so it was slightly above every other table in the hall. Judith and her parents were to be seated on the left side of the table while Nathan, his mother, and Saul sat on the right. Nathan concluded that the meal was to be rather informal, as the hall was nearly empty when they arrived. For the convenience of the guests, each table already contained appetizing platters of food and generous servings of wine. People could stroll in, take their places, and begin dining at their leisure. Judith assured him that the hall would be packed well before the time for the gifts.

Nathan and Judith had taken only a few bites before the well-wishers began lining up. Like a queen bee, Judith was soon swarmed and led off by female acquaintances. Nathan did not mind. This week belonged to Judith, and he felt a vicarious thrill watching her enjoy it to the full. The giggling and excited gasps from her entourage made him curious as to what secrets his wife might be sharing. However, the favorable glances sent his way convinced Nathan he had at least made a promising start as a husband.

Since the attention was on Judith for the moment, Nathan could appease his hunger and study the guests beginning to pour into the room. He was too preoccupied last night to notice anyone in the crowd, but now he identified some unexpected attendees. He counted at least a dozen men who had originally opposed Saul's selection as king. Their wedding invitation was most likely an attempt by Saul to mend fences. Nathan politely accepted their congratulations as they drifted by. Saul's entry to the hall created a stir in the assembly, and his former foes rushed to pay homage to their king. Their sudden change of heart made Nathan wary. He resolved to take note of anyone these men spoke with for any length of time.

Nathan was pleased to see Karaz and Jonathan make their way over. Karaz wasted little time paying his respects before finding a seat near the center of the hall. Nathan was amused the Hittite veteran seemed to be making an extra effort to remain upright. Apparently, Karaz had an incredibly good time last night. Jonathan, on the other hand, lingered, anxious to garner any advice for his own wedding night. The *man talk* was cut short when Judith returned to the table, and Nathan introduced the two most important people in his life to each other. He was pleased by how easily his wife charmed the bachelor prince with her wit and sagacity. Jonathan left the table gratified to hear how Judith held his future bride, Naomi, in high esteem.

Applause filled the chamber when the parents of the bride and groom entered. Nathan saw Saul end his current conversation to welcome and escort them to the main table. Affectionate greetings were then exchanged between each member of the newly formed family. Miriam warmly hugged and kissed Judith while giving Nathan her familiar *mother-knows-best* look. He dipped his head in acknowledgement before wrapping his arms around his mother. Once all the principals were seated, the festivities began in earnest.

An hour later, Jephunneh had a brief conversation with Saul, and then excused himself to get the main event underway. Nathan overheard Saul asking to make an announcement before the first wedding gift was presented. When Jephunneh returned, he whispered something to Saul before taking his seat. The king gestured to two servants standing just outside a side chamber and moved to stand in front of the main table. The two servants placed a table covered with a heavy cloth beside Saul while he waited for the audience to quiet.

"Honored friends, I have chosen this joyous occasion to confer royal title on a man who has performed mighty deeds for Israel. I hereby appoint Nathan Ben-Jotham as a *Prince of the Realm*. He and his descendants will be counted among the nobility of our nation. Within the Kingdom of Israel, the word of Nathan Ben-Jotham will be second only to one of royal blood. This title includes a yearly income of twelve talents of gold. Behold now the badges of his office!"

The crowd gasped as the servants pulled back the tablecloth to reveal a helmet, armor, shield, and sword finer than any Nathan had ever seen. The matching pieces were overlaid with highly burnished bronze. The shield had been engraved with the emblem of a rampant lion outlined in silver. One servant brought the sword over for Nathan to examine. The handle was encrusted with rubies in gold settings, and the iron blade was honed to a razor's edge. But when Nathan hefted his new weapon, he recognized that it could be worn only on formal occasions. The ornate handle could slip too easily from a sweaty and grimy hand in the heat of combat. However, the rest of his armor appeared to be quite serviceable.

Nathan had no doubt his unexpected promotion was meant to honor the tribe of Judah as much as himself. An obvious clue was the iconic *Lion of Judah* decorating his new shield. Saul might be marrying off Jonathan to the tribe of Ephraim, but he had elevated Judah's newest son-in-law almost as high. Nathan also appreciated the limits of his new title. It provided wealth and status, but no specific powers. The king had clearly subordinated Nathan to the likes of Abner, as well as the youngest child of the royal household. Still, to a million other Israelites, Nathan was a lord. This simple fact would enable him to carve out a significant niche in the kingdom.

Nathan stood and bowed deeply to Saul, swearing to be worthy of the king's trust. He sat down amid enthusiastic shouts of approval, but the rapt admiration of his wife pleased him the most. Judith laid her head on his shoulder and whispered in his ear.

"Does this make me a *princess*?"

"You've always been one, my Love."

It was now time for Jephunneh to step forward. As father of the bride, it was customary for him to present Judith's dowry as the first wedding gift. Jephunneh called Nathan forward and awarded him title to over one hundred acres of vineyards, farmland, and pasture less than a mile from Gibeah. A large house, servants' quarters, barns, and sheep pens also came with the property. Nathan was astonished, for he was familiar with this prosperous estate, almost within sight of Saul's new palace. He imagined numerous bargains had been struck and many promises made for a Judean family to acquire such a prized piece of land in Benjamin. Nathan also appreciated Jephunneh's shrewdness. Even if his new son-in-law proved to be a fool, Jephunneh's daughter and her children would be assured of food and shelter. Nathan graciously thanked his father-in-law as the guests applauded.

"Father, your gift is most generous...and wise. I promise you will never have cause to regret it."

Nathan's response was a pledge that Judith's dowry would be used solely for the care of their family. Jephunneh's broad smile indicated his satisfaction at reaching this understanding with his son-in-law. As the next scheduled guest readied his gift, Nathan decided to share a troubling thought with Jephunneh.

"The truth is that I know nothing about vineyards."

"You don't have to, my Son. The grapes will provide more than enough income to hire husbandmen skilled in their care."

"But I don't even know how to find such people."

"Don't worry. Judith does."

Nathan soon became familiar with these words. Later, he questioned Jephunneh about what to do with another wedding gift - a large flock of sheep. The answer was to hire shepherds...and Judith knew how to do that too. Managing household servants? Leave it to Judith. It seemed no matter what Nathan asked, Judith was to be found somewhere in the answer. Nathan finally stopped questioning Jephunneh after each gift. The two men would simply look at each other and nod.

It soon became apparent to Nathan why a whole week was set aside for the wedding festivities. Members of the audience were permitted to stand and praise each giver's generosity. Not everyone availed themselves of this privilege, but Nathan noticed that several dignitaries took advantage of every opportunity to be seen and heard. Only six gifts were received that first afternoon before the session adjourned for the evening meal. Seeing more than one hundred families in attendance, Nathan asked his wife if even a week were sufficient time. Judith provided him a glimpse into the mysteries of wedding etiquette. Wedding gifts were presented in order of clan and family status. This turned out to be the most crucial part of a successful wedding. Weeks had gone into negotiating each position on the final list. Naturally, the best gifts, which also drew the most praise, tended to be given first. As the week progressed, more gifts and less praise would be presented each day. According to Judith, nearly half the gifts typically were received on the final day.

Aghast at these new insights, Nathan privately resolved to father only sons.

It would be over an hour before the great hall was prepared for the evening meal, so Nathan and Judith retired to their new quarters. The bridal tent had been dismantled and the couple's belongings moved into an opulent guest house behind the main residence. Nathan found that their wardrobe selection had also increased during the day. They both chose new garments suitable for the night's activities. Naturally, they had to remove their current clothing, which naturally led to other activities before getting dressed again. Nathan and Judith were in no hurry since both knew the party could not start without them. Then after spending many hours enjoying food, wine and celebration, the cheerful couple returned to their house and resumed where they left off.

This daily cycle of lovemaking, meals, entertainment, and gifts repeated itself throughout the week, except on the fourth day. This was the Sabbath, when all work ceased from sundown to sundown to commemorate God's resting after the six Days of Creation. Before sunset, servants provisioned each guest room with a sumptuous selection of food requiring no preparation and plenty of fresh water. Oil lamps were lit, eliminating the effort required to spark a flame the next day. Bedrooms were left dark to facilitate sleeping. Everyone under Jephunneh's roof would be able to spend the Sabbath in sleep, quiet conversation or solemn meditation, except for Nathan. Judith made it abundantly clear her husband could expect little Sabbath rest.

The most lavish banquet was held on the last evening of the festivities and Nathan welcomed it wholeheartedly. He had enjoyed all the luxury, but Nathan was anxious to commence his new life with Judith. Nearly all the guests remained until this final farewell, but not just for the food. Such a broad spectrum of Israelite leaders rarely assembled in the same place. The numerous business and political meetings conducted during the week did not escape Nathan's eye. He need not overhear individual conversations to guess their purpose; he simply noted the participants, who spoke and how the listeners reacted. Nathan judged the majority to be quite harmless, but recognized Saul still had a few jealous rivals trying to drum up support.

Nathan and Judith were up the following morning at daybreak to see off the first of their guests. All had departed by midday, but new visitors arrived that afternoon. Laban showed up with the fifty-three surviving *Renegades* who had served at least one campaign with Nathan. Though not deemed worthy of a wedding invitation, these loyal commoners had come to escort the young couple to their new home in Gibeah. The *Renegades'* wedding gift to Nathan would be the sweat of their brow. These brawny men would serve as both porters and guards for the many valuable wedding gifts. Nathan felt safer in the protection of this small band than he would with any of Abner's regiments. Knowing better than to insult his proud friends by offering direct payment, Nathan had an entire cart loaded with Jephunneh's best wine and other delicacies for their enjoyment.

The moving schedule had already been worked out. Everyone would rest today, pack tomorrow and depart the following day for Gibeah. The coming week would allow Judith to become acquainted with her new life. Nathan was especially interested to see how his refined wife and the gruff *Renegades* got along. He had already regaled Judith with some tales of their bold exploits. His new wife's instincts proved to be excellent. She was a warrior's daughter after all. Judith could both act as a noble lady and still seem completely at ease with these rough men. She walked confidently among the *Renegades*, asked their names, and greeted each one warmly, as if old acquaintances. Nathan was amused by the men's attempts at polite behavior and temperate speech in Judith's presence. If anyone stumbled in their etiquette, she took no notice of it.

By nightfall, Judith's charms had tamed the *Renegades*.

The next day's packing and loading of ox carts went smoothly, thanks to Judith. Organizing a large caravan was no simple task. However, Nathan's wife demonstrated skills comparable to any military quartermaster, and she always gave her instructions with a smile. Judith soon earned the *Renegades*' respect, as well as their affection. They responded as if the young girl were just another officer, albeit one who never shouted or cursed.

The caravan's main body departed at sunrise, although a handful of *Renegades* were on the road much earlier. Laban had insisted on sending scouts ahead, just as on any campaign. Judith and Nathan both rode donkeys ahead of the ox carts. He usually walked places, but riding allowed him to easily converse with Judith. Her mind was brimming with ideas for their new home, as well as plans for its flocks, herds and vineyards. This was a particular concern to Nathan, for he knew royal business could keep him away for weeks at a time. They discussed these issues intently during the first day's travel. The gist of their agreement was that Nathan would always have final approval, but Judith would manage their household on a day-to-day basis as she saw fit. Nathan joked that his life was now quite simple. As long as he kept the king's favor and provided seed for children, Judith would take care of everything else. Judith assumed a demure expression, but never contradicted her husband's assessment.

The three-day journey over dusty roads to Gibeah was punctuated by very pleasant evenings in camp. Nathan thoroughly enjoyed spending time in the company of the *Renegades*. These plainspoken men were closer to his heart than any member of the nobility. He sat around the fire with his fellow warriors, sharing food, wine, and stories. This pleased

Nathan more than any of his recent wedding activities, except for the lovemaking, of course. He came to bed extremely late the first night and found Judith still waiting up for him in their tent. He instantly felt regret and asked if his time with the *Renegades* made her feel neglected. Her thoughtful response affected him profoundly.

"Of course not, Nathan. You are now a prince of Israel. You will rarely have a chance for such honest fellowship again."

Chapter 14 – A Chance for Redemption

Samuel said to King Saul: I am the one whom the LORD sent to anoint you king over Israel. Hear this Message from the LORD. "I will punish the Amalekites for attacking Israel when they came up out of Egypt. Go and attack the Amalekites. Destroy everything they own. Do not spare any of them. Kill their men, their women, their children, their cattle, their sheep, their camels and their donkeys."

From the book of I Samuel, chapter 15, verses 1 to 3

The royal palace in the Philistine City of Gath

The Philistine Kingdom of Gath's three preeminent citizens filed into the palace's most cramped and least accessible chamber. The humble compartment had only two things in its favor: tradition and security. Untold generations of kings had met here with their cronies to plot and scheme in absolute privacy. Few knew of its existence. Even fewer survived a visit. Intrigue permeated the very air of this eerie retreat. Some past kings of Gath had sworn they could sense their ancestors' eavesdropping.

An ancient chair creaked as King Achish took his place at the head of the bleak room's solitary worn-out table. He fretted more over his two closest allies than any spirit or superstition. Gath's *Archon*, Abimelek, adjusted his chair in relation to the oil lamps so that his face remained in the shadows when leaning back. Achish had inherited the kingdom's chief administrator, diplomat, and spymaster from his father. Abimelek had secured the throne for Achish, but his loyalty to the Crown was based solely on mutual benefit. General Davon, Commander of Gath's army, bolted the massive door before taking his seat. The talented soldier had been by Achish's side since their very first battle together, and he trusted Davon more than any other man. However, that was not saying much, as Achish still employed his own spies among Davon's staff. Honorable generals overthrowing their kings was a hoary tradition.

Achish decided to begin with the state of his army. Gath had suffered more losses at the devastating Battle of Michmash than any of the other Philistine kingdoms. Out of five frontline infantry regiments, barely a thousand demoralized survivors had returned to Gath. Davon's first assignment as commander was to rebuild the shattered units and replenish their ranks using dispirited veterans, untried trainees, garrison troops and raw recruits. His efforts were further hampered by the vast quantity of equipment lost to the Hebrews. Until recently, most of Gath's soldiers were armed with only fire-hardened wooden spears and ox-hide shields. Fortunately, Gath's excellent chariot corps came through the disaster unscathed. However, they could not possibly win a pitched battle without infantry support. A nod from Achish signaled Davon to begin.

"The good news is that we can now field five infantry regiments again. The bad news is that they would be hard pressed to defeat a herd of angry goats. Dividing five thousand men into regiments, companies and platoons was the easy part. The problem, no surprise, is the lack of junior officers, especially sergeants. I've had to promote men to leadership whom I wouldn't follow into a brothel."

"Would taking more volunteers from the chariot corps help?"

"You told me I could promote fifty to be officers, Achish. I've since taken one hundred more and it's still not enough."

"How are you replacing the charioteers?"

"I'm not. Typically, only one soldier in ten can be molded into a competent charioteer. Only one in five of those ever make officer. I'm temporarily disbanding five chariot squadrons instead."

"I don't like weakening our strongest force, Davon."

"We need quality somewhere, Achish. Unless you tell me differently, my orders stand."

"No, I won't interfere. I don't like it, but it's your neck...literally. What about weapons?"

"That has been the bright spot in an otherwise dreary month. Our noble *Archon* has been successfully converting his mysterious treasure into armaments. We got rid of the last wooden spears a few days ago. Next up is armor for some heavy infantry companies, but at least every man has a sword. Now we just have to teach the new recruits not to cut themselves."

"Well done, Abimelek. What's the view outside our borders?"

"Better than we have any right to expect, Achish. I have ended my treasonous negotiations with Kaftor of Gaza now that the army is in better shape. Surprisingly, there has not been a peep out of him. It appears the unexpected successes of the Hebrews have captured the attention of all the kings in Philistia."

"Not unexpected to you, *Archon*. You correctly predicted Saul's moves against Moab, Edom and Aramea. Now, how worried should I be?"

"This string of Hebrew victories, while impressive, was shallow. They plucked some valuable low-hanging fruit from its unwary owners. Saul might even try it again, but not against us. Note that all the recent Hebrew campaigns have been in regions where chariots are ineffective. Conquering Philistia would require capabilities that Saul does not appear to possess."

"So why are Kaftor and the other kings worried?"

"They do not have me advising them."

"Besides that."

"I suspect Kaftor is playing on the other kings' fears. Subterfuge has not brought Gaza the power which Kaftor craves. He may try to seek it on the battlefield...as the leader of a Philistine expedition against the Hebrews."

"Kaftor's a double-dealing scoundrel, Abimelek, not a general. He would lead Philistia to disaster."

"Yet I advise you to encourage Kaftor in this ambition. Subtly, of course, as part of your *deep strategy* against him for your father's murder. It will lead to victory over the Hebrews."

"Why would I want Kaftor to be victorious?"

"I'm not talking about Kaftor's campaign, Achish. I refer to the one that will follow."

Nathan's Estate near Gibeah in Benjamite Territory

A wail of despair caused Nathan to jerk upright in bed. Another few seconds passed before he realized it had come from his own lips. Nathan's eyes quickly adjusted to the early morning light streaming through the bedroom window. He was embarrassed to see the commotion also woke his pregnant wife Judith. Eight months had passed since their wedding and she was already great with child. Judith brushed back her tousled hair and gazed at her husband with concern. Nathan smiled to allay her fears and pulled his wife close to his side. Learning to share their bed with the growing baby and sleep at the same time had been a challenge. The experience was uncomfortable yet comforting.

"Was it the nightmare, Nathan? The one you told me about?"

Nathan closed his eyes and nodded. It had been over a year since the last occurrence. He had never intended to tell Judith about his horrible recurring dream. However, over the past few months, Nathan and Judith had opened their hearts to each other. He realized the nightmare might come again, and his wife deserved to be prepared for it. Undoubtedly, the excitement over their wedding and many happy months of marriage had driven it from his mind.

But the nightmare now returned with a vengeance. At age twelve, Nathan had witnessed the Philistines kill Jotham, his father, for the offense of making iron weapons for the tribe of Benjamin. That same night he had dreamed of his family happily watching Jotham working at the hidden forge. The dream changed to a nightmare as Nathan watched in horror as a demonic Philistine crept up behind his father. Nathan tried to shout a warning, but only silence came from his lips as the Philistine plunged a sword into his father's back. Jotham fell to his knees as blood soaked the ground. Yet this was not the worst part of the nightmare. That came when Jotham peered into Nathan's eyes with a disappointed expression. The message was clear. The son had done nothing to prevent the father's death. The nightmare returned to remind Nathan that he had still not avenged Jotham. The passage of time only made the horrifying images even more vivid.

Judith hugged her husband tightly and whispered soothing words. Nathan was tempted to spend the rest of the day with her, hiding from a troubled world. Instead, he kissed her deeply and claimed that he promised to meet with Prince Jonathan that morning. The excuse was part truth and part fiction because the two men had never agreed upon a date or time. Nathan felt that some kind of activity was required to prevent him from brooding.

The only drawback to their new home was that Nathan now had to walk for half an hour to reach the royal compound in Gibeah. Gone were the days when he and Jonathan could lean out their respective windows and call to each other. Despite being heir to the Throne, Jonathan had continued to live on his family's estate. However, Saul's new palace atop the highest point in Gibeah was nearly complete. The king, his wife and their minor children would soon take up residence there. Jonathan and his wife Naomi would be taking sole possession of Saul's original house, as well as obtaining an apartment at the palace for special occasions.

The stonemasons' hammering grew louder as Nathan approached the new palace. He was viewing their progress when he noticed a well-dressed throng descending the hilltop. Although the great hall was already being utilized for meetings, Nathan had not been invited to this one. He would wager Jonathan had not been invited either. It was yet another sign of their diminished influence since being married. They both still had seats on the War Council. Jonathan was still commander of Israel's tribal militia. Nathan went on diplomatic missions to soothe the feelings of disgruntled neighbors. Their roles were just not as vital after a year of peace.

Now was the time for men like Beker, the *Yameen*, the self-appointed *right hand of the king*. Governors, administrators, tax collectors, lawyers and scribes were those whose skills were presently in demand. Nathan knew part of the fault lay with both him and Jonathan. It was nice to be married, even with all the attendant responsibilities. Judith would deliver her baby within the month; Naomi probably six months after that. They could hardly demand new responsibilities that might take them away for lengthy periods. However, the two friends promised themselves that *next year* would be different.

Nathan found Jonathan pacing outside his home while watching the group departing from the palace mount. The prince greeted his friend warmly and ushered him quickly inside. Naomi served them wine, bread, and cheese in the cool antechamber before politely excusing herself. Nathan saw immediately that his friend was perturbed.

"You weren't invited either."

"I wouldn't mind, Nathan, if it was one of Beker's boring lectures. Except it wasn't. Abner was invited. That means it was a military meeting."

"The War Council still has the final word on any decision."

"I fear the decision has already been made. All Abner needs is my father's backing to have a majority."

Jonathan's next words were interrupted by the unexpected entrance of Karaz, their former mentor and current ally on the War Council. The Hittite mercenary pulled up a chair and helped himself to a goblet of wine and a generous portion of food. Karaz slurped and munched while Nathan and Jonathan waited for the older man to give them his attention. The prince finally grew impatient and sarcastic.

"By all means, Karaz, come in. Make yourself at home. Have something to eat."

"Sorry, but that miserly Beker didn't even provide breakfast. My belly growled through that whole meeting at the palace."

"YOU were invited?"

"No. I just went."

"How did you get in? Even more interesting, how did you stay?"

"Well, I trained all the guards, and they're still scared of me. Once inside, nobody dared throw me out. Saul would have been embarrassed in front of his visitor."

"What visitor?"

"Samuel."

Nathan and Jonathan stared at each other in shock while Karaz resumed eating. The Prophet Samuel had anointed Saul as king, but their relationship soon became fraught. Surprised by the Philistine capture of Michmash, the Royal Army of Israel had begun to disintegrate. Then Saul had panicked, defied Samuel's instructions, and usurped the role of a priest to offer a sacrifice to rally his soldiers. Samuel had denounced this sacrilege and declared that God would replace Saul's dynasty with another. The king and the prophet had not spoken since. Karaz finally raised his head to see Nathan and Jonathan sitting in stunned silence. He looked from one to the other while swallowing his last bite.

"Anybody want to know what Samuel said?"

"YES!"

"Seems your God wants a war, specifically against the Amalekites. Apparently, He's still angry over how they treated your ancestors a few hundred years ago. Angry enough that every last Amalekite man, woman and child are to be killed. All their animals too, although I didn't catch what they did wrong."

"When will the War Council respond to Samuel's request?"

"I doubt it matters, Jonathan. Who votes against God? No, Israel fighting Amalek is as certain as your taking a piss today."

"Even so, the Council must establish a strategy."

"Not this time, Lad. The king has already approved Abner's plan."

290

"Well, I'll have something to say about that. If Abner expects any help from the Tribal militia, he'll have to go through its commander. Me."

"No, Jonathan, he won't. This war will be entirely a Royal Army affair. No militia. Not even your precious *Renegades* as scouts."

"That's madness, Karaz. Amalek's army is at least our equal."

"The good general has been paying attention to what you did against Moab, Edom and Aramea. Abner expects to draw their soldiers into an ambush, cut them off and annihilate them. Then he can either assault or starve out their cities."

Nathan had kept his troubled thoughts to himself during this discussion. To him the concern was not Amalek or even Abner. It was Samuel. The two of them had a mixed history. Nathan had been at Saul's side during the future king's first encounter with the prophet. He even played a small role when Samuel had introduced the Nation of Israel to their new Ruler.

But Nathan's relationship with Samuel became rocky after that. The turning point had been Samuel's condemnation of Saul's sacrifice before the Battle of Michmash. Nathan believed the prophet's rash action played into the hands of the hated Philistines. He had even sought out and threatened to kill the old man unless he vindicated Saul. However, the encounter did not go as Nathan expected. Samuel had shrugged off the threat to his life and given a calm, reasoned justification for his actions. He even challenged Nathan to search his own soul regarding what was the will of God. Shoving these memories aside, Nathan voiced his immediate doubts to Jonathan.

"Samuel is forcing things to happen too fast. Why Amalek? Why now?"

"Besides the fact that they are blood-drinking pagans who have sworn to destroy Israel? Amalek has been quietly expanding their army as Egypt's hold over them weakens. Also, our lands are readily accessible to them for invasion. It's just a matter of time. If one of us does not wipe the other out, there will be endless fighting for generation after generation. Samuel's saying that God wants to put an end to it here and now."

"What if Samuel misunderstood God?"

"Nathan...he's a prophet. Talking to God is what prophets do."

"Still, Jonathan, what if he's wrong?"

"The short answer? Follow Karaz's emergency plan. We go into exile and find another kingdom to take over."

The new royal palace overlooking Gibeah

Beker ignored the gritty dust generated by the busy stonemasons as he observed Samuel inspecting their handiwork. The two men were rarely alone in the same proximity. The dignitaries summoned for the prophet's holy declaration were already wending their ways home. The *Yameen* beheld Samuel with a mixture of irritation and admiration. Beker's recent endeavors to expand his personal kingdom within the Kingdom of Israel were going so well. Nearly a year of peace had allowed him to surpass his more military focused competitors. Prince Jonathan and his devoted henchman, Nathan, were preoccupied with the joys and trials of married life. Their Hittite war dog, Karaz, had been idled along with his masters. Beker took advantage of their distraction to make King Saul ever more dependent on him for counsel. Abner ran the army and deferred to Beker in all other matters. Yet the veteran politician knew this period of good fortune could not last.

As the untimely intervention of Samuel now showed.

The prophet swept into Gibeah like a sandstorm yesterday to demand an audience with the king. Beker barely managed to stay ahead of the impending chaos. The *Yameen* argued that the king needed time to pray and prepare to receive a Divine message. Samuel reluctantly agreed to wait until the following morning. Beker used the delay to coach Saul on what to say and to assemble an audience composed of the *Yameen's* loyal minions. He effectively isolated Samuel so that none of his rivals even suspected the prophet's presence. Despite all his planning, Beker still held his breath as he escorted Samuel into the palace's great hall. He winced at the sight of Karaz in the crowd. Somehow, the Hittite mercenary had sniffed out the secret gathering, but at least Prince Jonathan and Nathan were nowhere to be seen.

Samuel's message proved to be more of an inconvenience than a disaster for Beker's ambitions. God commanded the destruction of Amalek. The *Yameen* would lose no sleep over the fate of heathens, but war always provided an opportunity for Jonathan's allies. He swiftly pulled Abner aside to recommend the general and his army take sole charge of the coming campaign. Abner had been delighted and easily persuaded his cousin Saul to agree. The last thing the insecure king desired was another popularity contest with his son. However, the most disturbing aspect to Beker was Saul's obvious desire for a reconciliation with Samuel.

Beker reflected on Samuel's cleverness in establishing Israel's first kingdom. The prophet had outfoxed all the Tribal leaders by selecting a warrior king whom he could keep under his thumb. Samuel's proclamations and edicts constantly reminded Saul who had placed him on the throne. Then came the Philistine invasion, where Beker felt Samuel had stumbled. The prophet tried to control the war by forbidding Saul to make a move without Samuel first offering a sacrifice. The prophet had tarried undoubtedly to emphasize his holy authority, never dreaming Saul would make the sacrifice himself. The frustrated Samuel desperately tried to reestablish his dominance over Israel by disinheriting Saul's family from the kingdom.

Despite this rejection by his patron, Saul's kingdom managed to survive by a hairsbreadth. Beker suspected that the insubordinate king's current prosperity caused Samuel to experience many second thoughts. That was why he secretly admired Samuel's deft performance that morning. The prophet had suddenly appeared without apology, bearing Saul the priceless gift of redemption. The king could get back in God's good graces, eliminate a dangerous enemy, gain new territory and bask in the gratitude of his people. And allow Samuel to slip back into his old role as the guiding light of Israel.

Not if Beker could help it. Samuel had given strict instructions for the coming war with Amalek. Beker was confident that he could find room for a few alterations.

On the Road outside Gibeah

Troubled thoughts had clouded Nathan's mind when he bid farewell to Jonathan and Karaz. He left both his friends hotly debating Abner's chances for success against the Amalekites without the support of Jonathan's militia. Nathan feared they were missing the bigger threat: Samuel. The last time the prophet interjected himself into a military operation, Israel's army had split into squabbling factions. The Philistines then rolled almost unopposed into the strategic pass at Michmash. Only a combination of Jonathan's boldness and Philistine incompetence won the day for Israel.

Now once again Samuel was playing the part of a warrior judge leading Israel into battle. Not literally leading this time. The actual bloodletting would be left to younger fighters such as Abner, but Samuel controlled everything else. He chose the enemy. He set the schedule. He established the rules of engagement. Samuel would undoubtedly use his close relationship with God to direct the entire course of the war. Saul and Abner would be mere tools in this holy endeavor.

Nathan suddenly became aware that he had been standing for some time at a fork in the road. Left led back to his home. Right was the route to Saul's new palace. As much as he desired the comfort and counsel of Judith, Nathan also longed to confront Samuel. Was the man a true voice of God? A power-hungry charlatan? A deluded old fool? Nathan longed to wring the answer out of him.

"Greetings, Nathan. Did you bring your dagger today?"

The unexpected voice caused Nathan to snap into a defensive stance. He relaxed marginally as a smirking Samuel strode towards him from the direction of the palace. A harem of beautiful women dancing down the road could not have been more startling. It was enough to make Nathan believe that God had just read his thoughts.

"No, but I can easily get one. Why do you ask?"

"Well, Nathan, last we spoke, I advised you to ask God whether I was a traitor. If He told you to kill me, I promised not to run. Naturally, I *am* somewhat curious about your decision."

"God has not spoken to me yet, Samuel, but the day is still young."

"Ah. You are anxious about the message I just delivered to the king. I looked for you at the palace but could not find you."

"I wasn't invited. Neither was Jonathan."

"Hmm. That is not a good sign. Saul's future depends on the outcome. Your absence decreases the likelihood of a favorable outcome."

"You doubt Saul will be victorious?"

"Oh, I am not worried that Saul will lose. I worry about how he might win."

"Yes, I heard about the conditions you set. Of course, you get to decide if Saul meets them."

"God will judge the king, not me. I am merely a messenger who wants only the best for Saul."

"Yet, God talks only to Samuel. How very convenient for you. The king must be quite grateful for your gift of redemption."

"I brought Saul a test, not a gift. This war against Amalek will prove Saul's fitness to rule. Or his unfitness."

"Israel has a veteran army now, Samuel. Saul's dynasty seems pretty secure to me."

"Your reasoning misses the mark, Nathan. Saul's test will take place in his heart, not on the battlefield. It is a question of obedience, not military skill."

"Granted, Saul disobeyed you, or rather disobeyed God, against the Philistines. Don't you think he has learned from that?"

"Then why has he surrounded himself with counselors like the one called Beker? That man has the cold eyes of a snake looking at its next meal. I fear he will undermine Saul's courage and tempt him into disobedience."

"I'm sure Beker is just as skeptical about your intentions, Samuel."

"Look, Nathan. God sought me out, not the other way around. I was barely five years old when He first spoke to me. Eli the High Priest had to explain it all to me."

"Why would God speak to a child?"

"Perhaps because He knew that I would listen. Very few grown men do, Nathan. You probably imagine that I glory in this awesome responsibility. I do not."

"Many men would love to take your place."

"Only out of ignorance. Bearing God's message to His people brings blessing and pain in equal measure."

"Why not quit?"

"One does not retire on God. If He keeps speaking, I will keep listening."

"What does His voice sound like?"

"More like a father than my own father."

"How can you know it is truly God and not your own imagination?"

Samuel eyes suddenly lost focus, as if staring through Nathan toward the distant hills. As the silence stretched on, Nathan began to fear for the prophet's health. Despite their fraught relationship, the last thing Nathan wanted was for the old man to drop dead at his feet. Fortunately, Samuel soon shook himself as if waking before gazing serenely into Nathan's eyes.

"Perhaps, Nathan, God will show you how one day."

Before Nathan could unravel this enigmatic statement, he heard his name carried by the wind. Coming over the nearest ridge was Nathan's twelve-year old sister, Leah, mounted on a donkey. She vigorously applied a switch to the poor animal's hindquarters. Nathan about to rebuke the girl for abusing the beast when his thoughts froze. There could be only one explanation for his sister's haste.

Nathan turned to race for home so quickly that he inadvertently kicked dirt on the ancient prophet's robe. Samuel's puzzled expression was soon replaced by a broad smile. He continued his own homeward trek while quietly uttering a blessing on Nathan and his family.

Nathan's Estate near Gibeah in Benjamite Territory

Sweat dripped from every pore on Nathan's body as he threw open the door to his house. He nearly trampled his mother Miriam in his haste to reach the main bedchamber. Nathan stumbled through a brief apology as he helped her stand upright again. However, Miriam grasped his chin firmly while glaring into his eyes.

"You may be the master of this house, Son, but I taught you to behave better than this."

"Sorry, Mother, I ...Leah on a donkey... Judith... the baby..."

"All in good time, Nathan. First, you must take a few minutes to compose yourself. Judith doesn't need you bursting in on her like a wild beast. Sit down, drink some water and then wash the grime off your face."

"No time...must see Judith...I"

"SIT!"

The little boy in Nathan plopped himself down on a bench. Miriam gave her son a satisfied nod as she held out a jug of water. Nathan was suddenly overcome with lightheadedness and a powerful thirst."

"Drink."

Nathan obeyed by draining the small jug and immediately felt better. He sheepishly handed it back to his smirking mother.

"Wash."

Miriam pointed to a basin of water and a towel on the table beside Nathan. The grime from his body quickly turned both the clear water and the towel a dirty brown. Nathan shuddered to think how he would have looked to his wife if Miriam had not intervened. Feeling more human now, he turned back to his mother.

"Now please tell me how Judith..."

"Shhhhh!"

Miriam then quietly led Nathan to the bedchamber and motioned him to enter. He almost trembled as the heavy door swung noisily on its hinges. Nathan peeked around the corner to get his first glimpse of Judith. He almost did not recognize her. Judith's normally lustrous hair hung down limply. Her gown and bedclothes were soaked in sweat. She looked as if she had just run a longer distance than Nathan. Everything about his young wife appeared fragile until Nathan gazed into her eyes. There gleamed a pride as fierce as any warrior after a battle won. A small movement immediately drew Nathan's attention to the tiny bundle at Judith's breast. She smiled and pulled back the blanket from a tiny form.

"Come here, Nathan, and meet Zabud. Your son."

Nathan crept to the edge of the bed and drank in the scene. A witticism died on his lips. He simply gathered his family into strong arms and wept soft tears of joy.

Chapter 15 – Partial Obedience

Then Saul attacked the Amalekites from Havilah to Shur and as far as the eastern border of Egypt. He destroyed all the people of Amalek with the sword. But Saul and the army took Agag, King of the Amalekites alive. They also kept the best of the sheep and cattle and everything else that was good. These they were unwilling to completely destroy. They only destroyed things that were worthless and weak."

From the book of I Samuel, chapter 15, verses 7 to 9

Samuel said to Saul, "The LORD told you to completely destroy the wicked Amalekites and all their possessions, to make war until they no longer existed. Why did you not obey the LORD? Why did you take their plunder and thereby do evil in the eyes of the LORD?"

Saul replied, "I did obey the LORD. I completed my mission. I destroyed the Amalekites and brought back Agag, their king. But it was the soldiers who took the cattle and sheep as plunder. Besides, they are going to sacrifice the best of them to the LORD here at Gilgal."

Then Samuel said to Saul, "To obey is better than sacrifice. Because you have rejected the LORD's words, He has rejected you as the King of Israel."

From the book of I Samuel, chapter 15, verses 18 to 23

The Plains of Gilgal in the Jordan River Valley

The smell of fresh animal dung hit Nathan's nostrils while he was at least five miles from the Israelite armory at Gilgal. His ears detected the cacophony of a stockyard with three miles to go. By the time the vast herds were in sight, Nathan could identify each type of sound separately. Enough sheep and cattle surrounded the Royal Army encampment to feed all three regiments indefinitely. The vast herds resembled a besieging army.

Although Nathan's initial impression of Gilgal was almost humorous, nothing seemed to justify the cryptic, but urgent, summons from his friend Prince Jonathan. Nathan had lived quietly for the past two years, his time consumed by married life, his rapidly growing son, the needs of his prosperous estate and various diplomatic missions to reassure skittish neighboring kingdoms and mollify disgruntled tribal Elders. Jonathan enjoyed a similar peaceful existence, but both men's sabbatical had been a direct result of a cunning scheme by rivals at Court. Besides strengthening the bonds between a Benjamite king and the two most powerful tribes in Israel, their political marriages had, by necessity, greatly limited the participation of Nathan and Jonathan in major policy decisions.

These limitations became painfully obvious seven months ago when the Prophet Samuel had presented God's latest command. Israel was to utterly destroy their sworn enemies, the Amalekites. Nathan and Jonathan had figured prominently in every previous military campaign of the young Kingdom of Israel. But the war on Amalek was to be different. King Saul gave total control of the operation to his cousin Abner, Commander of Israel's Royal Army. Nathan and Jonathan both fumed but ended up tending to their domestic affairs instead. And Abner had not done badly. He just missed several opportunities to be exceptional.

Jonathan, Nathan, and their Hittite mentor Karaz had built their military reputations by employing clever tactics. Abner intended to prove that he could do even better. Amalek's field army had been drawn into a cunning, but complex, ambush. The bulk of the enemy forces were trapped and annihilated; however, miscommunication between Abner's regimental commanders allowed far too many Amalekites to slip away. Abner partially redeemed himself with a skillful pursuit which hounded the fleeing soldiers mercilessly. Only a handful of pitiful refugees made it across the border into Egypt.

Unfortunately, the Amalekite king Agag and a few hundred soldiers withdrew into a fortress while Abner was chasing down stragglers. Abner's carelessness gave the Amalekites five precious days to gather supplies and fortify their position for a lengthy siege. The Royal Army of Israel was unprepared for this new challenge. Not since Joshua's conquest centuries before had Israelites required siege craft skills. It appeared that a swift victory over the hated Amalekites would elude King Saul.

Yet scarcely a fortnight later, Abner declared a momentous victory. The Amalekite fortress had fallen. Its defenders slain. God's command fulfilled. Israel's honor redeemed. Nathan wondered how these good tidings could have upset Jonathan. Had Abner *lied* to the Nation? The thought seemed preposterous. Abner had his flaws, but blatant stupidity was not one of them.

Nathan decided that circling around Gilgal would give him a better chance of spotting Jonathan's tent than entering the compound itself. He could also avoid the civilian foot traffic, which seemed much heavier than usual. He unexpectedly came across the reason a few minutes later. A newly erected platform loomed over the Gilgal plain. Thousands of people already waited on the rocky ground before it in anticipation of some great event. Nathan spied a highly polished bronze altar nearby being serviced by a score of white-robed priests. Everywhere was the air of celebration. Nathan was not surprised to see the king's tent pitched nearby. Nor to see Jonathan pacing a short distance away. He hailed his friend only to receive a distressed look in return.

"Ten thousand people and I manage to find the only one who looks grumpy."

"Only because they don't know the disaster about to be unleashed on them, Nathan."

"I didn't walk for three days for riddles, Jonathan. You called me. I came. Now talk."

"Samuel and my father have been arguing in his tent for nearly an hour."

"That can't be good."

"It seems Abner and the king decided to interpret Samuel's instructions regarding Amalek rather loosely."

"And we all know how touchy Samuel gets about things like that. What did they do?"

"They negotiated with King Agag."

"Let me guess, Jonathan. One of Agag's conditions was not to die."

"There's more. Agag offered a ransom. You passed most of it walking around camp on four legs. Anything made of gold or silver is probably in Beker's clutches. In return, Agag, his family, the senior officers and a few ministers were spared. Agag's common soldiers were not included."

"Amalekites were never known for loyalty."

"The outcome of these negotiations falls well short of the command *to completely destroy* the Amalekites and their livestock. My father has leaped headfirst into a huge dung heap."

"Abner had Agag penned up in his fortress. Why not finish the bastard off?"

"Abner also had a mutiny on his hands. His soldiers were already pissed over being denied what they saw as a soldier's fair share of the plunder. They had no siege equipment, and the men weren't keen to take a few hundred casualties going over the walls. Besides, they were tired and homesick. None of them wanted to wait a year or more for the Amalekites to get hungry and surrender."

"And then came Agag's offer?"

"I suspect Beker had something to do with that. I can almost hear our illustrious *Yameen* now. *Amalek as a nation is finished. Why should Israel expend any more blood and treasure just to exterminate a few holdouts?* It was a tidy solution. Everyone got what they wanted...except for a few hundred Amalekite soldiers, of course. Our army gets its plunder. Abner gets his victory. The king gets a monument on Mount Carmel. Agag gets his life. Beker gets everyone in his debt."

"And everyone is happy."

"Except Samuel and God. And that, Nathan, is a huge problem for my father."

"Samuel and Saul have fallen out before and yet your father still managed to keep his crown. Perhaps Saul can convince Samuel to overlook a few details."

"Care to make a wager on that?"

"Too late. Here they come."

A soldier had just pulled back a flap on the royal tent allowing Saul and Samuel to exit side by side. Saul was resplendent in a snow-white robe with a magnificent jeweled sword at his side. Nathan noted the king's attire closely resembled that of the priests who would make the celebratory sacrifices. Saul's appearance projected a combination of purity and power. In contrast, Samuel could have been mistaken for a peasant. The king exuded confidence as he strode forward. The prophet gritted his teeth as if he had just swallowed something bitter. Nathan began to hope a national crisis had been averted. Instead of calling on the assembly to depose their rebellious monarch, Samuel was submissively attending his king. Nathan almost laughed when Jonathan released a deep breath in obvious relief.

Nathan then noticed Abner waiting nearby with an honor guard for his royal cousin. However, one man stood out from the rest. Instead of armor, the stranger wore expensive, but obviously foreign, robes. Nathan's blood ran cold to realize he must be looking at Agag, the former King of Amalek. He nudged Jonathan and nodded toward the Amalekite. The prince's expression slowly changed from puzzlement to abject horror. Nathan's brief hopes for a peaceful ceremony began evaporating faster than piss on a hot stone. There could be only one explanation for Agag's presence. Saul intended to show off his war trophy to the Nation. This conquered king would ascend the massive platform, kneel and pay homage to Saul before the adoring multitude. Nathan could think of nothing that would infuriate Samuel more.

"The secret to getting around not being invited, Boys, is to move quickly, quietly and confidently."

Both Nathan and Jonathan spun round at the sound of Karaz's whisper. The Hittite mercenary gestured emphatically toward the rear of Abner's honor guard. Answering Jonathan's grin with his own, Nathan proceeded with his two friends at a leisurely pace toward the gleaming soldiers. A sergeant peered over his shoulder at them and frowned. However, a stern glare from the prince was enough to make the man face eyes front. A few seconds later, the entire formation fell in behind Saul and Samuel.

The King of Israel mounted the stairs alone before striking a majestic pose on the platform. The old prophet trudged along more slowly and took a position to one side of, but slightly behind, his sovereign. Nathan assumed he and his fellow interlopers were spotted when Saul's eyes briefly opened wide in shock. However, the king quickly recovered and instead settled his gaze upon the multitude. Abner and Agag halted at the bottom of the stairs while the honor guard lined up along the base of the platform. Nathan now faced an awkward choice.

Should he go up or stay down? He decided to follow Jonathan's lead. Unsurprisingly, the prince went straight up to stand at his father's side, opposite from Samuel. This was also the first indication Abner had that something was amiss. If the general was annoyed by Jonathan's and Nathan's unscheduled appearances, he was absolutely livid when Karaz pushed past him. Naturally, the Hittite chose to aggravate Abner further with a sly wink. Nathan avoided direct eye contact but heard Abner's muttered profanities all the way up the steps. Saul diplomatically chose to nod graciously to Nathan and Karaz as they took their usual spots behind Jonathan. As far as the thousands of spectators were concerned, everything was going just as their king wished.

That illusion was ruined a moment later by Samuel.

Saul's jaw tightened in anger as the prophet unexpectedly took two steps forward and ordered Agag to come up. The Amalekite's gaze moved from the perplexed Abner to the fuming Saul. Agag then shrugged at the impromptu change in the agenda and calmly ascended the stairs to stand before Samuel. However, he soon turned pale as the outraged prophet spat accusation after accusation in his face. Samuel concluded his brief prosecution of Agag with a final condemnation. Like everyone else, Nathan assumed Samuel was finished when the old man stepped back by Saul. No one in the vast throng anticipated what was coming next.

With a swiftness belying his age, Samuel drew Saul's ornate sword from its sheath. Nathan marveled at graceful way the prophet thrust the borrowed blade under Agag's rib cage and drove it up into the astonished man's heart and lungs. The executioner and the condemned momentarily embraced. Then

309

Samuel pulled the sword out as swiftly as he had plunged it in. The arc of the blade sprayed blood across Saul's face and white robe. Agag tottered briefly, crumbled to his knees, and toppled over on his right side. All without uttering a sound. Samuel then faced his king with a countenance full of holy wrath. Nathan feared at that instant the prophet meant to kill Saul as well. Instead, Samuel flung the bloody sword at Saul's feet in disgust. He descended the stairs without a word before disappearing into the stunned crowd. For a moment, Nathan thought he could hear Saul's frightened heart beating. Then he realized it was his own.

The images of that moment were forever stamped on Nathan's memory. Agag's blood pooling around his body. The crimson stains on Saul's white clothing, the king's trembling lips and his shaking hands. The look of utter despair on Jonathan's face. Abner's profane tirade. Soldiers vainly seeking orders. Confused priests milling about, ironically resembling their sacrificial sheep and cattle. Finally, the High Priest summoned up the courage to approach his paralyzed king.

"My King, can we proceed?"

"Proceed?"

"Apologies, my King. I mean with the sacrifices. We must thank the LORD for your great victory over the Amalekites. The animals are here. The priests are ready. Your people are waiting. God is watching."

"Send them away."

"Send who away, my King?"

"Everyone."

"My King! Refusing to honor the LORD would be sacrilege. I recommend…"

"SEND THEM AWAY!"

The shaken High Priest scurried off to instruct the other priests and the soldiers to break up the assembly. Now, Saul went from sullen silence to ceaseless talking. It seemed to Nathan as if the king were rehearsing the arguments he must have had with Samuel. He watched sadly as Jonathan attempted to gently guide his father off the platform and away from the gaping crowd. Nathan was startled when Karaz touched his shoulder.

"You all right, Lad? You seem pretty dazed."

"Who wouldn't be?"

"I feel a little shaky myself. Your Hebrew religion is full of surprises. I never dreamed it included human sacrifice."

"What? No, Karaz. That was not a sacrifice. It was an execution."

"Hah! Try telling that to Agag. Anyway, I need to start showing Samuel a lot more respect. That old man didn't learn how to handle a blade like that killing sheep. He must have been really dangerous in his prime."

"Never mind that. What will Saul do now?"

"I'm still learning your customs, Lad, but I think you should be asking, *what will your God do?*

The Royal Quarters in the City of Gilgal

Beker, the king's *right hand*, reckoned that he must be the only truly happy person within a day's journey from Gilgal.

The fact that the *Yameen* was enjoying a golden goblet of wine in a luxurious suite was only a small part of the reason. He shuddered to recall his early days of government service...shivering in dusty tents, sleeping on gravel, chewing cold meat, and otherwise grubbing about like a nomad. As soon as wealth began trickling into the Royal Treasury, Beker initiated a building campaign. Quarters suitable for the king now stood in every significant city, fortress, and crossroad across Israel, stretching from Judah in the south to Naphtali in the north.

Of course, the king could reside in only one place at a time. Yet Beker ensured that these valuable properties were rarely unoccupied. Besides his own use, the *Yameen* made these desirable accommodations available to his loyal ministers, influential Tribal leaders, and men of wealth. Travel was always an ordeal. Everyone appreciated comfort and pampering at the end of the day. And Beker never charged anyone for this opulent room and board. These were favors granted to friends, who repaid Beker with other favors in the future.

Beker reclined next to a table of tasty delicacies and reflected on the opportunities provided him by the day's chaos. He had wisely chosen to observe Saul's elaborate celebration from afar. Although the *Yameen* had no inkling what would transpire, he learned to be suspicious of the volatile and unpredictable Samuel. Thus, Beker avoided being publicly humiliated by the prophet on the great platform along with the others. Killing the king's prize prisoner and dousing Saul in blood conveyed to Israel a greater denunciation than any words.

Yet Samuel seemed destined to forever remain a mystery to Beker. Time and again, the old man would grasp political power in one hand, only to toss it away with the other. The prophet's selection of Saul as king was inspired. The handsome warrior was an unknown from the smallest tribe in Israel. Thus, Saul was no threat to the other tribes and dependent on Samuel to retain his crown. But Beker felt that the prophet erred by trying to control the king's every move. The first time Saul tried to be his own man, Samuel retaliated by declaring God would replace the current dynasty with a different one. But later events seem to contradict the prophet. Against all expectations and without Samuel's help, Saul managed to overcome the Philistines and save his kingdom. Naturally, Beker expected the discredited Samuel to simply fade away from the public eye.

But the elderly prophet made an amazing comeback. He apparently surmised that Saul secretly desired reconciliation with the man who had anointed him king. So, Samuel brought his king the war with Amalek as a gift. To get back in God's good graces, all Saul had to do was obey Samuel's instructions. Instead of tossing the old man out of the palace, Saul embraced him. The prophet was back in charge and all was right in Heaven and Israel. Except that everything was wrong from Beker's perspective.

The *Yameen* saw no room for another *right hand* of the king, or even a *left hand* for that matter. Somehow, he must separate the king from his prophet. Fortunately for Beker, Samuel was consistent in one key habit: the man never compromised. If Saul deviated in any way from God's holy decrees regarding the Amalekites, history showed that Samuel would abandon him. Beker's path was clear. It was simple, almost inevitable. All he had to do was nudge Saul to take a shortcut at the proper time.

War is chaos, and chaos is full of opportunities for the open-minded. Samuel should have seen from the start that finding and killing every single Amalekite was an unlikely prospect. Naturally, Beker pointed out to Saul that he had already failed to meet God's primary requirement before the dust of the first battle had settled. This fact made it even easier for the *Yameen* to suggest that the king spare Agag. Besides saving the lives of his soldiers and collecting a ransom, Saul would be able to trot out a captive king whenever he wanted to impress other rulers. Rewarding the Army with sheep and cattle was almost an afterthought.

So Beker had started the day feeling confident. He knew roughly *what* Samuel might do, just not precisely *how* the old man would do it. But as he expected, the details did not matter. Beker would turn Saul's rejection into his own good fortune. The relationship between king and prophet was irretrievably broken. The king left the grand platform today as a pathetic figure.

Beker could work with that.

Nathan's Estate near Gibeah in Benjamite Territory

Judith recognized Nathan's distress before her husband even entered their home. Driven by his worries over the fate of the kingdom, Nathan had completed the normally three-day journey from Gilgal in only two. Judith immediately handed their son, Zabud, over to his grandmother, so she could tend to her exhausted husband. Once they were seated comfortably inside, Nathan began relating the sad events of Gilgal and all their implications. Judith absorbed this disturbing information in silence. She comforted Nathan with hugs to ease his anguish and by gently stroking his hand when he started to choke up. Once her husband seemed talked out, Judith leaned back and stared off into the distance for several moments. Nathan knew she was sorting through his jumble of facts before offering any advice. He had grown to expect, and treasure, such well-considered counsel from his seventeen-year-old wife.

And Judith did not disappoint him this time. She first insisted that Nathan do nothing on his first day back except eat, sleep, and recover his strength. Nathan laughed aloud when Judith said that he looked like a donkey had ridden him from Gilgal, instead of the other way around. She also encouraged Nathan with sound advice. Judith recommended taking advantage of the fact that the news from Gilgal had not yet reached Gibeah. As a prince of Israel, Nathan could summon the Royal Court the next day and reassure them about King Saul. Judith also suggested that Nathan send a personal message to her father. As commander of Judah's militia, Jephunneh could diffuse any panic before it spread across one of Israel's most powerful tribes. However, Judith insisted that everything could wait until tomorrow.

The wisdom of Judith's advice to rest and eat soon became apparent. Nathan dozed off on his couch shortly after his wife went to check on their son. He was awakened several hours later by the mouth-watering aroma of supper. Nathan enjoyed a pleasant meal with his wife, son, mother, and sister. Any hint of politics was quashed by a disapproving look from Judith. Afterwards, Nathan played vigorously with Zabud for an hour before Judith bundled the boy off to bed. Then fatigue hit him with a vengeance. Nathan staggered to his bedroom, pulled off his dusty tunic and washed in a basin of cool water. He extinguished the oil lamp just before crawling under the inviting sheets of the bed.

Just as Nathan was surrendering to blissful sleep, Judith came through the door and quickly closed it behind her. Nathan heard her rustling around in the dark for a moment before sliding into bed next to him. He reached for his wife and felt nothing but warm, soft skin.

"I thought I was supposed to sleep now."

"Oh, I promise you. You'll sleep well afterwards."

Judith then began a familiar refrain.

"*We are going to found a great house, You and I...*"

Nathan completed the verse.

"*And we will require many strong sons and beautiful daughters.*"

"Now Zabud is a wonderful child, but..."

"Let me make a prediction, Judith. You wish to start on our next child right now."

"Why, Nathan! You should be a prophet."

Chapter 16 – The Harp Player

Saul said to Samuel, "I have sinned. But please honor me before the people of Israel. Come with me and help me worship the LORD."

So, Samuel went with Saul to Gilgal. But then Samuel said, "Bring me Agag, the Amalekite king." Agag approached Samuel without fear, thinking "Surely I will not be killed now." But Samuel said, "As your sword has made other women childless, so shall I make your mother childless." Then Samuel killed Agag before the LORD at Gilgal.

Samuel returned to his home in Ramah. Samuel never went to see Saul again, although Samuel mourned for Saul for the rest of his life. And the LORD regretted making Saul the King of Israel.

From the book of I Samuel, chapter 15, verses 30 to 35

The Spirit of the LORD departed from Saul and the LORD sent an evil spirit to torment him.

From the book of I Samuel, chapter 16, verse 14

The royal palace in the Philistine city of Gath

King Achish steered his *Archon*, Abimelek, away from the fawning sycophants crowding his Palace's great banquet hall. They were supposedly all here to celebrate the beginning of their monarch's twelfth year on the throne of Gath. In reality, the attendees were drawn by the opportunity to improve their position within the pecking order of the Royal Court. It was an unavoidable game which all courtiers, including the king, must play. The game itself could never actually be won. Dropping out resulted in disgrace at the very least and possibly death in extreme cases. The goal was to simply keep on playing for the rest of your life. Literally. So Achish spent hours expressing gratitude he did not feel in response to praise his well-wishers did not mean. However, even a king could stand only so much hypocrisy. And Achish had learned to stand a lot.

The two men backed away from the noisy throng toward a large tapestry decorating the adjacent wall. So far, the self-absorbed courtiers had not yet noticed their king's stealthy retreat. Achish whipped aside the tapestry while Abimelek opened a hidden door through which they made their escape. As king, Achish could leave his own party whenever he wished, but only at a cost. Many unpleasant hours would be required to sooth injured egos and repair damaged relationships. Disappearing was much simpler. No one would dare to admit that he had taken his eyes from the king.

Achish's private chamber was small, but pleasantly furnished. The perfect place for a peaceful getaway or romantic liaison. There was even a secluded balcony from which Achish could view his capital city without being seen himself. His stewards had already laid out food and drink in anticipation of their king's needs. Achish plopped down on a couch and rubbed his aching feet. Only thirty-four years of age and he was already feeling old. Achish suspected his discomfort stemmed more from growing softer than growing older. Over twelve years had passed since Philistia's horrid military debacle at the hands of the Hebrews. Achish had been a dashing figure then, deploying his chariots to protect the Philistine retreat from Michmash. The five kings of Philistia scrambled to rebuild their shattered armies while the Hebrews went on a rampage against their other neighbors. In short order, King Saul subdued the Moabites, the Edomites, the Arameans and finally the Amalekites. Achish and his allies braced to receive the expected Hebrew onslaught. The Philistines waited. And waited. For ten years they had waited without as much as a Hebrew sling stone hurled their way.

The Kingdom of Gath did not waste this fortuitous period of peace. The thousands of boys originally recruited into Achish's depleted Army had grown up. Their sharp sticks replaced by iron weapons. The resourceful General Davon managed to train up five field regiments, reestablish the reserve regiment, restore the garrisons to full strength and expand Gath's prized chariots corps. However, training could go only so far. A decade of peace provided few opportunities to blood amateurs in battle. Like their king, Gath's soldiers had grown soft. The Hebrews might possess numerous shortcomings, but softness was not one of them.

The Hebrew threat was the real reason Achish wanted to talk privately with Abimelek. Getting away from the denizens of the Royal Court was merely a bonus. The disadvantage of meeting alone with his *Archon* was the petty disrespect Abimelek privately showed toward his king. It was the old man's way of not so subtly reminding Achish who had placed him on the Throne of Gath. Even now, Abimelek served himself a goblet of wine and took a comfortable seat as if his sovereign were not even present. The goblet was nearly to the *Archon's* lips before he noticed the king's harsh expression. Abimelek cocked his head to one side briefly, shrugged and handed the goblet to Achish. As Abimelek turned to serve himself again, Achish chose to overlook this minor discourtesy. Actually, it was an improvement over the *Archon's* typical behavior.

"What news have your spies gleaned from the Hebrews?"

"Their leadership is uneasy, Achish. Almost fearful."

"Of us?"

"Certainly not."

"Then who?"

"Their king."

"That's hardly worth reporting, Abimelek. People are supposed to fear their king."

"Achish, there is good fear and then there is bad fear. Apparently, Saul has managed to anger the Hebrew God. In return, this God is driving Saul mad. Rumors like that produce the bad kind of fear."

"Is Saul mad?"

"Of course. Madness is a requirement for the office of king."

This unexpected answer caused Achish to choke on his wine. *Was the old man taunting him with a bad joke?* Achish glared at his *Archon* and refused to be baited into an outburst. After a lengthy silence, Abimelek finally sighed and defended his answer.

"It is a matter of perspective. A king must do outrageous things which a normal person would shrink from. If anyone else in Gath behaved as you do, Achish, they would be considered mad. Yet your people not only expect a king to act this way, they demand it."

"You still have not answered my question about Saul."

"Yes, I did. It is not my fault you asked a poor question."

"Quit dodging me, you old scoundrel. Does Saul have a *debilitating* madness?"

"Since that is a better question, I can give you an even better answer. The issue is not whether *Saul* is debilitated as a king by his madness. It is whether *his kingdom* is debilitated by his madness. My answer to that is a definite YES."

"You could have just said that in the first place, Abimelek."

"And only confused you, Achish. We need not know if some god is driving Saul mad. We need only recognize that a growing number of Hebrews believe it."

"Does Kaftor understand how Saul is struggling? He's been itching for years to lead Philistia against the Hebrews."

"I have already passed this information on to Gaza through Kaftor's own spies. Undoubtedly, he will soon call for a meeting of the *Sarney*. I expect the other Philistine kings will appoint him as the War Leader."

"Why should Kaftor lead instead of me?"

"Because the Hebrews are demoralized, not impotent. An invasion can make them forget their other fears for a while. Kaftor will be lucky to crawl back to Gaza in one piece."

"You could be wrong, Old Man. Kaftor may be a buffoon on the battlefield, but Gaza has a few good generals. They might win despite their king."

"Remember your *deep strategy*, Achish. Allow Kaftor to become entangled in his own snare. Nurture the disunity of the Hebrews. Be patient. Your time will come. Then your revenge on Kaftor will be absolute."

King Saul's palace in Gibeah, Benjamite Territory

Beker, the self-appointed *right hand* of King Saul, paced restlessly that night in his quarters at the royal palace. He had concluded long ago that politics was merely a continuation of war by other means. Men would always compete for food, shelter, land and power. War was simply the most effective way to separate the winners from the losers. However, war was just too damned expensive to use all the time. The deaths of productive citizens, the sacking of cities, the burning of crops, killing of livestock and the expenditure of treasure would eventually bleed any nation white. Long periods of peace were necessary to recover strength for the next round. Yet the needs of people inevitably increased during the lull between wars. Something had to fill this void, thus politics was born. It was a field where Beker had few peers. He learned early on that shrewd bargaining, combined with deception, often achieved more than open warfare. That was why wars were measured in months while politics spanned lifetimes.

This was not to say that politics was a safe occupation. The risks of a political leader could be just as deadly as those faced by a military leader. Assassination, imprisonment and execution were hazards for all who gambled and lost. The difference was that political deaths occurred more discreetly than those on the battlefield.

Yet it was these same well-established political axioms which now vexed Beker that evening. Israel enjoyed peace during the decade since its victory in the Amalekite War. His chief rival Samuel had retreated into self-imposed exile. The king depended on his counsel more than ever. He ran Israel's government without challenge. It was a time when the *Yameen* should have flourished. Instead, Beker struggled daily to maintain not only his status, but also his life.

There were numerous reasons. The prosperity of Israel's peace was not widespread. The king's standard of living, a multitude of administrators, various building projects and a standing army sucked up vast resources from the twelve tribes. The result was a stable kingdom, but stability alone did not bring joy to its people. Beker cared little for the masses themselves, but he rode on their backs like a small boat at sea. A violent upheaval could sink him. The murmurings of discontented Tribal Elders were of the greatest concern to Beker. Many had never wanted a king and longed for the days of greater Tribal independence. So far, Beker had successfully quashed any budding rebellion by cajoling, threatening and bribing the troublemakers. Yet, the *Yameen* recognized these were only short-lived remedies, not true solutions. Truth be told, Beker was winning minor battles but still losing the political war.

Ironically, Beker had identified both the cause of his troubles and the cure for it several years ago. The *Yameen* faced a true paradox. The greatest threat to the Kingdom of Israel was the king himself. Saul's growing depression and bouts of paranoia alienated his allies and emboldened his enemies. Beker traced it all back to the king's final break with the Prophet Samuel. Instead of moving on, Saul had brooded over when the next *anointed one* would appear and challenge him for the Throne. Beker remembered how Saul had originally been reluctant to become a king. Now he clung to the crown like a drowning man to a rope thrown his way.

However, the obvious cure for the kingdom's malaise was both simple and impossible. Saul must be replaced. The thought brought no tears to Beker's eyes. The *Yameen* had hitched his career to a king who no longer seemed able to pull his share of the load. Beker would happily replace the Benjamite Saul with someone from Ephraim, perhaps even one of his own relatives. That was the simple part of the cure. The impossible part was the king's cousin, Abner. While the general ran the Royal Army with an iron fist, no one dared depose Saul.

No, the king's fate and his *Yameen's* ambition seemed inextricably bound together for the present. This realization cost Beker many sleepless nights searching for another way. He interviewed numerous candidates offering cures for Saul's moodiness: healers, priests, courtesans, even a sorcerer. None were suitable. He then moved onto possible distractions for a king such as wars, travels, and the pleasures of the flesh. The *Yameen* had rejected these just as quickly. Beker pondered partnering with Jonathan to control his erratic father, even if it meant sharing power with the prince. If all else failed, this would be his last resort.

One final thought cropped up to disturb Beker's sleep. The Prophet Samuel had returned to his previous occupations of itinerant teaching and judging occasional disputes. Since Samuel's unpredictability and ability to awe the peasants were always a threat, Beker kept him under observation. Last week, however, the old man managed to elude Beker's spy in Ramah and disappear for several days. Samuel had finally surfaced to conduct sacrifices in the hamlet of Bethlehem. The tiny village itself was of no consequence to Beker. The fact that it belonged the powerful tribe of Judah was.

Nathan's Estate in Gibeah, Benjamite Territory

Evenings in Nathan's household were usually both hectic and satisfying. Eleven years of fruitful marriage had blessed Nathan and Judith with three rambunctious sons and two exasperating daughters. Even with the assistance of his mother, the hours between supper and bedtime could often be an adventure. His boys, even the toddler, were truly gifted at finding opportunities for mischief. The girls were much more refined in their scheming despite being only six and four years of age. They managed to elevate playing adults off against each other into an artform. Nathan found he was especially susceptible to little girl charms.

The children were more manageable during the day thanks to Judith's organizational skills. Their home was surrounded by olive trees, vineyards, and sheep. Work opportunities existed in abundance. The two older boys were assigned to fetch and carry for the hired men. The girls performed similar services for their mother and grandmother. Even the two-year-old had his tasks, albeit ones which were more busy work than true productivity. Today he had happily spent hours digging up weeds in a patch where nothing else grew.

However, family discipline became more of a challenge at the end of a workday. All children possess an innate ability to sense when their parents' guard was down. Truth be told, Nathan enjoyed frolicking with his brood, sometimes causing Judith to swear she really had six children to look after. He would always regain his wife's favor by restoring order and shepherding his little flock to bed. Nathan's favorite time came later when he held Judith as they silently observed their sleeping offspring. They would then imagine their children growing into impressive men and women. Provided they somehow survived their childhood misadventures.

Family memories caused Nathan's thoughts to drift to his younger sister, Leah, and her newborn son. Her husband Eri was a promising young officer in the elite company known as the *Renegades*, hand-picked warriors who served as Prince Jonathan's bodyguards. As head of the family, Nathan was responsible for his sister's well-being. Two years ago, when Leah turned fifteen, Nathan had despaired of arranging a suitable marriage for his sister. The combination of the girl's headstrong nature and Nathan's high position in the kingdom had intimidated several acceptable suitors. The rest seemed interested only in a political marriage to advance their ambitions.

Then one day, Judith was startled when a disheveled Leah came home in a furious rage. It seems she had stumbled into a muddy ditch along a busy road and needed help getting out. The handsome Eri immediately came to her rescue, but then committed an unforgivable sin. He laughed at the dripping wet Leah. Desperate to regain her dignity, the flustered girl rebuked Eri for his rudeness. He continued laughing. Leah then informed him of how important her family was. He only laughed harder. His offer to escort Leah safely home was instantly rejected. Judith listened sympathetically that afternoon to her indignant sister-in-law. Judith also listened that evening. And the next morning. And the following afternoon. The perceptive Judith then advised Nathan to seek out this offensive young man. Leah and Eri were betrothed the following week.

The rest of his family were already asleep that night when Nathan heard the knocking. Good tidings rarely arrived this late, so Nathan made sure his sword was handy before unbolting the door. The room's oil lamp illuminated the threshold to reveal Prince Jonathan and Karaz the Hittite. Nathan ushered his friends to a table where all three seated themselves in silence. Jonathan and Karaz exchanged looks as if unsure who should speak first. Nathan took their hesitation as a bad sign.

"Well, this is a first. Only one thing could make both of you shut up. There's trouble with Saul."

"The kingdom is slipping from my father's grasp."

"Everyone knows that. What's Saul done now?"

Jonathan responded by sighing and lowering his head in frustration. Nathan knew Saul was no longer the bold leader who had rallied a divided people to destroy the invading Ammonites and thereby won the hearts of Israel. Nathan had witnessed firsthand Saul's shortcomings as king during the last Philistine invasion. Only Jonathan's initiative at Michmash had

327

saved the day. However, Saul salvaged his reputation in a rapid series of punitive actions against Israel's aggressive eastern neighbors. The victory over an ancient enemy, the Amalekites, was Saul's crowning achievement, but it also marked the beginning of the king's mental decline. After agonizing silence, Jonathan finally spoke.

"My father's behavior worsened three nights ago. Even Abner is worried."

"So, the great general has finally acknowledged what others have been whispering about for years. Saul suffers nightmares for days at a stretch. That didn't bother Abner. The king cries uncontrollably for hours at a time. That didn't worry Abner either. How could Saul get any worse?"

"My father spent last evening terrorizing his attendants with a dagger, until he collapsed in exhaustion."

"Now that would be worse."

"Abner wants to meet with us. To discuss ways to restore the king to full health."

"I'll wager, Jonathan, that's not all Abner wants. He's also looking for dupes to share the blame if Saul's mind collapses. Be honest, Jonathan. We *all* know the real cure for what ails Saul. Reconciliation with Samuel."

"Not going to happen, Nathan. Both are too stubborn. Believe me, I have tried for years."

"Personally, I don't trust the old codger. But it's Samuel or nothing, my Friend."

"I may have an alternative. It came to me last week when I observed a shepherd bedding his flock down for the night. Nathan, I need your help to pull it off."

King Saul's palace in Gibeah, Benjamite Territory

A week later, Nathan stood alongside a hopeful Jonathan and a cranky Abner outside the palace entrance. They were all peering towards an unlikely applicant for the job of savior of Israel.

"Is that scruffy youngster the one we've been waiting for? Doesn't look like much."

"He's here for his skill, Abner, not his appearance."

"Waste of time if you ask me. Which nobody did."

"Nobody had to. This was my father's idea."

"*Somebody* put him up to it."

"Why, Abner. I thought you knew everything."

This testy exchange between Abner and Prince Jonathan brought a fleeting smile to Nathan's face. He normally enjoyed the proud general being needled, but a great deal was riding on the approaching boy, perhaps an entire kingdom. King Saul was the lynchpin which held Israel's fledgling monarchy together. Under Saul's reign, Israel's traditional enemies trembled, and the Nation prospered. Yet the man had been gradually descending into madness ever since his acrimonious schism with the Prophet Samuel over a decade before. This crisis of leadership now united rival Royal Court factions in a frantic search for a cure for their king. So far, their unity had produced only failure.

Prayers, sacrifices, soothsayers, potions, charms, and ever more exotic remedies had been applied to Saul over the past few months. Most did nothing. A few made him worse. The last had nearly been fatal. That was why so much tension surrounded a sixteen-year-old youth this day. One more fiasco would likely cause Saul to forbid any more attempts at a cure.

Despite the prince's seeming indifference, Nathan knew Jonathan was behind this day's trial. It was rooted in his chance observation of a shepherd soothing nervous sheep with a song. And so, an idea was born...music for the king. A simple concept, but one difficult for Jonathan to suggest to his father. The two men had a fraught relationship ever since the Battle of Michmash. Credit for the victory had gone to Jonathan, not Saul. The insecure king had tried to kill the insubordinate prince. The army had sided with Jonathan and forced Saul to back down. Ever since, the king had been suspicious of his heir's intentions. Saul's declining mental state only deepened the rift.

Thus, Jonathan had approached Nathan for assistance last week. Two things were required. The first obviously was to locate an extremely gifted musician. The second was to recruit a suitable advocate to broach the plan to Saul. Jonathan already had his proxy in mind: Nathan's father-in-law, Jephunneh. Saul still possessed great respect for the commander of Judah's tribal militia. Jephunneh had been largely responsible for Saul's first military triumph over the Ammonites. The marriage of Nathan and Judith had made the two men practically family. Naturally, Nathan agreed to speak to his father-in-law on Jonathan's behalf.

Jephunneh did much more than consent to Jonathan's request. He also supplied the all-important musician. One of Jephunneh's old regimental commanders was a man from Bethlehem named Jesse. The retired warrior had eight sons, the youngest of which was a shepherd renowned for his skills with a harp, his melodic voice, and a gift for composing songs. Jonathan arranged for Jephunneh to visit the royal palace during a period when Saul was especially distressed. Although the prince thought it prudent to be absent, he sent Karaz as support for Jephunneh. The two veteran warriors were old friends and worked Jonathan's plan to perfection. When Saul seemed tormented, Karaz extolled the benefits of harp music. After the king asked for someone who played the harp well, Jephunneh stepped up to provide a glowing recommendation for the son of Jesse. The ailing king then sent an urgent summons to Bethlehem for the young man.

Three donkeys now came to a halt before the royal palace. The first two bore the king's messengers. A tall, rugged looking teenager wearing homespun clothing dismounted from the third. Nathan noted a young goat trailing behind the boy. He chuckled upon realizing the young bumpkin must have brought the scrawny animal as a gift for the king. A sobering thought suddenly drove all humor from Nathan's mind. Jonathan had wagered everything on Jephunneh's judgment. Could this boy's music be as impressive in a palace as it was in a sheep pen? They were all about to find out.

Ironically, Nathan realized that he was just as skeptical of this shepherd as Abner.

Jonathan's chiding voice brought Nathan out of his musing. He hurried after the prince into a chamber reserved for the king's private audiences. Nathan's eyes were immediately drawn to the center of the room where Saul sat upright on an elevated couch. Even seated, the king's head towered over everyone else's. The early hour, the limited attendance and the closed door emphasized the secrecy of this session. Nathan sensed that Saul struggled to maintain his composure. The king was pale and noticeably thinner than when he was first crowned. His face was lined with fatigue. There were dark shadows under his eyes, which stared down vacantly. Nathan was most alarmed by the way Saul's right hand trembled. Nathan's concentration was broken by the sound of the main door being opened, and then quickly closed.

Nathan turned to see Abner leading the shepherd across the room. The boy seemed tall for his age. He wore a sand colored tunic which was plain and worn, but clean. Both his hair and skin bespoke long exposure to the sun. The harp he carried looked surprisingly delicate in his rugged hands. While the young man had the look of a shepherd, Nathan doubted the powerful muscles in the young man's limbs came from merely prodding sheep across a pasture. While the young shepherd appeared slightly uncomfortable, he was not intimidated. His dark brown eyes darted swiftly around the room, noting everything. At Abner's direction, the young man advanced to within a few paces in front of Saul and waited to be introduced. The sound of his cousin's voice finally caused the king to look up from the floor.

"My Lord King, this is the musician that you requested. Jephunneh has vouched for his skill with the harp. His name is David, youngest son of Jesse, from Bethlehem. Whenever you..."

Abner stopped short as Saul held up his hand for silence. As the king regarded the young musician, his mood seemed to brighten ever so slightly. Still, it required some effort for Saul to respond with a single word.

"Play."

In the brief silence that followed, David looked anxiously toward Abner. However, the general had already blended into the small audience, clearly abandoning the boy to his own devices. Nathan felt a sudden twinge of sympathy for the young shepherd. After a tiring journey, this teenager had been thrust before his king and ordered to perform the most important music of his life. Nathan expected to hear some simple folk ballad or a local village tune. Nathan tensed as a worrisome thought crossed his mind. Who knew the effect that some random song might have on Saul? Nathan's jaw tightened as he waited for the outcome.

If David felt any fear, he hid it well. The boy closed his eyes and took a deep breath. Nathan could see the musician's lips moving soundlessly. *Was this a prayer?* As David opened his eyes, he softly strummed the harp for a few introductory chords and then began to sing.

"The LORD is my Shepherd..."

The song seemed to catch everyone in the chamber off guard. Nathan expected soothing music, but the beauty of David's voice was an unexpected delight. When he glanced at the king, Nathan thought that Saul seemed entranced by the performance. Relieved by the king's favorable reaction, Nathan's tension eased as, he too, allowed the pleasant sounds to wash over him. The subjects of the song were rather mundane: sheep, green pastures, cool waters, and the like. But combined with the gentle strumming of the harp and the young man's soothing voice, the effect was wonderfully comforting.

With scarcely a pause, David launched into one lovely song after another. The subjects were different, but Nathan discerned a common theme: God loved and protected his people. Nathan did not realize how relaxed he had become until he felt Jonathan's grip on his shoulder after the fourth song. Coming fully alert, he followed Jonathan's gaze to an amazing sight.

Saul was reclining on his couch in a peaceful sleep.

Jonathan allowed David to finish his fifth song before signaling for a pause. The chamber was completely silent as the anxious courtiers studied their king. Saul's chest continued to rise and fall smoothly with each breath as his body experienced its first true rest in days. There was calmness on his face not seen since the Amalekite debacle. An attendant gathered up a shawl to place over Saul's shoulders. Another began extinguishing all the oil lamps save one. Seeing that the king continued to slumber, the men noiselessly departed, except for a solitary servant remaining to watch over Saul.

Jonathan led Nathan, Abner, and David to a secluded corner of the palace. Nathan thought Abner wanted to say something, but probably was unsure of how much to reveal in front of the young outsider. David began to fidget nervously as the others stared at him without speaking. It was Jonathan who finally broke the awkward silence.

"Are all the shepherds of Bethlehem as musically gifted as you?"

David shyly lowered his eyes before answering.

"I could not say, my Lord. We play for the sheep, not each other."

Nathan could not help grinning at the young man's modest, but very shrewd, response. David's manners might still be rough, but he showed an innate intelligence and the ability to quickly adapt to new situations. Jonathan smiled to put the young man at ease.

"That notwithstanding, your talent is undeniable... and deeply appreciated. Who taught you to play? Who is the author of your songs?"

"As a child, I listened to my father play and then borrowed his harp until I could produce similar sounds."

"Remarkable. And the source of the songs you played today?"

"They are my own."

Interpreting Jonathan's amazed expression as disbelief, David hurried to justify his answer.

"My ideas come from the stories of our people, the words of Moses, and what I see of everyday life. I always carry my harp with me to the pastures where I have much time to compose and refine songs. Singing helps keep the sheep calm and manageable."

"Relax, David. I believe you. It is just surprising to see so much depth in one so young."

Nathan could see Abner growing uneasy with the direction this discussion was taking. After all, the general had been almost derogatory of David less than an hour before. Abner's next words were an obvious attempt to justify himself.

"It doesn't surprise me. Being a shepherd is easy. The boy obviously has a great deal of time on his hands."

Jonathan frowned at Abner's thinly veiled insult. Nathan also disapproved of any noble denigrating a commoner, a position Abner himself had until recently occupied. However, David appeared to be unaffected by Abner's callous words as he enthusiastically responded.

"Caring for a large flock of sheep is harder than most people expect, Sir. Sheep require a surprising amount of land for grazing, and they need to drink frequently. One must always plan the journey carefully and be prepared for the unexpected. Otherwise, your sheep will begin to die. The flock must trust their shepherd during a time of danger, or they will scatter before predators and become easy prey. Sheep can be incredibly stupid, so a good shepherd must be both attentive and patient. Above all, a shepherd must truly care for his flock or else he will lose it."

David paused and gazed into the distance, as if he were considering an idea for the first time.

"Actually, Sir, the job of shepherd is similar to a general leading an army."

The shocked look on Abner's face was priceless. Nathan stifled a giggle at the thought of Abner explaining why his job was more demanding than herding sheep. Jonathan was obviously fighting for self-control and barely winning. On the other hand, David appeared to be the very essence of innocence and humility.

Nathan suddenly found himself re-evaluating this David. Obviously much more than some peasant with a harp and a voice. His intelligence was undeniable. The efficient grace of his movements belied some military training. However, the shepherd's deft verbal sparring with Abner really caught Nathan's attention. Was David bold enough to tug on the beard of one of the most powerful men in Israel? And clever enough to get away with it? This hinted at a gift for politics, one that would only increase as the young man gained experience. Nathan found David to be both impressive...and potentially dangerous.

The small talk came to an end when Jonathan gestured for attention. He turned toward David and gave the young man a warm smile.

"David, today you have been made privy to a national secret...the king has been ill. Will you swear on your honor never to reveal what you have witnessed here? Not even to your family?"

"Of course, my Prince."

"That is good because you may yet have a significant role to play here."

"I don't understand."

"Your harp and your voice have the power to ease the king's suffering. David, if you were offered a position as the king's musician, would you accept it?"

Nathan watched David's reaction carefully. He could not hear a man's thoughts, but he was experienced at reading facial expressions. Nathan saw nervousness and trepidation in the boy, which was a good sign. The total lack of fear would have indicated a failure to truly understand the situation. Nathan also observed strength and determination. Yet it was something he did not see that was disturbing. David did not seem the least bit surprised to be offered a position at court. It was almost as if the boy did not know *what* was going to happen, but that he had expected *something* to happen. David's quick response seemed to confirm Nathan's suspicions.

"I would like to, my Prince. My only concern is my family. Would I be able to return home from time to time?"

"That is understandable. I assume that as the king's health improves, you will not be required to play for him as frequently. You may visit your family during those times."

"Then, I await the pleasure of the king."

"Excellent. You must be famished from your long journey. The chamberlain here will provide you with food and lodging. We will discuss your duties later."

Nathan heard Abner clear his throat for attention as David was led away.

"The boy may have a divine talent, but I worry about him being seen at Court every day."

"Why, Abner?"

"Rumors spread at the Royal Court faster than a plague of locusts. People will wonder why the king is being followed around by a shepherd with a harp. We need a better excuse than David is here to keep the king from going mad."

Nathan was forced to admit Abner had a very good point. A new face like David's would be noticed by the palace regulars almost immediately. They could not hide him in Bethlehem every time someone became curious. Nathan looked up at the sound of Jonathan chuckling to himself.

"Gentlemen, the answer is simple. Give David another job. A position that will not attract attention. One that allows him play for my father when the need arises."

Nathan thought Jonathan was on to something, but he still had to ask a question.

"Remember, Jonathan, we're talking about a shepherd boy here. Wouldn't it arouse suspicion when he suddenly appears on the royal lists?"

"It will appear to be a favor to the friend of a friend that ensures a clan's loyalty to the throne. Trust me on this, Nathan. If there is one thing which courtiers understand, it's political patronage."

"You already have a suitable job in mind for David, don't you?"

"I was thinking of making him an armor bearer to my father."

"But will he accept it?"

"It would be his dream position. Becoming a royal armor bearer would be a significant increase in status for a shepherd. He'll receive training in arms and tactics, learn court etiquette, be taught to read and write. Who knows how far a talented youth like him could go?"

While the other two men walked away satisfied, Nathan was still re-evaluating this most unusual of shepherds. Thinking back to the emotions he had seen on the young man's face, Nathan thought he could add one final attribute to David's list. Ambition.

Chapter 17 – The Champion

The Philistines sent out a champion from the city of Gath named Goliath. He was nine feet tall.

From the book of I Samuel, chapter 17, verse 4

The Army Encampment outside the Philistine city of Gath

Abimelek trudged along a dusty trail from the royal palace to the army barracks on the outskirts of Gath. He was accompanied by his usual contingent of four bodyguards, two preceding the *Archon* and two following. The clash of iron weapons echoed from the training area to which he had been summoned by King Achish. Abimelek soon observed scores of sweating men hounded by implacable sergeants. These hard-pressed soldiers were hurling javelins, performing sword drills, and launching volleys of arrows under the critical eyes of their officers.

Abimelek spotted King Achish standing beneath a shade tree near the javelin range. After dismissing his escort, the *Archon* sauntered over and stood beside his sovereign in sullen silence. He was miffed that Achish had brought him all this way on such a hot afternoon without any explanation. Abimelek recognized the small slight as part of the ongoing pissing contest between the two most powerful men in the Philistine Kingdom of Gath. Naturally, he would not give Achish the satisfaction of admitting his discomfort. In turn, the king gave no more notice to his *Archon* than he would a common servant. Abimelek was soon contemplating suitable payback.

"Ah! There they are."

Achish's words brought Abimelek out of his musings. He turned to see four soldiers approaching, each bearing sword, shield and javelin. None wore any armor or helmet. Although all four were impressive physical specimens, one stood apart from the others. The man was nearly half again as tall as his fellows. Now Abimelek's curiosity was piqued.

"Which one of you is Goliath?"

Achish's tone was playful as he asked his seemingly innocent question. The soldiers momentarily looked confused before all four began laughing at their king's jest. The giant sheepishly raised his hand.

"I thought so. Now to business. You all volunteered for my challenge. This will be a fight to the death. Goliath against the three of you, one at a time. The prize is a talent's weight of silver, more than five years of a soldier's wages. While there may be multiple survivors, there will be only one prize given. If any of you three slay Goliath, that man wins. Goliath must kill all three of you to win. No questions? Good. Now decide who enters the arena to fight Goliath first."

All traces of humor disappeared from the warriors' faces. Even Abimelek found their deadly seriousness to be infectious. Goliath strode directly to the crude training arena which was dug a foot into the ground and covered with a thick layer of sand. It was in the shape of a square fifteen yards long on each side. The other three competitors began casting lots to determine their order of combat. Obviously, going last against a fatigued giant would be most advantageous. Abimelek noticed an unusual quiet spreading through the army camp. Entire platoons of soldiers abandoned their training to watch the coming battle to the death. Their officers came with them. A few enterprising men even began accepting wagers on the outcome.

The first challenger now stood just beyond the edge of the arena. Abimelek assumed that the combat would commence as soon as he entered. Goliath firmed up his footing in the gritty surface on the opposite side of the arena. The giant held a javelin in his right hand, gripped an iron-rimmed wooden shield with his left arm and carried a sword sheathed on his left hip. The challenger was armed in a similar fashion. The man was extremely muscular, and Abimelek would have considered him a giant in other circumstances. Goliath crouched forward slightly while waiting for his opponent to make the first move.

Abimelek was surprised when the silent challenger suddenly charged forward at full speed. The man led with his shield, placing all his body weight behind it during the charge. His javelin was held high in anticipation of delivering a killing thrust. Goliath required barely a second to analyze his opponent's tactics and responded in kind. Abimelek's jaw dropped in amazement at the giant's speed. If the smaller man thought he would enjoy an advantage in momentum at the point of impact, he would be sorely disappointed.

The two fighters met shield to shield in a resounding crash. Goliath flattened the smaller man onto the sand while simultaneously thrusting his javelin into the challenger's unprotected throat. The battle was over in the blink of an eye. It was not until after Goliath pulled the javelin out of his victim that Abimelek realized he had forgotten to breathe. Achish directed two spectators to remove the loser's body from the arena, leaving behind only a bloody spot of sand to mark the man's defeat. When asked if he wished a few minutes rest,

Goliath took a long drink of water and indicated he was ready to continue.

The second challenger entered the arena more cautiously and skulked around the edge. Abimelek speculated that since a violent charge had failed, this man would force the giant to make the first move. A challenge which Goliath readily accepted. The big man dropped his shield, gripped his javelin tightly with both hands and sprinted forward five broad paces. Goliath then drew the javelin back with his right arm and placed all his body weight behind the weapon as he hurled it forward. The result was spectacular. Goliath's javelin splintered through the challenger's wooden shield, penetrated his exposed chest and pinned the hapless man to the ground. The second combat ended more rapidly than the first. Abimelek remembered to breathe this time.

Abimelek now studied the third and final competitor, who happened to be the smallest of them all. Amazingly, the man was lounging on a large rock casually watching Goliath extract his javelin from the loser's corpse. He seemed to be totally unconcerned by the rapid slaughter of his comrades. As Abimelek studied the man's face, he found eyes which were alert and discerning. The *Archon's* career, and sometimes his life, often depended on his ability to quickly evaluate people. He concluded the last challenger was a deep thinker and that little escaped his notice.

After Goliath's latest victim was unceremoniously hauled away, the third challenger gathered his weapons and strode confidently toward the arena. Unlike the first two men, he entered without pausing. Abimelek felt this simple variation caught Goliath slightly off guard, but the giant grinned when his opponent began charging forward. However, any resemblance to the first battle ended when the smaller man lofted his javelin toward Goliath's head. The giant was forced to break stride and use his shield to swat the missile to one side. Abimelek realized later this simple distraction was the turning point of the fight. The challenger had gained precious seconds to close with Goliath and draw his sword. The giant began thrusting his javelin forward only to have it repeatedly deflected by the smaller man's shield. Abimelek now saw why javelins worked best at a distance. Despite his size advantage, Goliath could not get enough leverage behind his jabs in such close quarters. The giant then attempted to hammer the smaller man into the ground with his shield. However, his agile opponent constantly shifted position to thwart both weapons.

A frustrated Goliath tossed his useless javelin aside and attempted to draw his own sword. Quick as a viper, the challenger used this small opening to strike. The giant howled as blood flowed from his left shin. Another scarlet trickle appeared on his right thigh before Goliath had his sword in hand. Yet, the giant's blade did him little good. The smaller man danced away from each thrust and then counterattacked as the big man pulled his sword back. When a third wound appeared on Goliath's sword arm, Achish intervened.

"This is not what I asked for. No more delays. No more retreating. You will both close and finish this fight. Now!"

Abimelek barely managed to keep the smile off his face. Earlier, he had searched for a way to put the upstart king in his place. Now he found it.

"My King, will you also issue such an instruction to Goliath's future opponents?"

Achish's angry face turned a satisfying shade of purple. Abimelek was almost relishing the expected outburst when the king's expression unexpectedly turned thoughtful. Achish signaled the two fighters to stand down and drew near enough to Abimelek to whisper.

"Are you just taunting me, Old Man? Or do you have something useful to say?"

"If you are grooming Goliath to be your personal champion, I might."

"You know I am, but I must first see if he is worthy."

"Then stop this contest."

"Why?"

"If the fight continues, one of these men will die. You need them both."

"Again, why?"

"As formidable as Goliath is, he still has flaws. That little soldier understands the giant's weaknesses. The answer is obvious. *Pair* them together. One will be your champion, and the other will be his trainer."

Abimelek crossed his arms while Achish silently absorbed the suggested strategy. At a sign from the king, a flurry of servants descended on the shady spot bearing tables, a chair, food, and wine. Once Achish was seated, he invited both fighters to join him. The two soldiers looked at each other, shrugged and tossed their weapons aside. Seeing the entertainment was at an end, cursing sergeants began hustling their spectating troops back to the training fields. Abimelek was amused as Goliath hoisted a large jug of wine and drained it without pausing to breathe. The giant even ignored the team of healers as they began stitching up his wounds. The *Archon* noted that the other soldier drank more circumspectly, never taking his eyes from Achish. He obviously sensed that his life depended on the king's next words. Even Abimelek felt the tension until Achish spoke.

"What is your name, Soldier?"

"It is Ashron, my King."

"You fight well. Can you teach others to fight as well as you?"

"Depends on the student, my King."

"What about Goliath?"

"Most certainly, my King. There is *much* I can teach him."

Ashron's arrogant words earned a profane response from Goliath. Abimelek could not hear Ashron's whispered retort, but whatever it was, it made the giant laugh. The *Archon* took this soldierly banter as a good omen that the two men could work together. Apparently, so did Achish. He gestured for his chamberlain to come over to receive instructions.

"Goliath and Ashron are to be added to my household guard but will report directly to me. Assign them the best staff quarters and mess privileges. Provide them with any weapons, armor, and training facilities which they request. Send their expenses to Abimelek for payment."

"Yes, my King."

"Now here is what I expect from my new personal killers. Ashron, you will train up Goliath to be my champion. Prepare him for single combat to the death. The challenge could take place next month or next year. The time, place and circumstances do not concern you. Your job is to be ready at a moment's notice. *Both* your lives will depend on Goliath's success. Is that understood, Ashron?"

"I appreciate your clarity, my King."

"In return, you will enjoy all the benefits of palace life. But abuse my trust, and both your heads will be staked over the city gates. Questions?"

"What about the silver, my King?"

"What silver, Ashron?"

"My King, we were promised a talent's weight of silver for winning today's contest."

"But you did not win. Neither did Goliath. I spared you both."

"We didn't ask you to change the rules, my King. That was your choice."

Abimelek turned away to avoid chuckling at the perplexed look on the king's face. They both should have expected such a bold demand from Ashron. It was the man's nature, the reason he was the perfect tool for Achish's scheming. Ashron would have Abimelek's respect, provided the man survived the next few minutes. What happened next may have saved Ashron's life. Goliath moved beside his new partner, folded his arms, and glared at the king. While Achish might find another trainer, the giant would be difficult to replace. A smile slowly creased the king's face as he summoned the chamberlain once more. Abimelek recognized Achish had chosen the easy solution.

"Give a talent's weight of silver to each of them."

Both soldiers bowed deeply and departed with the chamberlain without further complaint. Ashron might be bold, but he was not stupid. Abimelek expected the combination of Ashron's brain with Goliath's body to be unbeatable. But for what? The *Archon* failed to see what Achish hoped to gain.

"You realize, Achish, that the *champion's challenge* has not been used in generations by our people. Too many of the losers would renege on the agreement."

"But it would be a new concept to the Hebrews."

"I doubt even they would accept it."

"Do not be so short sighted, Abimelek. With Goliath, I plan to win a *champion's challenge* whether the Hebrews accept it or not."

"I would enjoy seeing how that works, Achish."

"Oh, you will. Goliath will carry out only the first part of my scheme. You, my dear *Archon*, will handle the second part."

Chapter 18 – The Valley of Elah

Now the Philistines made their encampment at Ephes Dammim, between Socoh and Azekah. They then assembled their army for battle at Socoh in the territory of Judah. Saul and his soldiers camped in the Valley of Elah and formed their battle line opposite the Philistines. The Philistine army occupied a hill on one side of the Valley and the Israelite army occupied another hill on the other side.

From the book of I Samuel, chapter 17, verses 1 to 3

The Israelite Army Encampment on the Northern Slope of the Valley of Elah

Nathan strode briskly through the crisp morning air to the commanders meeting in the king's tent. He had kissed Judith and the children farewell five days ago in Gibeah before departing for the Valley of Elah. Rode a donkey for two days escorted by fifteen elite *Renegades* from Prince Jonathan's bodyguard. Spent a day organizing patrols and finding a suitable site for the army to camp. Argued with General Abner and his officers the following day about the patrol strategy and the choice of campsite. Praised God yesterday when Jonathan finally arrived with King Saul, and *they* took over arguing with Abner. Nathan knew only one thing could cause this much chaos and confusion.

The Philistines were on the move.

The last Philistine invasion had been narrowly beaten back at the battle of Michmash largely thanks to Prince Jonathan's boldness. Thousands of Philistine soldiers had been killed during the subsequent retreat with most of their horses and chariots being destroyed. Some hotheads had urged an immediate attack on Philistia to wipe out Israel's most hated enemy for all time. Fortunately, calmer thinking prevailed. The Philistines might have been battered and bloodied, but they were still the most formidable military force in Canaan. So, after thirteen years of licking their wounds, the Philistines were back under new leadership.

Israel's security was based on the mountainous spine running from north to south through its heartland. Philistine chariots might be the masters of the coastal plains, but this rugged terrain rendered them impotent. Access opportunities for invading armies were limited to a small number of defensible passes. The Valley of Elah was one such route. Starting at their city of Gath, the Philistines could easily traverse the Judean foothills known as the *Shephelah* and move east into the Valley. Judean militia in Azekah had detected the Philistine vanguard last week. When their report reached Gibeah a day later, panic ensued at the royal palace.

Two *Renegade* scouts were just beginning their reports as Nathan lifted the tent flap to enter. King Saul slouched in the only chair in the room with Prince Jonathan standing to his right and General Abner on his left. Nathan joined the other leaders gathered around the scouts. He nodded greetings to his father-in-law, Jephunneh, and the Hittite mercenary, Karaz. Jephunneh was the leader of Judah's militia and a temporary member of the War Council since the Philistine incursion was taking place in his tribal territory. Abner's three hand-picked regimental commanders ignored him, and Nathan returned the favor. Everyone listened dispassionately to the reports. Arguments would wait until the commoners had departed the tent.

The Philistines appeared to be setting up a base camp near Ephes Dammim, a few miles into the Valley of Elah. The first three enemy regiments to arrive bore the colors of Gaza, an indication that its king was the leader of the expedition. This was a bit surprising since Kaftor of Gaza was considered more of a politician than a warrior. At least one infantry regiment had been identified from each of the Kingdoms of Ekron, Ashdod and Ashkelon in the days which followed. Curiously, all the chariots wore the livery of Gath, but the horsemen lacked any supporting infantry from Gath. Additional military units and supply caravans had been spotted on the road, but the Philistines already in the Valley still outnumbered Israel's three army regiments by better than two to one.

After dismissing the two *Renegades*, the king asked for comments. Nathan noticed Abner made the mistake of taking a deep breath before speaking. This small delay provided the wily Karaz with all the opening he needed.

"Overall, my King, we're in pretty good shape."

"I hardly think the Philistines would agree, Karaz."

"Doesn't matter. Where can they go? What can they do?"

"They could conquer the entire Valley of Elah."

"But *they can't get out of it*, if we don't let them."

"The people who live there will suffer depredation."

"Not if you get them out first. Burning their crops would also be a good idea. They're already lost to the Philistines.

Besides, you have a good-sized treasury, my King. Make it up to them later."

"You are very generous with my gold, Karaz."

"It's still the cheapest way to defeat the Philistines. They'll go home when they get hungry."

"And what if they keep going east instead?"

"We should be so lucky. They'll just stick their heads farther into the noose. Then we can bag them all!"

There followed an uncomfortable silence as Saul began to stare off into space. Soon the commanders started to fidget while impatiently waiting for their king to provide guidance. Finally, Abner cleared his throat for attention. Nathan knew the proud general must be aggravated by Karaz stealing much of his thunder. He was curious to see how Abner regained the initiative in this discussion without contradicting Karaz's facts.

"The Hittite may be insensitive to our people's suffering, my King, but I can make two predictions based on his observations. First, we cannot drive the Philistines out of the valley. Second, I can turn the valley into a trap."

"How would you do that, Cousin?"

"By establishing a chain of camps along the northern side of the valley. An infantry company will be assigned to block each of the small passes and raid the enemy supply lines. If the Philistines try to force a passage, I'll send enough reinforcements to contain them."

"And if they choose to go through passes on the southern side?"

"They won't, my King. That direction leads only to mountains and desert."

"So, Abner, the Philistines come from the west. We block them to the north. They will not choose to go south. That still leaves the east."

"That is why I propose we establish our main encampment on the northern slope opposite the town of Socoh. The Philistines will see us and be forced to stop halfway into the Valley. If they attack, we'll retreat slowly up the steep slope and make them pay for every foot of ground until they quit. If they try to slip past us, I will advance and cut off the head of the snake."

"And if the enemy chooses to remain in Socoh?"

"As the Hittite has already observed, they will get very, very hungry."

Despite his aggressive instincts, Nathan found himself nodding in approval of the general's cautious strategy. The Philistines had murdered Nathan's father. Normally, he would have favored attacking Israel's most hated enemy as soon and for as long as possible. Yet while Abner might be full of himself, but the man was still a competent military leader. Nathan hoped that a Philistine retreat might still offer opportunities for a slaughter. After polling the other commanders, Saul endorsed his cousin's plan. The meeting was adjourned so the necessary orders could be issued to the army units. Upon exiting the tent, Nathan was pulled aside by Jonathan.

"What did you think of my father's performance today?"

"Seemed calm and reasonable to me. He asked thoughtful questions and accepted good advice."

"He was passive, Nathan, much too passive. When my father had the chance to make decisions, he hesitated. A king needs to lead, not let subordinates make the hard choices for him."

"You can't be upset just over this one meeting, Jonathan. There's more, isn't there?"

"My father often seems distracted when I speak with him. I'm not the only one to notice. Rumors are spreading that the king is frequently forgetful, unsure of himself and insecure."

"I thought your harp-playing shepherd was curing him of all that."

"He was. That's the problem. David is not around enough anymore."

"He's just a peasant, Jonathan. The boy can't wander off when the king needs him."

"Not David's fault. He's officially an armor bearer. That puts him under Abner's authority."

"And Abner never wanted him here in the first place."

"Neither does Beker, our illustrious *Yameen*. They keep David in Bethlehem unless the king becomes violent. I fear they conspire to keep my father dependent on them."

"Like today. Saul approved everything Abner asked him to."

"Like every day, Nathan. My father used to be a bold ruler. Now he desires plans with no risk, where he has to do nothing."

The Philistine Army Encampment at Ephes Dammim at the western end of the Valley of Elah

King Achish grinned as the last of his chariot companies roared into the Philistine compound. Gath was providing over five hundred chariots as its contribution to Kaftor's grand expedition. The other four Philistine kingdoms had not yet fully recovered from their chariot losses at Michmash, just as Gath's infantry was still rebuilding. Achish owned many more chariots, but it made little tactical sense to bring a greater number into the narrow Valley of Elah. Five hundred were more than enough to screen the advance of the Philistine army from Hebrew militia. It was also a force which Achish could swiftly withdraw if disaster struck.

Kaftor, King of Gaza, had spent over a decade cajoling, bribing and bluffing the Philistine council known as the *Sarney* into authorizing a punitive campaign against the Hebrews. His promises as War Leader proved irresistible. The humiliation of Michmash avenged. New territory added to Philistia. A troublesome foe crippled. Kaftor had assembled an overwhelming force which the Hebrews dare not face in a pitched battle. His regiments would sweep through to the Dead Sea and cut Judah off from the rest of Saul's kingdom. Kaftor then planned to swarm down over the Judean foothills and plains. The Hebrews' largest tribe would be strangled and reduced to a Philistine vassal state.

Yet for all its ambition, Kaftor's strategy was both mediocre and unimaginative. A hammer applied to a compliant nail. It was everything Achish could hope for.

Gath was the closest of the Philistine kingdoms to this battlefield. Achish's spies had secretly made a careful survey of the terrain in the Valley of Elah. He already recognized the flaws in Kaftor's strategy that would become agonizingly obvious to the other four kings over the coming days. The Hebrews were neither fools nor cowards. They would not march into the open to be slaughtered. They would not flee from Kaftor's mighty horde. No, the Hebrews would choose a third option. They would be patient.

All the Hebrews needed to do was to block the few narrow passes out of the valley. This would deny the Philistine foraging parties access to the local harvests. They could wait until the Philistine supply lines were overextended, cut them and thereby trap the invaders. However, Achish did not expect things to go that far. Once Kaftor's folly became apparent to all, the Philistines would simply make an embarrassing retreat. The King of Gaza would have conquered his way to nowhere.

However, Achish and the Kingdom of Gath would emerge as the true victors, albeit unrecognized ones. Kaftor's ambitions for Gaza to dominate Philistia would be in shambles. The other three Philistine kingdoms would be demoralized. The table would be set for Achish to assume leadership of the five Philistine kingdoms, before molding them into an empire. His empire. His father's dream turned into reality. Then Kaftor would suffer for the murder of Achish's father.

Of course, there was a chance that Kaftor would remain in denial regarding his blunder. The King of Gaza might stubbornly dig in for weeks just to save face. Achish hoped so. It would allow him to use a ploy he had been nurturing for months. One which would earn him even more power at the expense of the Hebrews. The first part depended on a giant. The second part involved the considerable diplomatic skills of his *Archon*, Abimelek.

Which was why Achish felt annoyed at the urgent request for a meeting from Goliath's trainer, Ashron. The fact that a king was expected to come to a commoner's tent sounded ominously like a summons. It showed little gratitude for the great wealth lavished on this special pair of fighters. He found both men waiting under a large fabric canopy outside their shared quarters. Remembering how crucial Goliath might be to the end game, the King of Gath calmed himself as he approached. However, Ashron's impertinent greeting nearly unhinged Achish.

"What's this *junk*?"

Such rudeness from a menial shocked the king into silence. Achish's eyes numbly followed Ashron's accusing finger toward a collection of highly polished metal artifacts carefully laid out on an expensively woven rug. A large skillfully forged bronze helmet. A coat of bronze scale armor weighing nearly one hundred and fifty pounds. Bronze greaves crafted to protect shins over two feet long. An iron rimmed, wooden shield five feet in diameter. A sleek bronze javelin. A ten-foot-long wooden spear which was thicker than a man's arm and capped with a fifteen-pound iron tip. Achish viewed these deadly implements with pride and admiration. They were not just weapons of war, but works of art. The perfect tools for his plan with Goliath. Yet for some insane reason the giant looked just as displeased as his trainer. Achish answered Ashron through clenched teeth.

"Armor. Expensive armor. For Goliath."

"Too bad about the cost, my King, but I never asked for it."

"You never...you seem confused about a few things, Ashron. I am the king. I tell you what to do. You do it."

"I thought you wanted Goliath to win your challenges. Then you provide equipment to ensure he loses them. You are correct, my King. I am confused."

"Let us take a step back, Ashron. Why do you disapprove of these weapons?"

"You asked me to make Goliath a better fighter. His greatest weakness then was an agile opponent at close quarters. I improved his tactics, his footwork, and the way he handles weapons. Now he defeats me two out of three times. We also prepared strategies for opponents who try to engage him at long range with missiles such as javelins, arrows or sling stones."

"Impressive. I am pleased."

"Yet, Goliath's success ultimately depends on one thing. Speed. Give Goliath a light shield, a sword, and a javelin. He'll destroy any man who challenges him up close. Or Goliath can swiftly close with an opponent keeping his distance. He'll deflect missiles with his shield until he either skewers his foe with the javelin or cuts him down with the sword."

"Then Goliath should be even more dangerous clad in this armor. It will make him *invulnerable*."

"No, my King. It will make him *more vulnerable*. I've made Goliath faster. That pretty armor will slow him down and undo everything I've achieved. Someone like me will wear him down until he's exhausted. An archer will keep launching arrows from a distance until he eventually finds a weak point."

"You really think it makes that big a difference, Ashron?"

"Try to pick up that coat of armor, my King. It weighs more than you do."

"There are things you do not know, Ashron. Plans within plans. What if I told you that I *do not want* Goliath to fight? I may be able to achieve my goals if he simply looks so formidable that no one will challenge him."

"Then you must make a choice, King Achish. A deadly killer or a pretty statue. You can't have both."

"I choose for Goliath to be a walking fortress. Your job is to make him an effective one."

"You are the king. You tell me what to do. I do it. But I must ask for a change in our arrangement."

"In what way?"

"You implied once that if Goliath died, so would I. I was willing to stake my life on my methods. It's not fair to force me to use yours."

"So be it, Ashron. My methods, my responsibility. You will help Goliath adjust to his new armor. In place of your life, a talent's weight of gold if he succeeds. For both of you."

Ashron quietly sighed as King Achish turned on his heel and walked away. Royals could be so fickle. He had done as Achish asked only to be burdened with this cursed armor. Fortunately, the king was in a good mood today and modified their agreement in Ashron's favor. Achish could just as easily be in a bad mood next week and have him executed. Ashron seriously considered for a moment whether desertion and exile might be his best options. Instead, he tossed the oversized helmet to Goliath.

"Come on, Big Guy. We've got work to do."

Chapter 19 – The Challenge

Goliath shouted to the soldiers of Israel as they stood in their ranks, "Did you come out here to fight? I am a Philistine. You serve Saul. Choose your best man and have him fight me. If he kills me, we will surrender to you; but if I kill him, you will surrender to us. This day I defy the Army of Israel! Give me someone to fight!"

After hearing the Philistine's words, Saul and all his soldiers became discouraged and terrified.

From the book of I Samuel, chapter 17, verses 6 to 11

Day 39 in the Israelite Army Encampment in the Valley of Elah

How could a strategy which seemed so promising turn into such a calamity?

Nathan gritted his teeth in frustration as he stomped toward the daily commanders' meeting. Less than six weeks ago, the Israelites thought they held the upper hand over the Philistine invaders. Soldiers blocking the exit passes confined the enemy to the Valley of Elah. People and animals were evacuated. The storage barns emptied. The green crops were left in the fields, but they were useless to Philistine bellies until they ripened. The Royal Army of Israel occupied a fortified hill halfway through the Valley at Socoh, daring the Philistines to advance. The enemy was forced to choose between fighting a costly battle, retreating, or starving. Faced with these unpleasant options, their invasion had stalled.

But since the Philistines were halted, nothing had gone as the Israelites expected. The Philistines did not attack. They did not retreat. Their enemies may have gotten a little hungry, but they did not starve. Instead they decided to wait out the Israelites. For over five weeks, the soldiers on both sides of the Valley of Elah formed up for battle at each sunrise. They spent the day staring at each other before returning to camp at sunset. Things did improve somewhat for the Israelites after the second week. Several of the Philistine kings grew impatient and took their regiments home. That still left five infantry regiments from Gaza and a few hundred chariots from Gath. Unfortunately, they still greatly outnumbered Saul's army. The smaller Philistine force was also easier to supply. They required fewer caravans from Philistia, which could be more heavily protected. This stalemate might have continued indefinitely, except the Israelites had been ambushed by the unexpected.

In the form of a nine-foot-tall giant.

The armored monster called Goliath appeared every morning after the armies assembled and every evening before they dispersed. The giant strutted menacingly up and down the battle lines. He mocked Saul and his soldiers as cowards for refusing battle. Goliath offered to fight any champion the Israelites might choose. Winner take all. The army of the loser would surrender. No one else need die. Nathan immediately recognized a fool's bargain when he heard one. Goliath, though huge, was just a common soldier. What value did his promises carry? Let the Philistine kings themselves come forth and make a serious offer to King Saul. Nathan suspected the Philistines were even less likely to honor such an agreement than the Israelites were. However, he soon recognized how insidious the Philistine strategy was.

Goliath was counting on most men being unwilling to die if there is a way to avoid it. The giant offered such a hope with his challenge. King Saul could let his soldiers off the hook by sending a champion to do the fighting, and possibly the dying, for everyone else. Surrender? That was a problem for kings, not commoners. The Israelite soldiers' fear slowly festered into resentment against their leaders. Day by day, their morale sagged.

Up to now, Nathan had not been overly worried by Goliath's antics. The Philistines showed little inclination to fight, even with a giant on their side. The level of fear among the Israelite troops was troublesome, but not fatal. They still occupied a strong defensive position. Nathan felt certain that most men could still find their courage if the Philistines came charging up the slopes. However, a single message today from the tribe of Judah changed everything for Nathan. It was the reason for his late arrival to the meeting. He lifted the flap to Saul's tent bearing tidings of disaster. Fear of Goliath had spread beyond the Valley of Elah.

"My King, I must speak!"

Nathan's abrupt entry had interrupted Abner in mid-sentence. He sensed anger from the general, indignation from the regimental commanders and confusion from King Saul. Only Prince Jonathan and the Hittite mercenary Karaz seemed curious about what Nathan might say. Jonathan whispered something to his father while Abner fumed. The prince's words caused Saul to hush his cousin and then signal Nathan to speak.

"I bear a message from my father-in-law, Jephunneh. A delegation of Judean Elders left for Gath three days ago. They were invited by that kingdom's *Archon* Abimelek to negotiate an alliance between Philistia and the tribe of Judah. Jephunneh believes they intend for Judah to become a vassal state to the Philistines."

Nathan thought he could hear his own heart beating in the ensuing silence. When all eyes turned to the king, Saul froze in his chair. Jonathan again whispered in his father's ear. After the king nodded numbly, Jonathan turned to Nathan.

"Why is Jephunneh not present?"

"He departed immediately for Judah in hopes of containing the damage done by these traitors. They represent only a minority, but the chaos caused by their actions could bring down the entire tribe."

"I assume your information is reliable, Nathan."

"It originated with my mother-in-law. A tribal elder who refused to join the conspiracy told her everything. Rumors are spreading that Saul is afraid to fight the Philistines. Supposedly he will offer them Judah to save the rest of his kingdom."

"Rumors spread by Philistine spies no doubt."

"The handful of Judean elders going to Gath feel abandoned by Saul. They want to save lives and get better terms."

"Was there anything else?"

"Yes. Unless the king attacks the Philistine army in the Valley of Elah in two days, those Judean Elders will surrender."

"Thank you, Nathan. This changes everything. We must..."

"It changes *nothing*!"

Nathan turned in shock with the others to behold the previously lethargic Saul foaming in a rage. Jonathan faltered momentarily after being interrupted by His father. Nathan sensed the prince was torn between saving the kingdom and protecting his father's dignity. However, this time when Jonathan tried to whisper to the king, Saul angrily shoved his son away. The prince looked to the other commanders for support, but none wished to get entangled in this royal squabble. Nonetheless, Jonathan forged ahead alone.

"We thought to tie down the Philistines here until they gave up. It is not working. Instead our soldiers have been losing heart for weeks. Now their fear spreads through the rest of Israel like a plague. Father, you must act now, before your kingdom crumbles."

"Oh, you would like some action, Jonathan. Wouldn't you? A chance to win the hearts of the army. Again. Save the nation. Again. Embarrass your father. AGAIN!"

"I apologize for speaking out of turn, Father. What do you propose?"

"I'll start with what we will *not* do. We will not attack the Philistines across the valley. They outnumber us, and their position is too strong."

"True, in daylight we have no chance. But a night attack gives us an edge. It is our people's specialty."

"Don't you think the Philistines know that, Jonathan? They have been expecting a night attack from the very first day.

Without the element of surprise, my army would be slaughtered."

"I ask again, Father. What do you propose?"

"First, I will snuff out this treason in Judah. Round up the conspirators. Arrest their families. Seize their lands. Execute the traitors. My *Yameen* Beker will know what to do."

"And then?"

"Seek a volunteer to fight Goliath. I'll offer the man wealth, one of my daughters in marriage, even freedom from taxes for his family. Everyone will say I made a good attempt to find a challenger."

"About time, too. And you can keep your gold, Father. I will fight Goliath."

"Not you, Jonathan. Not Abner. No one from the royal family. Not even Nathan. Losing to the giant would shame our family more than a few traitorous Judeans."

"It's too late for anyone else! You might have found some volunteers a few weeks ago. Now our men piss themselves whenever that giant glances their way. Do you really expect any of them to accept your offer?"

"No, but it will put the shame on them, not me. Israel cannot blame the king if their own soldiers are cowards."

"You really don't want someone to kill Goliath, Father. You never did. Why?"

"The reason has been obvious to me ever since that ungodly monster first appeared. Don't you see, Son? The man who could defeat Goliath could one day claim my crown."

"Very clever. Your plan was never to win. It was simply not to lose."

"Oh, we will be victorious, just not on the battlefield. By standing fast here in the Valley of Elah. By executing traitors. That, my Son, is how I will save Judah, my kingdom and my crown…from anyone and everyone."

The stunning revelations of the past few minutes threatened to overwhelm Nathan's mind. Saul's display of paranoia toward Jonathan was disturbing. His willingness to execute frightened people was cruel. The king's refusal to take military action was negligent. Yet they paled in comparison to Saul's thoughts on Goliath's challenge. The king was more frightened of an Israelite who could defeat Goliath than he was of the giant himself.

Saul dismissed everyone from the tent except his cousin Abner. No doubt the two were planning the fate of the supposed traitors. Nathan determined to send a message to Judith, so his wife could warn people to go into hiding until the crisis passed. He was not surprised to find an anxious Jonathan waiting nearby. Nathan followed the prince to where his bodyguard known as the *Renegades* camped. It was also the most secure place for a potentially seditious conversation. And Jonathan did not disappoint him.

"Nathan, I must save my father from himself. The kingdom as well."

"Sounds like treason."

"Does that frighten you?"

"Never has before. Let's get Karaz and make a plan."

"What I have in mind might be too radical for Karaz."

"*Now* you are scaring me, Jonathan."

"We must move quickly. If those foolish elders form an alliance with the Philistines, Judah will fall into civil war. Killing them afterwards won't stop that. So, any preventative action must take place tomorrow. That means everything must be prepared tonight. I don't have time to argue with Karaz."

"I hope it's not just the two of us again."

"No, Nathan. I'm going to use the *Renegades* too."

"Still, we can't defeat the Philistines with only eighty-four men. That leaves someone challenging Goliath. You?"

"There's no other choice. Think you can find another man who could defeat Goliath and not be a threat to my father? It has to be me."

"You might be dead either way, Jonathan. If Goliath doesn't kill you, Saul might do it out of jealousy."

"I may have a way around that, my friend. After all, challenging Goliath and fighting him are two different things."

Day 39 in the Gazan Encampment in the Valley of Elah

How could a strategy which seemed so promising turn into such a calamity?

Kaftor, King of Gaza, ground his teeth as he slunk back into his tent at the end of another wasted day. Another expensive day, too. Five thousand soldiers collecting a daily war bonus for staring at the enemy. Paying triple the normal costs to haul in provisions. A decade of careful preparation was coming to naught before his eyes.

His campaign into the Valley of Elah had begun so well. The powerful army under his command advanced without opposition as the Hebrews simply melted into the hills. Large areas of rich farmland fell under his control. Then came the stalemate. The Philistine vanguard finally stumbled across the Hebrew army occupying an unassailable hill halfway into the Valley. Kaftor set up camp there at Socoh and waited in vain for King Saul to give battle. Frustrated, Kaftor sent a regiment into the foothills to try to outflank his foe. After taking over a hundred casualties in the narrow passes, Kaftor's men returned empty handed.

The other Philistine kings refused to advance further with the enemy army in position to block their way home. They grumbled openly about Kaftor's failure to foresee Saul's defensive strategy and his inability to cope with it. One by one, the other kings began departing with their infantry. First, Ashkelon, then Ekron and finally Ashdod. Only the King of Gath remained with his chariots. In fact, Achish had provided the only Philistine tactic which seemed to discomfort the Hebrews. The man's use of his giant was as much a political stroke of genius as it was a military one. The Hebrew soldiers could actually be seen cringing when Goliath came within one hundred yards of their battle line. Yet bullying a few enemy foot soldiers was not enough to prevent Kaftor's position from growing steadily weaker.

After standing in formation day after day, awaiting a battle which never came, discipline in the Army of Gaza grew ever more slipshod. Two weeks ago, Kaftor admonished his commanders because many soldiers were mustering for the daily confrontation without their armor. Things improved for a few days, only to get worse. Now he estimated that over half his troops had marched from their tents that day without armor. Kaftor even witnessed a platoon of soldiers laughing at their lieutenant when he ordered them to fetch their equipment. The Hebrews might lack courage, but poor morale hampered his army.

As he poured himself a goblet of wine, Kaftor wondered whether the giant was a blessing or a curse. Perhaps the Hebrews would have sallied forth by now if they were not so intimidated by Goliath. He nurtured the faint hope that Saul might grow desperate enough to accept the challenge. It never even crossed Kaftor's mind that the giant might lose.

Day 39 in the Gath Encampment in the Valley of Elah

King Achish grinned broadly as the stealthy courier from Gath departed his tent and faded into the night. None saw him arrive. None would see him leave. The secrets the man carried into the Valley of Elah were known to Achish alone. And what wonderous secrets they were. He felt like a magician who had pulled off a trick while his audience was distracted. As far as Achish was concerned, that was what Kaftor's floundering military expedition really was. One magnificent distraction. It drew away the attention of every single Philistine and Hebrew in the valley while the real magic was taking place far away.

The day had ended satisfactorily enough with more bravado provided by Goliath. The big man's performance achieved two essential goals for Achish's ploy. It made the Hebrews fearful, and it kept them inactive. Kaftor may want Saul's soldiers to charge down from their hill or for some fool to challenge Goliath, but not Achish. He wanted the enemy army to stay right where it was and continue sending disheartening messages to their loved ones, particularly if they were from Judah. But Goliath was only the first phase of his grand strategy.

The courier from his *Archon* Abimelek had just brought word that the second phase was now bearing fruit. Abimelek's agents had been spreading tales about King Saul far and wide in Judah. The King of Israel was unwilling to drive the Philistines from Judean territory. Saul was prepared to sacrifice Judah to preserve the rest of his kingdom. Their ruler trembled before a single Philistine warrior. Most Judeans scoffed at such baseless rumors at first, but their number was dwindling. Abimelek soon found fertile ground in which to plant the seeds of doubt.

The news which cheered Achish this evening was that a delegation of eight Judean elders had agreed to come to Gath to negotiate an alliance between Judah and Philistia. Truth be told, they were only eight out of a possible forty-seven clan leaders, but these men had been carefully cultivated and selected by Abimelek. They were all influential, ambitious, and jealous of Saul, convinced that only they could save their tribe. If King Saul refused to act, they would.

Such action would play right into the hands of Achish. Those eight Judean elders could not possibly sway their entire tribe, but they could cause enough confusion to paralyze it. General Davon's infantry regiments were poised to march in from Gath and occupy the chief cities of Judah. Achish still expected opposition from thousands of Judean militia, but they would consist of small scattered bands without coordinated leadership. Tied down in the Valley of Elah, Saul would be helpless to stop the invasion. Likewise, Kaftor's Gazan regiments would be caught flatfooted. Achish would add Judah to his domain while everyone else was slinging blame around.

Of course, Achish was prepared for a Philistine backlash against Gath's sudden expansion. He was not worried about Gaza. Kaftor's blundering in the Valley of Elah had lost him any support from the other kings. Achish planned to mollify Ekron, Ashkelon and Ashdod with promises to restore the old balance of power. A future Philistine campaign would acquire more Hebrew territory from a crippled King Saul. A campaign led by Achish. All this was possible if the situation in the Valley of Elah remained the same while the Judean elders met with Abimelek in Gath.

One more day. That was all Achish needed.

Chapter 20 – The Shepherd

Goliath saw that David was only a boy and despised him. He said to David, "Do you think I am some dog that you can drive off with sticks?" Then the Philistine used his gods to curse David. Goliath said, "I will feed your flesh to the birds and wild animals!"

David responded, "You come against me with a sword, a spear and a javelin, but I come against you in the name of the LORD, the God of Israel's Army, whom you have defied. Today, the LORD will give you into my hand. I will kill you and cut off your head. Then I will feed the Philistine dead to the birds and wild animals, so the entire world will know there is a God in Israel."

From the book of I Samuel, chapter 17, verses 42 to 46

Day 40 in the Philistine Army forward command post in the Valley of Elah

Achish thought he might be the only man in the entire Valley of Elah to feel excitement at this moment. Kaftor, his fellow Philistine king, looked as if he had a mouthful of vinegar. The Gazan generals yawned whenever their sovereign looked away. Except for their uniforms, the thousands of Philistine soldiers arrayed on the slope below bore little resemblance to a professional army. Achish could hardly fault them. What little discipline their officers and sergeants could still call upon had been used to march the sleepy men from camp to battlefield before dawn. The steadily increasing heat from the sun assaulted the wretched souls worse than anything the Hebrews had yet done. Their helmets came off first, soon to be followed by armor and weapons. This late in the afternoon, the only men Achish could see standing were either on the way to relieve themselves or in search of water. The snoring from a thousand throats provided a fitting background. This type of behavior had given Kaftor fits during the first few weeks of the listless confrontation in the Valley of Elah. Now the King of Gaza strained not to notice.

The distant Hebrews appeared to be in a similarly pitiful condition on the opposite hill. Their ragged battle line was broken in numerous places where men had simply wandered off to seek out shade. Achish noted the enemy archers as an exception to the otherwise lax discipline. Scores of alert Hebrew bowmen were evenly spaced across the battlefront. Their arrows would disrupt a Philistine assault long enough to allow the Hebrew infantry to form up. Not that either army appeared so ambitious today.

Achish could only shake his head at this blatant waste of good soldiers on both sides of the valley. One army had to come out each morning because the other one did. Neither side could leave the battlefield before sunset and expose their rear to the enemy. Staying in camp during the day invited a surprise attack by an aggressive commander. Sometimes Achish wondered why the opposing soldiers did not just get together, agree to ignore their leaders, and simply go home. Apparently, as long as everyone was fed and paid, the soldiers were still content to obey their superiors. Nothing had happened the previous thirty-nine days, so why would today be any different?

And today would not be any different if Achish could help it. A swift chariot would leave tonight for Gath bearing news that King Saul had once again refused battle. Tomorrow, his *Archon* Abimelek would convince the small Judean delegation to form an alliance with Gath. General Davon would subsequently lead Achish's infantry regiments in the conquest of a divided tribe of Judah. The Gath chariot corps here in the Valley of Elah would prevent anyone from interfering, be they Hebrew or Philistine. As Goliath's trainer, Ashron, approached the command tent, Achish prepared to attend to one final detail.

"Goliath is ready for his usual afternoon performance, my King. Did you summon me to make any changes?"

"No changes, Ashron. However, this will be Goliath's final appearance, so it must be a memorable one."

"Ah! Something is finally going to happen. About damn time. Uh...I mean...yes, my King."

"A secret plan of mine is already in motion far from here, Ashron. *No one else* in this valley must know of it. Not the Hebrews. Not the damn Gazans."

"I won't even tell the Big Guy."

"Especially not Goliath. His words and actions must not arouse anyone's suspicions. I want another boring day to come to a boring end. Then tomorrow we can quit this fool's errand and return to Gath in triumph."

Late Afternoon on Day 40 in the Israelite Front Lines in the Valley of Elah

Nathan shifted restlessly from one foot to the other like a raw recruit awaiting his first battle. He admired the calmness of his friend Jonathan. No one gazing upon him would suspect the prince was about to risk his life in a desperate battle. Which was exactly as it should be. Not one of the thousands of Israelite soldiers lounging on the hillside could even suspect what was about to happen. Jonathan would soon challenge Goliath as a diversion. When all eyes were on the combatants, Nathan would sound his ram's horn *shofar*. Laban would lead the *Renegades* from their hiding place near the Philistine position. They would ambush the exposed enemy flank and drive up the hill. Hopefully, the Philistines would fear they had been surrounded and flee. Hopefully, the Royal Army of Israel would seize the opportunity to join in the pursuit. Jonathan's plan involved much more hope than Nathan felt comfortable with. The two men had deliberately avoided Saul and his commanders all day lest one of them interfere in Jonathan's daring scheme by accident. Both were even now lurking just behind the Israelite position nearest the Philistines to avoid anyone's attention.

Ironically, their efforts to remain inconspicuous were aided by Saul's unprecedented announcement. Every Israelite mind was focused on how the king would reward the man who killed Goliath. Wealth beyond a peasant's wildest fantasy. A beautiful princess of royal blood to wed. No taxes ever again for any member of his father's family. Yet, the only result so far to this generous offer was a noisy camp. Not a single man had come forth to accept the challenge. It was just as Jonathan predicted and Saul expected. The stalemate in the Valley of Elah would go on, but with the blame transferred from the king to his men.

Once again, Nathan's concentration was disrupted by a booming voice echoing across the narrow Valley. Goliath had been strutting back and forth across the front of the Israelite battle line for nearly an hour. It was a familiar routine. The giant would repeatedly harangue his captive audience for several minutes and then wait for a reaction. During the early days of the standoff, Israelite soldiers would sometimes hurl their own insults. Goliath always laughed and responded with threats that chilled even a brave man's blood. He attacked everything precious to the Israelite soul. Their God, their king, their family, their courage. Nothing was off limits to the Philistine's mocking tongue. Eventually the Israelites grew passive and simply listened. Their lack of response became a mute acknowledgement that everything Goliath said was true. This collective impotence proved far more demoralizing to Saul's soldiers than the giant's words.

The deteriorating Israelite cause had finally compelled Jonathan to act. Not only was the Royal Army suffering, but the Nation itself was losing faith in their king. Still, Saul refused to act; insisting he could weather this storm without risking his men or his reputation. So yesterday the prince had gathered his limited resources and embarked on a fateful course. Jonathan stood armed for battle. The eighty-two members of his bodyguard, the *Renegades*, were in position. Nathan held a *shofar*. The two friends exchanged glances. It was time. Then disaster struck in the form of a cheerful greeting.

"So, there you are! I've been looking for you two boys."

A grinning Karaz limped in front of his former protégées. Even in his late fifties, the Hittite mercenary still cut an imposing figure. Nathan struggled to keep any hint of guilt off his face in the presence of his old mentor. Jonathan chose to conceal his anxiety behind a mask of annoyance.

"Karaz, I've told you before. We are grown men. We have wives. We have children. We are no longer b*oys*!"

"Except the two of you still get into mischief like little boys."

"Mischief! What mischief?"

"Come on, Jonathan. It's me! Karaz! You both look as guilty as two harlots on the Sabbath."

"I am not in the mood for your Hittite wit."

"Very well, we'll do this the hard way. Jonathan's wearing every weapon he owns. There's a very big man over yonder saying very nasty things about him. Could the two of them *possibly* come to blows?"

"You're just guessing, Karaz."

"Now let's consider Nathan, who is trying unsuccessfully to hide a *shofar* behind his back. That would be useful for signaling someone to attack... like Jonathan's *Renegades*. Say where is your gang of bandits anyway?"

"Nosey little sod, aren't you? Fine. Laban hid them last night in a gully to the left of that grove of trees."

"Impressive. I know where to look. and I still can't see them. Too bad they spent a night in the rocks for nothing. Your sneaky gamble is over, Jonathan."

"I'm surprised to see you here and not my father."

"Your father didn't know you were going to do something stupid...but I knew you would. That's why I came alone."

"You won't be able to stop us by yourself, Karaz."

"Oh, I didn't come to stop you. I came to tell you that you're too late."

In response to Jonathan's perplexed expression, Karaz pointed to a solitary figure crossing the valley. Nathan made out a man dressed in a brown homespun tunic approaching the Philistine battle line. The stranger stooped down as he crossed a small stream and spent a few moments searching for something. Nathan assumed he was looking at a messenger from Saul to the Philistine commander, though it was curious that the man was pausing in midstream. He sought an answer from Karaz.

"Did Saul send him?"

"Of course."

"What message does he bear to the Philistines?"

"Only that he's going to kill Goliath."

"That's not funny, Karaz. The man is unarmed."

"He has a sling. I assume he's collecting some stones for it as we speak."

"What fool would attack a huge, armored warrior with rocks?"

"David."

"The harp player? The shepherd? *That David?* Has Saul lost his mind?"

"I suspect our good king is being cunning rather than crazy, Nathan. If David is killed, Saul can disavow him as just some delusional boy. And if David wins, he's still only a boy and no threat to Saul's crown. It's a rather clever move. The king has much to gain and little to lose."

"It's still insane."

"No. It's brilliant."

Both Nathan and Karaz turned at Jonathan's unexpected observation. The prince never took his eyes from David as the boy resumed walking directly toward Goliath.

"Don't you see? David has the advantages of speed and a distance weapon. I watched him as he trained with some soldiers a few months ago. He's smart, strong, and agile. Goliath won't be able to touch him. David can use his sling to pummel the big oaf and perhaps even wound him. At the very least, he will humiliate the giant and regain our honor."

"Unless Goliath skewers him with that javelin."

"Yes, Nathan, there is that. But I would still wager on David."

All three men's attention were drawn back to the coming battle. Goliath had just seen David and began advancing with the servant carrying his oversized shield. Karaz turned again toward Jonathan.

"There is one other possible reason why your father sent David out there."

"What would that be?"

"David claims that he will kill the giant because his God is going with him."

"Karaz, this simple shepherd grows more amazing by the minute."

"I'm still learning about your Hebrew God, Jonathan. Does He really work that way?"

The Hittite's naïve, yet poignant, question caught Nathan off guard. He had killed many Philistines in the years since they had murdered his father. Nathan assumed that God approved of his life's mission, but it had never occurred to him that the LORD might ever be at his side. He found himself anxious to hear Jonathan's thoughts. The prince chewed thoughtfully on his lower lip before answering.

"We will soon find out."

Late Afternoon on Day 40 in the Philistine Army forward command post in the Valley of Elah

Achish's senses suddenly became fully alert for no apparent reason. The other occupants of Kaftor's command post continued their routines undisturbed, but Achish's mind began to tingle. Several seconds passed before he identified a barely detectable sound. It reminded him of a tide coming in from the sea, beginning as a whisper before slowly growing into a roar with each passing moment. The noise soon became loud enough that the Gazan officers began looking around for a source. Achish located it before anyone else.

The Philistine army arrayed on the slope below them.

Soldiers lounging in the front ranks had apparently been roused by something from the Hebrew camp. They had then alerted the next rank of men higher up the hillside, who had progressively passed the message on to each succeeding rank. As more soldiers became aware of the disturbance, their collective voices became louder. Achish's eyes looked in the direction indicated by hundreds of pointing fingers to see a lone man traversing the valley. The Hebrew's lack of a beard identified him as an adolescent. Achish assumed the boy to be a herald of some sort due to his lack of armor or visible weapons. No matter what the young man's purpose might be, it appeared that Achish's hope for a quiet end to a quiet day had been quashed.

The effect on Kaftor's headquarters was electric. The conclusion to weeks of wasted inactivity appeared to be at hand. Kaftor was overjoyed at the prospect of salvaging his wretched military campaign. The King of Gaza issued a flurry of orders to his generals, who passed them on to regimental commanders, who sent their adjutants to seek out the captains of each infantry company. Achish suspected all their activity might be for naught. Whether the Hebrew herald brought acceptance of Goliath's challenge or even King Saul's surrender, the Gazan infantry regiments were far from combat ready. Achish had frequently observed Gazan officers sneaking back to their tents during the day's hottest hours and leaving their sergeants in charge. Hours might be required to get the sluggish

Philistine soldiers back into armor and organized for battle. He doubted Kaftor's men would be ready to fight before sunset.

The most likely scenario was that King Saul had finally found a champion to face Goliath. Achish had mixed feelings about that. If nothing unusual had happened today, all Achish's plans would move forward. Abimelek would formalize an alliance with the disaffected Judean delegation now in Gath based on Saul's refusal to fight. General Davon's regiments would occupy Judah while its leadership was divided and confused. Achish would return to Gath with his chariots and leave both Gaza and Israel locked in a hopeless stalemate in the Valley of Elah.

Of course, Goliath cutting off the head of a Hebrew champion would also work. There might even be an added benefit for Achish. The humiliation of defeat could possibly force Saul from his throne. At the very least, additional Hebrew territory might be added to Gath either by conquest or through treaty with a weakened King of Israel. Achish's greatest concern was some sort of trickery on Saul's part. The Hebrew king might attempt to regain face by dragging out the negotiations for a *champion's challenge*. Accompanying Goliath as his shield-bearer, Ashron had explicit instructions to reject such a ploy out of hand. Achish was more worried over the effects of any delay on his plans than the possibility of the giant losing. It just would be so much simpler to avoid a fight altogether.

A sudden commotion within the command post interrupted Achish's thoughts. The previously joyful Kaftor was now raging at his subordinates. The cause of the King of Gaza's anger quickly became apparent to Achish. The Philistine soldiers were streaming down the hillside in an uncontrollable flood of humanity. Achish was momentarily impressed by their aggressiveness until he noticed the thousands of pieces of armor and weapons left behind. The reason for the soldiers' delinquent behavior was soon revealed by their shouts.

"Goliath! Goliath! Goliath!"

Achish's jaw dropped in response to a shocking revelation. The boy was going to fight the giant. The Philistine army was not rushing to fight, but to be entertained. The men bunched together in an enormous semicircle about fifty yards behind their champion. Kaftor had completely lost control of his soldiers. Similar chaos was erupting on the other side of the Valley of Elah as a mob of Hebrew soldiers flowed into position behind their man. Achish recognized that Saul must be in the same dire straits as Kaftor. Both kings no longer commanded. Instead, all their soldiers were now enthralled by a giant and a teenager. However, Achish had no intention of being rendered helpless. He pulled the commander of his chariot corps away from the Gazans and whispered frantic orders.

"Prepare to abandon camp immediately. And quietly. Every man, horse and chariot must be ready to move on my signal."

"What about our equipment and supplies, my King? There are also hundreds of servants and camp followers to consider."

"Our soldiers must take only weapons, two days of food and all the water they can carry. Say nothing to the others. Those peasants will have to fend for themselves if everything goes to hell. And send me a good man with a trumpet."

The chariot commander bowed and scurried off toward the Gath encampment. Achish judged the situation to still be salvageable, despite Kaftor's incompetence. Once Goliath killed the foolishly brave youth, the Hebrews might tuck their tails between their legs and go home. Or they could choose to attack the woefully unprepared Philistines. If the Gazan infantry kept their composure, they would retreat uphill, recover their weapons and drive the Hebrews off. Or they might turn into a mindless mob and race each other back to Philistia. It did not matter to Achish. He was prepared to stay or retreat depending on which action better served Gath. A few moments later, a breathless soldier bearing a trumpet skidded to a halt before Achish.

"Stay by my side, Soldier. No matter what."

Achish ignored the man's response because of new activity on the valley floor. The Hebrew boy was unravelling a previously concealed sling, earning Achish's grudging respect. Goliath grabbed his oversized shield from Ashron. The giant tossed aside his humongous spear and reached for the sleek javelin on his back. This combat would be missile against missile...to the death. A strange sense of calm descended on Achish. The King of Gath had spent a great deal of time and treasure in preparation for this moment.

He might as well enjoy the performance.

Chapter 21 – The Impact

As Goliath came closer to attack, David ran forward to meet him. David took a stone from his bag, slung it and hit the Philistine in the forehead. The stone penetrated Goliath's forehead and the giant fell to the ground on his face.

From the book of I Samuel, chapter 17, verses 48 and 49

The Floor of the Valley of Elah in the Late Afternoon on Day 40

Ashron grew tense, but not overly worried, when the Hebrew youth deployed a simple sling. It consisted of two woolen cords, each about three feet long, joined by a woven pouch about the size of a man's palm. It was one of the simplest weapons on the battlefield, but one able to cripple or even kill a man over one hundred yards away. Both Ashron and Goliath had originally assumed the boy was just a messenger. After threatening to kill the giant, they thought him a fool. However, the appearance of the sling had changed their opinions in an instant. The two Philistines now viewed the young man as a deadly serious foe.

Slings were nothing new to the Philistines. Their army used them on the battlefield as needed, just not to the same extent as the Hebrews. It was a poor man's weapon commonly employed by peasant militia. The missile could be a small iron pellet or a stone as large as an apple. Naturally, Ashron had included defending against slings as part of Goliath's training. Philistine soldiers were taught to swing the sling in a circle parallel to their side. Launching the missile from its pouch was as simple as releasing one of the two strands. Depending on the direction of the rotation, the projectile was released at the top of the circle or at the bottom of it. If the opponent was on a higher elevation, such as a hillside, or at a long distance, the underhand release was used. If the enemy was closer and on lower ground, such as when attacking a fortress, the overhand release drove the pellet down with great force. Philistine slingers usually remained stationary during a battle to avoid entangling their legs in the rotating sling.

Assuming any challenge would be fought on level ground at an unknown distance, Ashron had practiced against Goliath using a sling with an underhand release. The giant's tactic would be to charge a slinger while carrying sword, shield, and javelin. An underhand release would propel the projectile into a high arching trajectory, most likely impacting Goliath on its downward path. The charging giant would tilt his head forward behind the shield just before the moment of impact. The missile would be deflected either by Goliath's shield or the crown of his bronze helmet. He would then locate the slinger and launch his javelin while the man was reloading. Goliath would then charge his foe and finish him off with the sword, if necessary.

However, timing was everything and Goliath had lost precious seconds with his failure to identify David as an immediate threat. The Hebrew's sling was already loaded and in motion by the time the giant had discarded his bulky spear, grabbed his shield from Ashron and unslung his javelin. After this brief delay, Goliath finally made his move. It was only after the big man began sprinting forward that Ashron recognized a potentially fatal flaw in his tactics.

David was using his sling in a totally unexpected manner.

Protecting sheep against predators requires different skills than fighting soldiers on a battlefield. Bears do not line up in ranks and march forward in step. Wolves move swiftly from side to side while stalking their prey. Lions must be pursued and driven from their hiding places. Therefore, the aggressive shepherd must be highly mobile to catch these wild animals in the open. He must be able to hit targets at close range before they find shelter. Spinning a sling to one side while running leads to tripping and inaccurate throws.

Experience had taught David to swing his sling in a circle over his head. This technique allowed him to stalk predators and launch a killing stone the instant they exposed themselves. His overhead release sent the projectile on a flatter trajectory with greater accuracy. The trade-off was that David's effective range was much shorter than normally required on the battlefield. However, today's battlefield happened to be exceedingly small. In a javelin versus sling stone contest, striking first would provide a tremendous advantage. Each combatant would likely get only one opportunity to let fly.

Goliath was drawing back his javelin in midstride as David launched his smooth river stone at just over thirty yards. The rock's flat trajectory propelled it toward the giant's most vulnerable point: above his eyes and below the crown of his head. Goliath was therefore unable to locate the projectile in flight and deflect it. The narrow leading edge of the stone struck the Philistine's forehead at over seventy miles an hour. The hurtling projectile delivered a tremendous amount of energy to an extremely small area. The impact fractured Goliath's skull while barely penetrating it. However, the stone still had a great deal of kinetic energy yet to be released. The resulting shock wave ruptured delicate blood vessels and pulverized small portions of Goliath's forebrain. Even though the cranial damage caused the running giant to black out, he still might have survived. Unfortunately for the huge Philistine, gravity, momentum and even his own body mass still had their own energy to add to the fatal equation.

As the stunned Goliath toppled forward at full running speed, the javelin slipped from his numb fingers. His momentum continued forward as gravity pulled him down. The giant landed flat on his shield, pinning his left arm between it and his body. The fatal blow occurred as Goliath's head snapped forward to smash against the rocky ground. The small skull fracture split wide open, and the deadly stone was thrust deep into his brain. The giant's lungs would take in a few more breaths. His heart would continue beat until blood loss shut it down. However, the man known as Goliath no longer existed.

Chapter 22 – The Hero

David defeated the Philistine using only a sling and a stone. Without even a sword, he knocked down and killed the Philistine. David then ran over and pulled the Philistine's sword from its sheath. After killing him, he cut off Goliath's head.

From the book of I Samuel, chapter 17, verses 50 and 51

Outside the Philistine Army Forward Command Post in the Late Afternoon on Day 40

The grating sound of Goliath sliding across the gravel on his shield caused Achish to clench his teeth. The limp body of the giant skidded over ten yards before finally coming to a halt just shy of the Hebrew youth. Friction had torn loose Goliath's chin strap and allowed the heavy bronze helmet to roll free for another few feet. Achish held his breath, praying this apparent disaster was actually a clever trick cooked up by Goliath and Ashron. As the Hebrew cautiously stepped forward, Achish hoped against hope that the giant would spring up to slay this impudent boy. The King of Gath was forced to admit defeat once the Hebrew began pulling Goliath's sword from its sheath. The giant was as dead as Achish's grand strategy. By then, Ashron had already taken to his heels to seek the safety of the Philistine lines.

Achish's thoughts raced as he sprinted toward his nearby chariot with the obedient trumpeter in tow. The acquisition of Judah was now beyond his reach, but smaller prizes might still be obtainable. The first step was to decide how to best make use of his chariot corps in the valley. Achish swiftly considered two options. The simplest was to simply withdraw to Gath and leave the incompetent Kaftor and his Gazan troops to their fate. The other option was risky but extremely tempting. After weeks of skulking in the hills, the bulk of the Hebrew army now lay exposed on the valley floor. A bold charge using hundreds of Gath chariots might finish them in a single killing stroke. The lack of reliable infantry to support those chariots caused Achish to hesitate. Everything would depend on the Hebrews panicking at the mere sight of his horses.

Less than a minute had passed since Goliath's demise. Achish hopped aboard his chariot followed by the trumpeter. He took one last look down into the valley before making his fateful decision. His eyes beheld a chilling spectacle. The Hebrew youth had just finished hacking off Goliath's head with the giant's own sword. The boy turned to face thousands of shocked Philistines while holding his gory trophy aloft with a single hand. The accompanying roar from the Hebrew ranks was deafening. Watching the giant's blood drip to the ground, Achish made the only choice possible. He turned to his trumpeter.

"Sound the withdrawal. We are going home."

Late Afternoon on Day 40 in the Israelite Front Lines in the Valley of Elah

Nathan had no idea what to do. He had expected a disaster. He was totally unprepared for a miracle. Jonathan was in even worse shape. The prince alternated between laughing hysterically and singing the praises of a humble shepherd. The astonishing sight of Goliath's bloody head swinging in David's grip seemed to perplex King Saul as much as everyone else. The junior army officers nervously waited for some superior to take the initiative. Fortunately for the Kingdom of Israel, one man was thinking clearly. And he was not even an Israelite. Nathan came out of his stupor as he felt Karaz firmly nudging him in the ribs.

"Now might be a good time to blow that *shofar*, Lad."

Laban and the *Renegades* burst from their concealment as the *shofar* howled between Nathan's lips. Jonathan's bodyguards were possibly the only people on the valley floor unaware of Goliath's death. Ironically, their ignorance proved to be a blessing. Unlike the thousands of other soldiers paralyzed by David's shocking victory, the *Renegades* fell on the exposed Philistine right flank like starving wolves. Laban's warriors cut down scores of their disorganized foes while pushing up the hill toward the enemy's camp. Few things frighten soldiers more than the idea of being surrounded. It did not matter whether there were eighty Israelites or eight thousand attacking from the rear. One quarter of the Gazan infantry instantly melted away to outrace the *Renegades* up the slope.

Nathan's call to arms also galvanized the Israelite horde into action. He could hear officers and sergeants profanely hounding the disorderly mob of soldiers back into their ranks. As each company formed up, it began charging independently toward the Philistine position. The sight made Nathan cringe. This lack of battlefield coordination normally guaranteed defeat against veteran soldiers. However, this was not a normal day for the Philistine army. Most of the Gazans had left their armor in camp as they expected sport today and not battle. A handful of Philistine officers attempted to gather a platoon here and there across their front, but these frantic efforts were too late. The small enemy units were swarmed under by enthusiastic Israelites before enough could be organized to make a difference. The bravest Philistines naturally died first and thereby spurred their demoralized comrades to save themselves.

"It's a crying shame, Nathan. You Hebrews missed a great opportunity today."

"Sometimes I don't understand you, Karaz. This morning, we were doomed. Tonight, we'll celebrate. Yet, you whine."

"Oh, I never said it was all bad. Those Philistines probably won't stop running until they reach the Mediterranean. It just could have been so much more. If Abner had his wits about him, your army could have bagged the whole lot. Now you'll have to fight those same regiments again in a year or two. A pity."

"Right now, Karaz, I'll settle for things going back to normal."

"Won't happen, Lad."

"Why not?"

"You really can't see it, can you? Jonathan can. Saul eventually will. That boy with the sling? He changed *everything*. This kingdom of yours will never be the same again."

An hour before sunset on Day 40 one mile west of the Philistine camp in the Valley of Elah

The sounds of battle were drawing nearer to Achish's chariot and yet diminishing in intensity. Bad news for Kaftor. His Gazan rearguard was being ground up and pushed back by the Hebrews. Only King Saul's incredible lack of foresight stood between the Philistines and a massacre of epic proportions. That and Achish's shrewd tactics. Once the Gath chariot corps was safely away from the pending annihilation, Achish chose not to drive straight home. Instead, he prepared to seize control of the road back to Philistia.

Units of five chariots held station at hundred-yard intervals westward along the route leading out of the Valley of Elah. Entire chariot squadrons aggressively patrolled the countryside. Their archers would discourage any Hebrew from leaving the safety of his home. Achish had positioned his remaining three chariot companies here where the valley provided sufficient room for them to maneuver. If the Hebrew Army rashly pursued Kaftor's retreating column out into open ground, the Gath chariots would crush them. Achish doubted it would come to that though.

For the only things in sight were hundreds of dejected Philistines.

The stream of fleeing Gazans was unbroken, as if the men feared to be caught in too small a group for safety. Achish saw none of the refugees wore armor and barely half carried any type of weapon. The lack of arms mattered little since the Gath horsemen provided their only real security. Achish's men gazed down from their chariots as they directed their Philistine cousins to safety. The King of Gath chuckled to himself as the similarity to herding sheep crossed his mind. His charioteers also were keen to remind the Gazans that their king was an idiot. Achish normally would have cracked down on any blatant disrespect to Philistine royalty. Today, he pretended to be hard of hearing.

The only six chariots in the valley not belonging to Achish now came into view. It was Kaftor and his bodyguard. Achish noted this small entourage rolled cautiously through the mass of foot soldiers. Kaftor would normally have sent men with whips ahead to clear his way, but the King of Gaza was being more circumspect today. For the first time, Achish sensed fear coming from the man. Kaftor was obviously loath to antagonize soldiers who might pull him down and beat him to death. Both Achish and his corps commander pulled themselves to a state of courteous attention as Kaftor's chariot came abreast of theirs. Only to be totally ignored by the King of Gaza as he passed.

Achish raised an eyebrow to his subordinate officer and received a look of amused surprise in return. Such rudeness from a fellow king could not be ignored. Achish mulled over his options. Kaftor would probably enjoy a shouting match with another ruler as a way to restore his tarnished reputation. However, Achish chose a more subtle and satisfying response.

He began to laugh. Loud enough for Kaftor to hear.

This created a predicament for the King of Gaza. Since Kaftor had refused to acknowledge Achish's presence, how could he be offended by seemingly random laughter? Achish grinned broadly at his nearest men to encourage them to join in. The hilarity spread slowly up the Gath chariot line at the same speed as Kaftor, but always just behind the man. Achish could not remember anything he had enjoyed more than the sight of the tight-lipped King of Gaza slowly fading from view.

Sunset on Day 40 in the abandoned Philistine camp in the Valley of Elah

Nathan beheld the chaotic scene in the Philistine encampment with a mixture of disgust and resignation. The best of an enemy's loot always seemed to go to the men who least deserved it. The *Renegades* had led the Israelite charge up the slope. Their commander Laban recognized the importance of maintaining contact with the enemy. The more numerous Philistines could not be allowed even a moment's respite to organize a counterattack. The most aggressive of the Israelite soldiers had caught the *Renegades'* enthusiasm and fought alongside the elite warriors every step of the way. However, the majority of the Royal Army of Israel had become distracted while passing through the Philistine tents. It appeared that most of their fighting this day was with their comrades over abandoned trinkets and treasures.

Remembering Karaz's recent words also soured Nathan's mood. The Hittite mercenary was right to claim Israel had missed a great opportunity. Too many Philistines had escaped to fight another day. Yet, Nathan was at a loss to imagine how it could have been otherwise. No one could have predicted David's shocking victory. The sight of an Israelite army preparing to attack would have only put the Philistines on their guard. Besides, the growing darkness prevented any sort of organized pursuit. And Laban's recent report now provided the final confirmation that today's fighting was over. Hundreds of

Philistine chariots blocked the road back to Philistia. Attacking such a deadly force in the dying light was pure folly.

Of course, the Israelites would resume their pursuit tomorrow. The Philistine chariots would be outflanked in the hills and forced to flee. Any stragglers on foot would be destroyed. The retreating enemy army would be chased out of the Valley of Elah and back to Philistia. The Philistines must be humiliated as well as defeated for daring to set foot on Israelite land. However, the Royal Army of Israel could accomplish nothing more this day. So, its soldiers might as well loot.

Nathan was also disturbed by Karaz's warning. *David had changed everything. The kingdom would never be the same.* The Hittite never said such things lightly, but Nathan struggled to see how this unsettling prediction could be true. The kingdom was more secure than ever. Saul seemed rejuvenated as a king now that his burdens of the recent weeks had been lifted. Jonathan could not be happier. The prince had warmly embraced David as the hero of the hour. His friend might be impulsive, but the man was a shrewd judge of character. And David? The boy seemed overwhelmed by the enormous attention being showered upon him. Saul had already promised him a command within the army despite his lack of experience. Nathan humorously recalled his and Jonathan's misadventures as teenagers leading their first regiment. David would either prove himself worthy of promotion or be quietly shuffled back home to tend sheep.

By himself, David hardly seemed a threat. Yet, Nathan's experience in politics taught him to always be wary of a good thing. Ambitious men might seek to take advantage of an innocent boy's fame for their own sinister purposes. They would waste no time in descending on David. Nathan would have to keep an eye on this shepherd, for the good of everyone.

Epilogue

*When the Philistines saw their hero Goliath was dead, they
turned around and fled. Then the soldiers of Israel and the men
of Judah charged after them with a shout. They chased the
Philistines to the border of Gath and the very gates of Ekron. The
Philistine dead lined the road all the way from Shaaraim to Gath
and Ekron. After the Israelites returned from their pursuit, they
plundered the Philistine camp.*

From the book of I Samuel, chapter 17, verses 51 to 53

The royal palace in the Philistine Kingdom of Ekron

Achish, King of Gath, slipped out of his robe and kicked
off his sandals once he was alone. The King of Ekron had
personally escorted him to the palace's guest quarters. Besides
being a good host, his fellow king wanted to pry more
information from him about the Valley of Elah debacle. Achish
begged off until tomorrow by truthfully pleading his exhaustion.
He had just endured several days of hard fighting followed by an
extremely long day of politics.

The Hebrews had initially been unprepared to exploit
their sudden advantage after the death of Goliath five days ago.
They swiftly made up for their laxness with a vengeance. The
Hebrew army raced along the slopes of the valley faster than
the retreating Philistines. Thanks to King Kaftor's complacency,
his five regiments of Gazan infantry had been driven from their
encampment without most of their equipment. Only Achish's
skillful deployment of several hundred Gath chariots had

preserved the lives of thousands of disorganized and largely defenseless Gazans.

Nonetheless, Achish's men could only do so much, especially where the road forked outside the valley between Gath and Ekron. They kept that vital junction open for an entire day until the pursuing Hebrews threatened to surround the Gath horsemen. Achish was then forced to take his surviving chariots home. Gath's losses were relatively light: twenty-seven chariots, forty-eight horses and sixty-three charioteers out of a corps of nearly five hundred chariots. The Hebrews gave up their pursuit of Achish's men at the border of Gath, but they chased the other Philistines right up to the gates of Ekron. The bulk of Kaftor's army survived, but hundreds of dead Gazans lined the road all the way back to Elah. The Hebrew warriors did not tarry long in Philistia. Saul's men were not prepared to conduct a siege nor to face chariots on the coastal plains.

Although fewer than one in ten Gazan soldiers were lost, the true damage was out of all proportion to mere numbers. Kaftor's best men had died fighting to the last. The loss of experienced sergeants and junior officers would be especially difficult to replace. Then Kaftor in a rage had compounded this calamity by ordering the execution of every Gazan officer above the rank of captain. Several centuries of accumulated battle experience were wiped out in a single stroke. More precisely, in twenty-three strokes of the executioner's axe, if Achish's sources were correct.

News of Kaftor's defeat spread through Philistia while the battlefield blood was still wet. The other three Philistine kings immediately called for an emergency meeting of the *Sarney* in Ekron. They had no love for Kaftor. His rivals would have happily danced on Gaza's grave except that the fall of one Philistine kingdom weakened them all. Ashkelon, Ashdod, Ekron and even Gath were compelled to prop up Gaza lest their opportunistic neighbors begin coveting Philistine territory.

Despite his fatigue, Achish found this day's session of the *Sarney* to be more intriguing than its usual council meetings. The agenda focused largely on roasting the hapless Kaftor. The King of Gaza was usually quite effective in the political arena, but even those considerable skills could not save his slimy hide today. The other three kings had witnessed Kaftor's shortcomings firsthand in the Valley of Elah. They collectively shredded Kaftor's flimsy excuses for the collapse of his army. The *Sarney* was especially displeased at the amount of Gazan armor and weapons which had fallen into Hebrew hands. In desperation, Kaftor began casting blame on Goliath. Achish was prepared to defend his unfortunate giant, but even that proved unnecessary. It was the King of Ashdod who eagerly drove the final nail into Kaftor's coffin.

"Just to be clear, Kaftor. You claim Goliath destroyed an army, but, unfortunately, it happened to be *your* army?"

The ensuing howls of laughter reduced the unrepentant Kaftor to sullen silence. Even the normally stone-faced guards and servants gave in to a few chuckles. Humiliation upon humiliation piled up for the King of Gaza.

Achish, on the other hand, emerged from the *Sarney's* investigation with his reputation enhanced. His Goliath tactic was considered the only good idea in the entire sorry campaign. Gath's chariots were credited with not only saving Gaza's army but also preventing a Hebrew invasion of Philistia. Through it all, Achish played to perfection the role of a humble ally doing his best in a difficult situation. The highlight for Achish came when an abashed Kaftor reluctantly praised Gath's performance against the Hebrews. Achish knew horse dung when he smelled it but enjoyed watching the little worm squirm.

Before ordering a bath, wine, and companionship for the evening, Achish reflected on the events of the past month. Overall, the good outweighed the bad. True, his plans to acquire Judah had failed. He also regretted the loss of valuable men, horses, and chariots. However, Achish had achieved his most important goal: breaking Kaftor's grip on power in Philistia. This was an essential step in Achish's *deep strategy* to avenge his father's murder by the King of Gaza. His bold actions also earned the respect of the other three Philistine kings, something vital for his next move. And although unsuccessful this time, Achish had confirmed the potential for Judah to be separated from the other Israelite tribes. This delectable piece of information would be tucked away for his future use.

Achish grinned while ringing for the palace steward assigned to cater to his every whim. Revenge. Power. Empire. They would all soon be within his grasp.

Saul's palace in the Israelite city of Gibeah

Beker was enjoying Saul's lavish victory banquet along with scores of other distinguished guests, but for different reasons than most. Several men had already ventured deeply into the expensive wine. Others devoured the platters of rich food faster than the sweating servants could replenish them from the kitchens. The musical entertainment was universally well received. The luxurious furnishings were especially pleasing to the eye.

Unlike the others, Beker appreciated the room's lighting most of all. The oil lamps burned low and cast exaggerated shadows of the attendees upon the stone walls. This subdued illumination created a warm, inviting, and cozy atmosphere where people felt free to share their thoughts with friends. Some might complain the great hall was too dark, but Beker did not mind. He had carefully arranged it that way. While everyone else was celebrating, the *Yameen* was working.

Beker knew from experience that people readily gave away secrets in a relaxed setting which otherwise could not be tortured out of them. Not that he hadn't tried on occasion. The trick was to gather secrets from others without giving away any of your own. Thus, the small size of the lamps. An attentive observer such as Beker could read unsuspecting faces in the dim light while subtly concealing his own within the shadows. He was also a master at plucking individual words from the numerous echoes bouncing around the chamber. Still, lighting was everything, although an overindulgence in wine helped. Unguarded reactions sometimes told far more than words alone.

One such example had played out earlier in the evening when Beker confirmed a potentially valuable rumor. Whispers had recently come to his attention concerning a plot to depose the Patriarch of the tribe of Asher. The name of only one conspirator was ever mentioned, but that man was in attendance tonight. Beker had unobtrusively noted the man in question meeting with three other Elders from Asher. Their words and expressions left no doubt that an agreement had been consummated. Beker knew exactly how to exploit this revelation. His swiftest courier would depart that night with a message for the Patriarch of Asher exposing the conspiracy. The four unsuspecting elders would journey to Asher only to find their titles revoked, their lands confiscated and their families living in tents. In return, Beker would have a tribal Patriarch firmly in his debt. Still, this small triumph paled in comparison to a greater threat to Beker's career posed by the banquet's guest of honor.

Beker noted cynically there were actually two guests of honor. One was a teenage boy, and the other a giant. Or rather the giant's head. The unlikely hero David sat prominently at the left hand of King Saul. The youth was trying so hard to be humble that it made the *Yameen* wince. If anyone could sniff out false modesty, it was Beker. David undoubtedly knew that he was something special and felt worthy of every honor coming his way. That one so young was shrewd enough to hide these feelings was disconcerting to Beker.

However, most eyes were drawn to the pitiful face perched on a shelf above and behind the boy. Goliath's head had been transported to the palace in a jar of wine to keep it from rotting. Saul planned to have it tanned like leather for display as a permanent trophy. The preservation would not be as skillful as what the Egyptians did, but it would still impress Saul's subjects. Beker thought the oversized head looked frightful enough already. The blood had all drained out leaving Goliath's skin a ghastly shade of grayish-white. Part of the fatal sling stone was still visible inside the large indentation in the giant's forehead. The sightless eyes were half-closed, and the immense mouth sagged open. Goliath's final expression had been widely mocked by guesses at what his last words were.

They ranged from a simple "Oh No!" to increasingly more profane exclamations.

Instead of the giant, Beker chose to focus his attention on David. The lad's future was secure. His incredible victory had earned him wealth and position within the Kingdom of Israel. The possibility of becoming royalty was also open to him, although Saul had backed off that somewhat. Rather than simply being given one of Saul's daughters in marriage, David would be able to earn the right to marry one. These facts alone made David no more a threat to Beker than dozens of other promising young men in Israel. The crucial difference was a single word.

Bethlehem.

Bethlehem was an insignificant village in a dusty corner of Judah. Bethlehem was David's home. Bethlehem was also where Judge Samuel had reappeared after eluding Beker's agents. Many loose threads had appeared in the kingdom since then, and Beker was busily binding them together.

Samuel had once anointed a nobody as king. Samuel had rejected that same king after a failed struggle for dominance. Later Samuel proclaimed God would start over with another king and establish a new dynasty. Then the judge had disappeared in an apparent search for a suitable successor. Another nobody? Beker thought he knew the answer.

David's rise from obscurity had been as rapid as it was suspicious. Someone had recommended David to be Saul's personal musician. This had led to David's training in the ways of the Royal Court. His familiarity with the king had caused Saul to grant David the opportunity to become a hero. Killing Goliath now opened a path to the throne for David. Beker saw the paths of Judge Samuel and David of Bethlehem crossing in a very disturbing way.

Beker did not see a king as he studied David making polite conversation. Instead, he saw a tool being sharpened by invisible hands, most likely Samuel's. The judge had attempted to bend one king to his will and failed. Samuel might try again by raising a pliable young hero to the Throne. Beker knew well the dangers of both underestimating and overestimating the old man. Samuel was incredibly cunning but tended to overreach himself. And Beker's position in Israel had also grown much stronger since their first encounter. The *Yameen* was confident in his ability to keep a young upstart off the Throne, but the boy could still be a threat.

The *Yameen* viewed the current power structure in Israel as a table with three chairs. Saul occupied the first chair due to his kingship, the loyalty of his people, his control of Israel's wealth and his command of the Royal Army. Prince Jonathan sat in the second chair. He wielded considerable influence as heir to the throne, enjoyed great popularity based on his brave deeds and was the nominal commander of Israel's tribal militias. This last title was not as powerful as it might seem, since the militia leaders were notorious for their infighting. It would require a national crisis for Jonathan to be able to get more than two tribes to follow him at the same time. The third chair belonged to Beker, the man who operated the sinews of the government. The kingdom's revenues and expenses all passed through the hands of his loyal minions. Nearly every magistrate and governor in Israel owed his position to the *Yameen*. Beker could never rule Israel directly, but he was secure as the power behind the Throne.

Now it appeared that someone was trying to add a fourth chair to that illustrious table. Having the callow David fill the new seat would be an inconvenience for Beker. There was only so much power at the top to go around after all. But the situation could rapidly escalate into a true crisis if someone like the wily Samuel held the young man's reins. Beker had pondered from where a new player might draw power. He was not pleased with the answers. David might steal some popularity from Saul. He could replace some of Jonathan's political influence with his own. However, David's greatest opportunities lay in Beker's domain. The *Yameen* might be hard pressed to fend off a charismatic hero operating under Samuel's guidance.

Beker's usual strategy in the past had been to assimilate, bribe, discredit or assassinate a troublesome rival. However, none of these tactics seemed viable against David. The influence of Samuel would negate the first three options and royal patronage protected the boy from murder. Beker could occasionally get his way by playing the king and his heir off against each other, but not now. It was obvious to Beker that both Saul and Jonathan were enamored with David, and for very strong reasons.

Rumors of cowardice had plagued the king since his apparent reluctance to fight in the Valley of Elah. In truth, Beker thought Saul's decision to wait out the Philistines was the correct strategy. Even more insane would have been to gamble the entire kingdom on a winner-take-all death match. However, the common people were ruled by their emotions and many Israelites were still jealous of a jumped-up Benjamite being their king. Now David offered the aging monarch a way out of this political quagmire. The young man had been sent off against

Goliath with the king's blessing. Therefore, David's triumph was also Saul's. Beker could foresee David as the king's surrogate on the battlefield. The boy's courage would become Saul's courage. The young warrior would win glory and victories for an old king.

Jonathan's attraction to David seemed more noble than his father's but no less pragmatic. Even the jaded Beker was forced to admit that the prince truly respected and had a genuine fondness for the young man. Still, Jonathan had rushed to make an astute alliance with Israel's newest hero. The royal father and his son had a fraught history. One which made Saul extremely wary of Jonathan's popularity with the people of Israel. The king might be tempted to use David to marginalize his own son. Beker recognized how a covenant between Jonathan and David would minimize that risk for the prince.

Beker soon became lost in his thoughts about David, totally unaware that the master observer was himself under observation.

A Benjamite such as Nathan learned stealth almost as soon as he was able to walk. He had served as both scout and spy since his early teens. His surveillance skills were furthered sharpened as a soldier on the battlefield. Seeing without being seen. Protecting his night vision when his foes were blinded. Hiding where one was least expected. Selecting the best vantage point. Nathan was doing all that this evening. The great banquet hall was just another battlefield to him.

Which was why Nathan stood quietly in the shadows near the kitchen entrance instead of feasting with everyone else. He was missing a grand party, but there would be plenty for him to eat later. If anyone had been looking for him, they would have been foiled by several layers of concealment. Nathan's first defense was to make no motion to attract the eye. Next, his body was partially masked by the frequent movement of servants in and out of the kitchen. Finally, anyone seated at a table gazing in Nathan's direction would be slightly blinded by the light of the kitchen. On the other hand, Nathan could view everyone in the dim hall quite clearly.

It was all Karaz's fault that Nathan could not enjoy the festivities. The Hittite's comment about David had been nagging him for days. *David and his sling changed everything. The kingdom would never be the same.* So, Nathan had decided to check up on the former shepherd. The suddenly cozy relationship between Jonathan and David was the first thing to tweak his interest. That and the fact that this young peasant seemed wise beyond his years. Still, Nathan found David's conduct to be beyond reproach. He hoped the evening's revelry would cause David to let his guard down. Nathan was not disappointed.

As the wine flowed, David became increasingly confident and self-assured among the assembled nobility, not the typical behavior of a humble shepherd. Even more unusual, David later began circulating around the room and introducing himself to various dignitaries. They were all delighted to bask in the attention of Israel's savior. Nathan found this part of David's conduct to be mildly disturbing. The young man acted more like someone recruiting supporters than making acquaintances. Then Nathan noticed David was under surveillance from someone else: Beker.

Nathan easily recognized another spy at work. The *Yameen* apparently believed no one else could detect his activity, but Nathan had honed his observational skills in life and death situations. Beker was intensely focused on David's every expression. The *Yameen* currently resembled a snake sizing up a mouse as a potential meal. Suddenly curious, Nathan switched his attention from David to the self-proclaimed *right hand of the king*. Minutes crept by slowly, but Nathan knew when to be patient. Then, he was rewarded by a tiny change in Beker's countenance. It occurred so quickly that Nathan almost missed it. Nonetheless, he was certain of what he had seen: *worry*. Beker never allowed anyone to see that he was worried. It would have been considered a fatal sign of weakness at the Royal Court. Yet, Beker was worried. Not only that, but Beker was worried about *David*.

This revelation chilled Nathan to his bones. Beker had numerous character flaws. You trusted the man at your own risk. He was ruled by his own self-interest. Yet, the *Yameen's* political instincts were second to none. In many ways, Beker was the government. If the self-centered Beker felt threatened, it was because his government was threatened. Combined with Karaz's belief, Jonathan's new behavior and his own observations, Nathan began viewing this simple shepherd in an entirely new way.

Nathan wondered if David might be a greater danger to Saul's kingdom than Goliath ever was.

****

Dear Reader:

I hope you enjoyed reading *A King to Fight*, the second book in my *Empire of Israel* series.

I would also greatly appreciate your writing a brief review on my book's detail page in Amazon. Your comments will provide feedback, so I can improve later books in the series.

This exciting Biblical saga continues with my third book, *A King to Die*.

Thanks!

Dale Ellis